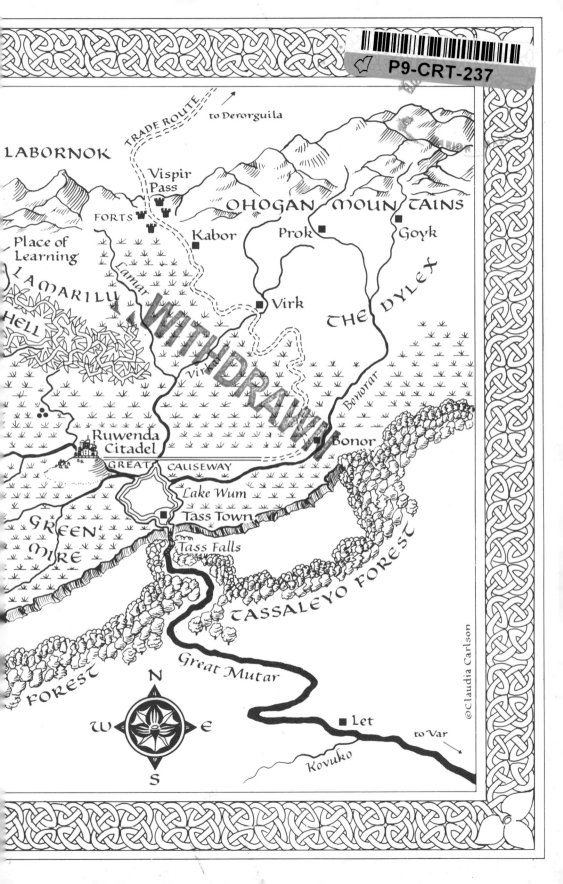

LABORNOK

TRADE ROUTE
to Derorguila

Vispir Pass

FORTS

Place of Learning

LAMARILU

HELL

OHOGAN MOUNTAINS

Kabor   Prok   Goyk

Lamar

Virk

THE DYLEX

Virkal

Bonorar

Ruwenda Citadel

GREAT CAUSEWAY

Bonor

Lake Wum

Tass Town

GREEN MIRE

Tass Falls

TASSALEYO FOREST

FOREST

Great Mutar

N
W   E
S

Let

to Var

Kovuko

©Claudia Carlson

BLACK TRILLIUM

BLACK TRILLIUM

Marion Zimmer Bradley,
Julian May,
∴ AND ∴
Andre Norton

A FOUNDATION BOOK
Doubleday
New York · London · Toronto · Sydney · Auckland

A FOUNDATION BOOK
PUBLISHED BY DOUBLEDAY
a division of Bantam Doubleday Dell Publishing Group, Inc.
666 Fifth Avenue, New York, New York 10103

FOUNDATION, DOUBLEDAY, and the portrayal of the letter F
are trademarks of Doubleday, a division of Bantam Doubleday
Dell Publishing Group, Inc.

BOOK DESIGN BY GUENET ABRAHAM

Library of Congress Cataloging-in-Publication Data

Bradley, Marion Zimmer.
Black Trillium / Marion Zimmer Bradley, Julian May, and Andre
Norton. — 1st ed.
p.   cm.
"A Foundation book."
I. May, Julian.   II. Norton, Andre.   III. Title.
PS3552.R228B56   1990
813'.54 — dc20   89-71544
                                        CIP
ISBN 0-385-26185-3

August 1990
First Edition

TO UWE LUSERKE
who planted the seed of the Black Trillium

PROLOGUE

From the Peninsular Chronicle
Of Lampiar, Late Savant of Labornok

I n the Eighth Hundred after those of Ruwenda came to rule over the swamp wilderness called the Mazy Mire (though not completely, for they never mastered the intractable Oddlings), legend and history both awoke to record one of those great changes which now and then alter the very balance of the world.

The civilized nations of the Peninsula — most especially we of neighboring Labornok — looked upon the wetland plateau of Ruwenda as a frustrating and vexing backwater, seeming to exist merely as a thorn in the flesh of more energetic and progressive peoples. In truth, Ruwenda was not at all a properly organized kingdom, owing to its failure to establish suzerainty over the peculiar aborigines dwelling within its claimed borders. Instead, the Ruwendian kings complaisantly allowed lawless enclaves of these so-called Oddlings to persist, ofttimes to the detriment of their legitimate subjects and the general peace and good order of the realm.

Of these aboriginal tribes, the bog-trotting little Nyssomu and the closely related but more aloof Uisgu (quite nonhuman and therefore clearly designed by Nature to serve their betters) were dealt with by both the crown and the merchant class of Ruwenda as putative equals, although no vows of fealty were ever demanded of them. Indeed, certain groups of Nyssomu were frequent visitors to the famed Ruwenda Citadel, and a few of the uncouth beings were actually accepted as upper servants of the royal court!

Two other Oddling tribes, the mountain-loving Vispi and the half-civilized Wyvilo of the southern rainforests, were inhospitable to humankind but deigned to trade with Ruwendian merchants on a regular basis. On the other hand, the shadowy Glismak, whose jungle haunts bordered those of the Wyvilo, were at this time seldom encountered by humans. They were vicious savages who delighted in the massacre of their Oddling neighbors. The last and largest tribe of Oddlings, the abominable Skritek, also called the Drowners, lived in most parts of the swamp, but were particularly numerous in the vast and noisome marshlands south of Ruwenda Citadel, as well as the Thorny Hell situated in the north-central region. These fiends of the Mazy Mire were notorious waylayers of caravans and attackers of isolated human manors and homesteads, either drowning their victims or torturing them with unspeakable brutality before consigning them to death in the quick-mires. Yet king followed king on the throne of Ruwenda, making no attempt to clear the land of that menace.

It was often whispered that the wetland rot had weakened both the minds and bodies of the human Ruwendians. Their rulers were a happy-go-lucky lot, utter strangers to proper feudal discipline. When the scholarly but obstinate Krain III ascended the throne, his manifest shortsightedness in dealing with his neighbor nations made it clear that the time was approaching when more enlightened and progressive methods would have to be applied to a festering situation, over which our own great kingdom of Labornok had stewed for years.

The unfortunate fact was that Labornok needed what these feckless and inefficient neighbors had to offer in trade. Our woodlands having long since been cut down and converted into farmland, we were dependent upon the Ruwendian rainforests not only for shiptimber to sustain our thriving maritime commerce, but also for fine woods to enhance and furnish the stately buildings at Derorguila. Also, by a heartless caprice of nature, the Labornoki slopes of the impenetrable Ohogan Mountains were virtually barren of useful minerals; while the Ruwendian side of the range contained lodes of gold and platinum, as well as many kinds of valuable gemstones, which were scoured out by the torrents and deposited here and there in the mountains. The precious metals and crystals were haphazardly gathered by the Vispi Oddlings, who traded them to the Uisgu; and eventually they passed into the hands of the human Ruwendians. Other tradegoods of the perverse little kingdom included valuable medicinal swampherbs and kitchen

spices, worram pelts and fedok skins, and certain curious ancient artifacts which the Oddlings procured from ruined cities deep in the most
inaccessible reaches of the Mires.

Even in the best of times, commerce between Labornok and Ruwenda
was a frustrating — occasionally perilous — business. More than a few
of our glorious kings, champing on the regal mustaches in fury over
some piece of Ruwendian insolence, had demanded that our generals
devise a scheme for conquering the smaller nation. But it is difficult to
invade a country to which there is only one door — the steep and narrow
Vispir Pass through the Ohogans, guarded by well-placed Ruwendian
forts. Those Labornoki kings of melancholy memory who made the
attempt did not return alive.

Surviving members of their defeated armies told tales of demonic
freezing fogs, whirlwinds from which inhuman eyes seemed to glare,
unseasonable mountain storms with snow, sleet, and hail, monstrous
rock slides, fulminating murrains that struck down the war-fronials,
and other calamities that had assailed them. It seemed almost as though
supernatural forces were arrayed in opposition to the invasions. But
even if the guardposts in the pass could have been taken, the sodden
morass beyond presented an even more formidable obstacle to an invading force.

As every Labornoki Master-Trader knew only too well.

This audacious and free-wheeling guild of merchants, which passed
its franchise and certain life-protecting incantations from father to son,
included the only citizens of our kingdom who knew the secret route
into the heart of Ruwenda. It was suspected by more than one Labornoki general, infuriated and frustrated in futile attempts to pry coherent
directions or even a useful map out of the uncooperative Masters, that
dark magic had been evoked to lock their lips during questioning.
Eventually, however, the route would be revealed through the craft of
the mighty sorcerer Orogastus, about whom more anon. But in earlier
days the Masters kept their secret well, and enjoyed not only a pros-
perous monopoly but also a sizable measure of political power.

A typical caravan led by four Master-Traders was small, consisting
of no more than twenty volumnial-drawn wagons and perhaps fifty
men. After giving the hill-fort commanders certain passwords, the Masters would lead the wagon-train into the Mire along an unmarked and
treacherous elevated roadway. Only a few isolated places between the

mountainous borderlands and the Ruwenda Citadel two hundred leagues hence were blessed with solid, unquakable land. The largest dry region, lying east of the Trade Road, was the Dylex Country, where polders or diked and drained fields contained well-cultivated farms, pastures, and scattered townships. Virk, the largest of these, engaged in the simple refining of minerals brought in by the Uisgu or Nyssomu Oddlings and was a secondary center of the Ruwenda gem and precious metal trade. By far the greater portion of this commerce, however, took place at the Citadel, the capital of Ruwenda, which perched upon a sizable rock dome upthrust in the midst of the Mazy Mire.

Once at the Citadel, Master-Traders paid the royal road-tax. (They also paid a capriciously variable wholesale goods tax upon departure, one of the great sore points in Ruwendian-Labornoki relations.) Then they were free to sell their own merchandise in the great Citadel Market, after which they might proceed to commodity exchanges dealing in minerals or timber. The latter was obtained by Ruwendian agents from the forest-dwelling Wyvilo Oddlings. Masters in search of more exotic trade goods would travel some one hundred leagues further, via Ruwendian punt or flatboat, up the sluggish Lower Mutar River to its confluence with the Vispar, where lay the ruined city of Trevista — and in its plazas, the fabulous trading fairs of the swamp Oddlings. These fairs were held only during the dry seasons, since the monsoons roaring up from the Southern Sea otherwise made passage of the bogland watercourses impossible. Only the Oddlings ventured about the Mazy Mire then, by ways they knew and methods they had perfected many hundreds ago.

Trevista remains one of the great mysteries of our Peninsula. It is of unimaginable age, and breathtakingly beautiful even in its present state of near-total dilapidation. The labyrinthine canals, crumblings bridges, and majestic ruined buildings are overgrown with a profusion of exquisite jungle flowers. Enough of the original urban design remains to demonstrate that Trevista's builders possessed a sophistication and a technical expertise far above that of the most advanced Peninsular civilization.

There is speculation by those interested in such matters that most of Ruwenda was once a huge glacier-fed lake dotted with islands that are now mere elevations in the swamp. Many of these are known to be crowned by similar ruins. Even the Oddlings are unable to account for

∴

the ancient cities, saying only that they were built by the Vanished Ones, and existed when their ancestors came into the swamp country. Ruwenda Citadel itself, a veritable mountain of intricate stone walls, bastions, keeps, towers, and interconnected buildings, also dates from remote antiquity and is said to have been the seat of whatever primordial rulers the Peninsula then bowed to.

The more isolated ruins, accessible only to the aborigines, were the source of the most coveted trade items — antique art-objects and mysterious small mechanisms which brought very high prices, not only from collectors in Labornok, but also from would-be students of occult knowledge in the farthest reaches of the known world. This trade, for reasons that will become plain, languished after Crown Prince Voltrik became heir to the throne of Labornok and set in motion events that would bring about the long-awaited conquest of our pestilential little southern neighbor.

Voltrik was forced to wait a long time for his crown, since his uncle, King Sporikar, lived well over his one hundred allotted years. During this time of waiting, Voltrik diverted himself by planning the acquisition of yet another crown, and also traveled widely. From one such expedition to the lands north of Raktum he returned with a new companion who was to provide him with the key to Ruwenda — the sorcerer Orogastus.

Voltrik was then in his eight-and-thirtieth year, a man of formidable physical presence, black-bearded and granitically handsome, with a temper as unpredictable and shocking as a thunderclap. His first wife, the beloved Princess Janeel, died giving birth to Voltrik's only son, Antar. His second wife, Shonda, perished under suspicious circumstances while on a lothok-hunt, having failed to conceive after ten years of marriage. The frivolous Princess Narice, his third wife, suffered the penalty for high treason after attempting to run away with an equerry. She and her paramour were tumbled together in a large sack of thornfleece, and then burnt alive.

The sorcerer Orogastus became Voltrik's chief adviser and before long commanded respect and fear throughout all Labornok. It was he who urged the Crown Prince to bide his time before taking a fourth bride, and possess his soul in patience if he wished to see his great ambitions fulfilled.

(Prudently, the magician did not disclose to the impetuous Prince that he would have to wait another seventeen years for the doddering King Sporikar to die.)

In the meantime, Oragastus established a stronghold high on the northern slope of the Ohogan Mountains on the flank of Mount Brom, where he set about to perfect his magical arts. All unusual antique artifacts procured by the Master-Traders of Labornok from the swamp Oddlings now came directly into his hands, for a vision had hinted to him that enormous power might be tapped through certain of the curious devices. Orogastus later took as assistants three sinister individuals who were known as his Voices. They served as the sorcerer's acolytes and agents, and were feared very nearly as much as their master.

On the opposite slope of the ice-crowned Ohogan Mountains, in the Ruwendian foothills where the River Nothar's precipitous descent eased and the watercourse broadened, lay the home of another occult practitioner. She was the Archimage Binah, also called the White Lady, who had lived for untold years in the ruins of Noth, one of the ancient cities of the Vanished Ones. She was little more than a legend to the human population of Ruwenda, whose common people never saw her. Yet they persistently invoked her name in times of trouble, and had revered her as the guardian of their land from time immemorial.

Only the Oddlings and the Ruwendian royalty knew the truth that lay behind the legend: It was Binah's benevolent enchantment, not the difficult terrain, the human fortifications, inclement weather, nor natural disasters, that had kept the Mazy Mire safe from would-be despoilers. But the weight of years bows down the wielders of magic even as it does those who do not exercise the powers. During the reign of Krain III the undetected safeguards Binah had set up around Ruwenda became increasingly more difficult for her to maintain. And as her faculties waned, those of the evil Orogastus became stronger and stronger.

There came a time when Queen Kalanthe of Ruwenda was finally brought to childbed after many years of barrenness, and all was not going well. King Krain knelt beside his stricken wife and called upon powers long near forgotten, which he had not named since childhood.

Out of the night-murk which hung thick and stagnant over the great swamp came a bird so immense that, with its wings spread, it could

∴

have covered most of the Citadel's High Tower roof. Beyond a doubt it was one of the awesome lammergeiers that haunted the most inaccessible crags of the Ohogan Range. From its back the Archimage Binah dismounted, and those on guard and those in service in the halls were awestruck and fell to their knees at the sight of her. In appearance she seemed to be only an aged woman, clad in a silver-bordered white cloak that changed with movement to that pale blue sometimes seen in snow shadows; but there was something about her that muted all question, and it was unthinkable that anyone should try to stop or hinder her as she hurried to the bedside of the Queen.

Those who stood close to the suffering lady now wept and sighed and prayed aloud, for it was plain that Kalanthe was unable to bring forth the new life that struggled for existence within her, and was nigh unto death. Her beautiful russet hair was darkened and plastered to her head by the sweat of her ordeal, and she gripped King Krain's hand as one drowning might cling to a rope.

Drawing near, the Archimage said: "Be at peace. All will yet be well. Kalanthe, dear daughter, look at me."

The Queen's eyes opened wide and her moaning ceased. Poor Krain did not want to leave his wife's side, but a single gesture from the Archimage filled him with sudden hope and he stepped back, motioning the courtiers and the Queen's women to make room for the visitor.

The royal midwife, who was an Oddling named Immu, stood by holding a goblet containing a potion of herbs, which she had not been able to get the Queen to swallow. The Archimage Binah beckoned the little nonhuman female to come forward and raise the cup, and then there was revealed a great wonder. All who were in the room, even the dying Queen, uttered cries of amazement, for Binah held over the goblet a Black Trillium plant — root, leaves, and a single tripartite blossom — a fabled swampherb so rare that not even the palace Oddlings could say where or if it still grew. Yet this same plant was the badge of the Ruwendian royal house, and among the most precious of the crown jewels were certain pieces of honey-amber, which had embedded in them minute fossil specimens of the bloom, no larger than the head of a pin.

But this flower was not small. It was fully as wide as the palm of the Archimage's hand, and of a rich black deeper than silk velvet. Binah plucked the trillium blossom and dropped it into the cup, but the plant

∴

she hid away beneath her cloak. She waited for the counting of ten breaths while the flower dissolved, then took the cup of tisane from the Oddling midwife and signaled to the King.

Krain rushed forward, raised his dear lady in his arms, and supported her while she sipped at the drink and then drank steadily until the goblet was empty.

The Queen now lay back upon her pillows. Suddenly she uttered a mighty cry — not of pain but rather of triumph — and the midwife Immu said: "She is giving birth!"

Three Princesses, one babe following swiftly upon another, appeared. And this was a great prodigy since multiple births are uncommon among the human aristocracy.

The babes cried lustily, and although small were perfect in form, each differing slightly in feature and coloring from the other. As each Princess was welcomed into the waiting birth-cloth the Archimage spoke a name and laid upon the small breast a strangely wrought golden pendant inlaid with honey-amber, containing a bud of the Black Trillium flower.

"Haramis," she said to the first child, in the tone of one welcoming a beloved friend or fosterling; and "Kadiya," she hailed the second; while "Anigel" greeted the third.

Then she looked beyond the infants to the King and Queen, who both were staring at her in wonder, and spoke with such a note of foreboding in her voice as to impress her words deeply upon the memories of all who heard them.

"Years come and go with speed. That which is lofty may fall, that which is cherished may be lost, that which is hidden must, in time, be revealed. And yet I tell you that all will be well. My day slides now into evening, although I shall do what I must and can until the coming of full night. These three Petals of the Living Trillium, children of your house, Krain and Kalanthe, have a fearsome destiny awaiting them and terrible tasks, but the time for that is not yet."

Before the King and Queen could ask the meaning of her warning, the Archimage Binah turned and went swiftly from the room. The howling babes and the necessary duties attending the Queen's deliverance fully occupied the royal women and the midwife Immu, while the King went forth to announce the joyful news and proclaim a time of celebration. The magical trillium amulets were hung on fine golden chains, and the Princesses wore them waking or sleeping.

As the Archimage had said, time passes; and with it treads also a measure of forgetfulness. The three Princesses grew up to be strong and beautiful girls, who heard often from their nurses and their parents the story of that strange scene attending their birth. However, to the girls it began to seem more and more to be a fanciful tale, especially the baleful warning, for there was nothing to disturb the comfort of their days as they matured, and like most young people they were much more interested in the present than the past.

Princess Haramis was her scholarly father's favorite. While she was yet a small child, she craved such knowledge as is to be found in books, pestering the royal scribes and sages with questions unbecoming to royal females. She also found magic in music, especially that drawn from the flute and the strings of the ladu-wood harp. She spent much of her time with the Oddling Uzun, who was a famous singer of songs and raconteur. He could change the most melancholy mood into one of good cheer through his jolly tale-spinning and wise counsel.

Princess Kadiya early proved to be a lover of animals and birds, especially the queer creatures of the deep swamp. Her passion was to live under the open sky and explore the wilder reaches of the realm, and for her guide and teacher in matters of natural history she turned to the Oddling Jagun, who was the royal Master of Animals and chief huntsman of the Citadel.

Princess Anigel, as dainty and delicate as one of the flowers she loved so much, was a shy child, although much given to laughter, and had a tender heart that went out to any sick or suffering thing. She was a special delight to Queen Kalanthe, taking pleasure in domestic and ceremonial duties that her sisters scorned. Her closest friend was that same Immu who had been the royal midwife and her nurse, who now served as the Citadel apothecary, brewing not only potions and simples but also sweet perfumes, confectionary essences, and very good beer.

The time came when the three Princesses were of marriageable age, Ruwenda having prospered for seventeen years at the expense of Labornok. At the behest of the sorcerer Orogastus, Crown Prince Voltrik sued for the hand of Haramis, the heiress. To his fury he was rejected, King Krain having decided that, failing a male heir, he would on the

∴

next Feast of the Three Moons betroth his eldest daughter to the second son of King Fiodelon of Var. This Prince, named Fiomakai, would then share the Ruwendian throne as co-monarch with Haramis. The nation of Var, lying to the south of the Tassaleyo Forest on the fertile plain of the Great Mutar, had very little commercial or diplomatic intercourse with Ruwenda. (It was, however, a notable maritime trade rival of Labornok!) But if the savage Glismak Oddlings could ever be subdued and the Great Mutar subsequently opened to the mercantile vessels of Var, Labornok might very well find the lucrative Ruwendian trade cut out from under it . . .

At this critical junction in Peninsular history, old King Sporikar finally closed his eyes to the world and Voltrik became King of Labornok. At the urging of Orogastus, his newly appointed Grand Minister of State, Voltrik summoned his grown son Crown Prince Antar and the Labornoki commander-in-chief General Hamil. He told them to prepare for the immediate invasion of Ruwenda.

Once again, from down in the outer ward of the beleaguered Citadel, a blazing blue-white light dazzled the eyes of the watching royal family, and those of the courtiers and the Oathed Companions gathered with them on a balcony at the mid-level of the great keep. An attendant clap of thunder hit their ears a split second later.

King Krain uttered a groan of despair. "By the White Lady, this time there can be no doubt! The sorcerer Orogastus has indeed called down lightning from a clear sky, and this stroke has breached the wall of the inner ward!"

Labornoki foot soldiery came surging by the hundreds through the broad, newly made gap. They were closely followed by mounted knights led by the brutal General Hamil. The charging attackers flattened the valiant Citadel defenders as easily as the hurricane blasts marshgrass. Moments later there was a third blinding magical flash, and then a fourth, and after each one enemy hordes poured through fresh breaks in the fortifications.

"It is the end," said the King. "If that ancient rampart with its multiple bastions can be pierced by the uncanny bolts of Orogastus, then there is no way the great keep itself can long remain secure."

He turned to one of the Oathed Companions. "Lord Sotolain, bring my armor. And you, Lord Manoparo, I charge with the safety of our dear Queen and Princesses. Take them to the innermost stronghold of the keep, where you and your knights must defend them to the last drop of your blood. The rest of you, prepare to engage the foe at my side."

Queen Kalanthe simply nodded; but Princess Anigel broke out in piteous weeping, and so did the ladies-in-waiting. Princess Haramis stood like a frowning image of marble, only her great blue eyes and shining black tresses relieving the pallor of her skin and the white gown and cloak she wore. Princess Kadiya, dressed in her mannish green leather hunting kit, unsheathed her dagger and brandished it.

"Sire — dear Father! — let me fight and fall at your side! Rather this than I cower away with sniveling women while the flatlander bastards conquer Ruwenda!"

The Queen and the nobles gasped, and Princess Anigel and the ladies left off their bewailing in astonishment.

Princess Haramis only smiled coldly. "I think, Sister, that you put rash stock in your prowess as a fighter. These are not larval raffins fleeing your toy spear in a hunt, but armed stalwarts of King Voltrik shielded by the enchantment of a black-hearted sorcerer."

"It is said by the Oddlings," Kadiya retorted, "that a woman of the royal house of Ruwenda shall bring about the fall of Labornok by slaying its wicked king!"

"And you have nominated yourself as our savior?" Haramis uttered a bitter laugh, and then tears sprang into her eyes, sparkling like a freshet bathing blue glacier ice. She cried: "Leave be, silly one! Spare us your foolish posturing. Can't you see how you distress our Mother?"

The Queen drew herself up proudly. She, like Anigel, wore the traditional Ruwendian court day-dress of unadorned satin, with its lattice-smocked sleeves and bodice. The girl's dress was a soft rose-color; but that morning the Queen had bid her handmaidens tire her in a gown and cape as crimson as blood.

Kalanthe said: "My heart is filled with sorrow and fear for all of us, but I know my duty. Kadiya, put not your faith in Oddling prophecies. Our Nyssomu servants have fled the Citadel for the safety of the Mazy Mire, leaving us to face the foe. As to your warrior pretensions . . ." She began to cough, for billows of smoke were rising up the wall as other magical devices of the invaders cast fireballs that ignited the wooden buildings of the inner ward. "You must remain with us, as befits your rank and station."

"Then I will be *your* defender," cried Princess Kadiya, "and that of my sisters. For if the Oddling prophecy is known to King Voltrik, then he dare not leave one of us royal women alive! I intend to sell my life dearly, and I will join Lord Manoparo and the Oathed Companions shielding you, and die with them if fate decrees."

"Oh, Kadi, you can't!" sobbed the Princess Anigel. "We must hide and pray for the White Lady to rescue us!"

"The White Lady is a myth!" Kadiya said. "We can only save ourselves."

"She is no myth," Anigel murmured, so softly that her voice was almost drowned in the clamor of the fighting going on twenty ells beneath.

"Perhaps not," Haramis conceded, "but it seems that she has abdicated her guardianship of this unhappy country. How else could the Labornoki host have crossed the pass, traversed the Mire, and fallen upon the Citadel with impunity?"

"My daughters, be silent!" said the King. "The enemy will attack the keep at any time, and I must soon leave you."

He bade them all withdraw from the open balcony into the chamber beyond, which had been furnished as a solar for the royal women. The bright silken cushions and gilded chairs had been kicked aside by mailed feet, and a tapestry frame lay sadly overturned near the cold hearth, together with abandoned books and a dulcimer with its painted sounding-board all cracked. The King now addressed himself to his second daughter, speaking with great sternness.

"Kadiya, you do ill to dismay your mother and sisters with foolhardy behavior and talk of Oddling nonsense. Would King Voltrik have asked for Haramis's hand if he gave credence to this fairytale about female warriors? It is my duty as lord of this realm to defend it or perish in the trying. But it is your duty to live and comfort your mother and sisters. And be assured that your burden is lighter than that of our poor Haramis, who will no doubt in the end have to submit to Voltrik after all."

At that all of the ladies-in-waiting burst into fresh wails, and the knights began to shout, and there was such a tumult of weeping and cries of "Nay, never!" that they scarcely heard the new fusillade of smaller occult explosions outside, and the clash of arms, and the screams of the wounded and dying.

"Quiet! Quiet, all of you!" cried King Krain.

∴

But they would not, for he was not a monarch who ruled absolutely, through force of character, but rather one who had always encouraged his subjects to treat him as a father and adviser.

For four hundreds, ever since the failed invasion of Labornok's King Pribinik the Foolhardy, the nation had been at peace. Crime and domestic strife had been almost nonexistent in Ruwenda—except for the occasional thief or homicidal madman, and the seasonal depredations of the abominable Skritek, which gave an excuse for knightly quests. During the extended peacetime military science had languished and the Oathed Companions forgot all they had ever known of strategy or tactics. The Kings of Ruwenda let their subjects do almost as they pleased, provided that justice and tranquillity generally prevailed and the usual revenues poured into the royal treasury. Traditionally, Ruwenda had no standing army. The Oathed Companions were the designated enforcement arm of the throne, and the hill-forts were manned by rotating cadres of free citizens from the Dylex Country, who were excused from taxes thereby. Ruwendian lords and ladies of the manor governed their tiny fiefdoms with a light hand, following the example of the throne, and everyone had prospered except the lazy, who did not deserve to.

Isolated little Ruwenda had seemed to be the happiest land in the entire Peninsula, if not in the known world . . . until the magic spells of Orogastus unlocked the Vispir Pass to covetous Labornok and traced out the secret route that King Voltrik's army had followed through the Mazy Mire to the Citadel.

Ten days was all it had taken. None of the magical storms or fog-phantoms or other disasters that had defeated King Pribinik plagued Voltrik. In fact, the abominable Skritek themselves were rumored to have allied with him! Under the aegis of the sorcerer Orogastus, Labornoki forces had quickly reduced the hill-forts to rubble, sacked the nearby Dylex townships and sent their inhabitants fleeing to the remote eastern counties, and come almost without hindrance to the outer bulwarks of the ancient Citadel itself. Soon it would fall to Voltrik, and the kingdom with it.

As the beleaguered Ruwendian royalty and their courtiers wrangled and wept, there suddenly came another tremendous flash of light and an ear-splitting detonation. The thick walls of the keep shook like a wattle hut before the winter monsoon. For an instant shocked silence prevailed within and without the Citadel. Then from below arose a roar from ten thousand throats and a triumphant sounding of buglehorns. It was plain that the gate of the huge central structure itself had been blasted open and the invaders were rushing inside.

Now Lord Sotolain came with the King's armor and quickly helped him to harness, and Krain sighed as he hefted the heavy sword of his great-great-great-grandsire Karaborlo, which he and his Companions knew he would wield bravely but ineptly. Neither the magnificent suit of shining steel inset with sapphires nor the crowned battle-helmet with its effigy of a platinum lammergeier could make King Krain more than he was—a mild-tempered middle-aged man, great of heart and mind but hopelessly unfit to be a warrior.

When his helm had been laced on he made his final farewell to his family. "I have been a scholar and not a fighter, and this I do not regret. For long generations our beloved land has known only peace. We have been protected—or so we were taught to believe—by the Archimage Binah: she who is called the White Lady, the Lady of the Flower, the Guardian, the Keeper of the Black Trillium. Numbers of us standing here on this day of misfortune saw her and heard her as she wrought marvelously at the birth of our triplet Princesses. The Archimage told us that all would be well, but she also spoke mysteriously of a particular destiny and dreadful tasks awaiting the royal daughters. We did not understand her words, and most of us—even I myself—all but lost the memory of them. But let us ponder them now, for they may give us a measure of hope. Frankly, I do not know where else to look for it."

He opened his metal-clad arms and gently embraced and kissed the Queen. Then came Haramis, whose face alone was still unstained by tears, and Kadiya, submissive at last, and golden-haired Anigel who could not leave off from sobbing.

After bidding goodbye to his friends, he once again most solemnly charged the venerable Lord Manoparo and the four knights with him, who smote their armored bosoms in a gesture of fealty and drew their swords. Then the King turned away. With his highborn squire Barnipo bearing the royal shield ahead of him, he strode through the solar door with most of the Oathed Companions following after. It was time for him to fulfill his own destiny, and not a one of those left in the room doubted what it would be.

As night fell on that day of conquest, the fires of the Citadel dwindled and merged their smoke with the miasma rising from the Mire. The

∴

knoll on which the Ruwendian capital stood seemed to be an island in a sea of turbulent cloud. Labornoki knights under General Hamil, who had emerged victorious from the last stand of the Oathed Companions, brought the vanquished King Krain and his squire Barnipo before King Voltrik, Crown Prince Antar, and the sorcerer Orogastus. A few score other noble Ruwendian captives were there in the throne room, heavily fettered and well guarded, in order to witness the capitulation of their nation. The banner of Labornok, scarlet with three golden crossed swords, hung on the wall behind the throne, where Voltrik now sat.

Krain was now near death, bleeding heavily from deep wounds in the right arm and groin, and had to be supported by two of Hamil's knights as he was led forward and forced to his knees at the feet of King Voltrik. One of his captors flung down Krain's battered azure shield with its Black Trillium device all but obliterated, and the other knight cast atop it the King's broken sword. Hamil himself tore off Krain's helmet, removed the platinum royal coronet set with sapphires and amber, and held it high for all to see. The squire Barnipo, unhurt and unbound, trembled behind his liege in the grip of Lord Osorkon, Hamil's second-in-command, a gigantic knight wearing gory black armor.

"Well met, Royal Brother," Voltrik said to Krain. His fang-edged helmet visor was open and he seemed to smile at the defeated Ruwendian monarch from within the open jaws of some fantastic, bejeweled saurian. Voltrik's chased and oranmented armor of gold-plated steel shone brilliantly in the torchlight, and he lounged akimbo on the throne of Ruwenda with one leg crossed jauntily over the other. "And do you now submit to me?"

"It seems I have little choice." Krain's voice was a husky whisper.

"Do you submit without condition," Voltrik demanded, thrusting the Ruwendian coronet beneath the stricken ruler's nose, "knowing that only by swearing thus will the noble and common inhabitants of your vanquished Citadel be spared death?"

"I will surrender . . . if you spare also the lives of my Queen and three daughters."

"That," said the sorcerer Orogastus, in tones as implacable as the strokes of a death-gong, "cannot be. They must die, as you must. And as part of your submission you shall tell us where in this great warren of crumbling masonry they have secreted themselves."

∴

"Never," Krain said.

Now Crown Prince Antar ventured to step forth and confront his royal father. "But surely, Sire, we do not make war on helpless women!"

"They must die," Orogatus repeated flatly. And King Voltrik nodded assent.

"Your wizard fears them because of the ridiculous Oddling prophecy!" Krain exclaimed. "But it is arrant nonsense, Voltrik — a nursery tale! Only a few months ago, you would have taken my eldest daughter Haramis as your bride —"

"But you scorned an alliance with Labornok," Voltrik said suavely, rolling the coronet around and around one finger as casually as an embroidery hoop. "And you replied to my gracious suit in words of haughty disdain."

"Tact never being a long suit of you snotty Ruwendians," General Hamil injected, grinning. "And now may you choke on the insolent fruit you have so long cultivated."

The gathering of Labornoki knights and nobles roared with laughter until King Voltrik lifted one hand. "I put my trust in the mighty Orogastus, who is my Grand Minister of State as well as the Court Sorcerer. And it is he who has foreseen disaster to my house at the hands of a royal Ruwendian woman, not some slime-skinned Oddling tale-teller. So your wife and daughters must die, Brother Krain, as must you. But if you submit to me humbly and turn them over to me, then your passing and that of your womenfolk shall be merciful, with a single sword stroke, and those of your people who swear fidelity to Labornok shall be spared."

Krain lifted his bruised chin. "I will not submit, and I will not deliver my women into your hands."

Voltrik held high the coronet, and then crushed it to a twisted mass between metal-gauntleted hands and dropped it in front of the kneeling Krain. "Do you know your family's fate if you do not surrender to me? And that of your knights here gathered in chains?"

King Krain did not answer.

Voltrik's craggy brow darkened with anger and his fingers drummed impatiently on one shining golden cuisse. When the King of Ruwenda remained stubbornly silent, Voltrik commanded: "Bring in four chargers!"

One of the Labornoki captains hastened to obey.

A shocked murmur came from the prisoners, and the squire Barnipo blanched in sudden fear and twisted in the grip of his captor.

"Ho!" General Hamil laughed. "This white-livered youth knows full well what manner of death the mockers of Labornok may expect. See how unstained his armor is — a coward, beyond a doubt. It would be a salutary thing if *he* were to be the first to participate in this small demonstration of Your Majesty's just punishment."

"No! No!" shrieked Barnipo. "God and the Lords of the Air have mercy on me!" He struggled frantically until the black-armored Lord Osorkon smote him in the face with his closed bare fist, whereupon the boy subsided weeping and groaning.

At that moment, the Labornoki captain and four hostlers returned to the spacious throne room leading four great war-fronials, still saddled and caparisoned. The animals' eyes rolled furiously red, and they tossed their gilded antlers and snorted and pranced, and their metal-shod cloven hooves rang on the marble floor.

"No!" Barnipo screamed.

"Yes," said King Voltrik quietly. His eyes met those of Krain. "I will show you, Royal Brother, just what fate awaits you and yours if you continue to defy me." And to the captain: "Take the craven, and tie one of his limbs to the pommel of each saddle, and then whip the beasts apart until he is well and truly quartered."

Barnipo let out a howl of despair and writhed in Osorkon's arms, while the Ruwendian knights bellowed curses upon the head of Voltrik until they were silenced by the prick of daggers at their throats.

King Krain said, "Let the poor lad be, and inflict this death rather upon me."

The sorcerer Orogastus said: "We will let the boy go free, and vouchsafe to you an honorable death rather than the ignominy of rending, if you will reveal to us the hiding place of your women."

"No," said Krain.

"Sire?" General Hamil asked of Voltrik.

The Labornoki King climbed to his feet. His red-violet cloak billowed about him and reflected garishly on his golden armor. "Krain of Ruwenda, you have chosen your own death. Lash him tightly to the beasts."

"Sire! Sire!" wept the boy. "Let it be me! Forgive my cowardice!"

"I forgive you with all my heart, Barni," Krain said.

The lackeys took the King, stripped him of his armor, and laid him supine out in the middle of the wide throne room floor. When they began to tie him with rawhide thongs, blood flowed from his reopened wounds and soon lay in a pool beneath him. Throughout all this, in spite of the shouts of the furious Ruwendian captives and the penitent blubbering of the squire Barnipo, Krain's countenance remained unperturbed. When everything was ready, the four great antilopine chargers ramping and squealing with excitement so that it took three men to hold each of them in place, the captain stood at attention and awaited Voltrik's command.

But now Orogastus whispered something to his King, who nodded and then beckoned Lord Osorkon to bring the fainting squire close to the throne.

"Boy," the sorcerer said, fixing the terrified Barnipo with his penetrating gaze, "you have it in your power to save your Liege Lord from this hideous death. And to save your own skin and that of the other captives as well."

Barnipo could barely mouth a reply. "I, my Lord?"

"You," said Orogastus.

Of all the invaders, the sorcerer alone was unarmored, wearing simple robes of white covered with a black cowled cloak. A platinum chain hung about his neck, and from it was suspended a heavy medallion engraved with a many-rayed star. He now pushed his hood back to disclose features that were comely and unlined, even though his long hair was as white as snow. His face seemed benign as he addressed the squire.

"Listen carefully to me, boy. Do as I say and you may yet save the lives of the Queen and the three Princesses. I confess that I am much amazed at the courage shown by King Krain, and I deem it meet that my gracious sovereign should wed your Princess Haramis after all, since the daughter must inherit the virtue of the father and pass it on to her sons."

"Really, my Lord?" A wild hope lit the squire's face.

"Really. And so that Princess Haramis may accept the betrothal in good heart, I have advised His Majesty to spare the lives of all the royal Ruwendian women. The only thing you have to do to bring about this fortunate resolution is to tell us where they are concealed."

The boy's eyes darted from sorcerer to King and he hesitated. "You will also spare my life?"

"By my crown," said Voltrik, touching the coronet atop his fearsome helmet, "you will live. But do not tarry, for the fronials grow restless."

∴

"And our King?"

"He must die," Orogastus told him, "for that is our law. But you can ensure that his passing is swift and painless. If you but speak."

Tears poured down the boy's cheeks. "So say you on your honor?"

"I swear it by the Lords of the Air," Orogastus said.

Barnipo took a deep breath. "Then . . . they are hid in a secret stronghold on the chapel floor of the great keep, reached through a hidden passage within the choir-loft, which opens by pressing the central boss of the great trillium carved on the wall. Lord Manoparo and four Oathed Companions guard them."

The sorcerer's deep eyes gleamed. "Ah!"

And King Voltrik and General Hamil echoed: "Ah."

"You swore not to hurt them!" The boy's teary face flushed and his lip trembled. "By the Lords of the Air —"

"A formidable oath," Orogastus said nonchalantly, "for those who believe in such fancies."

"But you also swore!" Barnipo turned frantically to the King.

"To spare your despicable life," Voltrik said, "and I will, so that you may serve as a cess-pit drudge for the rest of your miserable days." And he cuffed the horrified boy smartly with his metal gauntlet, so that he crumpled and fell off the dais and lay as one dead.

"My King," General Hamil said, "I will take a force and seek out the royal bitch and her three whelps."

"No," said Voltrik. "My son and I will lead the search party. You will deal with the Ruwendian scum gathered here . . . and with their worthless leader."

Beckoning to Prince Antar, Voltrik strode off the dais. He called to them a group of twenty knights, and they set off for the great spiral staircase that led up to the chapel.

Hamil, mailed fists resting on mailed hips, surveyed the throne room with its mob of Labornoki and their wretched prisoners ranged about the perimeter. In the center of the hall King Krain still lay tied to the shying war-frontials.

"Disposing of prisoners in chains is dull stuff," Hamil remarked to Osorkon, "and it has been a wearying day. Let us first have some entertainment." Then he shouted, "Hostlers! Use your whips!"

In the horror that followed, Barnipo made a quick recovery from his sham faint, scuttled away unseen, and raced up a back stairway to warn the Queen and Princesses of their peril.

∴

2

Barni had run so fast that his breath failed. There was in his side a pain as dire as a knife-wound, and his head ached so much from the blow King Voltrik had dealt that he had begun to see two of everything. Now as he staggered up the cramped little staircase to the choir-loft he heard afar off the measured clank of armored feet and an enemy voice shouting: "This way!"

The chapel was almost pitch-black, lit only by a few votive lamps, and the staircase unlighted at all. This changed in an instant as King Voltrik and his torchbearing knights rushed in through the central portal and crowded into the vestibule.

Seized with panic, the squire tripped and fell near the stairway top, striking his swollen head. All his strength ebbed away and it seemed he would fail his duty yet again. "White Lady!" he sobbed aloud. "Help me. Help our poor Queen and Princesses."

Sweet air filled his congested lungs and his vision cleared. There was still sore pain in his head, but he could move again. More like a scrambling many-legged worram than a man, he crawled up the rest of the stairs and across the splintery floor-boards to the wall behind the ranks of choir stools. It was of dressed stone, with a carved and painted panel of the Royal Seal of Ruwenda, an azure field having a great heraldic Black Trillium with a golden boss at the center.

Barni crawled to it and pressed the boss with both hands. At once the stone square swung inward, making a small doorway through which a man could squeeze with difficulty. No sooner had he entered and swung the panel closed, than the greybearded Lord Manoparo and two other Ruwendian knights, Korban and Wederal, came out into the cramped secret passageway from a lighted inner sanctum, weapons bared.

"Hold, hold, it's only me!" the squire croaked, rising to his knees.

"By the Flower! Young Barni!" Manoparo sheathed his sword and drew the draggled boy to his feet. "Now then, my lad —"

"Quickly! If you would save the ladies, bolt fast the outer door and break its opening mechanism so that the foe may not enter!"

Uttering curses, Korban and Wederal hastened to shoot home four great steel sliding bolts and chop up the secret panel's wooden machinery with their swords. No sooner had they accomplished this, than a mighty battering commenced from the outside, accompanied by martial shouts. And then, even more ominously, the pounding stopped.

"They have gone to get a ram," Wederal said.

"More likely the sorcerer!" snapped Manoparo. "Back inside the stronghold."

They dragged the squire with them to the secret chamber, which was about seven ells square and equipped for a siege, having a massive door of heavy gonda-wood strapped with iron, barred by three stout baulks of timber. The walls were covered with ancient tapestries and the floor with thick carpets and sleeping mats. There were no windows, only two embrasures high up, so narrow that a finger would barely pass through the slot. The room had a small table and one stool, upon which Queen Kalanthe sat, guarded by a fourth knight, Lord Jalindo. A tiny fireplace hardly larger than a brazier was flanked by chests of foodstuffs and kegs of wine and water. A standing candlestick of battered silver-gilt and other candles in a wall sconce gave fitful light.

Lord Manoparo made obeisance to the Queen, who sat pale and calm with her three daughters huddled against her skirts. She had put on her great platinum Crown of State, blazing with emeralds and rubies, surmounted by a glittering diamond sunburst centered with a drop of amber as large as an egg. At the amber's heart was a fossil Black Trillium the size of a thumbnail.

"My Queen, the foe have found us," Manoparo indicated the drooping Barnipo. "This squire gave warning and we have made shift to block the way as well as may be. But they are sure to bring up the sorcerer to break the doors with his black magic and make an end of us."

∴

Little Princess Anigel gave a rending shriek of terror, and would have fallen into hysterics had not her sister Kadiya slapped her smartly and admonished her to be still. Haramis took the sobbing girl into her arms while the Queen questioned Barnipo.

"What of my royal husband?"

The squire dropped to his knees, tears coursing down his dirty cheeks. "Oh, my Lady, he is dead and our poor Ruwenda lost."

The four knights groaned and the royal daughters cried out in horror. Queen Kalanthe only inclined her head and asked, "How did my Lord fall?"

"Alas!" cried the boy. "God and the Lords of the Air forgive me, for it was all my fault." And he continued on in this manner reviling himself until Lord Jalindo laid a hand on his shoulder.

"Come now. You are not yet fifteen years old, and no one of us can believe that such a youngling contrives the death of kings. Tell us plainly what happened."

So Barni did. And when he related the manner of shameful death that King Krain had suffered, the Princess Anigel fainted dead away into the arms of her sister Haramis, and Princess Kadiya exclaimed in a broken voice, "They shall pay!" But the Queen sat still, staring at the barred door opposite, holding in her lap the sweaty and bloodstained head of the King's squire, who wept as though his heart would break.

"It is not your fault, poor Barni," she soothed him. "The foul Orogastus deceived you. No one holds you to blame. The blame be upon the sorcerer and King Voltrik, and upon that monster Hamil, who gave the order that tore my beloved asunder."

"They shall pay," Kadiya whispered, but no one except Haramis heard.

Suddenly there was a great detonation. The knights drew their swords and arranged themselves in a line between the women and the door. The Queen leapt to her feet, letting the squire slide to the carpeted floor.

"A woman of our house," Kalanthe said, her eyes alight with resolution. "That is what the diabolical Voltrik fears! So the prophecy is not merely an Oddling tale after all, since the Labornoki soothsayer himself confirms it!"

She faced her daughters. Anigel had recovered herself, and the three pairs of eyes were fixed on their mother. "The fall of Labornok shall be compassed by a woman of our house. *You will live, daughters* — and prove the prophecy true."

Now the foe was smashing with bludgeons and axes at the very door of the sanctum, Orogastus not being able to use his magical destructive bolts in such a confined space for fear of toppling the walls. Queen Kalanthe pulled aside one of the hanging tapestries, which were made of an antique fabric, still to be found here and there in the Citadel, that had outlasted those who had built the great pile and awed the humans who had called the place home for eight hundreds. The cloth was grey, and as the Queen thrust it aside it turned blue, and on it or in it shadows moved, and yet one could never see just what those shadows were.

Behind this wondrous drapery lay a homely necessity, the stronghold garderobe, a tiny closet just large enough for a single occupant. Kalanthe flung open its small door and commanded: "Daughters, inside!"

Haramis moved quickly, dragging with her Anigel, whose fragile body again shook with sobs. The fit was very tight for two, and Kadiya drew her dagger and said: "No matter: I will remain with you, Mother —"

"Inside!" the Queen commanded, in a terrible voice none of the girls had ever heard before. Kadiya gaped at her, then hastened to push and cram the other two within until there was room for her, but only barely, and the door to the garderobe would not shut tightly.

"One last thing," the Queen said, and she took off her great Crown and passed it to the waiting hands of Haramis. "And now pray, my darlings, and may we meet again in a happier world."

She let the dusty tapestry fall. There remained a small gap between the hangings through which the three Princesses saw what happened next.

The gonda-wood door was now in splinters from the blows of Labornoki battleaxes. They hewed at the doorframe itself until the hinges holding the metal strapping gave way, and the timber bars collapsed, and then the final melee began.

Prince Antar, wearing blue-enameled armor and a winged helmet, was among the first to penetrate the broken door. He engaged Lord Manoparo, the two of them smiting one another with two-handed swords that rang like bells with the force of the blows. Other knights of Labornok rushed into the room and had at the other four Oathed Companions, while King Voltrik and Orogastus stood aside. The Queen

∴

had withdrawn to the front of the hearth, as far as possible from the place where her daughters were concealed, and the hidden girls saw her clearly, as well as the pitched battle taking place in the room.

Lord Manoparo gave a mighty thrust at the winged helm of Prince Antar. Its laces broke, and it fell from the Prince's head. His face, strangely, was not contorted with battle-lust but rather full of anguish. Nevertheless, Antar laid about with skill and great strength, and at a fortuitous moment caught Lord Manoparo disengaged and lifted his huge sword above his head and struck downward, using such force that the Ruwendian's head, helmet and all, was cloven in two.

Then Korban and Wederal were mortally wounded and disarmed, and only Lord Jalindo still fought on until he was overwhelmed by the press of Labornoki. When the last Oathed Companion fell, the victors began to hack him and his fallen fellows to collops.

Oh, the horror! Princess Kadiya's eyes burned and she snarled in silent, helpless fury, as might a voiceless lothok kit taken for taming from the breast of its slain dam. The barbarous wretches were actually enjoying themselves as they dismembered the fallen Ruwendians and made mock of their dying cries. Kadiya was overwhelmed by the need to burst forth from the hiding place and take revenge. Gripping her blade, crushed between her sisters, her every muscle tensed in readiness —

"Stay!" hissed Haramis. "By the Flower, stay where you are! Would you kill us all?"

Anigel had pulled her trillium amulet on its chain from her bodice and now pressed it to her lips. "Pray to the White Lady, guardian of our land!"

"Pray that those devilish brutes won't find us," muttered Haramis, holding her own amulet.

"Pray that someone will come to save us," Anigel urged.

Shivering with fear and rage, Kadiya nevertheless felt her grip on the dagger handle ease. Almost without volition her hand stole to the neck opening of her doublet. The amulet was there under her silken shirt, warm against her pounding heart.

"I pray that I will be the one," she whispered, "the one to make Voltrik and Antar and General Hamil and the sorcerer pay with their blood for the deeds of this day!"

"Pray also for self-control," said Haramis, "or else your foolhardy bravery may yet doom us all. And cease your wriggling, plague take you, lest we tumble out at Voltrik's feet!"

"Hush, hush! They will hear," Anigel pleaded. The dreadful chopping and the laughter of the evil knights had ceased, and King Voltrik himself was speaking.

Against her will, Kadiya silently uttered a plea for self-mastery. The anger still burned within her, but slowly the emotion was covered, as one banks the coals of a campfire so that the flames may be summoned again into life when the proper hour comes.

"Look!" Anigel whispered, her voice almost inaudible for terror. "Our Mother!"

King Voltrik had been addressing the Queen, evidently questioning her about the whereabouts of the Princesses. It was close and smoky in the stronghold, with the candles in the wall sconce gutttering and a few of the floor mats asmoulder, having been burnt when the big standing candlestick was upset. The King had unhelmed and removed his gauntlets, and from the fierce scowl that darkened his countenance it was evident that Queen Kalanthe had defied him.

She stood straight, with the disheveled squire Barnipo crouched at her feet in a daze, and said: "Never will I tell you where my daughters are."

"Orogastus, force her!" bellowed Voltrik. "Or spy out the royal brats with your farseeing eye!"

"I cannot force her will, my King," the sorcerer replied. "She is beyond fear. And I cannot descry the hidden ones, no more than I could do so down in the throne room. This ancient Citadel must be pervaded with some arcane enchantment that blocks my seeking Sight. I own a magical device that would accomplish the task no matter what obstacles intervened, but it is bulky and of a great weight, and it cannot be removed from my eyrie on Mount Brom."

"Then we shall have to use other means to unlock the lady's tongue." King Voltrik came slowly toward the Queen with sword drawn, and took hold of her right wrist.

"Enough of this, royal bitch! You will tell me quickly where the girls are, or I will strike your hand from your arm. And do you still fail to speak, then I will strike off the other hand, and proceed to your feet, and then your limbs little by little until you give answer, for thus does Labornok repay insolence in its enemies."

"Sire!" exclaimed Prince Antar, his face aghast. "She is a queen, and that punishment is one for rebellious slaves —"

"Silence!" thundered Voltrik. There was a murmuring among the other men, but this died away as the King raised his sword arm. "Will you speak, woman?"

Then a thing happened so swiftly that the watching knights and the Prince could not grasp it, but the Princesses saw clearly. The fainting squire Barnipo was energized and sprang at King Voltrik like a marauding fedok attacking its farmyard prey. Having no blade, he sank his teeth into the King's left hand, that which gripped the Queen.

Voltrik uttered a roar of pain and drew back with the boy still hanging onto him. The King laid about every which way with his great sword, and by misadventure slashed the Queen in the throat, and she fell with her life's blood pouring forth on the hearth. All of the Labornoki knights began to yell and to thrust at the still-clinging youth — but gingerly, lest the flailing monarch also by chance strike them. The squire Barnipo was pierced by a dozen blades and fell away at last, laughing in his pain, until the King himself smote off the brave boy's head.

Then Voltrik gave vent to black fury, cursing so vilely that even his henchmen flinched, for Queen Kalanthe was also dead, beyond coercion, and the three Princesses still at large.

"What are we to do?" Prince Antar asked.

Orogastus said: "They cannot have gone far. It is certain that they must have been with their mother up until the time that this lowborn whelp" — and he kicked the squire's body — "went by some shortcut from the throne room and gave warning. We must mount a search of the entire keep."

Calming himself, Voltrik said: "Orogastus speaks truly. You, Milotis, will take charge of these knights and begin searching the chapel and its environs immediately. Be alert for secret passages and 'tween-wall stairways! After that, search the High Tower above. Antar and Orogastus, come with me. We'll roust out the rest of our fellows and ransack this pile from the highest parapet to the lowest dungeon."

Then the King began to mutter maledictions upon the soul of Barnipo, who had taken a fair chunk of flesh from the heel of his hand, which now was exceedingly painful. Orogastus undertook to bind the wound, saying that Voltrik would have to take great care, human bites being likely to carry dangerous infection.

∴

"May the member putrefy," Kadiya whispered ferociously, "and the poisoned blood ascend into Voltrik's already rotten heart!"

"And may the Lords of the Air carry poor Barni into highest heaven," Haramis breathed, "for by his brave action, he spared our Mother torture, and gained us time to save our lives."

The King, his son, and the sorcerer went off; and after a short search of the blind passage outside the stronghold, Sir Milotis and his men also withdrew to begin their scrutiny of the choir-loft. They banged about and shouted and overturned furniture for some minutes, and then trooped down the stairs to examine the chapel.

Kadiya said: "I think it's safe to come out."

So they did, all stiff-jointed and trembling, creeping from the garde-robe into the awful shambles of the chamber. The full reality of their situation now struck them like a splash of icy water. Anigel clung to Haramis's hand and bit her lower lip until a trickle of blood stole down her chin. Kadiya stepped over the tangled bodies to the fallen Queen.

"She seems at peace," the girl marveled. "Her eyes are closed and her aspect gentle." She took a black silk cloak that someone had dropped and would have covered her mother's body; but Haramis said:

"Fool! What if one of them should come back and discover it?"

Chagrined, Kadiya admitted: "You are wiser than I, Sister."

"Give the cloak to me," Haramis said, "so that I may wrap the Crown. I will carry it with me — although there is small chance I shall ever wear it."

Anigel let out a smothered squeak of fear. Her sapphire eyes were enormous as she pointed without words to one corner of the room athwart the door.

There were no bodies there, and yet a pile of cushions was moving.

"Stand back," Kadiya ordered, drawing her dagger and advancing. One by one, she plucked up the pillows with her blade's point and threw them aside, until there was revealed the carpet, pushed up like a tent and rising higher by the moment.

"By the Flower, a trapdoor!" Haramis said. "Quick, Kadi, draw aside the rug."

"Oh, beware," Anigel cried. "Perhaps it is the foe!"

"Foe foe foe indeed!" said a crabby little voice. "Move lively, girl, or else they'll cut off our escape."

The three Princesses gasped, and when Kadiya got the trap uncovered there in its mouth stood a female creature of short stature, neatly dressed in a fustian robe, a green plait-work shawl, and a leather apron. Her sallow face was broad, as was her mouth, and her beautiful golden eyes bulged inhumanly above two tiny slitted nostrils. Narrow pointed ears tipped with silvery baubles thrust up from the folds of her lawn headdress. Her hands were broadly two-fingered with opposing thumbs, stained and scarred from many years of mixing strange concoctions.

"Immu!" cried Anigel in a transport of joy and relief. "Dearest Immu, you've come to save us after all. We thought you'd fled with the rest of the Oddlings —"

"Fled fled fled! What rubbish!" Immu climbed up into the chamber, then pointed dramatically into the hole. "Get you down the ladder, for I'll have to contrive a way to cover the trapdoor behind us."

Haramis and Anigel kilted up their long skirts and went awkwardly, while Kadiya scrambled down agile as a tree-vart. In the rough vaulted passage below was another surprise.

"Uzun!" Haramis exclaimed. "And Jagun, too!"

Two other small figures stood waiting, carrying green-glowing lanterns in which luminous swamp-worms were enclosed. They were males of the same Nyssomu race as Immu. Jagun wore a fedok-skin hunter's cap and brown leathers cut very similarly to those of Kadiya, while the musician Uzun had on his usual embroidered maroon velvet smock. His gold brocade beret was besmirched with sticky black lingit webbing from the secret passage.

Kadiya embraced her small mentor. "You didn't desert us, Jagun!"

"Desert? Desert?" The Master of Animals was indignant. "We simply hid, which was the prudent thing to do. Only you humans are foolish enough to stand still like silly togars mesmerized in the moonlight, watching death march down the causeway right into your front door!"

"Honor demanded our defense of the Citadel," said Kadiya hotly.

"Well, see what your honor's bought you," said Uzun the musician. "If only you had gone away into the Mazy Mire, to our people at Trevista, we could have taken you in."

"And then what?" Kadiya demanded.

"Then . . ." The Master of Animals shrugged his narrow shoulders. "You might have lived with us."

"But this is our home," Anigel protested gently.

∴

"And now it's *theirs*," said Immu, her voice brusque. She had finished her camouflaging and came quickly down the ladder, picking up her own lantern. "And they're bound and determined to slay you. Us as well, if they catch us."

"But you came anyway to save us," Anigel said softly. She had hold of the trillium amulet. "The White Lady answered our prayers."

"That is so." Uzun sketched a mystic three-lobed sign above his head in reverence. "My own mastery of domestic magic is puny, as you know, dear Princesses. I am much more accomplished on the harp and fipple flute! But yesterday I did the water-scry, seeking to discover that which would tell us three Nyssomu whether our destiny lay with humankind whom we have served so long or with our own people. And the Archimage spoke."

Haramis said: "Archimage! That's one of the names of the White Lady."

"Lady lady lady!" scolded Immu. "Hush, child, and let Uzun explain, for we must be away at once."

Haramis lowered her head. "Say on, friend Uzun."

"The White Lady is actually named Binah. Archimage is her title, for she is an enchantress, the most mighty in all our Peninsula."

"Or was," said Jagun gloomily. "She is dying, being of a vast age, and her failing powers could not countervail those of the terrible Orogastus."

"She bade us bring you to her," Uzun said.

"Why?" asked Kadiya, rather tartly. "If she is dying, she can be of scant help, and it is hardly a time for sick-visits."

To which Haramis appended, "We would do better, it seems to me, to go to Trevista. There we can wait out the Winter Rains, which will be here in a few weeks. Perhaps later we can disguise ourselves and join a caravan, and eventually make our way to the coast and take ship to Var. There King Fiodelon will surely give us sanctuary."

Uzun spoke with simple dignity. "As to that course of action, I know not. The Archimage charged us to bring you to her — just as she charged the three of us, many long years ago, to serve in this human castle against a day of great need for all Folk dwelling in the Mazy Mire."

"Which day is *today*," Immu said, "or I'm a ringtailed volumnial!"

She clamped her wide lips shut and cocked her head, listening intently, her long, sensitive ears swiveling about so that the ornaments winked in the living lamplight. "They leave the chapel," she said at length. "But other searchers will be swarming about the keep at King Voltrik's command. Even those three lackeys of the sorcerer, who are called his Voices and who consort with the Skritek! It's time to leave."

"Haramis, Eldest Daughter of the King, you will come with me," Uzun said. "Jagun and Immu will take your sisters by another way. This was commanded by the Archimage."

For a moment it seemed Haramis would refuse. Abandon her sisters? Her hand went to her breast and her fingers closed about the amulet that had never left her after the hour of her birth.

"But I cannot leave them! I am the eldest, and heir to the throne, responsible for them. And when matters demanded, it has always been I who decided for us all."

"Hara, do as he says," Anigel urged. "Trust the White Lady."

"I like this not, Sisters," said Kadiya. Her tanned brow was creased and her hair, russet like that of the Queen, was all awry, escaping from what had been neatly coiled braids. "If we stay together, my blade offers us all some measure of protection. Gladly I would lay down my life—"

"Life life life!" Immu was totally exasperated. "Why are you always so hotheaded? And why must Haramis make the decisions? Anigel is not strongminded like you two, and yet she shows the greatest wisdom! Tell them, Uzun! Tell them the other words of the Archimage."

"I forbore," the musician admitted sheepishly, "wanting not to dismay you. The Archimage Binah bids you come to her because you are unready to pursue your great destiny. Indeed, you do not even recognize it yet."

Haramis and Kadiya bridled at this, but Uzun went on. "You three, Petals of the Living Trillium, have it within you to save this land from the oppressive rule of King Voltrik and Orogastus, but only if your flaws and weaknesses are mended can you succeed. The Archimage will tell you how this may be done when you come to her."

Anigel took the hands of her two sisters. "Hara . . . Kadi . . . please!"

Kadiya veiled her fierce brown eyes and slowly nodded. A moment later Haramis said: "Very well."

"By the Flower, it's about time!" Immu exclaimed. She continued: "Haramis, you must follow Uzun. Anigel and Kadiya, come with Jagun and me."

∴

So saying, the Oddling woman pulled Anigel off down the narrow dusty passage, and the huntsman followed after, shooing Kadiya ahead of him as a farmwife herds her togars. In a moment the light of their living torches was lost in thick darkness.

"And we two must fare forth together," Haramis said to the musician. "Old friend, I hope the White Lady has strengthened your puny magic, for your flute ditties, excellent as they are, will not long fend off the warriors of Labornok or their storm-beckoning sorcerer."

"I, too, am afraid, Princess," Uzun admitted. "But I put my trust in the Archimage, as you must. And she has ordered that you be taken to the top of the High Tower of the great keep."

Dismay paled the girl's face. With its framing blue-black hair, it was spectral in the gloom. "We shall be trapped up there! The searchers will surely discover us! Oh, why didn't I listen to Kadi?"

"Come," Uzun insisted, and went hurrying off with the lantern, and Haramis had no choice but to follow.

∴

3

Kadiya, Anigel, and the two Oddlings fled through dark and narrow spaces between the stone walls of the Citadel keep, sometimes passing other secret doors, their machinery furred with the dust of ages. At length, after they had descended a steep stairway, they came to a passage where there was a peephole giving onto the throne room.

Jagun spied through this into the now silent and lifeless chamber. Then Immu looked, and then Princess Kadiya, who uttered a low cry of grief and struck her small fists against the stone wall while she wept, not uttering a sound.

They begged Princess Anigel not to look, fearing that the appalling sight would strike her senseless, but she would not move from the spot until Jagun stepped aside. She put her eye to the hole in the wall and saw from above the mutilated remains of the captive Oathed Companions and King Krain, and to the amazement of the others she neither cringed nor cried, but only closed her eyes and held tight to her trillium amulet.

After a moment she sighed raggedly and asked: "Immu, you are old and wise. Tell me why the Labornoki did this, when our Father and his knights were already in their power and surrendered?"

"It is a hard thing for such as you to understand, child. You are gentle and loving yourself, and you have known only love and gentleness throughout your life. But there are those to whom cruelty vouchsafes a dark thrill, a rushing sense of power. Small-souled and fearful themselves, surrounded by others who would wreak cruelty on them and finding scant happiness in life, they fall prey to the basest of all lusts — that which finds pleasure in destruction and in the pain of others. The cruel one feels himself exalted above all by his action. He feels more alive because of the death of others. He defies the Creator by rending creation. He scorns love and embraces hate, because it alone enkindles his cold and stagnant soul. There is no pity, no stricken conscience, no remorse in the wantonly vicious. There is only a hunger for more and more cruelty, because these persons can never be sated. Gentle folk may not safely respond to them gently, because evildoers do not know what love is, mistaking it for weakness. For this reason you, who are a gentle and loving Princess, must find a sterner way of dealing with such ones."

"Oh, I could not," Anigel said, trembling. "Never could I — not even after viewing this terrible sight!"

Princess Kadiya flung her arms around her sister. "Never mind, Ani dear. *I'll* see that the brutes get what's coming to them."

Then Jagun made them move on, and they walked and walked, always moving deeper into the Citadel's lower levels, until finally the secret way ended in a wall of modern brick that formed a dead end.

Anigel began to whimper in a panic, but Immu hushed her while Jagun held his lamp close and made finger play on the wall, first in this direction and then in that. Suddenly a section of brickwork shifted, and torchlight shone through, and the girls caught a familiar malty smell and knew where they must be. They hurried between ranks of barrels and big copper vessels with beer puddled beneath, for this was the Citadel brewery that Immu supervised, although all the workers had fled and the fires had gone out, and the huge vat of wort was untended.

Immu led them now, and they entered the grain store, where the two Oddlings and the girls had to shift a large pile of sacks. In back of it was a mouldering wooden door that yielded with loud and reluctant creakings when Jagun prized it open with a fire-poker. The door led to a precipitous stairway hewn from living rock, wet and slippery from water that dripped from cracks overhead. They descended, the walls glistening as the wan lantern light reflected off occasional flows of greasy mud.

"This way leads to the uttermost depths of the Citadel," Jagun said, "to dungeons and oubliettes and cisterns and drains that have never before been seen by Ruwendian eyes, built by the Vanished Ones."

There had been a few web-building lingits in the upper passages, tiny harmless creatures that fed on household bugs. But at the bottom of the stairs they came into a low-roofed chamber hung with dripping mud-stalactites, and among these were much larger lingits, with bodies the size of ladu-fruit and nasty teeth. The creatures had spun clumsy sticky nets as big as black bed-sheets, and Jagun and Kadiya drew their blades and hacked through those that impeded their passage. Anigel shrank back in loathing when Immu kicked aside the indignant displaced spinners, which cheeped and squeaked and tried to bite through the shoes and boots of the intruders.

Once past this obstacle, they descended another flight of roughly carved stairs, and the smell of tainted water grew offensively strong. They came to a rusted gate that stood half-open. Beyond it was another portal gaping wide, and on the walls empty torch-holders and pegs holding bunches of keys so attacked by verdigris that they crumbled to greenish clots when Kadiya ventured to touch them. The floor was covered with pools of water, and as they hurried down a corridor, becoming more mud-splashed by the moment, the gloom lightened and a yellowish radiance shone forth.

They entered a large arched room and the girls exclaimed aloud, for the place was a kind of prison ward, with rotting cells all around it, and the floor and ceiling and walls were streaked with slippery glowing matter. Shapeless little creatures slithered languidly about, leaving shining trails behind them.

"They are the slime-dawdlers," Jagun said. "Such also dwell in the remote reaches of the Misty Mire."

"Ugh!" cried Anigel. And she pointed in horror to one cell where the door had fallen from its decayed frame, and within lay a skeleton still chained to the wall by rusted fetters. The eye sockets glowed, for slime-dawdlers had made their dwelling inside it.

"What a nauseating place. Look! There are rusted instruments of torture in that corner. And these horrid slimy things — ! They lurk in every nook and cranny. See, this old bucket is crawling with them. Oh! There is one climbing up my shoe!" She tried in vain to scrape the clinging thing off against a stone plinth, shuddering all the while with abhorrence, and then burst into helpless tears.

Immu went to her darling's rescue, skewering the slug expertly with

∴

the dagger she wore sheathed behind her apron, and flipping it away. She drew out a dry kerchief and wiped Anigel's muddy and tear-stained face, murmuring words of solace.

"How much farther must we go?" Kadiya demanded of Jagun. "My poor sister's court slippers give scant protection from the wet, and her gown and light cloak are soaked through. She will catch her death."

"There will be warm, dry clothing waiting," Jagun said, "but we shall get wetter still before quitting this place — *hark!*"

They all stood stock-still. Jagun snatched off his hunter's cap to give his great ears full play. His face became a mask, the skin drawn tightly over the bones, the eyes like refulgent globes of amber, the wide lips parted a little to show those fanglike foreteeth that humans usually did not notice, reminders that even the peaceful Nyssomu had been in their time hunters who went equipped with more than blowpipes and spears.

The girls heard nothing but the tinkle of dripping water; but Jagun said: "They have followed us! Doubtless they discovered our tracks in the brewery. Quickly!"

He dashed to a low opening on the other side of the dungeon, which proved to be the entry to another steep staircase. It had a kind of railing at Oddling waist-height, and a good thing, for the steps were fiendishly slippery. The girls held on for their lives as they all went hurtling downward, not noticing that they left behind them faint luminous footprints that became less and less bright as they descended.

The wildly swinging lanterns of the Oddlings revealed nothing of what lay ahead until they reached the very bottom. There they found themselves in a dark cavernous chamber, ankle-deep in mud and water. The place was crowded with strange, rusting machinery and broken pipes thicker than tree-trunks, which harbored more of the glowing slime-dawdlers as well as larger flying creatures that took fright at their presence and skittered off hooting into the darkness. Jagun led them to a circular paved platform in the chamber's center. In the middle of it was a round black hole about two ells in width, circled by a low stone curb.

Now, from above came faintly the sound of armor clanking, and human voices. Anigel cried out in terror. Jagun peered into the well-like opening and then picked up a stone that lay nearby and cast it in. A long moment later there was a faint splash.

"Good!" he exclaimed. "I feared that, it being still the dry season, the great cistern would have drained. But all is well and our escape route is at hand." He beckoned to Kadiya. "Come, my brave kit! The cistern is the ancient water storage chamber of the Citadel, built long ages before the edifice attained its present size. It is fed by a conduit leading to the Mutar River north of Citadel Knoll. The Archimage has commanded my brother Rapahun to bring a punt to the conduit's secret mouth. All we have to do is jump."

"Jump?" Kadiya repeated incredulously.

Jagun tucked his lantern into his belt-wallet. A wetting would not harm it at all. "I'll go first, and assist each of you as you splash down."

"But I can't swim!" Anigel wailed.

"The rest of us can, sweeting," said Immu encouragingly. "We'll hold you up."

The noise of the approaching Labornoki force was becoming louder.

"No time to waste," Jagun said. "I'm off!"

With a cheery wave, he stepped over the edge and vanished. There was a distant splash, and a hollow call: "Jump! It's quite all right!"

Kadiya took a deep breath. "May the Lords of the Air grant me courage!"

She took hold of her trillium amulet, approached the well's lip, and jumped before her rising panic could freeze her muscles.

She fell.

White Lady, help! Oh, let me land softly . . .

She floated.

What is this? Kadiya's fear turned to stupefaction. She still gripped the amulet. A light breeze, seeming to blow upward in the darkness, told her that she drifted slowly into the depths. Down, down, down — and then she slipped into cool water as easily as a knife into an oiled sheath. She found herself afloat. Jagun's strong nonhuman hand towed her along until she bumped squared stones.

"There is a narrow walkway," the Oddling said. "Climb up and I will pass the lantern."

But she did not climb. Bemused, clinging to the ledge in the dark, water dripping into her eyes, she whispered: "Jagun . . . old friend . . . I did not fall but wafted through the air like a winged salith seed!"

"What say you, girl?" The Oddling's voice, usually kind and diffident, had sharpened.

"I clasped tight my trillium amulet, and prayed that I would land soft, and it happened. The very Lords of the Air bore me up."

"Triune God! This cannot be!"

"I did float, I tell you! And landed easily in the water."

Suddenly there was light, as Jagun hauled out his lantern and set it on the cistern ledge. Kadiya saw the little being in the black water beside her, his great eyes bulging, his face working, torn between consternation and anxiety.

"The prophecy — but there is no time for this!" he groaned. "The mystery must wait upon our safe deliverance." He lifted his head and called out to Princess Anigel to jump, his words echoing in the vast hollow dark.

Up in the well-chamber, Anigel heard and approached the lip of the hole, with Immu encouraging her.

"Jump!" the faraway voice urged. "Jump, daughter of the King. Fear not!"

And then came Kadiya's voice, strangely exultant. "Jump, Ani! Hold fast to your amulet and pray that you will fall slowly, *and it will happen!* The trillium amulet is magical, and we can command it!"

"What's this?" Immu leaned over the edge. "Princess Kadiya! Did this really happen?"

"It did, it did, dear Immu! And to think we never suspected! . . . Jump, Ani, and trust the White Lady's gift!"

Anigel gritted her teeth, clutched the pendant, and began to tremble so violently that Immu feared she would fall in a fit. "I cannot jump! I'm afraid! What if the magic won't work for me?"

Orange flamelight now flickered dimly from the stairwell. The clashing of armor and arms mingled with the sound of men cursing the slime-dawdlers. Someone cried: "Prince Antar! This way! Follow the glowing footprints down the stairs!"

"You must jump," Immu pleaded. "Dearest Ani, they will soon be upon us. Here, let me take one hand, and do you hold your amulet with the other, and we will step off together."

But the girl leapt back from the brink, eyes wide. "No! No!"

Jagun's voice rose hollowly from the depths. "What are you waiting for, silly women? Hurry! The knights dare not follow, for they would sink from the weight of their iron. Jump! Jump!"

∴

"The Princess is afraid, and I cannot abandon her," Immu called.

"Then *push* her, lackwit!" Jagun screeched.

Immu turned to the cowering Princess, lantern high, but the girl drew back, shaking her head wildly, eyes now rolling and mouth wide in a grimace of fear-madness. The little Oddling female took hold of Anigel's wrist and pulled, but the girl fought back. Both of them slipped and fell off the platform into the shallow muck, where they howled and thrashed about like Skritek worrying their prey.

It was thus that Prince Antar and his men found and laid hold of them.

Sodden and weeping, Anigel and Immu were forced to their feet. They stood with hanging heads amidst the twelve armed men, who held high their smoking torches and made rude jests. But Prince Antar, his face taut, said: "Where are the others?"

Immu stuck out her long prehensile tongue at him. One of the knights drew his sword and would have slain her on the spot, but the Prince cried: "Hold, Rinutar!" The man stepped back, grumbling.

Gently, the Prince took bedraggled Anigel and looked into her face. It was without expression, the eyes turned dull and dead. "Lady," said he, "have they gone into yon well?"

Anigel said softly: "Yes. They have escaped. So kill us, but remember that my sister Kadiya now possesses great magic, and will one day wreak vengeance for the foul deeds you have done today."

The assembled knights exclaimed at this, and threw questions at the girl, but she would say no more.

"Shall I put them to death, my Prince?" asked Sir Rinutar.

"Nay. They will have to be questioned, so that we know what manner of enchantment — if any — opposes our rule of Ruwenda."

"Just let me have the Oddling slut," Rinutar said eagerly, sheathing his sword and drawing a glittering poniard, "If I only toy with her a bit before the eyes of the Princess, she shall soon tell us all that we want to know."

"Oh, no! Please, no . . ." Anigel's voice trailed off into a moan, and she fell senseless into the muddy water.

Prince Antar bent to lift her, and as he held her frail body in his arms and looked down upon her, pallid in the flickering torchlight, he thought that he had never seen so beautiful a woman, for all her sad

∴

and besmirched state. He was relieved that he would now not be obliged to condone the torture of the Oddling hag, much less slay the lovely, helpless creature whose head lay against his armored breast.

"We can do nothing more here," the Prince said. "It is plain that the others have eluded us, and that it is impossible for us to follow. We must abandon this pursuit and take these prisoners to my Royal Father. Let their disposition be up to him."

The knights concurred with enthusiasm, for the eeriness of the Citadel bowels had all but unmanned them. Antar commanded his marshal Sir Owanon to bind Immu and carry her across his shoulder, and he himself did likewise with Princess Anigel. Then they began the long slow climb upward.

4

Haramis ran, following the pattering, uneven steps of the Oddling court musician, and her headlong flight told her things about her courage — or lack of it — that she had never suspected.

They traveled upward through secret passages and stairways that became ever more cramped and choked with dust and webbing, places where Uzun assured her no foot but theirs had trod since the first Ruwendians took over the ancient Citadel. Finally the hidden way ended, and they were forced into the open to face the broad stone spiral staircase of the keep's High Tower, which was Ruwendian-made. The wall fixtures, wrought-iron baskets that held tubs of oil with wicks, had been lighted, and it was clear that Labornoki searchers were already abroad in the tower.

Haramis and Uzun toiled upward floor after floor, past the enormous royal library, where Haramis had spent many long happy days in study, her greatest pleasure. The library levels were deserted, but Haramis gasped with indignation at the sight of toppled shelves and precious volumes left in random heaps on the floor. Still, nothing seemed to be maliciously detroyed. *No doubt Orogastus has given orders to preserve this,* she thought. *I certainly would, in his place.*

In spite of herself she felt a grudging admiration for the enemy sorcerer, a man who had learned to command the lightning, who had traced out the convoluted pathway through the Mazy Mire with his clairvoyant eye. It was only through the power of Orogastus that Ruwenda had fallen, and Haramis respected competence, even when it was turned against her and hers. She was curious about him; even as she followed Uzun upward, she wondered about their enemy. *What sort of man can he be, if he is a man at all?*

Haramis and Uzun cautiously moved past the open iron gate of the antechamber to the tower's fifteenth floor, where the crown jewels were kept. The Princess faltered when she heard the sound of searchers within the closed doors of the strongroom, but no one appeared to challenge them. They continued climbing past the next locked and barred level, where cut and uncut gems and fresh-minted specie were stored, to the seventeenth floor, a kind of fortified workroom, where damaged precious articles were repaired or melted down. There were only two more levels, Haramis knew, between them and the roof: first a small armory, then the dormitory for guards and certain other tower workers.

Uzun paused to rest. He took off his beret, mopped his sweating, lined forehead, and struggled to catch his breath, while Haramis regarded him with concern. The Oddling musician had been her friend from early childhood, and she was fond of him and trusted him, even though he was not human. The Nyssomu, of all the aborigines, in external appearance most resembled humans, but their blood was a queer dusky red, and their bones were oddly shaped within, and their hearts beat on the other side of the breast. All of them claimed to have the Sight, and it was certain that at times they could speak to one another from a distance, communicating by means of the speech without words. But most Ruwendians believed them to be inferior beings for all that, lacking in culture and barely civilized, even though they learned human ways quickly enough and sometimes even excelled humans at their own arts and crafts. As a small child, Haramis had thought for a time that the Nyssomu Oddlings belonged to her Father the King, as the animals did. But her Father had explained to her that the little aborigines were free, and had souls, and must be treated as true people . . .

When Uzun had rested, they resumed their stealthy climb. As they approached the last section of stairs, Uzun made Haramis hang back while he went to spy that all was clear ahead. She was becoming increasingly anxious about what would happen when they reached the tower's battlements. As Uzun peeked over the edge of the top-floor landing, Haramis frowned and drew her cloak tightly about her. A cold wind whistled through the unglazed embrasures and flattened the flames of the blazing wall-cressets.

Haramis was dismayed when Uzun failed to beckon her on. He crept back down with one wide, clipped talon pressed to his lips. Alarm shone in his huge yellow eyes. When he reached her side, he whispered: "A single knight on guard, Princess. No doubt others are searching the rest of this level."

"I knew it!" Haramis whispered. "We are trapped up here, with enemy soldiers above and below us! Your White Lady's plan has failed."

"Hush, hush," the Oddling pleaded. "I think there may be a way past, but it will demand that you be brave, and move quickly. Can you tie up your gown?"

She nodded grimly, dropped her cloak, and set the Crown carefully on top of it. Then she kilted her skirts through her jeweled belt until they hung bloused to her knees. She wrapped the Crown in her cloak, tied the corners together, and slung the bundle over her shoulder. She looked to Uzun. "And now?"

"The parapet is reached by a ladder near to the stairs, perhaps four ells from where the guard stands. He has been wounded in one arm and it is bound up, but his sword-arm is quite whole. He is very likely fatigued and sick of the futile searching, which has deprived him of the anticipated joys of looting, feasting, and drinking."

"And violating the Citadel women," Haramis added. "Such will doubtless now be my fate, before they slit my throat and cast my body into the cess-pit."

Uzun looked at her reproachfully. "Princess, you will be harmed only over my dead body. Trust in the White Lady and listen to my plan, I beg of you."

Haramis played nervously with the trillium amulet, running one thumb over and over the smooth amber that encased the small black flower-bud. *I don't doubt your dedication,* she thought, *but "over your dead body" may not be difficult for armed soldiers to achieve.* Not wanting to hurt the little Oddling's feelings, she said merely: "I am listening, Uzun."

"I shall spring suddenly up from the stairwell and dart toward the knight, pretending to be scared out of my wits."

"If you are as frightened as I am, that should present no difficulty."

"I shall caper and gibber and roll my eyes in and out on their stalks."

She knew that what he was saying was a real sacrifice; she had not seen him extrude his eyes since she was a very small child, when he had sometimes done it to amuse her or her sisters. However, she had learned before she was six or so that no adult Nyssomu would show such a lack of control unless he was virtually beside himself.

"I shall distract the villain," Uzun continued. "Meanwhile, you must climb up the ladder and open the upper trap. I shall follow, and together we'll overthrow the ladder and slam shut the trapdoor and bar it against him."

"And then? Even if we can hold off the soldiers — and assuming their sorcerer doesn't blast us with one of his damnable lightning bolts — the top of the tower is no place for a siege. We could, of course, die heroically of starvation and thirst, but that will hardly help Ruwenda!"

"I don't *know* what happens then!" Uzun snapped. "I only follow the White Lady's commands! Oh, Princess, can you not leave off your incessant questioning? More knights may appear at any minute! Just give me a moment to seize this man's attention, and then follow quickly."

He hopped up the steps and into the guards' anteroom.

Haramis heard the soldier curse, and then came the ringing swish of a drawn sword. But Uzun was cackling like an insane thing, his footsteps dancing over the boards, and the knight's filthy language changed to a startled guffaw. Tensing, Haramis looked over the top step and saw the normally staid musician cavorting about, long pointed ears comically aflap like the wings of a night-caroler drunk on fermented fruit. His eyes popped in and out of their sockets on stalks, and his lolling tongue coiled and uncoiled while their owner hooted ridiculously up and down the musical scale.

The knight doubled over with laughter, lowering his sword, and in a flash Haramis scrambled up the ladder and flung open the ceiling-trap.

"Uzun! Come up! Hurry!" She knelt on the roof and gripped the heavy ladder just as the Oddling streaked over to it and began clambering up the rungs. The bamboozled knight cried out an alarm and stumbled toward the ladder waving his sword at Uzun. Haramis grabbed Uzun's wrist and hauled him up beside her. The sword, aimed at his ankle, became embedded in the ladder's rung. Together they gave a mighty heave and thrust the ladder away, while the knight was still clumsily trying to pull his sword from the wood.

Entangled and unbalanced, the armored form fell with an ear-splitting crash. Shouts came from within the dormitory, and as Uzun slammed shut the trapdoor and barred it, more knights of Labornok rushed forth to investigate.

There was a strong wind up on the High Tower roof; redolent of the marshes, it tore at the low-lying fog that hid the Mazy Mire and the lower reaches of the Citadel. The blood-colored Labornoki banner snapped from the tall flagstaff at the side of the tower facing the river. Directly below, some fires still burned among the buildings of the inner ward, flickering eerily beneath the mist. The deep blue sky was bright with stars, and in the west the Triple Moons moved toward their conjunction, which would occur at full phase, four weeks hence.

Fear and indignation over her plight now suffused the Princess with a burning anger. They were in a cul-de-sac with no exit. Knights were smashing on the trapdoor with swords and battleaxes, and soon it would give way. But she would not let the Labornoki take her alive! Better to leap from the tower's battlements —

The trapdoor broke open and a knight whose helmet was a grotesque iron mask hauled himself up, whooping in triumph.

Haramis stood with Uzun at the very brink of the parapet, clutching her amulet as she had when terrified by nightmares as a child. But this nightmare was real.

"Lords of the Air, protect us!"

Uzun cried: "White Lady! Be thou at her aid!"

Three armored men bounded toward them with weapons raised. But at the same moment there was a great blast of wind, and the stars were blotted out by two huge dark forms swooping down. They gave voice like monstrous brazen trumpets, and one stooped and dropped straight at the thunderstruck armored trio.

"Lammergeiers!" one of the knights yelped. "Beware!" But an instant later, a gigantic wing bowled the three men over like dolls and swept them over the edge of the parapet. Their voices blended in one scream, which lasted for several seconds before stopping abruptly. Their companions, who were just emerging from the trapdoor, dodged back down to safety. There was a clanging and a smashing and yells of pain and fury as several presumably fell from the ladder. Others of the Labornoki kept their footing and watched, although none dared to venture out.

Later they would tell King Voltrik and the sorcerer Orogastus what they had seen: two gigantic creatures with white bodies and wings banded black and white, soaring down to land on the High Tower roof, their talons striking sparks from the stones, and their eyes and toothed beaks glistening in the dim moonlight. Princess Haramis mounted one, and the Oddling musician Uzun clambered onto the back of the other.

Then the great lammergeiers spread their wings and took flight, bearing the fugitives away to the northwest, toward the distant rampart of the Ohogan Mountains.

∴

5

The ignominious retreat added fuel to Kadiya's anger. She thought of them being discovered creeping on hands and knees along the narrow, slippery ledge of the conduit. Since it had been disused for countless hundreds, the Ruwendians having built a new water supply system when they took over the ancient citadel, this way was not only falling to pieces but was nearly choked with noisome and rotting debris. Jagun had slung the lantern about his neck, but time after time he was forced to pause and pass the light back to Kadiya until he had broken away a mass of dead branches or pawed up a soggy haystack of marsh grass. In some places the masonry had crumbled utterly, so that they waded, swam, and worked their way around obstacles. The knees of Kadiya's leather trews were soon worn through, the skin beneath scraped raw. Under her breath she muttered words she had heard in the stables but never before voiced aloud.

"Is the river far?" she demanded at last, nursing hands torn painfully by thorn ferns she had taken an equal part in clearing away.

"Not far. If it were day we could see the light ahead, for these accursed ferns cannot grow in total darkness. Take special care now, for this is an excellent lurking place for gradoliks or water-worms."

Kadiya spat out a lump of foul-tasting mud and felt, rising to flame within her, that anger which had been born at the first alarm.

"May the everlasting mud sink them all! May the vipers of Viborn lace them throat and wrist —"

"Save your breath, King's Daughter. Doubtless in time the spirits will provide fates for your enemies even you may find adequate."

"No fate save that I deal myself!" she flared back.

His hand grabbed her wrist in a hold Kadiya knew of old to be a warning. She swallowed and was still.

Now they waded, slipped and slid over quaking mud, netted by a web of small riverlets, until they at last found a time-rusted grill and worked their way around it where part of the stone which had anchored it had fallen away. Above was open sky at last. Once again Jagun cautioned her with outstretched hand.

He moved a little farther from her, his head high. Apparently he was listening intently, as well as using his hunter's sense of smell to test the safety of that small stretch of forgotten wasteland.

"The Labornoki must have established an outpost not far from here."

Kadiya looked up over her shoulder, having to strain her head at an angle to see better. Fire above, looping flames. There was little enough within the Citadel to fuel that victory blaze unless those who had riven its defenses had ripped old hangings from the walls, smashed all the furnishings. Distant shouts, shrill screams, against which Kadiya tried to steel herself—striving to shut out of her mind what must be happening there.

"May I live to give you new mouths to laugh with straight across your filthy throats!" Her lacerated hand crossed her breast to seek her belt knife, touched the amulet which had slipped out through a tear in her shirt.

If the power of this had been able to waft her down into the cistern . . . well, it might have even more to offer. She clutched the amber in one hand so tightly that she might be trying to force it into her wounded flesh.

Will—will and strength—and what words she could summon:

"Lords of the Air, all ye who hold by the God Triune, may thy power be lent to mine, thy will to mine for this, that these be brought to death even as they have slain those who call upon you. Pay blood price, ye of the upper ways, grant me blood price!"

With the amulet gripped as tightly as she would have held a sword, Kadiya pointed to the light of the holocaust behind her.

Her answer was a tortured scream out of the night, a hoarse call for another keg.

∴

Kadiya's lips tightened against her teeth. "It does not work!" Almost she made to fling the amulet from her, but her fingers were so locked that she could not loose them.

"No," Jagun answered quietly, as he might speak to soothe an impatient child.

"But I used my will! I did so more strongly than when I went into the well." She opened her fingers one by one to survey what she held. "Or does it work for me alone? Will it carry me to the White Lady? Or both of us —?"

Jagun watched her patiently. "One can only try, King's Daughter."

Again Kadiya's fingers imprisoned the amulet.

"By what power lives within you — bring us now to she who made you — the Archimage!"

The night held fast about them.

"Carry me, then, if there be any virtue within you, sorceress's gift!"

No answer.

"So! Did I then dream it all?" Kadiya asked of the night. "Was I so bereft of my senses, Jagun?"

"Little one, I cannot answer you truly, it was too dark within. Perhaps I mistook the time of your jump. I am no dealer in old wisdom."

She dropped the pendant, to let it dangle on its chain. "Magic seems to have deserted us, Jagun — if it ever touched us at all. Well, at least that flatland scum cannot hope to trace us through the Mazy Mire."

Kadiya had been many times in the swamps — but only along well-marked Oddling routes. There were other secret ones, some being the jealously guarded knowledge of single-family clans. It was a point of honor not to remember any guidances if one was not of the Kin. Now she bent her head closer to the hunched shadow of Jagun to ask grimly:

"Those plains-crawlers dare not follow us there, is that not so?"

Half concealed by bushes, the Oddling was groping in the water near a tumble of rocks.

"Their sorcerer has called the Skritek. Also Pellan has joined them."

"Pellan!" That one of the merchants' guides — lored almost from birth in the matter of hidden trails — would betray them seemed utterly impossible. But before yesterday she would have sworn that it was impossible that Kadiya of the House of Krain would have bellied like a snake across sucking mud.

"Voltrik holds that which some find it difficult to refuse." Jagun's

∴

voice was cold and hard. He straightened up, bringing out of the mud a stout rope which ended in deep water. On this he pulled with care. "The Labornoki King has power which rests on wealth. And wealth comes from the efforts of men. What king grubs in the mountain for precious ores, lays hand to axe to down trees, bespeaks strange and rare finds from the swamp people? It is those of Pellan's kin who gather these riches. Voltrik takes a mighty share, yes. But he can grant the leavings to those who serve him, and even those leavings will make many men rich. Come, Farseer." He used now the name she had been so proud to gain half a year earlier — a swamp-given name that brought with it respect. "Farseer, there is yet a long way to go."

She was not really listening, still shaken at the thought of Pellan's treachery. Why, she knew him — smiling, pleasant, he had even guided her to one of the strange ruins.

"Did Pellan truly act for gain as you say, Jagun? Or out of fear? He has kin within the flatlands. We have seen this murderous King and what he would do to those who cross him. Fear is mightier perhaps than magic. Did not Anigel surrender to fear?"

"Judge not so quickly, King's Daughter. Your sister made no willing surrender. Fear can become so great as to give birth to madness. In that there is no guilt."

"Only weakness," Kadiya muttered.

"Weakness you may taste of also, and even you may know great fear. Speak not against any one whose burden you have not weighed yourself."

Jagun gave a jerk to the rope and there glided out of the swamp mist a stout punt stocked with poles and a sculling oar, as well as a large bundle well wrapped against the damp.

"Blessings be upon my brother!" Jagun said. "He has followed very well the Archimage's instructions. Now we have our way of travel, food, and clothing also."

The punt was big enough for four passengers, and Kadiya realized with a stab of sorrow that Anigel and Immu had been meant to travel with them. But surely they were now helpless within enemy hands. And Haramis? Kadiya had no way of knowing. This night she stood alone, and on her would doubtless fall the burden of resistance against the invaders.

They embarked and Jagun mounted the sculling oar at the stern.

Their craft began to move up the sluggish stream which skirted the northeastern part of the Citadel. For a moment the mists parted and Kadiya caught a glimpse of the mighty castle-crowned rock and a star or two above it.

Her home — in the hands of the enemy! And where were her sisters? They might be already dead — or worse.

NO! Her hands went to her head as if she could reach inside and pull out the pictures forming there. She must not think of that — she must not!

"Where do we go?" There were many kinds of resistance possible. While vengeance would certainly be hers, she could not bring down King Voltrik alone. Haramis, Anigel — if they lived — might they join with her?

She had not spoken those names aloud, yet Jagun answered, and not for the first time she was startled, for now he said:

"For your sisters are roads waiting also. It is only our own way we must keep in mind now."

"Where do we go?" she demanded again.

"You must answer that, Farseer."

"How?" She had settled into the punt, glancing back once more at the Citadel. The fire there was dying. Still she felt that the swamp seemed unnaturally warm. She looked down. Under her mud-smeared, rent bodice there was a pale spot of light. She clapped a hand to it — the amulet!

Kadiya drew it forth. It seemed to move on her grimed palm. A spark of light pointed skyward as if from some strange candle. Her breath came raggedly. Perhaps after all it still held magic! But magic certainly did not work according to her own will, she had already proven that. Steel in the hand was more certain.

Voltrik's soothsayer Orogastus — he dealt in magic which obeyed him. He could even command his own King, treating him as though he were but a tool and a toy.

Tool and toy! That might be the story of her own birth, and the Archimage's gift-giving! Perhaps magic was like all else — it grew old, rusted, brittle, broken when it was called upon too late.

Under Jagun's stirring the punt made a sharp turn, carrying them in a new direction. She saw the spark move as might the needle of a compass.

∴

"Jagun, this is a guide!"

"What is?" asked the Oddling, weariness in his voice. He had drawn closer to the bank and anchored them with a stone-weighted rope. Now he was tugging at the wrappings of the bundle.

Kadiya held out her hand and told him excitedly of the change in the spark of light.

"So—then it points the way to the Archimage's dwelling at Noth. That is good, for I knew of few trails thither. None of the Nyssomu hunt there. That country, the Goldenmire, is Uisgu territory."

From the wrapping he had shaken out tunics and breeks woven from aromatic grass by his people. There were also hoodcapes of fedok skin, which could turn aside a torrent, and wood-soled sandals. After the clothing came two stoppered jars which he opened, and the scent of the well-crushed and creamed herbs within fought against the swamp odors.

"You can wash and dry your leathers later, if they can be repaired. But now you must be of the swamp."

She skinned out of her garments, which were indeed torn, and re-dressed, taking the cream from the jar to anoint her skin and even plaster through her tangled hair. The insect life of the swamp could make life a torture for any without such protection.

One more precaution Jagun produced, this time from a loop on his belt. It was a hunter's trick Kadiya had seen before. Between his fingers he held a pipe which was hardly more than a reed in thickness. This he put to his lips. The sound he produced was very thin and without a tune, but he was answered.

Passage along any waterway of the Mire could bring a betraying silence which would alert any tracker. Kadiya had not been truly aware of the quiet about them until Jagun's piping unleashed the normal sounds of life. Now she heard the buzz of insects, small gulping and peeping sounds, and the deepthroated call of a gulbard on the hunt, so close that she could see its soft grey-green body lurking just at the surface of the murky water. Ahead, all was darkness.

They sculled up the broad Mutar slowly, staying far out from the inhabited southern shore. Jagun was especially cautious as they passed the wharfs of Ruwenda Market at the Knoll's western edge, where the river swung away at last from its skirting of the high ground and entered the Blackmire. This densely forested region extended over many square leagues between the Citadel and the ruins of Trevista, and received its name from the sunless aspect of the swampland, where tall, intertwined trees were mated by leafy vines and other growth into a dense canopy, so that the surface was nearly always in shadow.

After a while the river broke up into braided watercourses without a clearly defined mainstream. There were thousands of swampy islands and mudbars without number in this part of the Blackmire, so that an ordinary human traveler would have become hopelessly lost trying to find the way in broad daylight — much less at night, in intermittent patches of mist. But Jagun sculled confidently onward.

Kadiya huddled in the bow, nibbling now and then at a piece of adop root, the tuber which made up much of their food stores. These seemed to suck all the moisture from the mouth and left a bitter aftertaste but she knew them for the travel ration of the Oddlings. To gnaw at one was to remember her first venture into the deep swamp with Jagun.

She had delighted so in the strange animals and plants he had brought to show her that she had pestered him to let her visit the Mazy Mire. Her father had very reluctantly given his permission and for a whole day she had traveled through a green gloaming alive with mysterious creatures and plants. That venture had changed her whole life. Kadiya had sworn then to learn the ways of the swamp and those dwelling within.

However, she had never gone where the amulet spark now pointed — toward the remotest and most secret lands. Ahead, the country of the friendly Nyssomu and the shyer Uisgu merged with that of the abominable Skritek.

Skritek! Their very appearance was a horror out of some nightmare. Though they strode two-legged, the skulls atop their sinewy, mottled bodies bore no resemblance to either human or Oddling. Flattened, the forepart elongated into a snout which split to show greenish fangs, dagger sharp, the head of a Skritek seemed designed by nature to rend and kill.

Their eyes were bulbous, as were those of all the swamp Folk, set high on their heads and somewhat to the side so they had a wide range of vision. Unlike the Oddlings', however, those eyes were not golden but a vivid orange, scarlet streaked. The green-blue of their bodies blended easily with the Mire vegetation except for those eyes; and so they usually awaited their prey almost submerged in the swamp, draped with water fern, and pulled their victims under. Thus were they spoken of in the swampland as the Drowners.

Most knew them only through travelers' tales, which were grisly enough. In their own country, which bordered on the farthest known Oddling territory, the Skritek were said to walk boldly, carrying spears and knives on occasion, although their strongest armament was their own fangs and the talons on their three-fingered hands. Their passage was noiseless but the choking musky odor of their bodies betrayed them. They were known to roll in mud wallows into which they tossed ill-smelling herbs to mask their stench. In their own territory they attacked without warning, frenzied by blood lust, either tearing their victims apart and devouring them — sometimes still living — or carrying them away to torture them to death.

"You spoke of the Skritek." Kadiya had wrapped her arms around herself, chilled now. "By what kind of power could those monsters be made to obey any will save their own?"

Jagun answered: "By the will of that one whose shadow overreaches even that of the King he is supposed to serve — Orogastus. Do not down-say him as a soothsayer, a purveyor of petty trickery. He is not one who follows fairs to read the future by casting colored sands. There are those born with unusual talents, King's Daughter, and most do not misuse their gifts. However, there are some adepts who tread a darker path in their search for strange knowledge, and such will spend a lifetime searching for that which gives them power — that power which is not of hand or sword, but rather of thought and will — over others. There are many stories of Orogastus which have come even to our ears here in the Mire. One can perhaps discount a half or two-thirds of such rumors — but what remains is dire enough! Like calls to like — it may be that the Skritek recognize in this King's wizard a force akin to what moves them. Perhaps, as yet, they are not his creatures; but their present alliance rests on a very old law: if your enemy is also mine, then until he is dead we shall walk a common path."

Kadiya sighed. "Jagun, you have long been my teacher and still you know much more that I must learn. I am sometimes hardly more than that child you humored when you first brought me into this country. Your people named me Farseer, but that is mere flattery. Yes, I may see some things well, but in other ways I am blind!"

"To know that one is blind is to begin to see," Jagun replied quietly.

∴

He was steering them toward one of the larger hummocks. Over their heads the patches of sky were greying. Dawn was not far off. "Peril not only threatens the body, it also strikes against the spirit."

"I do not understand."

"Persons, even those you once loved and trusted, might want to use you as a tool, even as I use this oar to steer by."

"Use me?" Kadiya was incredulous. "If they tried they would face my steel!"

"Fight, always fight," the Oddling's voice was gentle mockery. "My little Farseer, you have spied a tree-vart on a branch a hundred ells away, but have you ever tried to see the inner, not the outer? Seeing one's own self is the hardest of all. Now, day comes and with it we shall camp. Pull aside those branches, so."

As she obeyed, he sent the punt neatly into an indentation of the hummock toward which he had guided them. But even on shore, and with fatigue weighing her down, Kadiya was not to be denied her answers:

"You shall teach me wisdom," she stated, with a note of command.

"Not I," he told her somberly.

"That you will leave for the Archimage?" She made a challenge of it.

"Nor she. Understand: only experience teaches wisdom. Each of us must learn it in our own way and in our own time."

Before she could think of an answer to make he looked about him. "This is good solid earth." He stamped on the soil with one foot. "We can camp safely here until dark. We shall even be able to build a fire. A pelrik broiled, or a karuwok — will that not be better than adop roots?"

"We will travel by night?" Now Kadiya wished mostly for a nest of ribbon grass — and there was indeed some growing in sight — in which she could curl up and sleep.

"That will be safest until we pass the Upper Mutar River. Perhaps — if Voltrik is clever enough — he will approach the Nyssomu as a friend, or under the mask of one. Most of us Folk know very little concerning those of your blood, Farseer. To some of us you humans seem to be all of one kin, and since we have long trusted you Ruwendians it may be that smooth words from the Labornoki will keep us from the truth until too late."

"We can warn your people." Kadiya halted in her energetic pulling of the grass. "Perhaps other defeated Ruwendians will escape by river — surely the Nyssomu at Trevista would help such who flee."

Jagun had taken out his pouch of needle-sharp blow-gun darts and was inspecting each with care.

"Farseer, we dare not be seen by any along the Mutar. We have but a short time before the Winter Rains, when no one can travel."

Now he looked up and his golden eyes were webbed with dark veins raised by fatigue. Beads of slimy sweat had worked through the insect-repellent paste on his face and hands. "You must reach Noth. It lies in the very foothills of the Ohogan Mountains more than a hundred leagues to the north. Once we cross the Skritek country, we enter the Goldenmire wilderness. We will then need the help of the Uisgu."

Jagun smoothed a small space of ground with the side of his hand and then began to draw upon it.

"This," he made an indentation with one nail, "is where we are now. Here" — he drew with nail tip northward — "lies Noth, where we must go."

She had heard tales of Noth. Throughout the swamp there were many ruins on sturdy outcrops of earth such as the small one they now shared. Some of those remnants of an earlier time had not been so ill-treated by age as crumbling Trevista, but were said to be as sound as the Citadel. Great treasure was rumored to be hidden in some ruined cities. Now and then there appeared at the market in Trevista peculiar trinkets and mysterious artifacts which the visiting merchants eagerly bargained for. Many were brought in by the shy Uisgu clans who allowed their bolder kin, the Nyssomu, to sell on their behalf. Kadiya had heard of human adventurers who had ventured north and west seeking forgotten islands and what treasure they might hold. Men near crazed by hardships had returned to the Citadel, and one had babbled of a city greater than ruined Trevista standing locked and silent, its walls unmanned and no way to be found within. And that was Noth, or so he had said.

There might be only wraiths to guard that lost city, but all Ruwenda knew that Noth was the hold of the Archimage. Some said that she was of an elder race, out of a past when city-crowned islands dotted a great lake. By the history of Kadiya's own people, the Archimage had always been. If not the same woman always, then one who was twin, and twin, and twin . . .

∴

Jagun disappeared and was back before she had finished a second nest of grass for his bed place. He swung a pelrik by its broad flat tail and Kadiya proved her worth as a traveler in hunting out dry twigs and broken branches to build a neat pile of sticks ready for a spark from Jagun's fireshell. He skinned and cleaned his catch and quartered it with his hunter's long knife, spitting the raw meat on sticks near enough to the fire to roast.

Kadiya found herself nodding, even though the smell of the cooking meat set her mouth watering. She could not remember when she had been so tired — not realizing that the horrors just behind her had had their part in draining her strength.

6

Princess Anigel did not recover her wits until her captors had attained the brewery. There the Labornoki knights rested, since they were worn out from the long climb out of the Citadel's lower levels, which had followed upon a day's battle. Sir Rinutar proposed to Prince Antar that they catch their breath and sample the Ruwendian liquor, barrels of which stood about on every hand.

"Well spake, Rin," said Sir Owanon, "for this Oddling crone is a good deal heavier than she looks, and my back is nigh broken." He dropped Immu onto a heap of grain sacks. She groaned but kept her great eyes tightly closed.

Prince Antar cautioned them. "A brief refreshment only, then. King Voltrik and the sorcerer will be angered if we delay long in bringing these prisoners for questioning. If a one of you drinks to excess, I shall see that the drunken rascal is severely punished."

He set the Princess Anigel down with great gentleness, and smoothed her hair before joining his companions at a freshly broached barrel. Beer flowed merrily from the bunghole into waiting cannikins and then poured onto the floor.

"The cravens of Ruwenda brew a fairish batch of suds," said Sir Rinutar, wiping his mustaches after taking a long pull. "In fact, it's better than ours by a long sight." He drank again, draining the mug, and went for a refill before that barrel emptied.

"Small wonder," whispered Immu, "for ours is aged and eight percent, while the Labornoki brew is naught but infant's piddle."

"This is indeed excellent stuff," said another knight, Sir Penapat. "Why can we not obtain such back home in Derorguila?"

"The brewers in Derorguila Town are ever complaining about the antics of beer-witches," said Sir Owanon, "blaming suchlike evil dames for souring the brew or otherwise making it so often strange to taste. I heard they burnt a beer-witch at the stake just before the army marched. She was taken as she lurked about the kettlehouse, where she was clearly up to mischief. Women know nothing of brewing."

"Lothok dung!" snapped Immu. Her voice was muffled, for they had thrown her on her stomach, but this time her captors heard.

"Well, flay me alive and nail my hide to the wall," Sir Owanon laughed. "My late burden speaks! And saucily, too."

"Give her a good kick," Rinutar suggested.

Princess Anigel struggled up, with her hands tied behind her as Immu's were, and cried: "Hold off, you ruffian, and for shame! For if you think our beer is good, you have Immu to thank for it, since she is the brew-mistress of this Citadel."

"She lies," growled Sir Rinutar. "What scrawny Oddling hag could understand such mysteries?" He gestured at the great copper cookers, the maze of tubing, the complex system of troughs that delivered malted grain to the mash tun and then transferred the clarified wort to the huge brew-kettle. There were catwalks about the rims of these vessels, where the workers could stir and strain and otherwise inspect the liquors.

"I understand brewing very well." Immu, like the Princess, had turned over. Her voice was cool and confident. "And only a jelly-brain would blame soured beer on imaginary beer-witches. Such happens most times because the kettles and fermenting vessels and tubing are not scoured out properly, and fetid growths form therein and taint the liquor."

"Say you true?" Prince Antar was interested. "Perhaps we should let you live, and see if you could teach our Labornoki brewers to come up with better drink."

"A good idea," Sir Owanon said, but others shouted him down, and they began then to quarrel, striking the bungs from other barrels and refilling their cannikins as they emptied.

Then they were diverted, for clattering down the steps came General Hamil, leading another force of knights. They were also fatigued to the bone, and greeted their comrades' discovery with great enthusiasm.

Hamil came to Antar, who only sipped at his brew, and congratulated him upon his capture of Princess Anigel. Then the General took his Lord aside and spoke in a low voice, but Anigel and Immu heard it clearly.

"There has been a dire and portentous happening, my Prince. Milotis and his men were searching the upper reaches of the High Tower when they chanced upon Princess Haramis and an Oddling companion. They pursued them to the parapet, whereupon Haramis stood upon the very brink of the battlement, held tight to an amulet around her neck, and called upon the Lords of the Air."

"So would I have also," the Prince said wryly, "in her position."

"But two monstrous lammergeiers came," Hamil said, "and bore the two away on their backs!"

The Prince uttered an oath. "Milotis saw this prodigy with his own eyes?"

"He did. I communicated the news to the mighty Orogastus, who was stricken with fury. Milotis and all his men were put to death by order of the King."

The Prince muttered, "Madness. Milotis was a worthy captain, and how could he be expected to counter magic? That is Orogastus's business. And I wonder if he will demand my own slaughter, since I snared but one Princess, while the other got away." He described Kadiya's escape through the cistern, and Anigel's statement that her sister now was in possession of great magic.

General Hamil came to stand over the two captive women, a terrible figure in blood-red armor ornamented with gold. On his red-enameled helmet were mounted golden antlers, and the visor was made in the form of a volumnial's skull.

"Princess Anigel," he demanded, "is it true that your sisters have magic?"

But the terrified girl only burst into tears, and thrashed about piteously while Immu said: "Now look what you've done, you great lummox! By the Flower, I know not why the lammergeiers came, but you can be sure no magic was involved. Are the three Princesses not triplets? Would not all three possess magic if two of them did? Yet here lies poor Anigel in your power." She began to speak softly to the girl, but in an urgent manner.

"The Oddling granny makes good sense," said the Prince, frowning. "But we had better leave all this to Orogastus." He lifted his voice. "Companions, we must quit this place now and return to the throne room with our captives."

Immu left off whispering to the distraught Princess and addressed Prince Antar in wheedling tones. "My Lord, have pity on this doomed maiden. Before you carry on, untie her briefly and permit her to relieve herself behind yon pile of sacks, lest she humiliate herself and soil you."

Anigel hung her head in shame, and General Hamil chortled and made a crude remark. But the Prince knelt and undid Anigel's bonds. She thanked him with a woeful countenance and begged that he also release her serving-woman, to help with her garments.

"That I will, but the two of you be quick," said Antar. He made certain that there was no exit from the corner behind the sacks, then let the women go.

"There is another matter I would mention," Hamil said. "The King's hand is much inflamed after his being bitten by the rogue squire. He is in a foul temper from the pain, and both the royal physician and the sorcerer's Green Voice say that he must take to bed with a strong herb pultice over it, and drink hot infusions and rest, lest the wound fester and blood poisoning set in."

"The wizard himself can do nothing?"

"Evidently not, although he did pronounce an incantation over the poultice-pot. He concurs with the diagnosis of his minion and the leech that the King must rest, and so the search for the two eloped Princesses will fall upon us."

"The men are exhausted. They must have several days to recover before an intensive search can be mounted. The time can be used to seek out information — especially from the Oddlings. The aborigines of the swamp would know where the Princesses have gone if any do."

Hamil nodded. "All Oddlings have fled the Citadel, but we can go to Trevista, that ruined ancient city where they have their fair. The turncoat riverman Pellan, who commands a fleet of flatboats carrying merchants to Trevista, will cooperate fully. And there are those among the Master-Merchants of Labornok who may advise us what pressures to put upon the little bog-trotters to gain their help."

"I will speak to my Royal Father, and see that all is put in order. Perhaps you and I and this Pellan can go at daylight to Trevista with

∴

a small force, while the rest of the army briefly takes its ease. We ourselves can nap on the river."

"A splendid suggestion, my Prince."

Antar now frowned and cast an eye about. "The women — where are they?"

Hamil strode at once to peer behind the piled sacks. "Gone! By the Sacred Bowels of Zoto, they are gone! But where?"

He began shouting orders to the others, and the knights raced about, searching every cranny of the great brewery, even though there seemed no way that Immu and Anigel could have passed Prince Antar and General Hamil.

Then, when they were making such a din that no man could hear the other, Prince Antar saw the cloddish knight Rinutar go stomping across one of the catwalks that circled a great wooden fermentation vat. Suddenly Rinutar began to stagger about and push at the air, and howl words that no one could understand, and he overbalanced and fell into the foam-topped, strong-smelling liquor with a great splash.

Every man fell silent from astonishment, and then they began roaring with laughter. Some went to fish the spluttering Rinutar out. His face was as black with fury as his armor was white with suds, and when they had hauled him up he screamed:

"Who pushed me?"

"Drunken numskull," the Prince said, disgusted. "No one pushed you. You simply lost your footing."

"Nay," Rinutar contradicted stoutly. "I was pushed — and more than that, I heard a voice say: 'Take a good long drink' as I fell."

Many knights greeted this protestation with skeptical guffaws, but General Hamil's brow darkened. He bellowed: "Silence, everyone!"

Every mouth clamped shut. In the sudden stillness that followed one could hear dripping beer, and men breathing heavily from exertion . . . and the quick patter of footsteps on the catwalk, and then on the open stairway leading down to the tapping room where the barrels were filled.

"Magic!" Hamil howled. "Magic at work! They have gone invisible! Down to the lower level, all! And go softly, damn you, and listen!"

Anigel, clutching her amulet, whispered anxiously to Immu. "We will be found. We are leaving wet footprints!"

"This way," hissed her invisible companion. "To the dumb-waiter that hoists the barrels to the kitchen level."

They ran to the lift, which was counterweighted and would carry them up with the simple release of a lever. Anigel climbed on, but Immu said: "Wait one minute, Princess." Her wet footprints turned back and approached a great stack of empty kegs waiting in serried ranks to be filled.

As the knights led by the Labornoki General dashed down the stairway, the pile of barrels began to teeter at the end nearest the dumb-waiter. One barrel nudged another, and before the knights knew what was happening the whole stack collapsed with a rumbling crash. Large kegs and small rolled about, tripping up the men and shattering as the knights stamped futilely upon them with mailed feet. But the way to the dumb-waiter was blocked completely.

Princess Anigel let loose of her amulet for a moment from laughing, and so the Labornoki saw the two fugitives clearly as they ascended out of sight.

"I prayed your idea would work," Anigel said, "but I was still sore afraid."

Immu smiled in the dimness of the Citadel Gatehouse, where they had paused to rest, hidden in a deserted sentry kiosk. "But you did not doubt and that was the important thing. Hearing that your sister Haramis also escaped with the aid of her amulet, you had confidence at last that yours would respond to your command, and render us invisible. And it did. So now all we have to do is walk away!"

Anigel sagged back against the flimsy wall. "Good friend, have mercy and let me stay here a little, for if we continue on now, I will surely collapse."

"Lie easy, sweeting." Immu took off her shawl and tucked it around the girl's shoulders. "We are safe for a while. There is no hue and cry out here."

The Labornoki believed that the Princess and Immu were still inside the central keep, and so General Hamil had barred all its doors. But Immu had known of a secret exit from the kitchens, where lazy scullions had been wont to slip away from their duties. This led to the ward outside the keep, and the two women had crossed it swiftly, invisible, dodging knots of Labornoki soldiers dozing around their watchfires.

Although Anigel was exhausted, she felt that she dare not close her eyes, fearing that sleep would cancel the beneficent magic that had brought them safely to the sentry kiosk.

"I still can scarce believe that we truly became invisible," she whispered. "The talisman would not save me at the rim of the cistern . . . why did it act later?"

"At the cistern, you were without hope and mad with fear. In the brewery, more useful emotions inclined you to follow my counsel."

"It's true that I was angry there," the Princess said slowly. "I despised myself for the cowardice that had caused us both to be captured. And I was mortified by the undignified stratagem that you used to make the villains loose our bonds —"

Immu chuckled. "Your anger clarified your mind, banishing the fear that paralyzed your will. You finally believed me when I bade you call upon your amulet's magic. Anger is a much more useful emotion than fear. You must learn to make more use of it, sweeting. In the state you now find yourself, meekness and dainty manners will do you little good."

"And magic will?" Anigel spoke wearily.

"That remains to be seen."

The Princess was lost in thought for several minutes, then asked: "Do . . . do your people make common use of magic, then?"

"Oh, no. It is a special thing, not to be invoked lightly. Sometimes it is there and sometimes not, no matter how desperately one wishes for its help. For your poor Mother and Father, there was no magical assistance —"

"And that was cruel! It makes no good sense that the King and Queen of Ruwenda perish and the country be conquered while magic shields me and my sisters!"

"Peace, child, peace. Magic is a mystery, like so much of life. It can be wielded for good or evil, and we do not always know which is which, any more than we really understand what magic *is*."

Anigel sighed. "Perhaps the Archimage will tell us."

She huddled down close to her old nurse and finally her eyes closed; but the Princess still held tightly to the trillium amber even when she was sound asleep.

They had not rested more than two hours when they heard bugle-horns sounding, and the soldiers sleeping about the Gatehouse began

∴

to awake snarling and growling. It was nearly dawn. The men were in
an evil mood because looting of the Citadel had been forbidden. They
built up their fires against the chill, prepared scanty breakfasts from
field rations, and relieved themselves most offensively in any place at
all.

"Don't look outside, Princess," Immu said. "The cultureless bump-
kins!"

"Oh, Immu, I don't care about that. What worries me is what we
are to do next. How will we ever get to the home of the Archimage?"

"Jagun had our escape all planned, and his brother brought a boat.
But doubtless Jagun and Kadiya have embarked in the punt long ago,
giving us up for lost." Immu's brow furrowed in thought. "We shall
have to find another way to get up the Mutar. If we can reach Trevista,
my Folk will help us contact the Uisgu, in whose lands the ruins of
Noth lie."

"But Trevista is so far away, with the Blackmire lying between it
and the Citadel!"

Outside there was a flourish of trumpets. Immu peered through a
crack in the door to see what was happening. A knight-commander
and his escort came cantering into the forecourt of the inner ward, and
pulled up not a dozen ells from the guard kiosk. There a sergeant-
quartermaster was supervising the distribution of supplies from a train
of covered wagons. The knight said: "The company will move out in
one hour. We shall march across the Knoll to Ruwenda Market on the
western side, and there board flatboats for Trevista. Be sure to bring
adequate food and materiel, and fodder for the beasts."

The sergeant saluted and the knight wheeled his war-fronial about
and clattered away with his escort through the Gatehouse and into the
outer ward.

Immu laughed softly. "Our problem is solved. The foemen themselves
will carry us to Trevista, all unawares! Are you hungry, my child?"

"Yes, Immu. And very tired."

"You cannot render us invisible while you sleep, but I think we will
be able to find a suitable place of concealment after we have had our
breakfast." She explained her plan, and the eyes of Princess Anigel
began to dance, and she hugged the Oddling woman.

Then Anigel clasped her amulet and made them disappear, and they
started off to find a suitable wagon.

∴

7

High over the fogbound Mazy Mire the lammergeiers flew, carrying Haramis and Uzun toward the ruins of Noth.

When her thudding heart slowed, and her senses told her that what she experienced was indeed real and not some fantastic dream, Haramis took stock of her situation. She was unharmed, and the appearance of the powerful creature had saved her from almost certain death. Was this the magic of the Archimage? Did the White Lady retain some power, even though her magic had not been sufficient to stand against Orogastus and prevent the invasion of Ruwenda?

The lammergeier's enormous wings beat strongly and regularly, making a faint thrumming sound as they stroked the air. Its white-plumed back was as wide and as soft as a bed quilted in down. Haramis sank so deeply into the hollow behind the bird's great black-streaked neck that it was hardly necessary to cling tightly to the plumage. When they had been aloft for nearly an hour, the lammergeier's crested head turned to regard its strange burden, but the dark eyes were mild and the toothed beak offered no threat.

Not knowing whether it understood, she said to it: "My thanks for rescuing me and my companion."

There might have been a miniscule nod, or perhaps not. The creature looked upon her no more, but flew steadily onward. Haramis waved to Uzun, but they could not converse, since the two lammergeiers were too far apart.

The world below was a pale cloud deck and in the clear night sky above, familiar constellations glittered: the Drawn Bow, the Kettle, the Ladu-Tree, the Great Worm, the Northern Crown.

Crown . . .

She still had, knotted and slung over one shoulder, the bundled black cloak with her Mother's blood on the folds. She divested herself of it, unknotted the fabric, and gazed upon the Queen's Crown of State with its finial of trillium amber until grief blurred her vision. *At least Voltrik does not have this,* she thought grimly, *nor shall he while I live! He killed my parents, but I still live, and Ruwenda is mine!*

She fought back tears, afraid that if she started crying she would not be able to stop. *I am Queen of Ruwenda now, and it is my duty to safeguard the country and its people, and to marry and raise my children to continue the task when I am gone.* Her throat was tight, and it was difficult for her to breathe, but she was determined. She was also, however, afraid. *I always knew that I would be Queen one day — but I never expected it to be so soon . . . or under these circumstances! I hope the White Lady can help me; I certainly am going to need help from somewhere!*

Was there truly magic in the strange fossilized blossoms encased in the Crown and her amulet, or had it only been good luck that had brought the Archimage's lammergeiers to the rescue in the nick of time?

I shall experiment, she thought. And she took hold of the amulet on its neck-chain, closed her eyes, and said, "Transport me instantly to the dwelling of the White Lady!"

But nothing happened, and the lammergeier flew on serenely.

She tried a simpler request: "Bring me a savory pasty, for I am dying of hunger."

Again there was nothing, and her stomack contracted painfully.

So much for magic. Ah, well. What did it matter?

A profound depression enveloped her. There was no kingdom for her to rule and no royal spouse to sit at her side. Haramis tried to be glad, to seek the compensations of her present predicament. She had always hated the pomp and ceremony of court life, the endless meetings with ministers that her Father had patiently endured, the tedious banquets and entertainments her Mother had supervised, always surrounded by her twittering ladies. There had been a deeper side to Queen Kalanthe as well, for she had written poetry and taken a keen interest in the affairs of the less fortunate in Ruwenda, always seeking to improve their lot without stifling their initiative. But queenship was a job that Haramis had dreaded. Dutiful, she had accepted it as her natural lot. But now her obligation had been, at the very least, altered somewhat . . .

She snuggled down into the cushiony hollow, letting the wind sing above her, and awaited sleep's release. The bundled Crown she tied to her jeweled girdle so that it might not be lost. The Archimage would know what to do with it.

And what to do with her.

Who was this woman, really? That she was real and not a legend, Haramis no longer doubted. The fabulous events at her birth must also now be counted as real, and the ominous speech of the Archimage as well. If this White Lady was truly nigh unto death, how would she be able to give aid and advice? And why had she said so long ago that *all would be well?*

These thoughts circled dizzily in her mind, and she mulled over a score of ways whereby Ruwenda might yet be saved — and she riding triumphant at the head of a Ruwendian host, having herself effectuated the victory. But these were nothing but foolish fantasies. She was seventeen, clever and book-learned beyond a doubt, but hardly a warleader. If this Archimage had chosen her as an instrument of destiny, she must be senile indeed . . .

I shall have to be on my guard, Haramis thought. *Who knows what foolhardy schemes this old woman may urge upon me? But I shall be wary, and form my own decisions. I am Queen now and the responsibility is mine, no matter who advises me. I must not meekly submit to another's will.*

Trillium or no trillium.

When she woke it was dawn, and the two lammergeiers still flew on. The Ohogan range now thrust up to fill fully half of the sky, forbidding fangs of granite and basalt, entirely snowclad above the tree-line. Rosy sunlight gave the glaciers and icefields a false softness. Haramis looked on them with a sinking heart. What if the Archimage told her that her destiny lay up there?

The mist was burning off the marshland below as the sun grew stronger, and the land was changing from jungle into a vast undulating sea of tall grass, yellowish in color, unlike any part of the Mazy Mire she had ever seen before. Only rare patches of dry land broke the monotonous wet plain. These slight elevations had hardwood trees, shrubs, and other green vegetation upon them — and, she supposed, the secret habitations of the Uisgu, those diminuitive kin to the Nyssomu who dwelt in the northern reaches of the Mazy Mire.

There were aborigines in the mountains also, she knew, called Vispi; but humans had no contact with them. Further east, where the range was cleft by the Vispir Pass, the men who had stood guard claimed that the elusive Vispi emerged on moonlit nights to dance on the new-fallen snow. And there were horror stories of the mountain Oddlings as well. They were called the demons of the frozen mist, and their eyes glared from the icy whirlwind, and it was said that those who looked upon them died. Nevertheless, no one doubted that the Vispi were real folk and not supernatural, for they traded gemstones and precious metals to the Uisgu. These eventually made their way to human markets via the Nyssomu, and the Vispi demanded in return certain foodstuffs, sturdy domestic animals such as fronials and volumnials, woven fabrics, and a few other trade items. But what the beings really looked like, no human being could tell — except perhaps those luckless ancient armies of Labornok who had dared the Vispir Pass ages ago and (if the old stories were to be believed) perished at the hands of these minions of the Guardian White Lady.

Sunlight reflected mirrorlike from the Goldenmire pools and small rivers as the day advanced. Haramis spied now and then thin twisting water-trails, which she presumed were the thoroughfares of the Uisgu. Then, after more hours during which they followed the course of a somewhat larger river northward, the terrain rose and the Goldenmire came to an end in foothills thinly forested with strange trees, interspersed with flower-decked highland bogs. The lammergeiers began to circle round and round, descending.

There were ruins down there, beside the river, all overgrown with creepers and with trees perched boldly on tumbledown walls and poking up through broken cupolas. Unlike her sister Kadiya, Haramis had no wish to explore such sites. Only the peculiar artifacts they contained interested her. She had owned a few — a small featureless box that played a different ethereal tune when set on each of its several sides, a writing instrument that seemed never to run dry of ink, and a weird bracelet of some unknown hard, white substance that was not bone, nor wood, nor any mineral the sages of Ruwenda knew. The Vanished Ones had certainly had some power, but their secrets had been lost long ago. If, however, the Archimage did truly share in the ancient wisdom, then Haramis might still have some faint chance of fulfilling her birth-prophecy.

She clutched the amulet automatically, praying: "But dear God and Lords of the Air, let me not be deceived! Above all, let me not be encouraged to rash behavior, then fail. I could not bear to fail!"

They were floating slowly, in a long shallow glide, approaching a small stone structure, towerlike in shape, that was almost buried in thick greenery. The winged creatures touched down softly on a kind of natural lawn all dotted with bright wildflowers that spread out before a lowered drawbridge. There were also water-blossoms of vivid blue growing in the moat, and a sweet fragrance in the air.

Haramis slid from the lammergeier's back and curtseyed low to it. "My fervent thanks to you, master of the sky, for having brought me and my good servant to this safe haven."

When she lifted her head, the two lammergeiers had already taken wing. They both uttered clarion cries before disappearing beyond the trees.

Uzun stood beside her. He was a sadly comical sight, his beret lost, his long silky hair all asnarl from the wind, and his once dapper maroon velvet smock stained and rumpled. But his grin was indomitable.

"Here we are," he chirped. "Let us enter, for our arrival has been announced by the lammergeiers."

Slowly, they walked across the meadow to the drawbridge. The building was shrouded in moss and girt about with tiny lacy ferns, each hewn stone softened in outline by flowers springing forth from the crumbling mortar. Plants grew on the bridge planking as well. The Princess stepped gingerly for fear of rot, but the span seemed sturdy enough. There were no retainers about to give welcome, no sign that any person inhabited the overgrown pile at all. But Uzun strode forward confidently, and Haramis followed, marveling at strangely carved pillars and wall-panels, and ornate floor mosaics barely visible through the mosses and lichens underfoot. They passed a splashing fountain, and went through archways hung with dripping strands of vines, into tangled gardens glorious with flowers of many colors.

They stopped at last in front of a wooden door of polished black wood with no moss upon it, but having hinges and fittings and a great ring-latch of what appeared to be solid gold. In the center was a carved

∴

ornament fashioned from the same wood, all fimbriate with shining platinum; and it had the image of a Black Trillium.

"This is the chamber of the Archimage Binah herself," Uzun said. "But only you may enter." He bowed to Haramis, and stepped back.

She hesitated. "But—you must accompany me!"

"Nay, my Princess. I will wait for you."

Haramis drew herself up. "Very well." Forcing her hand not to tremble, she took hold of the golden ring and pulled. The tall door swung open easily, and she stepped inside.

The room was dim and warm, without windows. There were many pieces of furniture half visible in it—cupboards and presses and bookshelves and tables strewn with strange implements, padded stools and settles, and a huge bed with dark hangings. At one wall was a hearth with a small peat fire burning, and before it stood a handsome table with a single place-setting of crystal, and a golden knife and spoon. Covered golden dishes steamed and gave forth a delicious smell. A flagon of honey-wine stood by, and a beautiful lamp with a shade of leaded opalescent glass cast light over all. There were two carved chairs, one before the food and another opposite, before which on the table sat a plainly wrought small casket of platinum, very dented and battered and dulled from long use.

"Welcome, my child," said a soft but resonant voice. "I have been waiting for you."

Haramis started, and looked about, and saw a pale shape move in the great bed. "My Lady?" she said, curtseying almost automatically.

"Come and assist me, and I will sit with you while you dine."

Wondering, Haramis asked, "Are you the Archimage Binah?"

"I am she. Do not be afraid. I am the one who stood by at your birth and who summoned you here. I have long awaited your coming and that of your sisters, and I give thanks that you have arrived safely."

Haramis stood stock-still. "Kadiya and Anigel—they are alive?"

"They are. Do not worry about them now, for they must follow their own paths and you yours. Come. Help me to enrobe."

Haramis could not move. A great fear had taken hold of her. She knew now that, like it or not, she was going to have to embark on some terrible adventure.

In the bed lay a woman with beautiful flowing white hair, who sat up slowly and beckoned to the girl. Her face was smooth and unlined,

∴

and only her eyes, dark-shadowed and set so deep in the skull that their color was unguessable, betrayed her great age. Her gaze ensnared Haramis and drew her forward with irresistible power. Haramis set down the Crown-bundle on the floor and walked in terror to the bed. But then she was suddenly set free, and the panic left her, and it seemed that the person sitting there was only a poor sick old woman needing help.

Haramis assisted the Archimage to don a long white robe that shimmered blue in its foldings, and put fur slippers on her long, slender feet. When the woman stood up, Haramis saw that she was very tall. Her figure was not stooped, but erect and supple, and she moved slowly to the table before the fire and sat down.

"Please be seated also, my child, and eat. You must be famished after your ordeal at the Citadel and your journey here."

"My companion, the musician Uzun —" Haramis began.

"He is being attended to by my own steward, Damatole, and will not want for rest and refreshment."

"I thank you," Haramis said, "for I owe my life to him, and I would not have him suffer for his devotion to me."

Then she fell upon the food with the fierce appetite of the young and healthy, for she had not eaten since the previous morning. There was a roast fowl, and creamy soup with pungent herbs, and a dish of baked dorun tubers all crusted with brown alga-cheese, and a bitter-cress salad, and a tartlet full of some plump, unknown fruit that was tangy on her palate after the heavy repast — of which Haramis devoured the last crumb.

Then she sighed, and sat back sipping at the exquisite wine. The Archimage smiled, and Haramis laughed ruefully and said: "I did not even think to wash my hands before dining. And I gobbled your delicious meal like an ill-bred serf. For this lack of good manners, I beg your pardon, Lady Binah. I would clear the table and clean up the dishes in amends, but I confess I do not know how such scullery matters are managed."

"Here in Noth," said the Archimage, "one fortunately need not bother with trivialities." She gestured, whereupon the table was clear of all except the wine-flagon, Haramis's goblet, and the mysterious platinum casket.

"So you are a sorceress indeed," murmured the girl.

"Such tricks require only small skill," Binah admitted. "It is the larger enchantments that are now beyond my waning powers."

"Since your lammergeiers brought me here, I suppose you know what has happened."

"The great flyers are not mine," the sorceress corrected. "They are free creatures, belonging only to themselves. It is true that I bade them bring you, for they may choose to obey certain of their friends. As to your question — yes, I do know what has happened. I have seen it all, and wept for my impotence to prevent it."

Haramis preserved a neutral expression. "Your mastery of magic is then insufficient to deliver Ruwenda from the murderer Voltrik and his conjurer Orogastus?"

"Even so. I warn you not to underestimate Orogastus, my child. He is no common trickster as are the magicians of your limited acquaintance. He is a man of profound accomplishment who not only commands the storm but holds the key to many other fearsome enchantments. He seeks power wherever he can find it and use it as he wills for his own purposes. He now transcends me in all powers save that of fargazing; for this he requires the ice-mirror hidden deep in his mountain lair."

"Then you cannot help me to bring down Ruwenda's enemies?"

"I did not say that. But the restoration of Ruwenda is a threefold task requiring the cooperation of all three of the Trillium's Petals —"

"You mean my sisters?" Haramis's voice was horrified and incredulous. "I don't think we may depend on them for very much constructive aid. I had to restrain Kadiya from rushing out to attack our Mother's murderers with her belt-knife! And Anigel does nothing but huddle in a corner and weep."

"Nevertheless, my Sight assures me that all three of you must accomplish your foreordained tasks, mastering your own selves above all, before Ruwenda may cast off the yoke of Labornok. And if any one of you fails, all fail."

"But that's not fair!" Haramis protested.

"No." The Archimage spoke gently. "That is only how it *is*."

Disgruntled, Haramis fingered her trillium amulet. "I had thought that these tokens of ours, which you gave us, were magical. But when I put this one to the test, it failed."

"They can only assist you in times of mortal danger, and their powers are limited."

∴

"So I discovered," Haramis sighed. "Well, my first prayer was well-answered, and my second and third were not so urgent as I then thought. Is this amulet to have a role in the tasks you will assign me?"

"That I do not know. You must find out its secrets, just as you must learn the secret within you and conquer the flaws and weaknesses that would deflect you from your destiny. But this I do know: when your preliminary work is accomplished, then you will be given a sign. A new talisman, the Three-Winged Circle, will come to you. Then you will know that the final struggle for Ruwenda and for your own soul is at hand."

"And my sisters?"

"They will have their own work. And, if they succeed, their own talismans. The Three Petals of the Trillium will then call out to one another and unite, and from this will come the resolution — the restoration of the lost balance of the world."

Haramis slumped in her chair. "This task. Must I begin it at once? I am so weary. And I mean you no disrespect, but what you say is hard to believe. I did not even believe in your existence —"

"What you believe, even at this moment, does not matter, for you are worn down from sorrow and fear. You must pray for strength and courage, and above all you must learn to trust yourself and the Triune Power that loves and guides us all."

Haramis uttered an ironic small laugh. "I am in sore need of more concrete help."

"The aborigines will help you on your quest as they are able — the Folk of the swamp, the forest, and the mountains. They revere the Black Trillium, as do the human inhabitants of Ruwenda."

"Am I to take Uzun with me? He is elderly —"

"He will accompany you part way on the long journey you must now undertake. It is *his* destiny to help you achieve yours. But the greatest challenges you must face alone."

Haramis was lost in introspection, staring at the peat flames burning low in the hearth, and fingering her amulet. "Can you tell me the nature of this soul-perfecting quest?"

"No. But you will know it."

She cried out, "Can you do *anything* to help me, aside from this supper and your advice and good wishes?"

"That I can."

The Archimage opened the platinum casket and reached inside with both hands. Lifting, she rose to her feet, and in some miraculous manner she brought out a great green growing plant, much larger than could have fit inside the casket by any normal means. It was a trillium nearly as tall as Haramis herself, bare-rooted, with spreading glossy leaves, and seedpods, and a myriad of night-black blossoms each as large as an outstretched hand. This the Archimage set upon the table.

Haramis cried out in astonishment. "How beautiful! And it is alive, not a tiny fossil entombed in amber!"

"It is the last living Black Trillium plant in the known world."

"And through it we three shall conquer King Voltrik and Orogastus! I know this is true, Binah! I know it!" Haramis sprang to her feet, all weariness fallen away, drinking in the sight of the wondrous plant whose flowers were the color of her hair.

The enchantress stretched out her hand and plucked something from beneath one of the great leaves. This she pressed into Haramis's palm and closed the girl's fingers about it. Then she lifted the plant, somehow put it again into the small platinum casket, and lowered the lid.

Haramis blinked as though a bright light had been extinguished, along with the certainty she had just felt. "But . . . is that all?"

The Archimage took her by the arm and led her to the outer door. "What I have given you will set you on your way. I shall keep the Crown of Ruwenda safe here for you. No enemy shall ever touch it. Only remember that Orogastus, not King Voltrik, is your true enemy. But he lives by the laws of magic, which declare that for every strength there must be a corresponding vulnerability or weakness. If you can find his weakness and vanquish your own, you will triumph. I can tell you no more. Now you must go. When you achieve your goal of the Three-Winged Circle, return to me."

"But what is the Three-Winged Circle?" Haramis asked anxiously.

"You will know it when you find it," Binah assured her. "Farewell."

Suddenly Haramis stood again on the flower-strewn greensward before the mossy tower, and Uzun was beside her, dressed in fresh new clothes. She looked down and saw that her own dirty and wilted white gown and cloak had disappeared, and she now wore a suit of white wool trimmed with albino fedok-fur, over which lay the amulet on its chain, and a fur-lined cloak, and strong white-leather boots. On the ground lay two knapsacks, and two stout walking sticks with iron-shod points.

"I am ready, Princess," Uzun said. He grinned up at her, and his round cheeks were as rosy as ripe cloudberries. "The White Lady has even given me a new fipple flute, so that I can cheer our journey with music!"

"But which way are we to go?" Haramis clenched her hands in vexation. Then she was reminded that the Archimage had put something in her hand. She uncurled her fingers, and in her palm lay a pod of the Black Trillium, dry and shiny. Unthinking, she cracked it open. Inside were rows of winged seeds. Again without conscious thought she plucked one seed forth and cast it into the air. To her surprise, instead of drifting off on the wind, it floated northward, toward the mountains.

The way seemed a trackless high bogland. But then Haramis looked more closely, following the floating seed, and saw a faint path, such as might have been made by a small animal moving through the grass tufts and sedges.

"So," said she. "I suppose this is as good a guide as we may expect. Shall we start?"

Her eye fixed on the tiny floating speck of white, she hoisted her pack, took up the stick, and led the way into the bog, Uzun following at her heels.

∴

t was mid-afternoon when the lookout on the leading flatboat sang out: "Trevista in view!"

The trade-guide Pellan, who was the skipper in charge
of the improvised Labornoki flotilla, raised a small golden horn to his
lips and blew a three-note call. Immediately the rowers in all fourteen
of the boats lifted their sweeps, and crews in the bow and stern of each
craft dropped anchors into the shallow muddy water. Pellan sounded
another more complex horn-call and gave orders for the sweating rivermen to take their ease.

A bellow of fury arose from the foredeck, and a gravelly voice shouted
Pellan's name, embroidered with colorful obscenities. In spite of the
fact that the journey up-river from the Citadel had been completed in
record time, General Hamil had still discovered something fresh to
complain about.

Sighing, the skipper made his way from the tiller-house in the stern-
sheets across the smelly afterdeck. Unlike the other boats in the train,
this one did not carry supply wagons or draft animals. But the mounts
of the high nobility were tethered back here (God only knowing what
use the conquerors hoped to make of them in the trackless swamps
around Trevista), together with their feed and tack, leather sacks full
of arms and armor, and a gang of twenty or thirty hostlers, soldiers,
and assorted lackeys who lounged about gambling, snoozing, or trading
bitter jests with the oarsmen.

Pellan paused at the little midships deckhouse that housed the galley
and his own small accommodation—the latter commandeered by the

sorcerer Orogastus and his two malevolent attendants — to order the messmen to serve a sizable ration of wine to the exhausted rowers and a token drink to the Labornoki commoners to forestall grumbling.

Then he slipped past a knot of sergeants, who glowered at him because the flotilla's halt had deprived them of the cooling breeze of passage, and arrived at last on the foredeck. An awning had been erected there to shade the privileged passengers, who included Prince Antar's knightly party, General Hamil and the handful of ranking officers he had brought on the reconnoitering expedition, and the Master-Trader Edzar, newly dubbed official spokesman to the Trevista aborigines on behalf of the occupying forces of Labornok.

Most of the younger knights were hanging over the rails, peering into the distance in a vain attempt to catch a glimpse of the fabulous Oddling city. Without their flamboyant enameled armor they were a rough and tatty-looking crew, dressed in rusty, sweat-stained smocks and trews. The nobles and high officers were similarly attired in a simple style of undress, distinguished from the knights' only for being fairly clean. The stout Master-Trader, on the other hand, was as elaborately garbed as a courtier at a royal audience, wearing his guild's gold-embroidered green tabard over a gauzy robe of cadmium-orange. His ensemble was topped off by an extraordinary broad-brimmed hat woven of a green leafy material and decorated with a band of living flowers.

"Why have we stopped?" General Hamil demanded rudely of Pellan. "If that's Trevista up ahead there, then shake your lazy tail and get a move on! You were told we wanted to get there as quickly as possible."

The flotilla had come to a standstill out in the middle of the Lower Mutar, which was so broad at this point that the Blackmire banks were nearly a league away on either side. Pellan gave a negligent salute to the scowling officer. "We must follow the Master-Traders' Protocols, my General, and wait for our Nyssomu escort into Trevista."

"Traders?!" exclaimed the Labornoki commander-in-chief. "We're not a pack of peddlers, we're conquerors — and we follow no Protocols but our own! Up anchor, you slugwit, and move on!"

"Sir, that would be most unwise. I couldn't take responsibility for what might happen." The Ruwendian turncoat had a face as brown and tough as the old leather garments he wore. His jowls were scratchy with white stubble from their three-day journey upstream, and his expression verged on the insolent. "These wild Oddlings are a touchy lot. No telling what they'd do if we just barged into Trevista on our own —"

"Ruwenda is ours and we do as we please!" Hamil roared. He drew his sword. "Now get a move on, or I'll ventilate your gullet!"

Pellan, unperturbed by the threat, turned to the Labornoki Master-Trader, who had been regaling the General and his cronies with stories of the fabulous hidden cities of the Vanished Ones. "You talk to him, Master Edzar. He just doesn't seem to understand the situation —" The boatman's voice broke off in a screech as Hamil gripped a handful of his grizzled hair and raised his sword.

"General! Hold, I say!"

Prince Antar, who had suffered from a mood of dejection throughout most of the journey and was sitting by himself up in the bows, pushed through the crowd of knights, who were waiting hopefully for bloodshed, and confronted the burly old soldier. Grudgingly, Hamil let the skipper go. Pellan scuttled out of reach and the Master-Trader stepped forward to bow to the Prince.

"Do let me explain, High Lord. I assure you that our new ally Pellan has only the best interests of Labornok at heart."

"He'd better," Hamil muttered, "or he'll find himself at the bottom of the Mutar with swamp-worms nibbling on his family jewels."

Most of the knights laughed, but the Prince said, "Say on, Master Edzar."

"Yonder lies Trevista." The Master-Trader gestured directly upstream toward a mass of low hillocks, distant blobs of green with deep purple shadows that shimmered in the heat-haze and filled the main channel of the Mutar from one side to the other. "It lies on that group of islands, at the confluence of the Vispar River and the Upper Mutar. But the place is not the kind of city that we Labornoki are familiar with — nor even the Ruwendians — and the so-called Trevista Fair is not an event that always takes place in the same location. Rather, it moves about Trevista as the mood strikes the local Nyssomu, so that not even trader-guides such as our worthy friend Pellan may say for certain where it may be found this day."

Osorkon, Hamil's gargantuan deputy, gave a derisive snort. "A city on an island — and you can't track down a wretched Oddling market even if it does skip about like a springfish on hot mud."

∴

"Trevista does not lie on one island, Lord Osorkon." Edzar's hand swept the horizon. "It is on all of them."

The company gasped.

"It is — or was — the crowning architectural glory of the Vanished Ones. Beside it, the immensity of Ruwenda Citadel is but a crude stronghold, a refuge against whatever disaster ultimately brought down the ancient race. Every one of those hundreds of islands is crowded with ruins, and between them is an intricate maze of canals with walls sunk deep into the riverbed. There are watergates, huge bridges, crumbling dockyards — every manner of riparian structure, to say nothing of derelict public buildings, gorgeous decayed dwellings, and great plazas and arcades all choked with dense jungle growth in places where the Nyssomu have forborne to interfere."

"How much of the city is inhabited by the aborigines?" the Prince asked.

"No one knows, High Lord. The wildling Nyssomu disdain social contact with humanity. We traders are led to the fair location, and there the individual Oddlings proffer such goods as they think will interest us." Avoiding Hamil's glare, he added: "If this flotilla were to penetrate Trevista without permission — you will notice that I do *not* say unannounced, because they always know when we are coming — it is likely that not a single Nyssomu would condescend to show its face. We would find the place deserted. As for invading Trevista with a view to conquest, such a venture would be futile. The value of that vast assemblage of ruins lies only in its tradegoods, and for those we must cultivate the good will of the Oddlings."

"Well spoken, Master Edzar." The Prince cast a meaningful look at the General. "And if we do gain their confidence — assuring them that trade will continue without a break under Labornok's rule of Ruwenda — do you believe that they will cooperate?"

"One can hope so, High Lord."

"We're damn well going to establish a Trevista garrison!" Hamil declared. "That was King Voltrik's order. And those little swamp-stompers had better not collude in any treason with the fugitive Princesses if they know what's good for them!"

"It's clear," said the Prince quietly, "that Nyssomu loyalties are stronger for the Princesses than for us. We shall have to locate the girls by subtlety rather than by a crude show of force." His gaze swept the assembled knights, finally coming to rest on the face of General Hamil. "Is that clear?"

"Perfectly," Hamil rumbled, adding a belated, "my Prince."

"Wherry from Trevista in view!" the lookout sang.

Most of the knights rushed back to the rails to watch the approach of the strange little craft. It was not propelled by oars or a sail, yet came toward the flatboat train at a high rate of speed, leaving a gleaming V-shaped wake on the sluggish water. It seemed to carry a single occupant and it was lavishly decorated with flowers from stem to stern.

"What in the world provides its motive power?" asked the amazed Sir Owanon.

Pellan, well out of General Hamil's reach and with his dignity restored, replied: "It is hauled along by a pair of rimoriks, aquatic creatures resembling large pelriks. Unfortunately, the beasts resist domestication by humans. Even among the Nyssomu, not too many have the knack of driving them, for this is a trick they must learn from their unsociable cousins, the Uisgu. Members of this latter tribe come regularly to Trevista, bringing trade items from the northern reaches of the Mire."

The Prince took Edzar by the shoulder and led him apart from the others, toward the midships deckhouse. "Explain to me what you meant by our flotilla not being unannounced. Do you mean to say that the Trevista Oddlings have been able to keep track of our voyaging, in spite of the double-time pace we maintained coming up-river?"

The Master-Trader shrugged. "High Lord, they speak to one another at a distance, using speech without words, even as the Lord Orogastus bespeaks his attendant Voices."

The door to Pellan's cabin opened so abruptly that both the Prince and the Master started. The tall, black-and-white-clad sorcerer himself stood there, hooded so that the upper part of his face was in deep shadow. Behind him were two other caped and cowled figures, the acolytes known as Voices, a stocky one dressed in red and a tall rangy one wearing blue.

"That is correct," Orogastus intoned. "The nonhumans employ a crude form of telepathy, and on occasion are even able to descry events at a distance through the Sight — although their command of both powers is greatly inferior to my own."

The Prince ordered the Master-Trader to leave them; and when the man was gone he said coldly to Orogastus: "Grand Minister, you never spoke of this to me before."

"There was no need. The matter was of no consequence during the invasion, and we never intended to wage war on the aborigines. On the contrary . . . We will be making very good use of the creatures."

"Then you have a plan for gaining an alliance with these small Oddlings, as we did with the Skritek? My Royal Father hinted as much to me during the march to the Citadel." Antar spoke stiffly, his manner combining deference and resentment. Even though he was six-and-twenty years of age, neither the King nor his mysterious Grand Minister of State had seen fit to confide any of their long-range plans to him.

"With certain of the tribes, when the time is ripe, we will enter into political alliance." Orogastus waved his hand in a dismissive gesture. "Not with these paltry Nyssomu, however. They are only useful to us for the herbs, spices, and other products of the swamp that they sell. They have long since gleaned the most interesting antique artifacts from Trevista itself and from the nearer abandoned cities, and because of their close ties to the fallen Ruwendians I do not trust them to exert themselves in supplying us with fresh quantities of the ancient devices. However, one way or another I intend to have Oddlings loyal to us comb the more remote parts of the Mazy Mire, where I know that there are hidden certain extraordinary magical machines of the Vanished Ones. These, properly utilized, will enable Labornok to extend its rule not only across the entire Peninsula — but eventually throughout the known world."

The Prince felt his heart contract. So this was why King Voltrik had appointed this upstart his Grand Minister, against the advice of his more conservative counselors! Was the sorcerer merely playing upon Voltrik's credulity, or might the mad scheme have a basis in fact?

Antar's face showed tolerant skepticism. "So say you? Labornok one day rule the world — ? No wonder you were so determined that we should declare war on Ruwenda! But this, too, is news to me. What is the nature of this portentous gadgetry you seek, and how do you have knowledge of it?"

"We will discuss this another time, my Prince. The boat from Trevista is almost upon us, and your request involves matters of the highest royal policy that must be enunciated by the King himself."

∴

A sibilant whisper came from the crimson-robed minion behind the sorcerer, and Orogastus nodded.

"The Red Voice reminds me to inform you that your Royal Father's condition has somewhat worsened. My Green Voice in attendance at his bedside bespoke the news to us just a short time ago. King Voltrik suffers from fever, and his wounded hand has become afflicted with noxious humors. I have directed my Green Voice to administer the most potent remedy at my command, the Golden Pastille. This should bring relief to our King within two or three days."

The Prince frowned. "Why was not this miracle pill given earlier?"

"It is a medication of the Vanished Ones, my Prince, in very short supply and suited only to the treatment of life-threatening ailments. I had hoped that King Voltrik's wound would respond to the usual ministrations of the royal physician. Since it has not, the more drastic therapy of the Golden Pastille is indicated."

"And this will certainly cure him?"

The sorcerer hesitated. "I have never known it to fail. But I have dared to use it only five times before — thrice upon myself, once upon the Blue Voice, and once upon the late Princess Shonda, your father's second wife, when a thorn-wound in her foot became mortified. Your Royal Father's injury is, unfortunately, of a peculiarly dangerous sort. This is why I farspeak my attending acolyte at frequent intervals and also keep a close watch upon our King by means of the Sight."

Prince Antar's face was somber, lost in thought. "I will remember my Royal Father in my prayers . . . And *you* should also most fervently commend our King to whatever exotic gods you acknowledge, sorcerer. For if Voltrik should die, the grief of Labornok will be profound. And who knows what brave plans may then be confounded?"

Antar turned abruptly, and went away.

The Red Voice whispered: "That one will be less pliable than his father, Almighty Master."

The lanky Blue Voice, who stood close behind the right shoulder of the enchanter, murmured: "It would be our pleasure to arrange for his reconciliation."

"No," said Orogastus firmly. "Not yet. But your zeal pleases me. And when the appropriate moment does arrive you shall be assigned the task of modifying the princely attitude, and be richly rewarded for your successful efforts."

9

The flower-bedecked Nyssomu wherry, proceeding at a more stately pace, conducted the flotilla to Trevista's outermost island, which was evidently the destination of choice. The blood-red banner of Labornok was now held high in the bows of the leading flatboat by Lord Osorkon, and the knights and the troops aboard the other thirteen boats carrying the supply wagons had donned their armor and capes to present an imposing appearance when they entered the city.

"A pity we won't be going to the inner islands this time," Master-Trader Edzar remarked cheerfully. "There are some spectacular bridges and a remarkable ruin of an astronomical observatory in there, with curious pedestals remaining where some sort of arcane equipment once stood. However, I think you'll find that this outer island is rather interesting, and the important thing isn't sight-seeing, after all, but a satisfactory initial meeting with the Discerner Frolotu and her associates."

"This Discerner is the female ruler of Trevista that you spoke of earlier?" Prince Antar inquired. He and his men and the army officers were also attired in their armor now, and Antar wore a coronet on his winged blue helmet.

"The Discerner doesn't rule, my Prince, she only speaks on behalf of her people and acts as a liason between the Master-Traders and the Nyssomu. But she is the closest thing to a central authority that the city has — and just about impossible to hoodwink. It's said she can read minds."

"And is this true?" Orogastus asked, stepping forward with his two assistants to join the others on the foredeck.

The Master cleared his throat nervously. "I can't say for certain, my Lord. In my own experience, she has shown uncanny insight into one's *disposition* — if you take my meaning."

"You mean," Antar stated, cutting off a response by the sorcerer, "that this Discerner knows a true-speaker from a liar."

"Almost certainly. And — uh — this will present difficulties in our negotiations. Especially as regards the search for the Princesses. We will have to be tactful —"

"Damn your tact!" General Hamil exploded. "If the Oddlings refuse to help us in our search, then we'll take hostages and force them. Perhaps this Discerner herself would like a taste of Lord Osorkon's famous hospitality!"

Hamil's deputy, who was once again clad in fearsome black-painted plate, gave a sardonic laugh. "It would be my privilege."

Edzar shrugged. "If you took Discerner Frolotu prisoner, the Nyssomu would simply appoint another Discerner. And it's very likely that the whole tribe would vanish like the mist at noontide, and our trade with them would be terminated. As I have tried to explain, my General, our options in dealing with these peculiar creatures are limited."

Hamil swung about to address the sorcerer. "Then you must use your magic to coerce them!"

"We will see," Orogastus replied smoothly.

"Since I am in command of this expedition," Prince Antar said, "let it be understood that I will be the only one to negotiate with this Discerner. Labornok's invasion of Ruwenda was undertaken for one principal reason: to redress our longstanding trade grievances and ensure a steady supply of vital commodities such as minerals and timber. I speak for my Royal Father when I say that *nothing* must jeopardize that trade. Not the Grand Minister of State's coveting of mysterious ancient gimcracks — and most especially not our General's singleminded pursuit of the three luckless girls. You will obey me in this!"

"Certainly, my Prince," said Orogastus, smiling.

Hamil's eyes darted back and forth between Antar, whose cadre of twenty fully armed knights had unobtrusively moved in to stand by him, and the sorcerer with his enigmatic attending Voices. Finally he said: "I am a soldier who follows the orders of my King, and it is true

∴

that he has set you, my Prince, in authority over this expedition. Therefore I will do as you say — unless King Voltrik himself should command otherwise."

Antar sighed. "That will suffice." He relaxed visibly and so did all his knights, and then everyone hurriedly returned to the rails so as not to miss the first close view of Trevista.

The wherry with its lone Nyssomu pilot led the procession into a channel that seemed nothing more than an opening into thick jungle. Gigantic trees of an unfamiliar species, with subsidiary trunks like flying buttresses, soared up several hundred ells high. They formed an emerald ceiling above tangled undergrowth that seemed even more rankly impenetrable than any part of the Mire that the invaders had already traversed. At the edge of the channel were masses of strange plants with varicolored red-and-green leaves the size of doors, their midribs and veins all studded with golden spines. Vines as thick as cables, bearing swags of purple, white, and pink flowers, hung from the overarching tree buttresses and trailed languidly in the dark water. The muggy air was full of lush fragrances and the less pleasant smell of decay. Birds, insects, and other forest creatures set up a shrieking cacophony just as soon as the boats entered the channel, and this lasted until the aborigine in the wherry climbed to his feet and uttered a shrill, warbling cry.

Suddenly silence prevailed, except for the slow dipping of the oars. The Master-Trader Edzar pointed wordlessly ahead as the flotilla swung slowly around a bend.

At first the men of Labornok could discern nothing but a continuing expanse of greenery. But then, as if their eyes became accustomed to a new manner of seeing, monumental shapes began to loom up on every hand, all but buried in the rampant vegetation. There were dwellings — palaces, rather — that made the mansions of Derorguila seem like peasant huts. They stood shoulder to shoulder along the water, splendid even in desolation, and their foundations formed the walls of a great canal fifty ells wide. The knights and soldiers gawked and yelped like excited children as they floated past one wonder after another.

Examples of magnificent stonework and carving were everywhere. Many of the ancient edifices were ornamented with mosaic facades as brightly colored as the riotous tropical flowers. Some had stacked setback gardens. Others featured the remains of exquisitely designed porticos, or open galleries with fluted pillars partially fallen down, or

∴

crumbling esplanades railed off by richly carved balustrades. Remnants of mysterious statuary and huge, broken urns were almost concealed by verdant shrouds. Trees and shrubs had thrust up and buckled the multicolored expanses of pavement that had once been open plazas. But no one would dare say that the jungle had reclaimed Trevista: the ancient metropolis still exuded an aura of power and sophisticated beauty that the passing of ages had scarcely diminished.

Now the guiding wherry led the boats from the arterial canal into a side channel, and almost immediately the vegetation masking the ruins began to change in character. Most of the colossal structures still appeared to be as overgrown as ever; but some of the streets and byways between them had been cleared. The flotilla drew close to a broad public square with an operating fountain at its center, which lay on the right bank. A great flight of shallow steps flanked by pillarlike lamp-standards led from the plaza to the water's edge. At the head of the stairs waited a compact group of some two dozen Nyssomu. There were no other native people in sight.

"But, where is the fair?" General Hamil demanded. "By Zoto's Holy Guts — the Oddlings have run away after all!"

The Master-Trader winced and hissed, "Softly, please, my General! The Discerner Frolotu and her tribal delegation may take offense."

"Spy them out, wizard!" Hamil persisted. "Are the slime-skinned little mud-lovers lurking in ambush?"

"Be quiet, you fool," Orogastus retorted. With a curt gesture he summoned the two Voices, who fell to their knees, side by side on the flatboat deck facing the plaza. Both Hamil and Prince Antar had seen the sorcerer utilize his minions in the Sight before; but the knights and officers and the Master-Trader watched curiously as Orogastus took up a position behind the pair, unceremoniously yanked down the blue and red hoods, and rested his hands on the two shaven heads.

The sorcerer's own head was bare, and his snowy hair seemed to glow in the green gloaming of the tropical afternoon. Slowly he closed his eyes. Those who were watching closely saw the eye-sockets of the submissive Voices seem to turn abruptly into black, empty pits. There were low curses and gasps of amazement from the knights that trailed off into stunned silence as Orogastus's eyelids reopened to reveal two small stars blazing beneath his dark brows. He lifted his hands into the air and turned his entire body about slowly, apparently scanning the entire region surrounding the square as well as the overgrown cluster of domed structures on the opposite side of the canal.

Then his eyes closed. The two rigid acolytes gave convulsive jerks and groaned, and their own eyes rolled normally in their heads again before they slumped down unconscious. The face of the sorcerer also regained its usual aspect before he drew up his shadowing hood.

"There are nearly four hundred Nyssomu concealed in the buildings across the canal," said Orogastus calmly. "They are watching us, and have neither hostile intent nor fear. I recommend that we land and proceed with the meeting. There is no danger."

Casually, he bent down and took hold of the noses of his inert associates. The two flowed to their feet as though drifting up through water and stood with heads lolling, mouths open, and eyes still tightly shut. Orogastus turned and headed for Pellan's cabin, beckoning, and the semicomatose Red Voice and Blue Voice shuffled after him.

"The two ensorcelled flunkies will recover after resting," Prince Antar told his awe-struck men curtly. "Now pull yourselves together, and for God's sake hold your shields high and form a decent honor guard when we disembark."

The wherry had already pulled up to the landing stage, which was easily large enough to accommodate all fourteen of the big flatboats at once. A few Nyssomu trudged down the steps to help tie up, and Pellan steered the leading boat to the very center of the stairs, called for up-oars, and brought them smartly to dock.

Preceded by the Master-Trader, Lord Osorkon bearing the Labornoki banner, and General Hamil with his four aides, Prince Antar marched down the gangplank onto the quay and waited, twenty knights ranged behind him with shields on their arms and pennoned lances at parade rest. The common soldiers and their sergeants lined the rails of the flatboats, crossbows and other weapons ported.

"Greetings to the Nyssomu people of Trevista!" Master Edzar exclaimed solemnly, using the tongue that all nations of the Peninsula spoke. He repeated the salutation in the Nyssomu language, and continued to translate throughout the rest of the speech.

"'The great nation of Labornok, which has traded peacefully with the Nyssomu people of Trevista for over four hundreds by means of Ruwendian intermediaries, now declares that its commerce will be conducted freely and directly, no longer through venal middlemen, and

∴

both the Nyssomu and Labornok will profit by the change! . . . Following many a grave insult to Labornok delivered by arrogant and greedy Ruwendian officials, the patience of our great King Voltrik was strained beyond endurance . . . He led a mighty Labornoki host southward and wreaked just vengeance upon the craven Ruwendians, who surrendered to him without condition three days ago . . . Now Ruwenda and Labornok will be united into one great nation. Trade caravans will continue to come to Trevista, just as before. The Nyssomu may rejoice together with Labornok, since the lifting of the unjust burden of Ruwendian taxation from their commercial intercourse will allow both peoples to thrive, and peace and prosperity will prevail amongst all persons of good will!"

The Master-Trader threw his arms open wide. Buglers on each of the flatboats brayed a fanfare in unison. All of the Nyssomu blinked their huge yellow eyes, but otherwise made no move. Edzar cleared his throat and resumed:

"Good King Voltrik sends you his beloved son Crown Prince Antar, bearing the authority of the Labornoki throne. Over the next few days the Prince will discuss with you the new relationship between our peoples, which will be closer and more amicable than ever before! . . . And now Prince Antar desires to convey his felicitations to the worthy Discerner of Trevista."

The Master-Trader stepped aside and made a deep obeisance to the Prince, who came forward. For a moment, the tight little group of aborigines at the head of the stairs stood immobile. Then one of them descended and approached Antar. Her robe was of woven dried grasses with a deep collar and cuffs of living sky-blue flowers. A wreath of similar flowers crowned her head and she carried a simple green reed which she pointed without ceremony at the disconcerted Prince.

"Antar of Labornok," she said, using the human language. Her voice was musical and far-carrying. "This one is Frolotu, chosen Discerner by our people. It is our custom to be straightforward with humans and this one will do you the honor of addressing you without artifice. We have listened to your trader's fine speech and scrutinized its content, separating truth from falsehood. Now this one asks your permission to question you."

The reed pointed unwaveringly at the Prince's heart and he found that he was sweating heavily inside his handsome suit of enameled parade armor. "You may ask your questions," he said in a low voice.

"Does Labornok mean to do harm to the Nyssomu?"

"I declare that we will do you no harm."

"Will your traders continue to give us a fair price for our goods?"

"I declare that they will."

"What else, besides the resumption of trade, do you ask of the Trevista Nyssomu?"

"We — we wish to have a small settlement here, as a base for exploring the interior of the Mazy Mire."

"You wish to quarter armed troops here."

"Yes. This is my Royal Father's command, so that fugitive Ruwendians who are enemies of the new regime may not disrupt commerce."

The Discerner's enormous eyes shone with sadness, but she continued to speak without emotion and the reed never trembled. "Those that you call your enemies have long been our friends. You have conquered them by means of black sorcery and an overwhelming force of arms. You have cruelly executed the King and Queen of Ruwenda and their noble cohort whose only fault was defending their country against your invasion. You now pursue the Three Petals of the Living Trillium, the Princesses of Ruwenda, and would put them also to death." ·

"Yes," said the Prince. "But these human matters have nothing to do with you. We do not seek your help in the search for the Princesses. If you hinder us, you may expect our anger. If you leave be, I tell you that no citizen of Labornok will offer you harm nor insult. We will pay for the accommodation and provisioning of the garrison here, and resume normal trade as soon as it is possible to do so."

The Discerner sketched a three-lobed pattern in the air about the Prince. Then she stood silent for a moment before saying: "Antar of Labornok, you have spoken the truth to this one. The Nyssomu of Trevista agree to reopen the fair and deal with your Master-Traders in our usual fashion. The fair will be held upon another island, the location of which will be vouchsafed to you in good time."

"Thank you," said the Prince.

"We will permit you to set up your garrison here, in the area of this square, which is called Lusagira. You may use the buildings surrounding it as you choose, and a market will convene daily about the fountain where foodstuffs and certain other goods may be purchased from us at just prices."

∴

"Again I thank you."

The little being outlined restrictions that would be placed upon the garrison: the soldiers might travel the canals of Trevista freely, but were forbidden to land unless invited by the Nyssomu. The region directly across the canal from Lusagira Square, where numbers of Nyssomu had made homes among the ruins, was completely off-limits to humans unless the Discerner herself declared an exception. On the other hand, the local aborigines were to have free access to the square during daylight, although the humans could close off the buildings to them.

"All these things are agreeable to us," Antar said. "And now, since the sun is sinking, we ask your permission to land our men and set up a temporary encampment before nightfall."

"All may disembark" — Frolotu swung the reed in an arc to the Prince's right, indicating three figures still on board the leading flat-boat — "except *him.*"

Antar and his companions turned to see Orogastus, who stood with his Voices near the midships cabin. The sorcerer gave a mocking bow of acknowledgment to the Discerner.

She continued: "He must leave this place tomorrow, and not return, or else everything that the Nyssomu have agreed to will be voided." Tears began to trickle down her cheeks even though her expression was still stony.

Antar sighed. Mist was rising from the canal and he was wretchedly uncomfortable in the sticky armor and famished as well. "I agree to this also, Discerner Frolotu. Is there anything further?"

The green reed was lowered, and the flower-crowned figure's aura of power and irresistible integrity seemed to drain away palpably, leaving only a weeping inhuman little female whose fortitude finally neared the breaking point. She said:

"We have nothing else to say to each other, Prince. This is a time of mourning and all Nyssomu hearts are heavy. Nevertheless my people will bring fresh fruit and meat for your expedition's refreshment. This is our free gift, together with the use of the buildings. Perhaps we will meet again at the Feast of the Three Moons . . . if the Lords of the Air grant that we both live so long."

She went back up the stairs like a person exhausted after running a long race. Then she and the rest of the Nyssomu walked slowly across

∴

the broad square into an overgrown passageway between two broken buildings, and disappeared into the deepening shadows.

Much later that night, when the men were quartered in their tents and the campfires burned low, Antar came out of his own pavilion and walked restlessly along the quay. The night-noises were loud and irritating and no breeze moved the humid air. Across the channel dim little lights of many different colors bobbed about in the Oddling settlement. A sickly greenish radiance shone from the window of the flatboat cabin where Orogastus and his minions were sequestered, and the Prince could hear a sound of chanting from there, barely audible over the din of the nocturnal jungle creatures. With a grimace, Antar turned away from that part of the landing and went down the string of deserted boats to the very last one, where a single soldier stood guard on the foredeck with a lantern at his feet.

Identifying himself, the Prince came aboard. "All quiet on the canal, my man?"

"Aye, Lord." The fellow gave a nod toward the twinkling lights on the other side of the water. "The Oddies are movin' about over yonder. Now and then somethin' or other moves in front of their lights. And some big creetur with glowin' eyeballs came swimmin' by a time ago, and caught and ate somethin' that squealed pitiful. Other 'n that, all's well."

Antar wandered to the bow rail and looked across the black water. "What think you of these Oddlings? Are they a kind of intelligent animal, as our sages have always taught, or are they true persons?"

The soldier hawked and spat. "By their outlandish looks, I'd judge them creeturs. But the slippery one that spoke got her way with you crafty enough, Lord."

"True," admitted the Prince, with a rueful chuckle.

"And I never heard of any creetur could weep for sorrow over dead friends."

Antar forbore to comment on that. "Were you chosen to remain here with the garrison?"

"No. I'll be returnin' to the Citadel in the mornin' with the wizard."

"And glad of it?"

"I'd be most glad to set my hoofies on the road back to Derorguila, Lord. I'm a plainsman and I don't much fancy the swamp country, and these big old hulks o' dead buildings give me the quiverin' creeps."

Antar laughed heartily. "Me, too."

He strolled over to one of the now emptied supply wagons that the boat carried. There would be scant need for wheeled vehicles at the garrison. The thoroughfares around about Lusagira Square dead-ended in jungle not a quarter league away. The Prince idly kicked one of the wagon-wheels, and then bent down to pluck at a bit of cloth caught on a nail of the tailgate. The fabric shimmered strangely in the lantern light.

It was a torn piece of expensive rose-colored silk, soiled with dried mud. As he studied it he felt an eerie conviction insinuate itself into his mind: he had seen — and touched — this material before.

Held in his arms a human form clad in it.

It was hers, from her dress.

Here? Impossible! There was no way that the Princess Anigel could have secreted herself on board the flatboat and dared to accompany the ones who had vowed to kill her. No way she could have avoided the farseeing eye of Orogastus —

But the sorcerer had admitted that his magic was unable to spy out the hiding place of the Princesses. She could have stayed concealed, since the unloading of the wagons had not been completed until full dark. And then . . . all evening long, the punts of the local Oddlings had shuttled back and forth across the canal, bringing food and drink to their unwelcome guests.

So she could be at large in Trevista, the beautiful golden-haired young woman whose very existence threatened his father's throne. She could be in the Nyssomu settlement across the water at this very moment.

What in God's name was he to do?

Antar straightened. He tucked the scrap of satin away into his belt, said goodnight to the soldier, and walked back up the landing stage. The queasy green light still shone in the sorcerer's cabin, pulsating rhythmically to the sound of the chanting. The Prince stopped, fingering the piece of cloth.

He stooped, picked up a small stone, and knotted the satin tightly about it. Then he flung the little missile out into midstream with all his strength, and went off to bed.

10

Kadiya sat up, bits of grass clinging to her sticky skin and hair. She was gasping as one who had run a punishing race to collapse at the end of it. She looked about her, shaken and dazzed, unable for a moment or two to understand where she was or what had happened. There was the muck-fueled warmth of the swamp, small splotches of sunlight on the short lengths of water she could catch sight of through the rank growing brush. In spite of the heat she shivered and hunkered in upon herself. *It* was still there—

She forced herself to breathe more slowly, to shake out of the daze which had held her. What *was* it? Nothing she could set name to. Yet she felt as if she were held under some great eye, entrapped and helpless. She had to try twice before she could croak out:

"Jagun!"

There was a stir not too far away. The Oddling hunter had so buried himself in the grass of his own nest that his arising made him look as if he were emerging from the ground itself.

His eyes were narrowed against the light but his long knife was bared in his hand.

"Someone"—her voice shook so that she was ashamed of her own state and made an effort at control—"someone is seeking us."

Jagun was on his feet, shuffling free of the nest grass. His slitted nostrils flared as he raised his head to sniff as might a hunted animal. Very slowly he pivoted, testing the air in each direction. She, too, shifted about. "Farseer" they called her because of her sharp sight, but now she noticed nothing but the swamp as it had always been. Yet somehow (and this was more alarming than any visible foe) she was certain that the watcher was not near them now . . .

Magic? Of what kind? Used by whom?

"There is nothing save that which is natural here," Jagun said slowly, and now he was staring at her. "You have been dreaming, King's Daughter. Rest: what guards one can set in the swamp are present — Nothing can come upon us that I shall not know." He yawned.

She subsided back into the roll of grass, her hand clasped about her amulet. With all her might she listened. There was plenty of swamp life abroad, and none of that seemed to have reason for fear. She tried to sort out sound from sound to identify each. Just as the night swarmed with one set of hunters so did others go about their work by day.

But the one that had sought her had passed her by, frustrated.

Softly she spoke: "Jagun, I no longer feel that someone is seeking us." She shifted her hand so that the amulet might be within his range of vision. "My trillium-amber has shielded us — perhaps from the magical Sight of Orogastus!"

Jagun stood up, casting the grass aside. "Farseer, I do not understand such as that." He gestured to the amulet. "But this I feel, we shall not wait for night to move on."

"Skritek?" Kadiya looked toward those parts of the surrounding swamp she could see from where she now sat. She let the amulet drop, to swing by its chain as she drew her dagger.

He shook his head. "Skritek, I would know. This — I can only guess."

His vehemence impressed her and a feeling of helplessness was coming back.

"Orogastus has followers of his own." Jagun was already busy tramping the soft soil over the remains of their fire. "They are called 'Voices,' having surrendered their full will to his so as to become only extensions of himself. It might very well be that he has sent such persons to cruise the swamp with whatever armed force goes to secure Trevista —"

"And follows me! But what do these Voices do, Jagun? Can they so disguise themselves that you who know the swamp well cannot search them out?"

"Farseer, do you remember how at the last trade fair there was that one Ustrel, of whom people asked questions concerning things which troubled them?"

Yes, certainly she recalled the old woman who was so lamed that she needed two staffs to aid her in walking. And Kadiya had watched her squat before a wide, curl-edged drogo leaf into which she had shaken some drops of water. There had been another female Oddling crouching on the other side of that leaf, waiting tensely to hear the muttering of the ancient seeress, but the dialect the latter used had been one Kadiya did not know.

"You said she could read fate in the water drops," Kadiya said now, "but surely that was merely a piece of trickery. Such is impossible—"

"Not quite, Farseer. Each of us differs one from the other, not only as to our bodies but also our minds, in what we are able to learn easily and what we cannot grasp without great labor, if at all. Are you like unto either of your sisters, King's Daughter? I am a hunter of beasts, a trainer of such upon occasion. This is my talent. I do not set carven wood pieces cunningly together, nor do I brew herbs, nor work with the gleanings from ruins. Those are other crafts and arts.

"Thus it is also with crafts of the mind. Yes, there are those who can cast their Sight distant, and they can read, if fleetingly and falteringly, what happens to another far away. Ustrel cannot always do it, and seldom very clearly. But there have been times when she has foreseen the truth and had her farseeing proven so. Orogastus is a man of great knowledge, most of it unmeasured by any of us. If his Voices are well taught and they begin with some talent, then it could be that he uses them to extend his own senses."

"Then they are searching for us and will continue to do so! What is your craft of water-trailing against that?" Kadiya shivered. Steel against steel she could understand, even the cruelties of the invaders; but that they could command such powers was daunting indeed.

Jagun shook his head slowly. "It is not an easy thing to do and it takes time and preparation. Also it is exhausting for the seer. It may be that there is a Voice with a search party on the river behind us. But the more distance we put between us and the Citadel, the less easy we shall be to find."

Kadiya cradled the glowing amber amulet in her hand. "Does magic call to magic?" Almost she was ready to drop what might be such an ill-omened thing into the water.

"Farseer, your amulet is of the Light, the Archimage's own gift. I do not believe that it would play you false. However, I would be away from here. We must take a route which goes around Trevista. The Labornoki will keep to the river. Neither Pellan, nor the Skritek, if they have such with them, know this Blackmire country away from the major trails."

Though she had been to Trevista several times and prided herself on an excellent memory for landmarks, Kadiya was totally bewildered as Jagun's punt carried them on through twisting waterways while the afternoon waned. They skirted an islet where broken walls thrust up from the undergrowth, plainly one of the ruin sites. The swamp vegetation here consisted of banks of reeds and tough grass, fleshy stemmed vines, and looming trees. There were a few spots of color, puff-petaled flowers which had a most unpleasant look and which Kadiya recognized as the bait for plants which fed upon unwary insects.

The spark in the amulet continued to glow, leading them on. They did not stop for food but chewed on the tubers, and sometimes ate fruit that Jagun picked. Out of the night rose more isles crowned by ruins, and around them danced points of filmy light born of the marshlands.

The grey of dawn was showing again when they swung aside to slide through an inlet Kadiya would have thought too narrow to allow them passage, into an open space which looked more pool than river. Kadiya's legs were cramped and she wondered if she could stand erect. Jagun was also tiring. He sculled the punt slowly along the edge of the pool to where a tree, its roots undercut during one of the monsoon floods, thrust out from the bank. On the other side stones stood above the water forming a line that led back into the jungle-like tangle beyond.

When they were ashore Jagun pulled the punt closer to the trees and draped over it some bunches of reeds. Kadiya's legs and back were very painful, but she stooped and caught up the larger of the two hunters' bags. If she were so worn out, how must Jagun feel?

He made no move to chop a way for them with his knife, but instead turned and twisted to avoid the thickest of the vegetation. Insects arose about them in a cloud, and then Jagun did chop fiercely downward. Between him and Kadiya there lay a thick object that might have been a vine; but it had no leaves and it threshed back and forth, while from the severed end dripped a yellowish stuff with the unhealthy look of discharge from an infected wound. There arose on the air a sweetish odor of putrid decay. A tangle-foot! The other end had snapped back into a dusky cavern of thick growth, and Kadiya took a wide stride to avoid the carnivorous plant that had come seeking them.

Although the bushes grew high here, the trees had thinned out. Kadiya and Jagun came into the light of morning in a place where stood the remains of a number of shattered pillars set in a circle upon a pavement of dull black-grey stone. Kadiya uttered an exclamation. The open patch was deserted, but in the very middle smouldered a fire, and a wandering breeze brought from it a stench as well as puffs of greasy smoke. There had fallen across the pieces of firewood a thicker and longer pole now charred nearly through in the middle. However, it was what was mounted on the end pointing toward the newcomers that brought a gasp from Kadiya.

Fastened to the blackened and scorched wood was a skull.

"Jagun!"

His hand went up in a gesture of command as he leaned forward to inspect it more closely. The bone was yellowed and smeared with slime, cracked as if it had been dragged through some of the most muck-filled ways of the Mire.

"Skritek!" the hunter breathed.

The swamp was dank and warm even though the sun was not fully up, but in that moment Kadiya felt a chill which roughened her skin as if she stood full face to a storm wind.

"A warn." Jagun walked around the fire as he might around a trap. "But — here?"

Kadiya looked about her uneasily. "Do the Skritek come so close then to Trevista or" — she drew a deep breath — "do they war here?"

It seemed as if Jagun had not heard her. He pounced suddenly and picked up what looked to be a braided-fiber string, the kind used to lace on water-skimmers. Taking good hold of either end he snapped it taut.

"Uisgu!" He threw back his head, and from deep in his throat sounded the call of questing made by the armored horiks which laired on such islets. Three times he called so, and then added, after a moment of silence, another trilling sound, high and thin, which Kadiya had never heard before.

Slowly he pivoted where he stood, his body tense as if every cell of it was now engaged in listening for an answer.

∴

It came in a single horik's call. Then out of the thick brush surrounding the circle of pillars there crawled another Oddling. Unlike Jagun he did not wear the finely woven clothing of the Nyssomu, only a short, kilt-like garment of golden yellow with a feathery edging of grass heads. A knife hilt, cord-wrapped in red, showed above the belt which supported his kilt. He held a blowpipe in one hand.

Around his protruding eyes had been painted rings of red-brown which enlarged the eyes themselves, and on his furred chest were three circles interlocked at a center point.

He looked at Kadiya and moved away from her toward the hunter. When he spoke, his words were strangely accented so that she, used only to the Nyssomu trade talk and some phrases of ceremony Jagun had carefully taught her, could only make out one word in three or four.

"—come—set pole—kill Unvis—kill." With that word he held up his blowpipe and shook it fiercely. "Those others—" Then he launched into an impassioned speech which Kadiya could not follow at all. When he was done he stood panting and there were flecks of spittle at the corners of his wide mouth.

Jagun looked to Kadiya. "Yesterday the Skritek were here. They captured one of Usos's clan whom they brought here. Then they set up one of their boundary poles, slaying the clan sister to seal what they did in blood."

Jagun turned back to the Uisgu and spoke again. The other replied in very limited words.

"They went on—toward Trevista," Jagun said. "I have told Usos of the trouble which faces us all now. He and his clan traders were going to Trevista with some finds. They will spread the warning as they now return."

The Uisgu then disappeared so quickly that Kadiya stood blinking. "Could we not go with them?"

Jagun gave a small grim sound which might have been a laugh. "The Uisgu travel with none but their kin, Farseer. It has always been so. Of the same blood we are." He nodded. "But to them we are very far kin indeed. Never have we carried war to them, or they to us. Long ago, in the very beginning, when the Vanished Ones ruled, it was set so. We are Nyssomu and they are Uisgu and so it has always been. Usos will take my warning, but he would not allow our company."

"And yet you are not enemies," Kadiya mused.

"King's Daughter, in the old days, we of the Nyssomu were, so our legends tell us, speakers for the Vanished Ones. Now we are servants of the Lady of Noth, who commanded us to befriend the humans who came to live in the Mazy Mire. But the Uisgu have always feared your people. Only a few very daring clansmen will trade with us, that we may in turn trade with you."

"They will discover that the Labornoki are not of *our* kind," Kadiya broke out. "Jagun, I believe that Voltrik will try to set his heel as firmly upon the Mires as he has upon the Citadel. Can the Uisgu hide so well that the Skritek cannot sniff them out?"

Jagun shrugged. "Farseer, who can say? But now we must rest, and since this is a place defiled we must search out another camp."

That they did, farther along the shore of the pool. There were no remains of the Vanished Ones here and Jagun said they must share sentry duties. Kadiya insisted that she take the first watch since the hunter had had the wearing labor of bringing the punt into this hidden harbor.

Jagun immediately curled up on a small mound of leaves he raked together and fell asleep. But Kadiya sat cross-legged, setting herself grimly to the task of watching. Though she lacked most of the keen senses the Oddlings possessed, being unable to pick out of the air scents which were overborne by the usual swamp odors, and she could not without difficulty name the sounds, still she was somewhat swamp-wise.

Several times she arose to her feet to prowl around the campsite. She scratched at her scalp, overladen with the insect-repelling grease, and tried to comb her fingers through her badly tangled hair. At this moment she could well envy the Nyssomu their general hairlessness and the Uisgu their sleek covering of fur.

On her second round of the camp she caught sight of a brighter green down beneath one of the bushes, and in a moment had in her hand a stout-rooted plant she did know. A scramble of pulling brought out five more and she cleaned and divided their roots carefully, placing half of them aside for Jagun. Then she began to eat. Unlike the woody tubers of their sparse rations, these were full of juice and had a clean, pungent taste. They were called mafun, and they had even appeared on the table at the Citadel, where they were esteemed as a delicacy, although they could not be replanted from the wild into any polder field.

As she chewed, Kadiya thought of the Vanished Ones. She had heard, ever since she could remember, debates and guesses concerning them. They were suposed to have ruled this land countless ages ago. That they had had vast powers all thinking men admitted. Powers? She swallowed the last of the sweet pulp in her mouth. Magic was power! Was the Archimage really one of the Vanished Ones? Had she lived many hundreds, watching her land change, Noth slowly eroding about her? And who was Orogastus? Had he some connection to the Vanished Ones as well?

Kadiya began to wonder how large was this world of hers. What lay beyond the Peninsula? The Labornoki plains in the north led to the sea, and to the south were the vast woodlands of Var; but few other countries had she studied, and now she envied Haramis, who had spent time in the Citadel library while she, Kadiya, scorned books in favor of an active, outdoor life.

Had the Vanished Ones merely withdrawn from Ruwenda, to re-establish their rule elsewhere? Orogastus was said to have come from a distant land, brought back by Voltrik during his waiting years. Might the sorcerer also be a Vanished One? There was nothing, however, either in legends or in the bits of information she had picked up from the Oddlings, to suggest that the Vanished Ones had been workers of evil. Certainly the Archimage had never tried to dominate either the Oddlings or the Ruwendians.

Kadiya lifted her trillium-amber amulet. Its glow was steady, reassuring, perhaps even protective. And its spark still faithfully pointed the way to Noth . . . where perhaps her questions would be answered.

The Black Trillium seeds led Haramis and the musician Uzun on and on over the highland bogs of the Ohogan foothills. The seeds did not float too fast for them to follow. If either of them stumbled, or became momentarily enmired, or even had to stop for some necessary reason, the seed-of-the-day would wait — apparently becalmed by a diminishing of the wind, or caught upon some obstruction — only to fly free again when they were in a position to march on. It also determined when and where they would stop at night, dropping to earth each evening in what Haramis supposed it considered a suitable campsite. *Or perhaps,* she thought, *the seeds are choosing places for themselves to grow. If I survive, and return here next year, will I find trillium plants, spaced a day's march apart along this route?*

But the seeds would not let her dawdle, either, and after several days' journeying westward over the heath, Haramis was beginning almost to detest the fluffy flying things. There were times when a strange plant or an intriguing, unfamiliar creature caught her eye and she would have liked to pause and study them; but the seed-of-the-day would sail on, and she and Uzun would be constrained to follow.

Once, on their second day out from Noth, she had dared to defy the magical guide. The trail that they followed through the high bogland led them past a patch of the largest, most juicy, most sweetly fermented cloudberries that Haramis had ever tasted in her life, and she insisted upon ignoring the seed-guide and stopping to feast upon them. The seed had floated on out of sight. But when Haramis plucked another from the pod and cast it free to guide them, it drifted to the ground and refused to fly even when she breathed upon it.

In a panic, she tried another seed. This one took off with such celerity that she almost had to run to keep up with it, and poor old Uzun staggered and tottered and moaned following after. Although he spoke no word of rebuke, Haramis knew full well that she was to blame for his misery.

She took hold of her amulet and whispered with breathless asperity: "I was wrong! I should not have ignored the seed! Have pity upon Uzun, if not upon me! Slow down! Please!"

And the seed did, adjusting its flight at once to a more comfortable pace.

But Haramis remained resentful. Could not the Archimage have given her a more seemly way of pursuing this quest? Was she a babe or a dim-witted animal, needing to be hurried on in such an inflexible manner? The quests she had read of in legends were carried out in an atmosphere of dignity and nobility. But she, it seemed, would fulfill her great destiny trudging up hill and down vale after a silly bit of fluff, garnering blisters on her bog-soaked feet, gnat-bites on her neck, and an increasing distaste for the wholesome but boring rations the Archimage had seen fit to include in their packs.

The food was not over lavish in quantity, either.

On their fifth day of travel, when they reached a large river that Uzun thought might be the Upper Vispar, it occured to Haramis for the first time that they would soon run out of provisions if they continued to gobble them heedlessly. The countryside looked completely deserted, and Uzun seemed to think that neither his own Nyssomu tribe nor the Uisgu would live so far north, beyond the borders of the Mazy Mire. The piedmont was a no-man's-land, separating the swamp from the mountain territory of the Vispi.

Haramis sat on a rock overlooking the rushing torrent. It was nearly sundown, and the seed they had followed that day had fallen, signaling that the two might make camp. Uzun was gathering firewood and getting ready to prepare their meal, a task which he undertook each evening and morning, insisting upon serving the Princess with as much deference as though she were still at home in the Citadel.

"Uzun," she called, and the little musician hurried to her, smiling. "Do you think there would be fish in this river?"

"I should certainly think so, my Princess. Garsu for sure, and doubtless other kinds that I know not the names of."

"I have found in my pack some string and three hooks. Would you take them and catch me a nice fish for supper? I am so wearied of the mealcakes and dried meat. Besides, our supplies of food are dwindling, and I doubt we can count on finding any Folk in this godforsaken region to give us more."

Uzun's face fell. "But it lacks only an hour or so until nightfall, Princess. If I spend the time fishing, how will I have time to fetch wood or cook?" He grinned apologetically. "And I am loath to confess it, but I have never fished in my life, and would probably make a botch of it."

Haramis laughed. "How difficult can it be, if even the little children of the Citadel freeholders do it? I have a wonderful idea! *I* shall fish, and instead of cooking our dreary rations, you shall gather berries, and some of that nice-looking bittercress that we spied growing beside the bog-pool a short way back along the trail. And if you cast about, there are certain to be mushrooms — and we shall feast tonight!"

As always, Uzun agreed to her demands. After building a good woodpile, he trotted off to secure the other edibles, leaving Haramis alone.

Fishing was easy, the Princess told herself. One got a pole, and tied to it a line, and on the end of that the hook, and on the hook some bait —

Ooh. The bait must needs be *impaled*. And where did one find bait, anyhow?

She poked about among the driftwood on the riverbank and found a most satisfactory pole, and beneath a rotten log came upon some wriggling grubs that glowed dimly in the advancing twilight. Steeling herself (she did retch once, but fortunately Uzun was too far away to hear), she managed to thread one of the vile little creatures onto the hook, after two were crushed in her trembling fingers.

Then she cleaned off her beslimed hands, found a spot where the river ran deep, and cast her lure. Line and bait drifted swiftly downstream into a pother of whitewater and rocks, and Haramis hauled it back to the pool, only to see it float away again.

Very well. The problem was one any intelligent person could solve.

And come to think of it, she did recall the freeholder urchins using floats and weights to control the placement of the lure.

She pulled the line in. Of course the wretched grub was gone and another had to be put on. Just above the hook, she tied a small rock, and an ell or so above this on the line, tied a piece of dry wood for a float. When she moved to a better position and cast this rig into the water, it landed most satisfactorily in the pool and stayed there. Haramis sighed, sat down on the bank, and waited.

I will have to do this from now on, she thought. *I have been a perfect dolt, allowing poor Uzun to wait upon me hand and foot, as though we were on a picnic in the Citadel meadows. It is quite evident that we shall have to live off the land from now on and conserve what few traveling rations remain for emergencies. The Lords of the Air only know how long this quest will last — or where it will take us!*

Haramis let her eyes move upstream, over the heath with its sparse trees and heavy brush. The tiny trail turned here at the river and continued northward along the bank. Beyond a doubt the implacable seeds would follow it, taking them into the mountains.

The mountains . . .

They loomed beyond the dark foothills, snow-crowned and terrible, the land of the mysterious Vispi. Was her talisman hidden up there? If it was, how could two innocents in the wilds such as she and Uzun hope to find it? To say nothing of returning with it to Noth, as the White Lady had commanded.

The White Lady, who was sick, dying, possibly even deranged.

All they could do was follow the seeds — ordinary tiny brown things, each with a tuft of white silky threads, seeming to have nothing of magic about them at all, except the purposeful nature of their course through the air.

She gives them impetus, Haramis thought. *She knows where we are, and where we must go, and she drives the seeds onward while we follow. And she did not tell me where I must go, because she knew I would then be too frightened and disheartened even to begin the journey . . .*

"Princess! I have brought berries and cress and a plethora of most delicious-looking mushrooms —"

Haramis started in surprise. Lost in her thoughts, she had not heard Uzun approach. Then the fishpole gave a great jerk and nearly leapt

∴

from her hands. She got a grip on it, and something pulled so strongly that she was dragged to the lip of the riverbank.

She cried: "Uzun! Help me! A fish!" And then something green and silver sprang from the water, and fell back in with a great splash. The Oddling musician dropped his gleanings and came running to help, gabbling with excitement. The two of them wrestled and shrieked and almost dropped the pole, while the fish fought so strongly that they were nearly ready to surrender.

But Haramis yelled: "No! You shall *not* get away, you are our *dinner!*" And with that, the creature's strugglings ceased, and they drew it onto shore. It was a shining garsu as long as Haramis's leg.

"Perhaps you did not need the hook, Princess," Uzun teased, "if you can command dinner from the water."

"I hope it was merely coincidence," Haramis laughed. "I should hate to think that our dinner was an intelligent creature capable of under-standing human speech — or, worse yet, an enchanted prince!"

"Like in the old ballads?" Uzun said. "I shouldn't think it likely. It's a perfectly ordinary garsu, and it will be delicious — and there will be plenty left for breakfast and lunch also. Oh, well done, my Princess. Well done!"

They grinned at one another. And then Haramis stared at the big fish, and her joy turned to discomfiture, and she said: "Uzun? Do — do you know what must be done next? To — prepare it?"

Stricken, with mouth agape, Uzun shook his head.

Haramis sighed. "Never mind. Trial and error is supposed to be an effective method of learning."

Uzun looked dubious. "Praying for divine inspiration couldn't hurt either."

∴

12

Anigel had an extraordinary dream, and in it something happened that had never happened in all the history of Peninsular humankind: the Rains did not come.

Instead of the familiar storms that rolled up from the Southern Sea and drenched Zinora and Var and Ruwenda and Labornok and Raktum and the Islands of Engi for two seasons each year, there were unending months when the sun glared down from a cloudless sky and a hot wind blew day and night, scorching the small nations with its pitiless, deadly blast. The entire Peninsula was devastated; but Ruwenda, having no seacoast, suffered most of all.

From her bedroom window in the Citadel she watched the mighty Mutar dwindle to a trickle, and likewise the Skrokar River, the Virkar, and the Bonorar. And this caused Lake Wum, which the rivers fed, to dry up completely, so that there was no way to float the huge logs from the Tassaleyo Forest to the timber yards. River commerce became impossible; the Dylex farms were drought-striken; and monstrous starving Skritek rampaged from one end of Ruwenda to the other.

Her parents King Krain and Queen Kalanthe came to her, together with the rulers of the other five nations, and begged her to do something to bring back the Rains. She told them she did not know how, and they went away in despair.

In the dream her sister Kadiya came to tell her that the muck soil of the Ruwenda wetlands had all dried out. Flowering plants and grasses turned sere and bore neither blossom nor fruit. Juicy fungi withered, nutritious green lichens shriveled away, and jungle trees dropped their leaves.

"Pray!" Kadiya urged her, and she did, clasping the Black Trilliuim amulet in fevered hands. But the hot wind only blew more strongly around the Citadel, and Kadi stormed away angrily. In the dream she saw the bodies of pathetic dead creatures lying about everywhere, piles of skin and bones. And it was her fault.

Her sister Haramis came to warn her that the people would die next: all of the humans living in the Peninsula and the aborigines of the Mire and mountains as well. The dream-sister pointed out the window toward the north, where both the White Lady and the Black Sorcerer were said to live. Only those two would survive, Haramis warned, if Anigel did not bring the Rain.

Death would come from that way — not in the form of a dry hot wind but as a great storm of fire born of the final conflict between the Archimage Binah and Orogastus. The fire would consume the known world unless she, little helpless Anigel, stopped it.

"But I can't!" she moaned, terror-stricken to the depths of her soul. "I've tried, but I don't know how! My heart is sore pained, and I'm so horribly afraid, and — *I just can't!*"

In the dream, the Peninsular Kings and Queens and her father Krain and mother Kalanthe and brave Kadiya and clever Haramis looked at her with contemptuous pity. Then they left her locked alone in her room, in disgrace. She pounded on the door, sobbing, but no one came. Then she looked again out of the window, and saw a wall of flames that stretched from horizon to horizon and leapt higher than the Citadel's High Tower.

It roared straight toward her while she screamed and screamed . . .

"Wake up! Don't cry, sweeting, it's all right!"

The flames were black-streaked vermilion lilies, dancing as she thrashed wildly in a net hammock hung from their vines. She was in a corner of a room built of squared and carved stones, all girt about with flowering plants. Immu had hold of her, restraining her lest she fall from the hammock.

"A dream — it was only a dream," the old aboriginal woman crooned. "You're safe safe safe, my darling. Here with friends in Trevista."

Anigel's frenzied cries stopped finally, and she climbed out of the hammock still all atremble, and sat on a block of stone while Immu sponged her face and combed her hair and laced her into the rosy satin gown. In a low voice, the Princess said, "I would like to tell you about my dream. In fact, I *must* tell you."

Immu insisted on bringing something to eat first, even though Anigel had no appetite. And she added: "I will also bring along my best friend whose dwelling this is. If this dream of yours is important, then she is the one to interpret it, not I."

Immu vanished through a doorway draped with filamentous lichen that made a fairly opaque curtain. Anigel drew a deep breath, grasped her amulet, and told herself to be calm. Immediately, she felt better. She looked about the chamber. Although it was open to the sky, there were enough stout leafy vines laced overhead to provide shade — and the suspension for two hammocks. Almost the entire wall behind the hanging nets was alive with the glorious orange lilies; and when she looked at them more carefully, she discovered that the blossoms were insectivorous. What a clever way to insure bug-free slumber! . . .

On the previous night, uncertain that the trillium amulet would still render them invisible, she and Immu had emerged from their hiding place on the underside of the wagon-bed only after all the soldiers on board the flatboat had gone ashore. The two fugitives had crept down to the edge of the canal below the quay steps, where Immu had employed her speech without words to notify kinsmen on the other side of the water of their presence and need.

In time, a fleet of Nyssomu craft had floated across to the Labornoki camp with the provisions promised by the Discerner. Two of the native boatmen were Immu's cousins, Sithun and Trezilun. They found Anigel and Immu with no difficulty at all, and insisted jovially that the women were certainly *not* invisible. This had confirmed Anigel's suspicions. While they were on the river, she had speculated that the amulet might only act protectively when the Princess-wearer was in the most deadly danger. The amber had refused to provide any comforts for them when Anigel besought it during the frightening three-day trip from the Citadel to Trevista.

"Well, you're safe enough now," Trezilun had reassured them, as he helped them into the punt. It was a dugout some seven ells long with upswept pointed ends upon which glow-worm lanterns hung. The gunwales were festooned with flowers and both cousins wore chains of blossoms around their necks and tucked into the wispy hair between their upstanding ears.

All throughout the brief trip across the canal, Anigel crouched on the damp floor of the boat, fearful that some enemy would spy her after all and sound the alarm. She knew very well that Orogastus and his two thaumaturgical underlings were on board the first flatboat. What if the sorcerer should come out on deck and see her with his own eyes?

But nothing of the sort had happened. They landed safely at the Nyssomu settlement, which was called Karonagira, and the cousins conducted them down paved streets only partially cleared of encroaching vegetation, so that they seemed to be walking through a vast darkened tropical conservatory. There were other small figures moving about with will-o'-the-wisp lights, but none ventured near the newcomers. No illumination at all came from the ancient structures that loomed ghostly in the moonlight, so beautifully adorned with night-blooming plants that Anigel at first thought that the effect was artificial. The Trevista Nyssomu were simply besotted with flowers! They wore them, they draped their punts with them, they lived in the midst of them.

Sithun and Trezilun left their passengers at a modest-sized stone dwelling with a garden-verandah overlooking the canal. There was apparently no one at home, but this had not bothered Immu. Although she herself could see quite well in the filtered moonlight, she had borrowed Sithun's lantern so that the Princess would not be frightened by the strange house. Locating the guest bedroom, she had bustled the exhausted girl off to sleep . . .

"And now your real adventure begins," said a soft voice behind Anigel.

The Princess jumped and gave a little cry. Then she laughed when she turned around and saw the speaker was another Nyssomu woman, even more venerable than Immu, whose woven-grass robe was studded all over with saucer-sized white blossoms, their stems fastened in place with thorns. She wore two great pompons of the same flowers at the sides of her head. But around her neck was not a garland but a platinum chain, and at the end of it was an object like a small, ornate hand lens.

The Oddling woman raised the glass and peered through it at Anigel, who saw one yellow eye grotesquely magnified. "So you are the girl who dreams important dreams."

∴

That voice was very familiar. Anigel had listened to it yesterday while still hidden on the flatboat. "And you are the Discerner Frolotu! I did not recognize you differently attired."

"To humans," the woman said gently, "we Nyssomu tend to look all alike."

"I beg your pardon if I have offended you, Discerner. And I thank you for sheltering us."

"But you did not sleep peacefully."

"I had the most ghastly dream," the Princess said. "The worst nightmare of my life. Will you listen to me tell of it, and perhaps explain it to me?"

Frolotu's two fanglike lower front teeth glistened as she smiled. "We'll see if that's possible. Let us go onto the terrace, where Immu is laying out your meal."

Anigel hesitated. "I thank you, but I am not really very hungry. And if we go outside we will be within view of any who travel the canal. What if the sorcerer Orogastus or his minions should see me —"

"We are deep within the islands," the Discerner said. "You are safe enough for a while. Sit down here and eat and tell this one the dream."

When the Princess saw the food that Immu had prepared and set upon a graceful table of carved stone, she nearly burst into tears. During the three days of their upstream journey from the Citadel she had subsisted upon the rations Immu had carried: awful dried roots, sickly sweet mistberry leather, and nothing but water to drink. The amulet had ignored her pleas for something more edible. Here in Trevista she had expected to be served unpalatable Nyssomu dishes that would further affront her delicate digestion — but there was a surprise.

"Oh, Immu! *Real food!*"

The crockery and tableware were strange, but the meal itself was her familiar Citadel breakfast: little rice hotcakes drizzled with waterbee honey, a curd-omelet filled with fresh mushrooms, spicy broiled sausages, ladu juice, and a steaming pot of darci tea. There were large dishes of everything, and the Princess devoured it like a starving thing, which of course she was, babbling her gratitude with her mouth full while Immu pretended to be affronted.

"Real food, indeed! Silly spoiled girl. And I suppose you think the Nyssomu subsist on roots and berries and swampwater all of the time!"

Anigel was abashed. "I fear I never thought at all about what the wild Oddlings eat. Immu, I'm sorry. I should have taken an interest, as Kadiya did —"

"Never mind, love." The Discerner Frolotu was peering at her again through her lens and smiling. "Both Immu and this one know that there is no malice in your heart, only the heedlessness of youth."

"But where did you *get* this food?" Anigel asked.

"Questions questions questions!" Immu snapped. "From the nobles' commissary over in Lusagira Square, if you must know. I had Sithun and Trezilun steal a fairish amount, knowing how you suffered whilst eating our trail rations on the river. It will last for a little while on the journey to Noth. But in time you will have to master your tender stomach's preferences and accept what the country provides."

"I expect I will," the Princess said, between gulps of tea. "When I get hungry enough! But tell me — have you really found a way for us to travel to the home of the Archimage?"

"Thanks to Frolotu. She has friends among the Uisgu who have agreed to take you in a rimorik-drawn punt."

The Princess sprang up from her seat, knelt at the Discerner's feet, and kissed both her wrinkled taloned hands. "Thank you, dear Lady! I thank you with all my heart, and I will find some way to reward you."

The old woman tut-tutted as she disengaged herself. "Child, this one's reward will be your fulfillment of your destiny."

"You — you know something of it?"

"This one knows the prophecies concerning the Three Petals of the Living Trillium who will deliver our beloved Mazy Mire from mortal danger. And it seems that you are one of the designated."

Anigel flushed and turned away. "I wish it were not so. I am very much afraid — not brave or clever like my sisters. And my dream told me that I would fail."

Frolotu laughed. "Oh, it did, did it? Suppose you finish your tea and tell us this dream."

All three sat down at the table, and Anigel described her nightmare in detail while the Discerner toyed with the lens and occasionally scrutinized the girl through it. Anigel was too shy to ask what the device revealed, or why it was used instead of the pointing reed that had helped Frolotu read the heart of Prince Antar.

∴

"This one will tell you why!" the surprising old woman said. "The lens is a device of the Vanished Ones. It serves to focus thoughts upon the mind of another. But it teaches its user also, and after a time one need not always use it. If the wicked enchanter had seen it yesterday, he would have taken it no matter how Prince Antar attempted to forbid him. And so this one used the reed, which no human would value."

"You use the lens now, however," Anigel said.

"Yes, child. In the morning, the faculties of the elderly are at low ebb and we need all the help we can get . . . But finish telling of your dream."

Anigel related everything to the last detail, and the reliving was so distressing that she turned as wan as the terrace stonework and could barely finish speaking. At the end the Discerner sat back with her great eyes closed and her wide lips mumbling silent words.

Anigel waited, full of dread. All around the flower-banked terrace, birds and insects sang, and silver fishes leaped out in the canal. Then Frolotu's eyelids opened with an audible pop.

"Do you know what the dream means?" Anigel asked timidly.

"Of course! Now, the usual thing for a sage to do when queried about things like this is to demand that the dreamer herself analyze the dream. Or else the wise one must utter some mealy-mouthed cliche to the effect that understanding will come to you all in good time. But this one will not trifle with you, girl! Your path will be difficult enough, and the kindest thing to do is tell you plain: your dream means that you are a coward, and you would like to shirk your hard duty."

"But I *knew* that!" the Princess wailed.

"Hush, now, hush. Listen to the explanation. Dreams are sometimes vouchsafed by the Lords of the Air — but this sort of thing is very uncommon. Most dreams actually come from deep within our secret self. And a disturbing, important dream like this one means that *your* secret self — the most important part of you, that which is closest to reflecting the image of God — is full of anxiety about the way that you are behaving. It is both warning you and urging you to do better: to be true to the noble instincts that prompt you, and to overcome selfishness and cowardice."

"But I don't know how!"

"You will be told," the Discerner said softly. "You have already started on your path. This one has seen it all through the glass. What is necessary is that you *get on with it* — one day after another, determined and trusting."

The Princess looked doubtful. "But that seems too simple."

Both Frolotu and Immu laughed long and merrily. At first Anigel was hurt, then angry, and finally she had to laugh with them.

"You have escaped death through many miracles and with the help of good friends." Frolotu's face had become grave. "The next steps you must take are clearly set out for you. You must go resolutely, whether you are afraid or not. There is no shame in fear, Princess. We cannot help it. But sometimes we are solemnly obliged to carry on in spite of it."

The Princess looked down in her lap, where her hands were tightly clenched. "I — I will try."

"Good." Frolotu arose from her seat. "The Uisgu boat that we have summoned will be here this evening. Until then, you must remain sequestered. That foul sorcerer has left one of his minions behind at the garrison — we assume to begin the search for you and your sister Princesses. But you will be off to Noth before moonrise. If all goes well, you should reach the abode of the White Lady in about four days."

Anigel was downcast at the thought of resuming her journey so soon. But when she spoke her voice held a touch of healthy irony. "It would be very consoling to be able to have a good cry right now, mourning my dead and feeling very sorry for myself. I could not weep on the boat because the sound might have betrayed us. And now it seems there is no time for it. Well, perhaps this is another purpose of dreams. I can bawl my eyes out in that shadowland, and cower and refuse destiny night after night, and it is no sin nor weakness. But when I am awake I will do my best to simply . . . get on with it!"

"That's my girl," crowed Immu.

The Discerner smiled her approval. "Your secret self wishes to help you. By confronting your nightmares head-on, you will surely learn to fear them less."

A trace of the old panic momentarily resurfaced on Anigel's face. She appealed to her old friend. "But you will stand by me all the way, Immu, won't you? If I were alone — I don't think —"

"I will love and serve you all my days," Immu said. She reached out to the girl beside her and embraced her and kissed her cheek. "I am coming along with you to Noth, of course, and I will accompany you wherever the White Lady sends you. But there will come a time, as it comes for all of us, when you must stand fast by yourself."

Anigel buried her face in her old nurse's shoulder. "Not too soon. Please, not too soon."

∴

13

Kadiya awoke into twilight and the smell of broiling fish which immediately roused in her a hunger she found near to pain. It seemed that Jagun had dared a small fire and was tending a number of garsu, the longest hardly the length of her hand.

Kadiya crept through the thick brush which guarded their camp and came to the water, where she used leaves to scrub her face and her hands. She longed for the warm pool of water back in the Citadel where she and her sisters had sported and learned to swim, for the handful of sweet-scented crystals from the south which one could strew on the water until one's body rested in a scented froth. Stoutly woven as the Oddling clothing was, hers showed rents, and the grease with which she was forced to smear herself now smelt rancid. Her lank hair she could only twist back and anchor with a stout length of reed.

She came back to camp and Jagun was quick to hand her one of the spitted garsu which she ate with her fingers, licking them quickly when the heat and grease made them smart.

Jagun was silent as she ate. Nor was he more communicative as they erased, as best they could, the signs of their occupancy and returned to the punt, pulling it back into open water. Kadiya persuaded him that she should take a hand in their voyaging and he put aside the scull for a pole, giving her its twin.

This exercise was not new to the girl, but she found it took her a measure of time to fall into the pattern which matched Jagun's efforts. She found that once she had captured the proper rhythm there was something almost hypnotic about it. Plunge the pole, exert her strength, plunge again. She was in the bow and she glanced frequently at the spark riding in her amulet.

They rested from time to time. Once they paused to pull from the water the roots of certain lilies. The huge blossoms were still only buds so that the roots could be eaten with impunity. Those, with what was left of the garsu, formed their midnight meal.

This had been an evening of silence. Kadiya felt a constant unease. Even the hypnotic swing of the poles could not keep her from fearing some invisible, voiceless attack. Among his own people Jagun ranked very high in trailcraft, and she could be sure that he would be instantly alive to any natural threat. But those were attacks from the outer world, while this thing that she feared came from the inner which she had not even realized existed until its first manifestation.

"Jagun." She kept her voice very low, hardly higher than the buzz of the many insects about them. "What still lies before us?" How she wished now that she had paid more attention to that large mural map which had covered, in very faded colors, the wall of the Citadel council chamber.

"We head into the Goldenmire," he said. "Before that we touch at Vurenha —"

"Your own clan place!"

"Yes. I am of the outer clans. Beyond that lies what only a few of the Ancestors have ever seen. I cannot say what we will find there. We shall have to depend wholly on that which you wear."

"Uisgu country?" she pressed.

"Some of it, yes, but also the dark places where the Drowners set up their land poles. Of that we have tales in plenty, how much truth is in them we do not know. But we must cross that country to reach Noth, for if we go by the longer way we may be tracked by those who follow us."

"You have been to Noth, Jagun?"

"Once. It was when you were a babe. It is laid upon us who are hunters, that when we believe we are well skilled in our craft, we shall present ourselves to the Lady, that she may grant us the full freedom of the Mires. It was then that she instructed me to come to your Father's court, to serve as hunter and await the day of need she prophesied, that day which has so recently passed. Also it is laid upon us that any

∴

new discovery we may make of the Vanished Ones we report to her—"

"New discoveries?" Kadiya was intrigued. "Are there new discoveries still to be made then, Jagun? So many hundreds have passed since your people began to journey the Mires. What more might there be to find?"

For a moment Jagun did not answer her. When he did there was a reluctant note in his voice. "Farseer, the Vanished Ones had secrets beyond any we can guess. It is also true that any ancient artifact which is unlike those discovered before must be taken to the White Lady of Noth. Some she keeps, and we know such things are dangerous and that their secrets are part of her guardianship."

It was plain to Kadiya that he intended to say no more on that subject. But surely if he had seen the Archimage he could furnish her with some scraps of knowlege which would prepare her for her own meeting.

"What is she like, Jagun? I know that she is mighty in magic, but how does that make her different from others? They have said that Orogastus is one who has a body like any other man but that he is of kingly appearance and able to turn such eyes upon a person that one can deny him nothing. But then the enemy always grows the greater in tales. If Orogastus is truly more than any man—then what is the Archimage?"

"King's Daughter, she is the Lady, the Guardian. Life she knows and death, but with neither is she herself concerned. For life and death are the common lot of all. She has been ever the same since my people first looked upon her. She raises no hand to stop death and she beckons forth no new life. Instead she holds the balance true and we deal with time's passage after our nature. Only she holds the Mires against invasion, and now the balance has been over-weighted and must be set straight again. A thing, King's Daughter, for which you were born—"

Kadiya had thrust her pole deep. Now she did not withdraw it, but half turned in the punt to face Jagun.

"I was born?" Her voice scaled up.

"You three were born, Farseer. Time passes, and even the hardest stone must yield in the end to flowing years. She of Noth looks forward in time. Thus when she sees clouds gather it is her duty to prepare against the coming of the Winter Rains. Before the day of your birth,

King's Daughter, certain of my people and certain of the Uisgu, were summoned to Noth. They were warned that there was Darkness growing and that she who had stood between us and all manifestations of that in the past was not this time able to summon up a wall of strength. However, she promised us this: there would be those who would follow after and reestablish the balance."

Kadiya bit her lip. Once more her inner anger blazed up from the coals she carefully nourished.

"A warning — she could have given *us* warning!"

"Farseer, this is the first time in the memory of the history songs of my people that the White Lady of Noth has faced one of similar powers. He may be even greater than she had hitherto knowledge of. You wish to take blood price of Voltrik for your kin . . . perhaps that is but a small thing in comparison with that which you will have to claim before the end."

"I have no magic —" she began.

"Look you to those reeds." Jagun nodded to their right. "One such you can pull, and, with not much effort, you may snap it. Three you pull, twist well together, and you have a cord which will entrap a harfut. One you are, three you are . . ."

Kadiya gave an impatient heave to her pole. "Haramis, Anigel, and I are to be your rope?" She laughed. "I fear you can do little skillful hunting with such a snare as that!"

Magic — she had no magic, and certainly Anigel had never in her soft life showed any desire to play with forgotten lore. Magic! She did not want to think of that as a weapon. Let her meet Voltrik with true steel in her hands. She did not know how or when that would occur, but she believed that it would. And she would not depend upon any dubious magic to do then what must be done!

Sometimes during that long night of journeying she could not hold under those thoughts. But always she forced her attention back to what lay about them. Twice they stopped by the shelter of some hummock to rest and eat. She rubbed her aching arms and shoulders but she refused to utter any complaint: in fact she and Jagun had very few words between them.

Once there came a harsh, night-shattering scream. Kadiya, though she had never heard its like before, held steady. They were resting under the drooping limbs of a water-wyde tree and so screened and enshadowed. Above them the Triple Moons gleamed, and across the sky flew a black-winged shape which made the girl draw a deep breath in awe. The thing plainly was larger than the punt beneath her feet and its wingspread for a moment blotted out the stars. What it could be she had no idea; she had never even heard its like described before.

It screeched again and then was gone. Yet Jagun made no move to venture out of their hiding place. The girl heard him utter a very low hiss, and he whispered: "The voor — and it hunts!" All the unease of one who must face a vastly more powerful foe was in the hunter's voice.

"The voor?"

"It could not have flown here from choice, for it is a creature of the heart of the unknown." He spoke as if he talked to himself. "What brings it to this country? Surely there must be a fearsome stirring over all the world."

At length they began their advance once more, this time at a lesser pace. Kadiya took all the care she could to be as quiet as possible. Once more they heard that ear-torturing cry, but it sounded farther to the north, in the direction of their travel.

They made camp as the sun arose. At first Kadiya would have steered away from the higher land toward which Jagun urged them, for there was good evidence that it contained more ruins and she could not forget what they had found in the last such place. But Jagun was emphatic.

He pointed to some swirls in the dark water. "Sucbri — and surely a nesting of them. They do not allow themselves to be found near any place where there has been a camp."

They landed on the island and Jagun disappeared, blowpipe in hand. The girl gathered pieces of the driftwood carried by the river in the rainy season, and with care set up, ready for the lighting, such a fire as would be the least visible. As she sat quietly then to wait, she opened all her senses to what lay about her. The odors of the swamp commingled. She smelled the scent of flowers, a breath of decay and rottenness, even traces of animal musk. Though she was no holder of the gift Jagun and other hunters possessed in its entirety, Kadiya set herself now to try to separate one of those wisps of odor from another and to recognize and classify each as best she could.

Also she listened. There was life all about her, awaking into more strident sound as the sun arose. She recognized the click-clatter of a nas-beetle, and more distantly the half sleepy chirping of birds. There was such abundant life in the swamp and she and her kind were only intruders here. It would take more lifetimes than were accorded to those of her blood to be able to classify and know the swamp life even a small bit.

Kadiya took up the amulet and held it into the first ray of sunlight which reached the camp. The small bud within was tight closed — although the spark of light showed at its very tip. Black, the flower was truly black as no other was known to be. It was the badge of her house — though the reason for that was something even the oldest of legends did not tell.

Though she had not heard him coming Jagun was suddenly there. He had a pair of karawoks, water still dripping from their open mouths. His blowpipe was in his hand, and he looked, not toward her, but over his shoulder to his back trail.

She could have counted to ten while he stood there. Then the tense line of his shoulders relaxed a little. Once more his gaze went from right to left as far as his head could turn while he stared back the way he had come. At last he dropped down with a sigh. His skin had greyed during the grueling efforts of their flight. He had dropped the karawoks without a glance as if the fact he had done so well with his hunting no longer meant anything.

Instead, after resting his blowpipe over one knee, Jagun loosed from his belt a large misshapen bundle bound up in a leaf. This he unrolled quickly. With a gasp Kadiya drew back. The stench was so great it seemed as if whatever caused it had been hurled straight into her face. The thing was a lump of what looked like green-yellow solidified jelly.

"Skritek-spawn." Jagun let the thing lie, wiping his hand vigorously on a wad of grass. "It is a very young one, but deadly enough."

Kadiya simply stared. That the Skritek themselves had ventured this far south to set up a warn pole was beyond all reason. That they would have a weave-hive near here — Surely this could not happen!

"There was a voor place of feeding," Jagun continued. "It had fed — on this."

"How far does such a one fly?" she asked.

"Bearing a full-sized spawn? Not far from the nearest known Skritek holdings —"

Kadiya considered the threat behind that. "The Skritek are then moving south?"

∴

Jagun picked up the unrolled leaf, taking care not to touch what it held. He went away from their camp, dug a hole with a stick, and crammed the malodorous fragment in, pressing down dirt over it.

There was a grim note in his voice as he returned. "We have many routes within the Mires, and most we know well. But no one can cover all this country. There are places of quaking mud which swallow all invaders, past which we cannot go. What lies beyond—" He shrugged.

They ate and then Kadiya again took the first watch while Jagun rested. She found it harder than ever to stay awake, even when she set her thoughts on what might be the result of a deliberate change of Skritek territory. And she lapsed almost immediately into the deep sleep of one who has pushed her body to the limit when Jagun took her place.

It was in the late afternoon when he roused her. He had been hunting again, and this time he had not only some of the sweet lily roots but garsu fish, the very sight of which made her mouth water. They ate slowly, savoring each bite, and then left the refuge, following always the promise of the amulet's light.

That night they caught no sight of the voor, nor any trace that more existed along their path than the vegetation and usual inhabitants of the Mires. But now they were at last close to the Goldenmire, close enough to glimpse patches of the brilliantly colored flowering reeds which gave the district its name.

When dawn warned them of the need for shelter they were able to rest in a place very different from the rough camps they had made along the way. For a hooting cry rang out, which brought an eager answer from Jagun.

The bank of the great shallow river was now cleft by the mouth of a smaller stream. Jagun sent their craft straight into the opening. Now on either bank of the creek appeared Oddlings Kadiya thought to be Nyssomu by their woven garments. But when they called out to Jagun it was not in trade tongue, and she could only understand a word or two. Jagun nosed the punt closer to the left bank. One of the Folk stepped carefully into it, taking the pole from Kadiya and gesturing her to sit, as with powerful surges he sent the small craft forward.

Thus she came to Vurenha, the only true Nyssomu village she had ever seen. Those who had trading concerns in Trevista lived in the ruins there. But here was no sign of any other history than that of their own kind. Their houses were set on piles in a wide expanse of water. Each stood at the center of a platform raised about five ells above the surface, nuzzled on two sides by a number of punts similar to that which had brought her here.

Vines, with their roots in pots, were evenly spaced about the sides of each long house, and their growth had gone up the walls of the buildings until the leaves appeared to be sprouting from the structures themselves. The vines were now showing heavy pods of yellow, shading to scarlet, which weighed them down. Those Kadiya recognized as the raw materials from which a sustaining and tasty beverage was made. Along the shores of the small lake on which the village had been erected were crop plots, as well as pens for two of the food animals Nyssomu raised—woth and qubar—both larger than their wild cousins in the Mires.

Their punt was sent to the side of one of the houses. There were figures outside all the dwellings now, but the four awaiting their arrival were older and two of them were women, their faces painted with small iridescent patterns and their grass robes fringed with small shells or bits of glittering material which might have come from the ruins. The tallest and most impressive appearing of the women now stepped forward to bid them welcome.

"Greeting, First of the House." Jagun spoke slowly and this time Kadiya was able to understand every word. "May Those We Do Not Name bring honor and good life to all the clan and to this kinhold."

The Nyssomu inclined her head with the same grace Kadiya had seen her Mother use upon a formal occasion of meeting an official embassy.

"This one offers roof cover, Hunter," she said.

Then Jagun introduced Kadiya: "First, this one is King's Daughter out of the Great Place. There has come much evil into our land. She has been summoned by the White Lady of Noth that council may be taken."

The Nyssomu male who had poled the punt put out his hand and brought Kadiya up onto the platform to face the woman whom Jagun had greeted with such respect. Courtesy and custom the girl had been drilled in, but one needed a formal robe in which to make a proper curtsey. Instead she hastily improvised with the gesture she had seen used by one of the Oddling women of Trevista to another. Placing the palms of her hands together, she inclined her head forward.

"I, Kadiya, daughter of King Krain, do wish all well in this kinhold."

To her relief the woman replied with a gesture Kadiya did know — holding out her own hand palm up. Kadiya quickly fitted her palm to it.

"Be at rest, King's Daughter," the woman said, with that widening of the lips which was an Oddling smile. Then she was quickly sober again. "True, there is death abroad, and all praise to Those We Do Not Name that you have come safe to us. Those who drown walk our land." She hesitated before she continued. "There is much which is dark-born abroad. But to this kinhold be free, King's Daughter, and let us give guest aid."

The interior of the Nyssomu house was divided into a series of paired rooms opening off a hallway, and it appeared to Kadiya that each of these had been assigned to some special family or group. There were no men to be seen here, but by each door stood one or more women, all of whom bowed their heads as Kadiya and her hostess passed. Then they came to a door at hall's end and she did indeed discover that luxury, though it might not be of the same kind she was used to, was not unknown here.

She found a carven tub (which by the look of it might have been brought out of some ruin) awaiting her, filled with clear water on which floated violet-blue petals which she recognized as one of the trade wares out of Trevista. Crushed between the hands and rubbed across the skin these not only released a lasting fragrance but also lathered into a cleanser. Happily, Kadiya shed her clothes and got into the tub. She scrubbed herself with perfumed petals and cleansed her tangled, grease-plastered hair. Oh, how she relished being clean again!

Her hostess had seated herself on a bench across the room, and one by one six other Nyssomu females, as impressively mannered and dressed as she, came in to join her. Somehow, Kadiya did not find their presence disconcerting. There was in this place a feeling of calm and peace which was like a soothing balm of herbs laid upon the raw wound of her immediate past.

A younger female brought forth a long robe of very finely woven grass for Kadiya to slip into. Her hostess arose then and gestured to a cushioned stool. When Kadiya seated herself another of the young women brought a tray on which dried corfer rinds, fancifully carved, were set out.

When all had been served and they held their cups, the hostess tilted hers a fraction so a drop or two dripped to the floor. The others followed her example, as did Kadiya, trying to be alert to any point of etiquette which might bring the approval of these people. Many times at the Citadel she had been impatient of ceremony, sometimes inattentive enough to earn a rebuke from her Mother; but now she realized that she must indeed follow any gesture which would please the Nyssomu.

Her hostess took a small sip from her cup and then held it out. Kadiya quickly followed her example and they exchanged cups which, again following her hostess's example, Kadiya emptied. A warm feeling of relaxation flowed through her body.

"There is evil," her hostess broke the silence. "Those blood-eaters walk abroad, and with them another who is not of our country and who can bewilder thoughts. We have had messages from down-river. Many of our people have come out of Trevista, for that place is now held by dealers in death. We have sent a message to the White Lady of Noth. But as yet there has been no answer . . ."

"First of the House," Kadiya leaned forward on her stool, "those who have invaded Trevista are ones who have little knowledge of the Mires. But they are ordered by an evil one learned in the strange arts, and one of his servants travels with the Skritek. However, I do not believe that soldiers used to the plains of Labornok can fight within Mire country. Your people who know all its twists and turns can surely go up against them and free this part of the land —"

But her hostess was shaking her head slowly. "King's Daughter, it is not our custom to wage battles against those who come into our country. We have our own defenses but we do not carry death to others."

Kadiya bit her lip. So clearly had she seen the chance to harry the enemy force, using these Nyssomu who could turn every trick and terror of the countryside against the enemy if only they would! Deep in her anger gnawed once more. But what could she do? Impatience had driven her so many times in the past into some folly; but this time there must be no mistakes made if she could help it.

She fingered her amulet.

∴

"The Lady of Noth," she said carefully, "has summoned me. She has long been the Guardian of this land. Perhaps she will have an answer."

The Nyssomu woman nodded approvingly. "That is right, King's Daughter. Greater than any other living she is, and mistress of many strange powers. We shall give you what aid we can to reach her."

And with that Kadiya had to be content.

14

The melody played by the fipple flute was "The Rosy Sunset Pool," one of Haramis's favorites, a sad and soaring ballad of a lonely riverman far from his home and loved ones. When the last silvery note died away in echoes among the frosted crags, the Princess said, "That was beautiful indeed, old friend."

"I wish I could have played on," Uzun said apologetically, "but I am having difficulty moving my fingers quickly." He huddled more deeply into his fur-lined mantle and extended his wet boots closer to the little campfire of twisted sticks. Night was fast approaching, bringing with it a cold wind from the glaciers above that cut exposed skin like a knife.

"Never mind, Uzun. I think if you had played longer, I would have wept for melancholy. The riverman in the song at least had the hope of returning to his family and homeland, but for me there is no home, and those I loved are dead."

"Mayhap not your sisters, my Princess."

She looked across the bleak, rocky slope, beyond the torrent of the Vispar River that they had followed higher and higher into the Ohogan Range. Above shadowed ridges, the majestic bulk of Mount Rotolo was tinged ruddy against the cloud-streaked evening sky by the sun's afterglow.

"I pray that Kadiya and Anigel still live," Haramis said, "but you know as well as I that Kadiya was preparing to die bravely against overwhelming odds when we parted. As for Anigel, I should not be surprised to learn that she perished of fright!" She blinked back sudden tears. "Poor little idiots!" She forced her thoughts hastily back to her current problems. "And we may join them soon, if these wretched trillium seeds lead us much higher into the mountains. There is now almost no wood for fires, no more edible roots or berries. There are no fish in the river since it began to run white, and the water tastes odd. What is that powdery stuff in it, do you know?"

"It tastes like rock to me," Uzun said. "At any rate, if it were poisonous . . ."

"—we would be dead already," Haramis agreed. "But I still don't like it. And I worry about you, Uzun; you should not be up here in the cold. It cannot be good for you; your body was not meant to dwell here."

"I'm perfectly well!" Uzun protested. "All I need is to be warmed up a bit and have my boots dried out."

"But they'll be soaked through all over again, once we set out slogging through patches of wet snow tomorrow," Haramis pointed out. "My blood runs warmer than yours, Uzun, and I can bear it. But you are Nyssomu, born to dwell in the warmth of the Mire. I have seen your face grow more and more grey with pain all throughout this day, and your steps are slower."

"I am holding you back," he murmured miserably.

"That's not important, I am in no hurry to freeze to death, God knows! But I think it unlikely that you will get better: More likely you will become worse as it gets colder."

She rose from her place beside the fire, yanked off her fur-lined mittens, and began to remove his wet boots. "We must get these off, they will never dry while on your feet."

"No, no—I must serve *you!* Never you serve *me!*"

"Be silent," she commanded, with mock sternness. When she had stripped off his boots and soggy felt liners and the inner wadding of grass—insulating when dry, but reduced now to a useless mess that clung to his taloned toes—she pulled her warm mittens onto his feet like slippers. Then she set out his footgear carefully so that the fire's meager heat would penetrate them, and gave him a drink from the small, soot-blackened crock that they used to brew darci tea.

The elderly Oddling uttered a deep sigh. "That feels so much better. But you should not have demeaned yourself—"

∴

She pressed one finger to his lips, silencing him. "Now listen to me, Uzun. I have thought on this matter most carefully, and I have made up my mind. My wish is that you now turn back, having accompanied me as far as you are able, while I continue on alone."

"No! No!" he cried, spilling tea in his agitation.

"Did I not say my mind is made up?" she said. "We know that we have nearly reached that part of the mountains where no living thing — save perhaps the fabled Eyes in the Whirlwind — can long survive. Our food is nearly gone and there is no chance of getting more. Soon not even the dwarf trees will be able to grow, and there will be no firewood. If I am a person of high destiny, as the White Lady said, then we can assume that the Lords of the Air will shelter and sustain me somehow or other as I follow the trillium seeds. But you, my dear friend, must turn back. The quest is mine, and I must fulfill it alone. The Archimage told me that. Did she not tell you also that you must leave me before the end of my journey?"

Uzun bowed his head without speaking. He wiped his streaming eyes on his sleeve, then sipped slowly from their communal tea-crock.

"If you turn back now," Haramis continued, "you can be out of the snowfields within half a day. Another day will see you in the fertile portion of the Vispar River, where garsu and other fish abound, and there are plenty of ripe and nourishing berries, and the nights are frost-free. You can follow the river southward until you encounter friendly Uisgu, and they will bear you in their boats to Trevista and your kin."

"But how can I leave you all alone? The Triune knows that I am a wretched outdoorsman, but you — forgive me, Princess! — you are even less competent to survive in this wilderness than I!"

"I need no special survival skills now. There are no more fish to gut, no more bog-varts to snare, no more wild plant-foods to search out or prepare. The food that remains in my pack will keep me from starving for a little while, and I know enough to let the sediment settle from the river water before drinking it. I can climb rocks with fair agility — I've certainly had enough practice lately — and the seeds will undoubtedly find me dry dens to bed down in for a few more days, at least, until the entire landscape is covered with deep snow. If I have not come to my goal by then . . ." She shrugged. "Well, perhaps the Eyes in the Whirlwind will take pity on me and take me to one of the fabled green valleys of the high Ohogans, where the Vispi are said to dwell among hot springs, and flowers bloom while the blizzards pass harmless over-head."

Uzun said in a low, thoughtful voice: "Truly, I did wonder whether the White Lady had set us on the path to some such place."

"What do you know of the Vispi?"

"They never come out of the mountains. They trade precious metals and gemstones to the Uisgu, and these are passed to the Nyssomu, and thence make their way to humankind, either at the Trevista Fair, or at the smaller markets of the Dylex villages. They take in trade mainly domestic animals — especially the more rugged kind of volumnial, to-gars, and nunchiks with furry coats. They also crave salt and all kinds of sweets — water-bee honey is the mainstay of Uisgu trade with them — and a few other products."

"What do they look like?"

"No Nyssomu has seen one and lived, for their lands are forbidden to swamp Folk."

"Since you would obviously freeze to death before you reached them," Haramis muttered, "that makes sense."

Uzun continued: "The grassland Folk, the Uisgu, say that Vispi are taller than men but more slender. They *are* of the Folk, for they bear their young in a finished state of body, rather than as ravenous larvae, as the wretched Skritek do. The Eyes in the Whirlwind, those guardians of the mountain passes that once helped keep our land safe from in-vasion — they are said to belong to the Vispi, and to serve the White Lady."

Haramis said: "Some of our hill-fort guards told tales of Vispi dancing on newfallen snow. They were said to be beautiful."

"They are also said to be the oldest of Folk. But no one really knows. Our tale-tellers say that they live in deep valleys in the flanks of Mount Rotolo, Mount Gidris, and Mount Brom. There, hot springs and steam-ing rivers are supposed to flow, moderating the terrible cold and bar-renness, so that plants may grow. And there are ice-caves round about the Vispi lands that slowly thaw, giving forth jewels and nuggets of gold and platinum as well as baser stones, and these are washed downhill by the mountain torrents. Some of those ice-caves are said to have belonged to the Vanished Ones, and very rarely, one of their ancient devices will be offered by the Vispi in trade."

"How fascinating," Haramis murmured. She prodded the fire with the iron-shod tip of her walking-staff, moving unburned portions of twigs onto the scanty pile of glowing coals. For many minutes she was silent. Then she said suddenly, "Uzun, will you try to scry for me?"

"For your sisters?"

"No, not them. The Vispi."

He gasped. "I — I can but try. If they are truly Folk, they *should* have auras, as other natural beings do."

She pointed wordlessly at the tea-crock, which still had a finger-width of dark liquid remaining in its bottom. Uzun nodded and took it up. He swirled the tea in the bowl, causing it to rotate faster and faster while he stared into the small vortex. Then his body stiffened, and his gaze became fixed and unfocused, and beads of oily sweat made his forehead shine.

Haramis waited. The rosy glow that had suffused the snowy peaks faded to grey. The sky, which had been cloudless throughout the days of their journeying, now showed a few long pearly streamers of cirrus reaching forth from the south, the harbingers of the winter monsoon. Some years the storms came early. If this should happen, she was certainly doomed . . .

"Movis," Uzun whispered.

Startled, Haramis gripped his shoulder. "Have you seen something?"

"Movis," he repeated. His great golden eyes looked into hers as he came to himself and slowly set down the tea-crock. "The name of their great settlement is Movis, and it lies above us and to the west."

"Did you scry it clearly?" she demanded, her face alight with excitement. "How far from here is it?"

"I can't tell that, I only know that it is there, somewhere in that direction. The Vispi are able to hide it completely from searchers if they wish, but I bespoke your name, and they granted me a momentary view of Movis . . . and said that they await you."

Haramis felt her heart pounding. Her bare hand went into her tunic and took hold of the warm amber amulet nestling against her skin. Movis! A real place, not some fever-dream of the dying Archimage! It was not, after all, a fool's chase the winged seeds led her on, but a true quest. Or so she could hope . . .

To Uzun, she said: "You have served me well. This scrying of yours gives me renewed confidence, where before I had only uncertainty. I confess to you, Uzun, I had begun to fear that the White Lady was only a sick and deluded witch, sending me to certain death."

"Movis is not close by," the little musician said, worry creasing his brow. "It is surely several more days' journey away, over the most rugged sort of terrain."

"My seeds will guide me," she told him, smiling. "I will find the place, never fear, and the Vispi living there will surely help me on my quest for the Three-Winged Circle."

"They seemed to bespeak me with good will," Uzun admitted. He wriggled his feet, still enveloped in Haramis's furry mittens, and the concern ebbed slowly from his face. "Perhaps everything will be all right, after all." He yawned, then hastily begged the Princess's pardon.

She only laughed. "You are right, beyond a doubt. And while I shall miss your dear face and your music, you will serve me best by turning back. You can begin to turn this journey into a ballad, to be sung when I am Queen in Ruwenda. Indeed, from the way you speak at times, you appear to be working on it already."

"Very well," Uzun sighed. "I shall turn back. You will certainly travel much faster without me. I can leave you with a lighter heart, hoping that the Vispi have been commanded by the Archimage to assist you. And as I travel south, I will now and again try to scry you out, and thus reassure myself of your safety."

"Of course you shall," Haramis said. She took up his boots and felt socks, which were now nearly dry. "Tuck these in the bottom of your sleep-sack and they will finish drying while you rest."

She helped him to slip into the downy bag, and he curled up with his back against a large rock on the opposite side of the fire. Even before Haramis had laid out her own sleep-sack and drunk up the dregs of the tea, he was asleep and snoring.

She tidied up the campsite, then went slowly down to the stream. Hoarfrost was already forming on the bare rocks, and patches of snow among the sharp crags glimmered in the twilight. She half-filled their largest waterskin, flinching at the icy touch of the river. By morning, after freezing and thawing, the grey mud suspended within the water would settle, and the water would be fit to drink.

At her feet, something twinkled, and she saw it was a tiny pool reflecting a single star. A perfect scrying vessel . . .

Could I perform such magic myself? For that matter, is scrying truly magic or is it a mental skill, like the speech without words the Oddlings use? I wonder if I can scry my sisters . . . I know that they may well be dead, but I don't feel that they are. Of course, even if I can't see them, it proves nothing. Suppose the Archimage set some barrier about the three of us — a sort of concealing spell — to frustrate Labornoki adepts such as Orogastus who would seek us out in order to kill us? But perhaps if I searched for my sisters, whose destiny is said to be linked with mine, the barrier would not stop me . . . It can't hurt to try.

She knelt above the little pool, careful not to blot out the light of the star, and said a brief prayer. Then she swept all thought from her mind, let her only reality be the faint silver spark on the water, and the imagined face of her sister Kadiya.

Kadi . . . Kadi . . . Do you live? Let me see you!

A smile. A rich scent of perfumed water, soap bubbles, russet hair afloat —

Then nothing.

Haramis sat back on her heels. For a moment, for the merest flicker of a second, she had seemed to grasp certain elusive images. But there was no true vision of Kadi, only those scraps of sensation, having no source, surely, save her own imagination, over-sharpened by fatigue.

She sighed. Well, she had not expected to succeed. Scrying was an Oddling talent, not one humans possessed. She was a perfect idiot to squat here half-freezing beside a mountain river when she could be nestled in her sleep-sack, where such fancies belonged. Sighing, she trudged uphill to bed.

15

The Uisgu boat sped along by the light of the Triple Moons, and Anigel awoke with a smothered gasp. She had had the dream of drought and fire again, for the fourth night running, and her body was clammy and stiff with terror beneath the plant-down sleep-sack that Immu had tucked around her. Damn the dream! It was so *stupid* to live that painful unreality over and over. She took hold of the trillium amulet on the chain around her neck. It felt warm against her icy palm as she asked why her secret self had sent the wretched nightmare yet again. She knew what it meant! She had faced her shortcomings and promised to be brave, hadn't she? Why did the phantoms persist in tormenting her? It wasn't fair!

Screwing up her determination, she pushed the fearful dream-memories aside and concentrated on the here and now.

She was moving along in a watercraft that was pointed at both ends and about the same length as the Nyssomu punts; but instead of being carved from a kala-log it was fashioned from long bundles of reeds, tightly plaited together like a great basket and coated inside with some hard substance. The two rimoriks that hauled the Uisgu boat were streamlined furred creatures larger than a man, with sleek heads, enormous black eyes, and webbed paws with formidable claws. Their bodies were dapple-green and their only voice was a hiss. They did not like humans and had bared their tusks when Anigel tried to make friends with them. The creatures were hitched to the boat by means of a double harness attached to the stem, and the Uisgu drivers, whose names were Lebb and Tirebb, controlled their aquatic steeds by means of reins running through rings on each side of the bow. Anigel was obliged to ride and sleep on a little pallet in the boat's narrow stern, so as not to upset the rimoriks with her human aura. They stopped every six hours or so to exchange their tired beasts for fresh ones at a Uisgu village and allow the two drivers to spell one another.

The strange country of the Goldenmire, which they had traveled through for the past three days, was blazing hot during the daytime. Very few native animals were in evidence except for dense flocks of birds, gauzy-winged flies — some with a wingspan of half an ell — and myriads of fish. The sharp-edged grasses often grew to twice Anigel's height and were crowned by feathery golden-yellow flower panicles.

At first their boat followed a convoluted narrow channel through a very dense region of the glade north of Trevista, twisting and turning every which way until Anigel lost all sense of direction. On their second day of travel they passed into country where the grass was shorter and the waterways less distinct. The rimoriks then simply swam straight ahead through the trackless submerged prairie, and the boat swished along over the grass as though it were on a greased roadway, hardly touching the water.

Their stopping places were always small elevated islands thickly overgrown with hardwood trees and shrubs laden with all sorts of flowers and fruits. There the shy Uisgu had their small villages, where they subsisted upon raw fish, the abundant wild produce, and a "sacred" brown beverage named miton, the nature of which Immu refused to explain at the same time that she forbade Anigel to sample it. Unlike the Nyssomu, the Uisgu did not use fire. They dwelt in grass huts woven in the same massive basketry style as their boats, mounted on stilts for safety's sake during the monsoon-season floods. The Folk were much smaller than their Nyssomu kin, and wore nothing except for golden jewelry set with gems, which they obtained in trade from the Vispi of the northern mountains, and a short, kiltlike garment. Around their protruding eyes were painted colored rings, and the bare chests of the males were adorned with a painted design of three circles inter-locked at a center point. Their bodies were mostly covered in short hair, lubricated with a heavy oil having a powerful musky smell. Anigel hardly noticed the odor now; but when she had first met the two Uisgu boatmen, Lebb and Tirebb, back at the home of the Discerner, she had had to control her revulsion at their slimy hand-shake. No wonder certain crude Ruwendians referred to the little Oddlings as Slippery Devils! The boatmen and Immu could barely understand one another's dialect, but there was not much need for conversation. The two Uisgu knew very well where the ruined city of Noth lay, and they had promised Frolotu to conduct the Princess and Immu there as quickly as possible.

After dark, when the stars above the prairie were unobscured by mist and seemed twice as bright as normal, the Goldenmire had an orchestra of night-sounds completely different from those of the Lower Mutar or Trevista. No large animals howled or roared out here in the vast treeless region; instead, the swamp noises were percussive and syncopated, like hundreds of tiny drums, all with different pitches, playing an everchanging melody accompanying the hiss of the boat through the sea of grass. The sound was hypnotic, and Anigel felt herself dozing off again.

No dreams, no dreams, she begged feebly, letting oblivion claim her. And when she awoke the boat had stopped, and she felt greatly refreshed, and it was dawn.

Three peculiar little faces were staring at her over the gunwale, their expressions both fascinated and horrified. They had a familial resemblance to the Nyssomu, but their upstanding ears were proportionally larger, as were their sharp teeth, and their heads and necks and cheeks were covered with slick, oily fur. The eyes of one were ringed with yellow paint; the others wore eye-paint of pink and ochre.

The Princess gave a squeak of surprise and the three faces dropped down out of sight.

"Oh, I'm sorry," she said softly. "Don't be afraid, little Uisgu. I know that I look ugly and gigantic to you, but I won't hurt you."

First one head reappeared, and then the other two. They were no larger than the heads of human babies. The Uisgu children conversed among themselves in an agitated twitter, obviously arguing about the nature of the monster they had found asleep in a boat on their beach.

"It's quite all right," Anigel reassured them. She held up the trillium amulet on its chain—and suddenly everything seemed to be explained

The three young Uisgu uttered a joyous trill and showed their diminutive fangs in wide grins. They crawled up onto the gunwale and would have climbed right into the boat with her, but she laughed and told them: "No, no. Please sit there while I get dressed. Then you can take me to your village. I suppose Immu and Lebb and Tirebb have gone there already to arrange for fresh rimoriks, leaving me here to slug-abed!"

She pushed aside the sleep-sack and sat up, slipping a soft, woven-grass robe over her shift. She had worn Frolotu's gift of aboriginal clothing with reluctance at first; but the pale green robe proved to be much cooler than her torn, dirty court dress, and its long bell-sleeves and ample hood protected her from the powerful sun of the open grassland. She had also discarded her ruined slippers in favor of calf-high buskins with sturdy sandals strapped over them. The traveling outfit was completed by a braided fiber belt having a large leather wallet hung from it, in which the Princess carried her handkerchief, comb, knife, and a few other necessities.

One of the juvenile Uisgu had vanished from its perch on the rail. It now reappeared, giggling, and handed her a string of waxy white flowers that exuded a spicy perfume. Anigel thanked the little creature, formed the flowers into a garland, and set the gift on her hair. Then she clambered out of the boat and followed the trio down a narrow path.

The village was only a short distance away, and consisted of five huts on stilts and the usual open-air shelter built at ground level, where the Uisgu customarily gathered to socialize, confer, and prepare and eat meals during the dry season. Immu and the boatmen Lebb and Tirebb were being served breakfast from the community pot. The village headman welcomed Anigel with a kindly but incomprehensible speech and ordered that she be given food also.

By now she was used to the chopped raw fish, which had been marinated in acidic fruit juice until it was white, flaky, and very similar in texture to the cooked kind. She also took slices of melon and a handful of rich-flavored blok-nuts, but followed Immu's lead in politely declining the sacred miton drink.

"These people say that Noth is now only a few hours away," Immu told the Princess. "The submerged part of the Goldenmire that the rimoriks can swim through comes to an end a few leagues beyond the village, where the water becomes very shallow. We shall have to cut over to the River Nothar, slightly to the east, and follow it for a ways in order to reach the home of the Archimage. The Uisgu do not usually dare to approach her dwelling without invitation, but I have explained

∴

to them who you are and why the White Lady has summoned you."

The headman, who was distinguished from the other eight adult males of the village by the ornateness of his golden collar and bracelets, his kilt of glittering fish-scales, and the triple rings of white paint around his eyes, approached the Princess when she had finished eating and harangued her at some length in his own language. Anigel tried not to flinch as his taloned fingers lifted the trillium amulet that hung at her throat and displayed it to his people.

The little band of Uisgu uttered a low, marveling cry that was cut short by the chattering of the three children, who were no doubt informing their elders that they had recognized Anigel already.

"These Uisgu who live in the western part of the Mazy Mire keep in close mental contact with their fellows," Immu said to the Princess in a low voice. "This headman says that you are not the only Petal of the Trillium en route to Noth. There is another — beyond a doubt your sister Kadiya — who has survived the perils of the Blackmire. She and her companion — this must be Jagun — have reached a Nyssomu village near the confluence of the Nothar River and the Upper Mutar."

"How wonderful!" Anigel exclaimed. "We can wait at Noth for her to arrive!"

Immu's expression was dubious. "That is for the Archimage to decide."

The headman spoke again, this time gesturing toward the northern sky and frowning, then wiping the palms of his hands on his hairy flanks in an indication of extreme disapproval.

"By the Flower!" Immu muttered. "He says that a *third* person wearing the trillium amulet set out from Noth over a week ago, moving northward into the foothills and then ascending into the snowfields of the high Ohogan Mountains. He says that this person is — is very unwise to enter this territory, which the Vispi have declared forbidden to all other races upon pain of death."

"He can only be speaking of Haramis!" Anigel exclaimed. "And she would only go where the White Lady sent her! But how could she —"

"Hush," Immu warned her. "Say no more." She gave a small speech of thanks to the villagers, then indicated to Lebb and Tirebb that it was time for them to be off. A pair of fresh rimoriks had already been harnessed up.

∴

The headman politely barred their way. Giving a curt order, he received from one of the Uisgu females a small stoppered drinking gourd that had been stained a bright red and enclosed in a knotted carrying net. This he solemnly presented to Anigel.

"Is it miton?" the Princess whispered to Immu.

"Yes. And this time you will have to take it, for it is a special gift that they rarely make to non-Uisgu — much less to humans. Thanks be to the Lords of the Air that they do not demand that you drink it down . . ."

Anigel bowed her head and thanked the Folk in her own tongue. They seemed to understand. One wizened little Oddling granny trotted after them as they walked back to the boat, patting Anigel's shoulder and pointing again and again to the gourd with an encouraging smile.

"Miton!" she said. "Miton! Miton ka poru ti!"

They climbed into the boat, the Uisgu drivers at the bow, Immu and Anigel in their usual places in the stern. As they drew away from the island the villagers on shore raised their hands in farewell. The squeaky voice of the matron shouted one last time: "Miton ka poru ti!"

"What do her words mean?" Anigel asked Immu. She held the gourd in her lap, examining the curious knots of the mesh that enclosed it.

"She says, 'Miton gives strength and courage,'" Immu translated reluctantly. "This is why they call it a sacred drink."

"But that's wonderful!" the Princess exclaimed in relief. "I'll have some right now, for I confess that the prospect of meeting the White Lady at last scares me witless."

Immu turned away. As if speaking to herself, she said: "There is between the rimoriks and the Uisgu a strange symbiosis whereby each aids and cherishes the other. The people and the beasts are friends of the heart, not masters and domestic animals. The rimoriks are strong and courageous, while the weaker Uisgu have greater intelligence. Their bonding is continually reinforced by means of the miton, which both drink . . . and in it is mingled the blood of both species."

The Princess sat as if turned to stone. One hand had gone instinctively to her amulet.

"I cannot say," Immu concluded, "whether this drink gives courage or not. My people, the Nyssomu, generally view it with dread. Those few of us who have dared to take it — the rimorik drivers among us — become a breed apart. Certainly there is some strong magic in it, but

∴

you would be wise to turn this gift over to the Archimage, or at least consult her about its potential."

"I — I will," said the girl. She sat for a long time without speaking, staring now at the scarlet gourd and then at the landscape ahead, where mountains had begun to loom against the northern horizon.

After nearly an hour had passed, Anigel turned to Immu and smiled. "Only the Lords of the Air know whether this miton drink actually stiffens the backbone of one who drinks it. But a strange thing has happened . . . By simply sitting her and holding it, I have overcome my fear of meeting the White Lady. And that is magic enough for now."

The ruins of Noth, although extensive, had much less grandeur than Trevista's, and Anigel was somehwat disappointed. The Uisgu boat brought them through an area of derelict and overgrown stone buildings to a lagoon all clogged with rank-smelling yellow purse-flowers, stuffed to the stamens with putrefying insect prey. They landed at a surprisingly tidy little dock. The sloping shore behind it was an expanse of short-clipped grass and civilized flower gardens that had been carved out of luxuriant jungle growth. Long-necked domesticated togars waddled about, just as they would have done in a freeholder's farmyard on the Knoll, now and then nibbling at the grass or some tidbit. A few dozen ells uphill, at the head of rustic flagstone steps, stood a cottage unlike any that Anigel had ever seen before.

Its roof was a thick mound of dried grass and its walls were white-painted plaster with the dark wooden framing-beams visible. There was a stone chimney from which a small plume of smoke curled. The windows had lozenge-shaped leaded panes, and boxes at the sills holding flowers, and there were wooden shutters that could be closed over the glass during stormy weather. The front door was cut right across the middle — and only the bottom half was shut. Beside it was a wicker bench with a small striped furry animal asleep on it and a spinning wheel with a basket of fleece and a bowl full of yarn balls. The total effect was so charming and unthreatening after the somber ruins of the lost city that Anigel wondered out loud if they had come to the right place.

Immu questioned the Uisgu Lebb and Tirebb, who were in an uncommon hurry to let off their passengers and retreat. The two little beings nodded vigorously and pointed to the house. One tossed out the

∴

traveling packs of Immu and the Princess, and the other sounded the hissing whistle that signaled the rimoriks to swim off.

"Well!" Immu watched the boat speed away with evident consternation. "What do you think of *that!*"

Anigel was already on her way up the garden steps. She called out: "Come quickly! You won't believe what I've found growing up here!"

"Come come come," Immu grumbled, following on her short legs. There were several small trees laden with spherical orange fruit between the water and the house, and they had concealed another plant that Anigel now stood contemplating with awed admiration.

It was a Black Trillium plant two ells tall, covered with huge blossoms.

Immu fell to her knees and burst into tears. "It's true! We've found her! Oh, thanks be to the Lords of the Air!" The Princess knelt to comfort her friend; but a moment later both of them gasped with shock and clung to each other when a shadowy figure suddenly appeared, standing between them and the brilliant midday sun.

"Lady?" Immu ventured, her voice quavering.

The figure moved, and light fell on the face of an aged woman, a face so seamed and crumpled and worn that the features were nearly obliterated, except for filmed blue eyes sunk deep in dark sockets. She wore plain garments of white homespun, and a veil of embroidered lawn covered her straggling white hair. The hand she extended was emaciated, with swollen joints and prominent veins, and she wore a single great ring of platinum filigree set with amber, and in the glowing stone was a fossil trillium.

"I am the Archimage Binah," she said. "Welcome."

Anigel stumbled to her feet, leaving Immu sitting paralyzed on the ground. Something burned at her breast and she drew forth her amulet on its chain. Its amber was aglow, pulsing with her heartbeat, and the bud within had changed: it was partially unfurled.

The old woman smiled and turned, gesturing for Anigel to follow. The Archimage walked with a painful, stooped shuffle, supporting herself with a silvery staff. The Princess followed without a trace of fear. How could anyone be afraid of this poor, dying White Lady?

"Oh, you would be surprised," the Archimage responded, chuckling with a sound like dry leaves rustling over stones. "But you shall not fear me, dear child. I am your godmother who loves you. You must trust me."

∴

"I do," Anigel said.

The Archimage paused at the tall trillium plant. "It is the only one of its kind that still grows in our land, and although it seems strong, it is dying, like me."

Anigel cried out in dismay. But the old woman lifted one finger to her lips. "Another kind of Trillium will take its place, if God wills. Do you know what I speak of, daughter?"

"Yes," the girl admitted. "But I am a weakling, and I may confound your great scheme if—"

"Be still," Binah admonished. "Such fatuous speculation may call forth the very failure it rails against! You must cultivate serenity, little love, for that is the garment of true royalty. See how serene these flowers are, accepting nourishment from leaf and root, turning their faces always toward the sun, cherishing seeds deep within their hearts. And they will die serene, since otherwise their seeds may not be set free."

Anigel shook her head in perplexity. "Please, Lady . . . I'm sorry if I seem slow-witted. It is then my destiny to die for my country?"

"I don't know," the Archimage said. "I do know that you must do an important work which will be revealed to you. And you will also receive a sign: a talisman signaling that the final struggle for Ruwenda, and for your own soul, is about to begin. Your sister Haramis has already set forth on her quest. Your sister Kadiya will go in search of her destiny shortly. Each will find her own talisman and in time the Three Petals of the Living Trillium will come once again together. Beyond this, where the finalization lies, I cannot see."

Anigel had turned pale as chalk, but she stood calmly, still keeping a tight hold of her trillium amulet. "Will this gift, then, that you gave me at birth, guide me on my quest?"

"It will, and this also." The Archimage broke one of the large leaves from the great trillium plant and held it out, pointing to its surface with her other hand. "This leaf bears the very impress of our land. Look closely! Its veins and ribs make a map of Ruwenda. Here at the tip is Noth, and the golden vein twisting down from it is the watercourse you must follow to locate your talisman. First down the Nothar, then down the Upper Mutar into the Lower."

Anigel was studying the leaf with puzzled interest. "But the golden vein continues on to the very leaf-stem! Look — here is where the Mutar curves around the Citadel, and this marking must be Lake Wum, and beyond that is the Great Mutar that flows through the country of the Wyvilo and the savage Glismak!" Fear leapt into the girl's eyes. "Must I go *there?* To the dark Tassaleyo Forest?"

"So it seems," the Archimage said. "I did not know myself until the leaf was plucked." She shook her head. "Such a long way to go! My poor little love . . . but it is all downstream, so you will travel more swiftly than you did before."

"And the work I must do—"

"Will be revealed." The old woman's face twisted momentarily with pain and she tottered as she stood. Immu, who had been standing back respectfully, darted forward and took hold of one of the White Lady's arms. Anigel took the other, and together they helped the Archimage into her cottage, seated her in a great cushioned chair, and brought her a cup of water.

"Don't be concerned, my dears," the old woman said. "I shan't die on you yet. My work is not done. I am only very, very tired."

Anigel hesitated, then opened her belt-wallet and took out the small scarlet gourd of miton. "I was given this by the Uisgu. It is said to bestow strength and courage—"

"The gift was for you," Binah said wearily. "Keep it, but use it only when it becomes necessary."

"When will that be?" Anigel asked. But Binah's eyes had closed, and her head had sunk onto her breast, and she breathed slowly and noisily.

"Can you at least tell me where my talisman can be found?" Anigel pleaded.

"At . . . the end of the stem." The voice was barely audible.

"But you haven't told me what the talisman is!" Anigel cried in desperation.

The Archimage sighed.

"Please!" The girl was almost in tears. "Only tell me what it is that I seek!"

"The Three-Headed Monster," Binah whispered. And then she was sound asleep.

∴

16

The Green Voice paused at the door of the royal bedchamber, and with an apologetic grimace opened the pouch at his belt. He took out three curiously wrought masks designed to cover the lower face — two colored green and blue for himself and his colleague, and one more ornate and colored silver-and-black for his master.

"We should don these before presenting ourselves to King Voltrik," the Green Voice explained. "The necrosis of the royal flesh has progressed to such a point that the stench exceeds that of the foulest cesspit, so that strong men puke and weaklings may faint dead away. Aromatic herbs I have packed within the masks will grant us surcease from the noxious exhalations for a half-hour or so. Will this be sufficient for your purposes, Great Lord?"

Orogastus nodded. His eyes were steely above the mask, and if he dreaded the crucial task that lay ahead of him he gave no signal that his telepathic minions could perceive.

The royal physician — drunken, sobbing, and fearful of losing his head — had reluctantly delivered his diagnosis to the Green Voice while the sorcerer and his party were still half a day up-river from the Citadel: In spite of the administration of the magical Golden Pastille, the mortification of Voltrik's hand had progressed to a point where the King was clearly in danger of dying, and the physician had lacked the courage to undertake the only treatment that might save him.

When this dire news was transmitted to Orogastus, he had had the oarsmen flogged, speeding the boat home in five hours, at the cost of half a dozen human lives. Now the sorcerer himself must needs try to deliver the King, whose death would mean the ruin of all his ambitions.

"Open the door," Orogastus commanded.

The Green Voice bowed and complied.

The bedchamber that had once been tenanted by King Krain had been hastily refurbished in Labornoki crimson for its new occupant. It was now very dark, the only illumination coming from the glowing coals in the fireplace and a single candle on a table, which also held a basin, wound-wrappings, and other medical implements and potions with which the royal physician had futilely attempted to treat the King's infected hand. The huge bed stood in the center of the room on a platform, surrounded by empty chairs. Its hangings were drawn back.

Orogastus gave swift orders in a low voice. "Green Voice, bring the two standing candelabra close to the bed and light them, then clear the table and position it at the bedside nearest the King's infirmity. Blue Voice, prepare the magical device. I think we have barely arrived in time."

A form stirred within the sheets, groaning, "Who is there? Is it you again, damned leech, come to torment me with your incompetent fumbling? Get out! Let me at least die in peace!"

"It is I, my King," Orogastus said. "And you shall not die." He lifted the King's left arm most carefully, but still the monarch uttered an agonized scream.

"Whoreson! Let me be! Your miraculous pill helped me for but a single day, and then my sufferings grew worse than before. Ah, Zoto have mercy — it is *their* doing! The Princesses! They have cursed me from afar! It is their revenge that tortures and dooms me."

"He is delirious," Orogastus said. From a pocket deep within his robe he took a small box carved from green malachite and opened it. It held six tiny spheres that shone golden and transparent in the candle light.

"Only half the original number left," the sorcerer mused. He extracted one and carefully put the others away. Then he took up a goblet of water and prevailed upon King Voltrik to swallow the Golden Pastille. When he had done so, the monarch uttered a gusty exhalation and seemed to relax.

Orogastus now slit the voluminous bandages about the King's hand with a small sharp knife. Positioning the extended arm on the table, he unwrapped it, exposing the wound. The entire limb felt hot to the touch, and streaks of red extended from the wrist to the armpit. The hand itself was hideously swollen, with the finger-tips bluish-black, and the flesh sloughing away in the area of the bite and exuding a towering stench that not even the herbal masks could inhibit. The sorcerer gave the Blue Voice the bandages to be burnt and spoke swift instructions to his other assistant, who had unpacked a leather bag and laid its contents on the table. Now Orogastus gave the limb over to the Green Voice and stood close to the King's head. Voltrik was gaunt, flushed, and rheumy-eyed, his once immaculate beard straggling and filth-clotted.

"What are you doing?" the monarch cried, starting up from the damp pillows. "Let loose my arm, you treasonous worrams! I know who you are! You've been sent by the three Ruwendian witches to finish me off!"

"Look into my eyes," Orogastus commanded. "Look and find respite from your suffering." The masked enchanter took the King's sweat-drenched head in both hands and turned it so that their two gazes commingled. Voltrik moaned, then gave vent to a great sigh and fell back onto the bedclothes, bereft of consciousness.

Orogastus returned to the table and took up a singular device. It was cubical except for a snoutlike protrusion on one side, and colored a shimmering silvery blue. On its top were ranks of black and red wart-like excrescences with mysterious symbols beneath them, and an inset miniature frame with grey blankness instead of a picture. When the sorcerer's fingers moved over the warts, pressing now this one and now that, the blankness within the little frame turned bright, and moving lines of colored hieroglyphics appeared on it. The attending Voice gasped in awe. One of the red warts glowed, then turned gold.

"Hold the arm perfectly still, thus," Orogastus commanded. "Sing the Chant of Healing but avert your eyes, for this machine of the Vanished Ones can blind a man who looks unprotected upon its working."

The sorcerer positioned the device a handspan below the elbow of the wounded arm as the three Voices began to chant in unison. Then he took up a strange visor and put it on, and all being in readiness, he pressed the largest of the machine's warts. A dazzling beam of blue-white light no thicker than a flaxen thread sprang forth from the protruding nozzle, and Orogastus manipulated the device slowly so that the ray transected the royal limb, moving in a deep V-shape.

There was a sharp sizzling sound and a great puff of smoke. When the beam winked out, Voltrik's lower arm was severed and there was a narrow charred groove in a corresponding V-shape burned into the wooden tabletop. The Chant of Healing came to an end.

"It is done." Orogastus removed the visor and inspected the stump. The large blood vessels were cauterized, but the flesh was red and glistening surrounding the two white bones within.

"Good. The mortal putrefaction had not reached into the arm itself. Now the Golden Pastille may wreak its healing without having to contend against a reservoir of deadly poison within the doomed hand."

He pressed a wart and all of the glowing areas on the device went dark. "Blue Voice, wrap the dead member and burn it, taking care lest it befoul you. Then repack my device most carefully. Green Voice, wipe well the table and the undamaged skin of the arm with strong brandy-spirit. Sponge also the King's forehead and temples, and bring fresh linen and a clean bedrobe for him from the press over yonder. Scorch new bandages at the fire and then rewrap the stump loosely. It must still purge itself of certain noxious fluids before it is sewn. Later I will give you and that cretinous physician further instructions concerning care of the stump that are to be followed scrupulously."

"The leech is to be spared, Great Lord?" Green was mildly surprised.

"Unless you wish to spoon gruel, change dressings, and empty the royal chamber-pot yourself, fool! Now attend to the King."

While the two Voices ministered to Voltrik, Orogastus went to the double window of the bedchamber, threw back the heavy red curtain, and opened the casement wide. Outside the sun shone brightly and there was a light breeze from the north. With the rotten flesh consigned to the flames and the stink finally abated, Orogastus took off his mask. His handsome features were pinched and pale and his lips tight-pressed to a grim line. It had been a near thing, but the King would recover rapidly now with careful nursing and appropriate reassurances. Once again the sorcerer approached the royal bedside.

"Voltrik — hear me!" Orogastus spoke in a low, compelling tone.

The King murmured, "I hear you."

"You have hovered at the threshold of death, my Liege, but I saved you when all others had despaired. You will live. There will yet be some suffering to be endured, but within a few weeks you will be strong again. I, Orogastus, pledge this most solemnly."

"Thank you," whispered the King. His eyes were closed and his hectic flush had receded. "You have removed the hand?"

"Yes, Sire."

The King sighed. "So be it. At least it is not the sword hand lost, thanks be to Zoto the Compassionate — and you." He groaned a little as the Voices enrobed him in a clean garment and put fresh pillows beneath his head and the newly bandaged arm. The sorcerer himself drew up the coverlet over the royal breast, whereupon the King opened his eyes and spoke in a voice that was weak but nearly normal in timbre.

"Send your servants away. I wish to speak to you of vital matters."

Orogastus addressed his underlings: "I will leave for my tower on Mount Brom within the hour. See to it that my escort is heavily armed and mounted upon the swiftest and strongest fronials."

"Yes, Almighty Master." The Voices went out and closed the door.

"You are leaving? . . ." The King was dismayed.

"My Voices will see that you are well cared for. I must go back to Labornok in order to consult the ice-mirror at my mountain stronghold. Only through this powerful device will I be able to spy out the whereabouts of your enemies."

The King sighed gustily. "That it was I wished to speak of. There was no news of the three fugitive girls in Trevista?"

"None. The female leader of the aborigines refused point-blank to cooperate with any search. If we attempt to coerce the swamp Folk in this matter, she says that all trade between them and us will be abolished."

The King cursed painfully. "We must find those Princesses!"

"My acolytes and I exerted our occult powers to the utmost, scanning not only the Oddling city, but also the farthest reaches of Ruwenda. Our efforts were in vain. Some powerful enchantment balks my Sight, even when it is amplified by mental conjunction. The three Princesses are said to wear amulets containing buds of the Black Trillium. Perhaps these shield them. This herb is linked to Binah, the guardian witch of Ruwenda, and it is likely that she has channeled all of her remaining meager potency through it to defend her wards."

"Your mirror will be able to squelch this — this obfuscation?"

"Beyond a doubt. It is empowered by the magic of the Vanished

Ones. No enchantment in the known world can confute its farseeing eye. It can see for five thousand leagues — to the very western boundary of the continent, where the feathered barbarians dwell. Have no fear, my King. I will locate the Princesses, no matter where they have hidden."

"So you track the she-devils down. What then? They could skip away long before you returned to Ruwenda to give chase."

Orogastus laughed. "My King, leave it all to me. The Red Voice has remained in Trevista, awaiting orders with the garrison troops. When I have found the girls, I will bespeak their hiding places to each of my assistants and we will send out search parties at once. The Voices will guide them, and I will constantly transmit news of the Princesses' movements until at last your enemies are taken and dealt with as they deserve."

"Good. Good." The King was silent for a few moments. Then he said: "The girls really *did* cause my wound to mortify, didn't they?"

"Such things can happen because of magic, but also from the normal course of events. At any rate, Sire, you will soon be well. Unfortunately, the malady you suffered is one that cannot be cured except by the most drastic intervention."

The King had closed his eyes again. A wry smile played about his discolored lips. "But you intervened in time. And so my dear son Antar will have to content himself without the crown that was so nearly within his grasp."

The sorcerer's voice was neutral. "The Crown Prince comported himself with dignity and honor in Trevista and sends his prayers for your recovery."

"Hmmph! Your Green Voice passed on his brothers' vision of Antar's meeting with the Oddling Discerner. The damned boy caved in before her like a wedding cake in a monsoon!" The royal eyelids flicked open. "What do you think, sorcerer? Is my son loyal?"

"We will find out, my King. Since Prince Antar will certainly captain one of the search-parties we send in pursuit of the three Princesses."

∴

17

Haramis awoke the next morning with the sun in her eyes and the knowledge that something was very wrong. It took her a moment to gather her wits enough to realize that what disturbed her was the silence. Uzun always rose before she did, so that she generally woke to the sounds of him moving around the camp, humming to himself. But now it was full day, the winds were still, the birds were silent, and there was no sound from Uzun, not so much as a snore.

Haramis turned her head to look at her friend's sleep-sack, still nestled against the boulder where he had placed it the night before. Judging by its shape, he was still in it. Haramis pulled herself reluctantly out of her own sack, noting that the temperature was much lower than it had been the previous night, in spite of the bright sunlight. She squinted into the cloudless sky and belatedly realized that the pattern of clouds she had seen the day before had indicated the imminent arrival of a cold spell.

Crawling over to where Uzun lay, she pulled back the top of his sleep-sack to uncover his face. It was perfectly still and expressionless, and Haramis was convinced she was looking at a corpse.

"Lords of the Air," she whispered in horror. "I should have sent him back yesterday — no, days ago!"

She grabbed the little Oddling by the shoulders and shook him violently. "Please, Uzun, wake up! Don't be dead! Please!"

His body flopped loosely in her grasp, and what remained of the rational part of her mind remembered that bodies stiffened in death. Perhaps he was alive after all . . .

She laid him down gently, pulled off her left mitten, and held her palm just above his mouth. It seemed forever before she felt his breath flow against her hand and even longer before the next breath. He was alive, but she had to get him someplace warmer, and that soon.

She tucked his sleep-sack back around him, returned to her own, and pulled on her boots. Then she set her pack and walking-staff against the rock next to Uzun's sleep-sack, and cast another anxious glance at the sky. She was fairly certain it wasn't going to snow today, and with luck she'd be back here tonight. Her pack should remain undisturbed; there were no animals in this area likely to be attracted to it.

She shouldered Uzun's pack, and picked him up, still bundled. Shaking as much snow as possible off the sleep-sack, she maneuvered him into her own. The extra layer of insulation might help, even if it was unwieldy to carry such a bulky bundle. Fortunately Uzun was not heavy, and the path was downhill.

Haramis set off at the best pace she could manage, which was fairly quick, especially in the spots where she slipped and slid, clutching Uzun to her breast until she could dig in her heels enough to stop them. By mid-morning they were out of the snowfields, and by midday they were back at the place where they had camped the previous night.

It was an alcove in the rocks, dry, sheltered from wind, and currently flooded with the noonday sun. Even the rock walls were warm to the touch. Haramis set Uzun down against the back wall and went to scavenge for firewood. He had been the one to gather wood when they had been here before, but she remembered in which direction he had looked and that it hadn't taken him long to find it.

When she returned, she checked Uzun's condition again. He was still unconscious, but his breathing seemed to be a bit faster, which she took to be a good sign. She built the fire as close to him as she dared, heated some water, and made tea. Uzun was still asleep when the tea was ready; but the smell of it reminded her that she hadn't eaten or drunk anything that day, so she sipped some of it and ate a little of the food from Uzun's pack. *He won't need as much on his trip south. He'll be in areas where food can be obtained.* Then, feeling more alive herself, she took the bowl of tea over to Uzun, propped him up, and carefully dripped a small amount of it between his lips.

∴

To her immense relief, he roused slightly at the touch of warm liquid. "Gently, Uzun," she murmured. "Swallow."

He did, and she coaxed him to take a few more mouthfuls before he feebly pushed it away, murmuring: "Too tired."

"I'm tired, too," Haramis agreed, realizing that it was true. She was exhausted. She drank off the rest of the tea, leaned her back against the stone wall, and cradled Uzun in her lap. Perhaps keeping him close to her body would help; she was warm-blooded and should radiate at least some heat. And the sun shining on her felt so good. She closed her eyes and tilted her face toward the light . . .

"Princess!" The bundle in her lap was squirming frantically. "What are we doing sitting here? Surely the seed hasn't stopped us this early . . ." Uzun's head whipped back and forth as its owner tried to orient himself. "Where are we? What happened?"

Haramis shook her head, struggling to clear her thoughts. She almost never slept during the daytime — certainly never when she wasn't sick — and she felt groggy, as if she had been drugged or poisoned. "Tea," she muttered. "I need tea." Her hand fumbled at her side and found the bowl, and she started to push herself to her feet.

Uzun wriggled out of the two sleep-sacks. "I'll get it." He took the bowl from her, added more wood to the fire, and put more water on to boil. To Haramis's sleepy eyes, he appeared completely recovered. Could Oddlings be frozen then, and thawed out again with no ill effects? It seemed incredible. But at least Uzun should be able to return alone now.

He brought her the tea, and she sipped it slowly, feeling her disordered wits start to fall back into place. She drank half the bowl, then handed the rest to Uzun to finish.

"Uzun," she began, eager to share with him the insight she had achieved during her overburdened trek down the mountain, "I really believe that we have spent too much of our lives in the library and the music room. We've been acting like a couple of idiot heroes on a quest — as if we were destined to succeed and therefore had no need to use our brains and common sense. The White Lady said I would have to part with you before I finished my quest, but she certainly never said that I should do so by dragging you into cold weather your body couldn't handle and allowing you to freeze to death."

The Oddling looked at their surroundings carefully. "I know this place. But this isn't where we stopped last night, is it?"

"No, it's not," Haramis replied. "This is our camp of two nights ago. I woke up this morning to find you frozen almost to death — in fact, I thought at first that you *were* dead! Your skin was as cold as the air, and your breathing was so slow it took me quite a while to be sure you were still alive." She shuddered at the memory. "So I bundled you up in both our sleep-sacks and carried you back down here in the hope that you would thaw out and survive." She drew a deep breath. "Thank the Triune God, it worked. You are all right, aren't you?" she added anxiously.

Uzun appeared a bit shaken by her account, but after a moment's thought he nodded. "I feel well enough," he said. "I'm still a bit chilly, but it's nothing serious. I'll be well enough to go on later."

"Good," Haramis said. "Now that you are out of the snowfields, you should be able to return to Trevista on your own, while I continue my journey." She rummaged in his pack for the fishing gear. "For now, just get back in the sleep-sacks and rest. I'm going to see if I can catch a fish or two for supper. If I can get enough, we'll both have food for tomorrow as well."

"But, my Princess," Uzun protested, "you will lose at least two days of travel time. And you may run out of seeds to guide you."

"The two days are already lost, old friend," Haramis sighed; "even if I started back up immediately, I would not be able to reach last night's campsite until nearly dawn — assuming I could move at the same pace by moonlight as by daylight, which I very much doubt. But I won't need another seed for tomorrow — I was careful to notice landmarks as I came downhill, so that I can retrace my steps unaided. And it doesn't look as though it will snow tonight, which means that I will have my old tracks to follow. So don't worry about me, just stay by the fire and rest. By the Triune God, Uzun, you nearly died!"

"Do you think I would not rejoice to die in your service?" Uzun asked in offended tones.

"I am quite sure you *would*," Haramis snapped crossly. "That's precisely what I mean about having our heads echoing with old ballads. I assure you that when one is slogging through the snow carrying a childhood friend who may very well die because you were too stupid to notice he was getting sick from the cold, one's thoughts are *not*

occupied in finding rhyming couplets for a song of his heroic death. I
was stupid not to notice how sick you were getting, and *you* were stupid
not to tell me. Your freezing to death wouldn't help Ruwenda in the
slightest, and would have left me distracted with grief and guilt. The
loss of two days' travel is a small price to pay for your life. Maybe,"
she continued thoughtfully, "maybe a queen does sometimes have to
sacrifice the life of one of her people, but by the Lords of the Air, if I
have to do that, I'm going to have a good reason!"

"Would you deny me the chance to be faithful unto death?" Uzun's
voice was hurt.

"Not at all," Haramis assured him. "I simply do not feel that *now* is
the appropriate time for you to die in my service. After all, if you die
now, who is going to be my chief musician when I have my throne
back — and who will teach my children to play the fipple flute?"

Uzun's face brightened considerably at that. "Very well, my Princess,
it shall be as you desire. I shall return to my homeland and await your
return to the throne and my return to your service."

"I, too, look forward to that day," Haramis said smiling as she tucked
the second sleep-sack more tightly around him. "Sleep now, my friend."
Uzun's eyelids fluttered closed, and Haramis moved her hand over his
forehead. His skin was definitely warmer now; he was going to be all
right. Blinking back tears of relief, she went to the river in search of
fish.

"Princess, wake up!" Uzun was shaking her shoulder urgently. "There
will be snow today, so you need to get started as soon as possible."

Haramis opened her eyes. Sure enough, the sky was obscured by
heavy pewter-grey clouds obviously just waiting for the right moment
to start dumping snow all over the landscape. She groaned, dragging
herself to a sitting position. She was still tired from her exertions of
the previous day. Carrying Uzun had required muscles she had not
been using before. Now her arms ached down their entire inner length.

Uzun bustled about the fire, preparing tea, and brought it to her.
"Princess," he asked, looking about them, "where is your backpack?"

Haramis hastily drank her portion of tea. "I left it at the campsite
yesterday — I had best get back up there to retrieve it before it gets
buried!" She got up, hastily rolled up her sleep-sack, and tied it around

her waist. "And you had better get out of here quickly, too, Uzun; you don't want to be caught in the snow!"

"Very true," Uzun agreed, shoving a large chunk of journey bread into her hand. "Eat this on your way, and may the Lords of the Air go with you."

"And with you, my friend." Haramis hugged her old friend tightly, reluctant to part with him, then released him and started up the path. *At least I don't have to keep watching a floating seed, so I can pay more attention to where I'm putting my feet,* she thought. *Now if the snow will just hold off . . .*

She went up the mountain at a good speed, since she was more lightly burdened than the last time she had made this climb and knew exactly where she was going. By the time the snow started falling she had already gone halfway; and when she reached the rock where she and Uzun had camped two nights before, her pack was buried under only a handspan of snow.

She dug it out, ate some more journey bread, and hollowed out a sleeping space in the lee of the rock. It was getting very dark, but with the snow falling she did not think she could keep a fire lit, so she crawled into her sleep-sack, pulling her pack in with her, and waited for sleep to come.

But her nerves, which had been shouting *hurry, hurry, hurry* at her all day, were not so easily quieted. Haramis had never felt so bereft and alone in her life, and she suddenly realized that this was the first time she ever *had* been alone. Before the invasion, she had always had her parents, her sisters, Uzun, and the rest of the inhabitants of the Citadel. Since then Uzun had been with her, except for the hours she had spent with the Archimage. And while at times during her life at home she had wished for more privacy, now that she had all the privacy anyone could possibly desire she wasn't at all sure she liked it.

In addition to her loneliness, there were other things troubling her. Chief among these was Uzun. She prayed to the Lords of the Air that he would make his way safely out of the mountains, but now that she had time to think about the situation and nothing else to do but think, several questions occurred to her. Why had Uzun not told her he couldn't go on before he nearly froze to death? Why hadn't the Archimage warned her to leave Uzun behind before she entered the snowfields, instead of simply saying that the elderly musician would be leaving her before she found her talisman? For all the help either of them had been, Uzun might have died!

Of course, the fault lay as much with her as with them; her judgment had been equally bad, but they were older. Shouldn't they have known better than she?

I am Queen of Ruwenda, she thought soberly, *and the responsibility is mine, but I still need counsel I can trust — and how much can I trust either of them? Uzun doesn't seem any more aware of his limitations than Kadiya is of hers, or if he is, he won't admit them without a struggle. As for the Archimage, did she not realize how susceptible Uzun would be to cold, or did she merely not think him important enough to worry about?*

Even her beloved parents, she belatedly realized, had hardly been masters of worldly wisdom and diplomacy. Labornok's covetous interest in Ruwenda had been well-known in the Ruwendian court; and while Haramis certainly did not want to marry Voltrik, her parents could at least have pretended to negotiate, or expressed concern about the great discrepancy in age between Haramis and Voltrik and suggested a union with Voltrik's son instead. What was his name? Oh yes, Prince Antar. And if Ruwenda wanted an alliance with Var, an idea which certainly had merit, Haramis was not the only royal daughter. Haramis had trouble visualizing Kadiya as anyone's wife, but Anigel would make a splendid bride for a diplomatic alliance. She was so gentle and yielding that she could get along with anyone. *And if I can think of all this off the top of my head*, Haramis thought, *what were my parents and their advisers doing? Trusting in the White Lady?*

Obviously, she decided, *it is necessary to consider people's capabilities as well as their intentions when one takes counsel of them or depends on them for aid.* So who, if anyone, remained who could help her now? Still pondering that question, Haramis fell asleep.

P rincess Anigel had nearly swooned when the White Lady revealed the nature of the talisman she must seek. A Three-Headed Monster! Such a prospect would have daunted even bold Kadiya or the confident Haramis. That *she* should be expected to find and subdue such a thing was laughable. No, impossible!

She said as much to Immu, speaking through a storm of furious weeping (for the Archimage had fallen asleep and could not be wakened), but the Nyssomu woman only counseled patience.

"There are many kinds of monsters," Immu said, "and not all are like the Skritek, with glowing eyes and rending fangs and claws, for the word has many meanings. Until you behold your monstrous talisman with your own eyes, Princess, you had better reserve judgment upon whether or not to be afraid of it."

Immu's good sense gave the Princess a certain grim comfort. Since the White Lady slept on oblivious, the two guests made themselves at home in her cottage, refreshing themselves, cooking a fine dinner from the well-stocked larder, and finally going to sleep on the floor in front of the fire, one on either side of the Lady's chair, in case she should need help during the night.

In the morning, the Archimage was gone.

So was the cottage, the neat yard with the lawn-clipping togars, the Black Trillium plant and the little orchard, even the flight of stone steps and the dock where they had landed.

Anigel and Immu lay in their plant-down sacks on a jungle slope beneath the huge leaves of a bruddok, the plant called by the Nyssomu the "traveler's friend" because of its sheltering foliage and sweet, juicy fruit. The only indication that they were not in the midst of a wilderness was a glimpse of the ruins of Noth, visible behind the trees across the river from the little lagoon, on the shore of which the cottage had once stood.

Anigel broke into exclamations of dismay and wept at the shocking discovery. For a moment she even wondered whether their meeting with the Archimage yesterday had all been a dream. But then she found beneath her sleep-sack a large green leaf with a golden vein tracing a winding path from tip to stem; and Immu, investigating down near the edge of the water, gave a sudden cry:

"Look look look! The White Lady left us a present!"

Still sniffling, Anigel crawled from her covers and came to the lagoonside. There among the tall reeds and putrid yellow water-flowers was a boat. It was not a Uisgu craft made of reeds, such as had carried them to Noth, but the larger Nyssomu model carved from a kala-trunk that commonly plied the waters around the Citadel. Only one thing was different about this boat — in addition to the usual sweeps and rowlocks (which were demounted and strapped to the inside of the hull) it had at the stem a stout fitting to which a pair of traces were snapped, and at the bow twin rings, through which two leather straps came and rested on the forward thwart. The lengths of leather led from the boat down into the murky water.

Anigel studied this arrangement for a moment, wondering. "You don't suppose — " And then she gave a shriek as two large heads clothed in dapple-green fur rose out of the water, sleek and fierce, with big black eyes, bristling whiskers, and fanged mouths open in a hostile hiss.

"Rimoriks!" said Immu. "Oh, dear . . ."

"But — but there are no Uisgu to drive them," the Princess faltered.

"And yet it seems that the Archimage intends for us to use this very efficient means of transport."

Anigel bit her lip. She could not look Immu in the eye. "Do you think that you could manage?"

"No, Princess Anigel," the Oddling woman said, solemnly. "The beasts work only in friendship, with those who drink the sacred miton."

∴

Trembling, Anigel turned to the two water-creatures. "Did the Arch-image send you to help us?" she asked them.

The only response was a vicious hiss. The rimoriks surged up and down in the water impatiently, revealing the harness that attached them to the boat, which rocked wildly in the waves they made and tugged at the mooring line that had been tied to a rock on the shore.

Anigel closed her eyes. "Immu, can you not drink the miton?"

"No, child." The old nurse's voice was gentle. "It was a gift to you from the Uisgu . . . and now we know why." Leaving the girl standing there, Immu went back up the slope and gathered their things, together with some of the bruddok fruit to eke out the trail rations that would be their breakfast. When she returned she put the packs into the boat and held out the scarlet miton gourd to the Princess.

Anigel took it. Her eyes were glazed and her cheeks still damp with tears. She removed the stopper and lifted the small netted container so that the rimoriks could see it. "*I* must drink — is that it?"

The great water-beasts closed their mouths and sank back into the lagoon so that only their noses and dark suspicious eyes were above the waves. They watched Anigel, motionless.

One of her hands groped for the trillium amulet. The other lifted the blood-drink to her pale lips. She took a small sip —

You see, Brother, how the human female fears us.

She fears the miton even more, and yet she has drunk of it. Human! Do you hear us? Do you wish to be our friend?

"Yes," whispered Anigel.

Then dip two fingers into the miton, wade into the water, and share the drink with us.

Dazed, she obeyed, tucking her grass robe up into her belt. The warm mud of the lagoon bottom oozed up between her bare toes as she walked out to where the water reached her knees. She extended her hand with brownish liquid dripping from the fingers.

The two great green-spotted animals glided up to her, resting on their forelimbs in the shallows and opening wide their glittering jaws. Whiplike tongues with pointed ends uncoiled, organs that could pierce the scaled bodies of fish as easily as a javelin. Anigel seemed to see herself from afar, as though she were a spectator at a fantastic drama, and the girl in the water and the rimoriks were mere play-actors. First one finger, then the other touched the terrible tongues. And as the rimoriks swallowed their faces seemed to change, radiating kindness instead of savagery, and she no longer feared them.

Anigel restoppered the gourd and put it into her belt-wallet, where the Black Trillium leaf also lay safe. She felt dizzy. The colors of the marshland foliage, of the algae-clothed lagoon water, even the carved wooden surfaces of the boat seemed sharpened and more vivid. She smelled subtle scents that had gone unnoticed before, and heard such a multitude of strange and overamplified sounds that for a moment there was pain in her ears. Her very skin seemed to crawl, shrinking from the light touch of the breeze and the suddenly scratchy and oppressive feel of her garments. Her submerged legs, on the other hand, felt caressed by the currents of the water, and the mud was velvety and soothing against her feet.

The miton will change you.

The miton will make you apprehensive at first, burdening your feeble human senses. But this malaise will pass. You will feel strong and brave, like us.

"Yes . . . I feel better already."

This is good. This means that we can indeed be friends with a human. You will share your intelligence with us, and you will partake of our audacity and strength.

"You call me intelligent. I have never thought of myself thus. But I will do my best to be so if you will only lend me bravery, for without it no amount of cleverness will enable me to fulfill my quest."

The White Lady bade us help you. We will do what we can.

"Do you have names?"

You could not say them. Call us friends.

"What — what do we do next?"

In her mind, Anigel heard the two rimoriks laugh. But it was good old crotchety Immu who replied.

"Do do do! And you are supposed to be the clever one — ? What a joke! The Tassaleyo Forest is over three hundred leagues away, and we cannot even begin your quest until we get there. Suppose you get into the punt, silly girl, and take up the reins, and get us started on our way!"

The rimoriks seemed to know exactly what route to follow, taking their cue from Anigel's study of the Black Trillium leaf. They sped down the River Nothar with reckless abandon, since there was no chance that the Labornoki enemy was abroad on its waters. Of Anigel's sister Princess Kadiya there was no trace, neither could the rimoriks tell what had become of her. When the punt moved into the broader Upper Mutar, Anigel instructed the beasts to slow down and progress more stealthily, keeping close to the banks so that there was less chance of any enemy explorers spotting them. Sure enough, they saw half a dozen punts full of Labornoki scouts prowling about in the waters above Trevista. But the enemy went about its business without noticing them, even though one of the Labornoki boats passed less than twenty ells away.

Each evening, they would find a safe stopping place. Anigel would unharness the beasts, standing in shallow water, and they would slip away to hunt. Some of the fish and other water-creatures that the rimoriks caught would be brought back and shared with their new friend, and in the morning the women would find a breakfast catch lying near the camp. But before Anigel could harness the rimoriks again, she would have to drink of the miton, then share it with the animals.

On the fourth morning of the down-river journey, the Princess awoke in the hushed darkness before dawn, when the night-creatures fell silent at last and those who went about in daylight were not yet stirring. A heavy fog enveloped their tiny campsite on an islet on the outskirts of Trevista, and all the foliage dripped. It had been a stray drop of water, falling from the overturned punt that was their improvised shelter, that had awakened Anigel.

Her sleep had again been free from dreams.

She lay there in her down sleep-sack, hearing only the irregular patter of the dripping dew and Immu's gentle snores, holding tight her warm amulet. No dreams of drought and fire. None since the night she and Immu had fallen asleep on the floor of the White lady's enchanted cottage. How strange that she had not noticed it before . . .

Am I really cured of the cowardice? she asked herself. No, that could not be. She knew that she was still desperately afraid — afraid of being captured by the Labornoki soldiers and killed, afraid of the trackless Tassaleyo Forest and the fierce, unfamiliar aborigines inhabiting it, afraid most of all of the dreadful talisman she sought, the Three-Headed Monster.

And yet the nightmare was gone — the warning from her secret self.

What did it mean? She thought of asking Immu, but the Oddling woman was sleeping soundly, murmuring sometimes in her own language, and the Princess had not the heart to wake her.

Still wondering, Anigel drifted back to sleep.

In the Lower Mutar there were many flatboats loaded with troops and supplies going up and down the river. It seemed as though the conquerors had commandeered the entire Ruwendian trade-fleet — for what purpose Anigel and Immu could not guess. They had a narrow escape one afternoon when, speeding around a bend, they met a Labornoki flatboat train dead ahead, coming at them on a collision course. Anigel clutched her amulet and tried to make them invisible, but the charm refused to work. Before she could panic, however, the rimoriks abruptly changed course, streaking off at a right angle and concealing them behind a great floating snag. The men of Labornok, half blinded by the westering sun, sailed heedlessly on.

As the punt approached more populous regions above the Citadel, the Princess directed the rimoriks to swim through the most obscure side-channels and backwaters that they could find, to keep them out of the enemy's sight. Their good luck began to seem almost supernatural. They did not travel as fast as they had from Trevista to Noth, since they could not change animals as the Uisgu drivers Lebb and Tirebb had done; but they managed a good rate of speed nevertheless, and were spared from many a natural danger to boaters, such as the giant flesh-eating milingal-fish infesting the Blackmire section of the Lower Mutar, because of the formidable nature of the rimoriks. Most other water-creatures gave the big green-furred carnivores a wide berth.

The first genuine disaster threatened on a day when they were encamped a few leagues above the Citadel, awaiting nightfall so as to pass the Knoll more safely in the dark. Anigel discovered that the red gourd of miton was empty. Its stopper had come loose, and the precious liquid had drained away.

"This is awful!" the Princess cried. "That this should happen here, at the most dangerous part of the river, where the enemy soldiers are everywhere! Without the miton, the rimoriks will not even allow us to get into the boat. You recall the one morning when I forgot the ritual — they bared their teeth at me as though I were a perfect stranger! Oh, Immu, what are we going to do? If the rimoriks don't help us, we'll never be able to reach the Tassaleyo Forest."

∴

Immu said: "There is only one possible course of action. You must make more miton."

"But how?" the girl fretted. And then her blue eyes went wide with the realization of what would have to be done. "But I can't do it!" she moaned. "Not even to myself — much less to *them.*"

"I can help draw your own blood," Immu said. "The process is not even painful, beyond the first prick. But you will have to cope with your fine sharp-toothed friends yourself. They would swallow me in one gulp if I came at them with my blade."

After an interlude of squeamish hesitation, the Princess finally submitted. Immu took certain thick leaves and squeezed a juice from them, then pierced a vein on the girl's wrist with her sharp little dagger. Anigel made not a sound. The leaf-liquor, dripped upon the small wound, inhibited the blood's clotting and a concave drogo leaf was soon filled. When this was done and the Princess's blood poured into the gourd, Immu washed the puncture with pure dew-water and bound it up tightly after pressing a medicinal blue flower to it.

"There!" The Oddling tied a neat knot to the wrist bandage of grass. "But how you will bleed the rimoriks, I have no idea."

"I will ask them," Anigel said. And the creatures told her:

Bring a dish-leaf into the boat.

The great animals were unharnessed, paddling around the stern of the partially beached punt. When Anigel crawled into the end that was afloat, they drew near. One after the other, they reared up, nipped the edges of their beclawed front flippers, and let blood flow into the drogo leaf. When it was filled one of the rimoriks swam off and returned with a red-flowered swampherb, which it had ripped up roots and all.

Crush a tuber of this plant and mix it with the blood. Thus is miton made. The swamp Folk customarily strain the liquid, but this is not really necessary.

"Thank you, my friends," Anigel said.

She followed their instructions, and when she had finished the gourd was full of the brown, salty-sweet-tasting sacred drink. The Princess was so used to it by now that she thought no ill of the drinking, and the subsequent heightening of her senses had begun to seem so normal to her that she did not feel that she was truly awake in the morning until she and the rimoriks had communed.

Much later, during the night-shrouded small hours of the next day, when they had nearly completed the perilous skirting of the Citadel Knoll and were racing through a backwater bordering the Greenmire,

Anigel thought to ask Immu whether or not the miton had changed her personality — as it was said to change that of the Nyssomu who drank it.

Immu said: "You are the same dear person I have always loved — although perhaps more mature and worldly-wise from our travels, and much less dainty about your food, and not nearly so hoity-toity about where you lay your head at night or relieve your body's needs. You have also turned into a demon boat-driver. Whether your own people would count all this an improvement, I cannot say."

Anigel spoke over her shoulder. "Since leaving Noth, I have not had the nightmares. Do you think this means I've grown brave, Immu?"

"Either brave or madcap," the old woman said grouchily. She was holding on for dear life as the punt zipped in and out of a dense grove of kalas north of the Great Causeway. For once there was no night-mist, and the Triple Moons glimmered through the moss-hung branches. "Just look at you, Princess, gripping the reins like a veteran volumnial-skinner as we charge through the darkness faster than ma-rauding Skritek! You have come a long way from the times when you thought yourself daring to attempt a new step on the dance floor or an unfamiliar embroidery stitch."

"And yet I still feel fear, Immu."

"Of course you do. So do I — for good reason! If you don't slow those wretched creatures down, we may end up wrapped around a tree with the night-warblers giggling over our broken bones."

Anigel reined in the rimoriks a little. "They see in the dark. There is no real danger here. It lies not far ahead, though. I — I feel it."

"That may be true."

"Do you suppose my sisters also are searching for their own fearsome talismans?"

"Probably."

"The White Lady is cruel to separate us!" Anigel cried out suddenly. "We were born together. We have lived our whole lives together. It would have been so much easier if she had let us share our quests. Had let us help one another!"

"No doubt," muttered the Nyssomu woman wearily. Her head drooped and her long ears lay blasted flat by the speed-wind against the dirty lawn of her old court headdress, which she persisted in wear-ing. "But you have not lacked for faithful servants."

The Princess bit off the fresh complaint that hovered on her lips. She *had* been helped by many aborigines, to say nothing of the rimoriks. But her most constant helper and companion had been Immu herself — and how much true appreciation had Anigel shown her dear old nurse since they set out on this terrible journey? She had taken Immu for granted, never thinking of how frightened and weary the old woman must be. And now they had both been awake for that whole day and most of the night, Immu having refused the Princess's suggestion that she nap during the night travel. Anigel was still charged with energy and excitement, eager to continue on, and the rimoriks, sensing her urgency, were willing. But Immu was plainly exhausted . . .

Find us a safe stopping place, she told the animals.

Yes, friend, they said. And the punt slowed, turned aside, and glided through a thick curtain of night-flowering vines. Ahead was a high, dry hummock. As the boat scraped bottom, Immu snorted. Her head flew up and her eyes popped open.

"Wake up, Immu," Anigel said softly. "It's bedtime."

19

T hey were being treated, Kadiya knew, as honored guests, and that portion of her which was rooted in patience, small though it was, told her that this was perhaps all she might expect. Still, on the second day after their arrival at the Nyssomu village, she made one last attempt to win fighting aid from those who hosted her. After all, it was not only her need to gather allies that mattered; these villagers should also prepare for the worst — the probable arrival of the Labornoki invaders.

She asked for another meeting with the First of the House, striving to set a rein on her usual headlong demand for what she believed was necessary.

"Lady," she schooled her voice into a low and level tone, "these humans who now come into your land are not as we Ruwendians. Let me tell you straightly of their deeds."

Her hands, which had been lying loosely in her lap, suddenly clutched each other in a punishing grip. She had to swallow twice before she launched into the terrible account of her Father's death. At the picture her words summoned up she forced nausea to become anger.

It was difficult to read subtle expression on any Oddling face. Kadiya watched very carefully for any sign that the First was moved by what she told baldly in all its horror.

"Thus they treated our people they took after honest battle," she concluded. "Lady, they hold your people in even greater contempt — what do you think they would do here, were they to take your village? The Mires hold your secrets and have been your walls of defense. But these Labornoki bring with them a sorcerer against whose will the Archimage's protection could not stand. To fight with honest steel, sword to sword, is one thing. To strive against black magic with no proper weapon is to face defeat before the battlehorns sound. This is your land, and one wholly unknown to the invaders. They seem to have already aligned with the Skritek — whose evil nature they certainly share. But that can be countered by your knowledge of the swamp itself. I say to you — even if your customs do not allow you to take up our cause, look to your own!"

The First sat for a moment in silence before she answered, and for that same moment Kadiya knew a faint stir of hope. Perhaps the sense of what she had told this Nyssomu woman would prevail after all. Let Hamil take Trevista; let him summon the Skritek; but if the Nyssomu arose and used the land itself as a weapon, surely there was a chance . . .

But when the First of the House spoke, her words were formal, holding no warmth. "King's Daughter, it is true that your people and we of the Mires have dealt easily together through many years. There is no record of any such horrors between us as those you have told me. Since these slain are your kin, it is certainly true you will look for any help you can gather to avenge them. But friends though we be, there is for us an older service, an old allegiance that rests with the Lady of Noth. She has summoned you and your sisters. It can well be that she has already some plan of action. Be sure, however, that we are well warned. Before your people came hither the Mires knew war . . ."

She was staring beyond Kadiya's shoulder as if she recognized there something of importance. "There was long ago a harvesting of lives beyond all accounting. How think you did this land become as it is: broken, in many parts, desolate, and filled with such perils that we have not ventured along certain paths for many hundreds? That war was not ours, but we were born of it — and when those who fought it were gone, we were newborns with a strange world before us which we had to make our own. Then we took oath that such a war would not come again through any of us Nyssomu. To the Lady of Noth we owe our lives. With her we have long kept peace. If we are attacked we fight, but we carry no war to others. You will find your answers at Noth, King's Daughter."

So it was that only Kadiya and Jagun set forth again on their journey,

∴

and the farther they went the stranger and more threatening became the land. Most of the swamp growth in the Blackmire forest had been various shades of green, save for the flowers. Here in the Goldenmire grew the tall reed-grass with yellow panicles which gave its name to this section of the swamp. Here, too, there were islets rising from the green-scummed water on which there were clumps of large fleshy-leaved plants, unlike any elsewhere. These were yellow-white with streaks of red across them. Seeming to hold the appearance of infected, unhealed wounds, they exuded a stench which appeared to attract insects. The farther Jagun and the Princess poled their way along, the more malignant became these outcroppings of vegetation.

She heard a hiss of breath from Jagun and balanced herself in the punt while the hunter moved with care. Moving toward them along the shore of an islet came what seemed to be one of the unwholesome leaves. At the village, Jagun had added to his equipment a short-hafted spear. Now his arm swung out and the blade caught under the edge of the wandering leaf, flipping it up into the air and back to the muddy earth it had just left. As it arose the girl could see fringe-like feet moving, vainly hunting purchase. Then the creature slammed against a mossy piece of wood and instantly curled about it.

"Snafi," Jagun said tersely. "We must watch for them here. Their clawed feet inject poison into the skin and once they have taken hold they cannot be pulled off."

Kadiya was glad that on leaving the Nyssomu village Jagun had decided that they were far enough away from the known trail to travel by day. This part of the Mire must be a series of vicious traps of one kind or another.

Against her breast the amulet lay warm and was a steadfast guide. According to its spark they were still bound in the right direction. Kadiya kept to the rhythm of the poles, fitting her swing to Jagun's for hour against hour, though they did halt at intervals to rest.

If she faced danger, Kadiya thought, what had Haramis found to fight against? And Anigel . . . *Had* her younger sister been taken? Somehow she felt more and more strongly that both of her sisters had escaped from the Citadel, were not helpless prey for King Voltrik.

The sky had steadily clouded over during the afternoon and it was near twilight when Jagun twisted a tough clump of grass to anchor their craft. Already those queer lights which were born of the swamp-

∴

gases were visible. This evening, they did not try to disembark from the punt but ate rations they had brought with them. And then Jagun said:

"Sleep."

Sleep! How could anyone sleep here; in the dark, not knowing what menace might come from either shore? But in spite of herself she found that her eyes were closing . . .

What followed seemed more vision than dream. Kadiya saw a city — not Trevista, but one far younger, its architecture lighter in spirit. However, no sentries walked its walls, nor passed through the open gate which appeared just before her. Was this Noth? She longed to enter it — it beckoned, called. It was a promise.

Then the vision was lost in a deeper dream of which she remembered nothing on waking. She roused at dawn, to discover Jagun already astir, digging into one of their food bags. A short time later, they resumed their journey to the Archimage's home, and in early afternoon they caught their first glimpse of it.

No such city as Kadiya had dreamt of rose before them as they approached their goal. They saw only a single monolithic tower, rising high above the golden-plumed grass. Kadiya stared up at it as Jagun negotiated the final twists of the waterway, and at length their boat grated, not against another mud bank, but on the edge of an area of stone blocks.

"This is Noth," Jagun said. "From here, only you who have been summoned may go. I shall await you."

The pavement was not much wider than the punt which had brought them here. Beyond stood the tower. It could have been carved from a single mountain-sized block of granite, as tall as one of the great royal trees of the southern forests. The huge door stood open.

Although the light did not reach far within that cavernous doorway, there was nothing about the tower which outwardly threatened. Still, Kadiya felt like a child about to answer for some act of disobedience as she strode resolutely forward, refusing to betray her unease.

"Welcome, Kadiya."

The voice did not echo down that narrow hall, nor did it sound other than a usual greeting. Still, she walked on with one hand at knife hilt and the other pressed over the amulet, which throbbed warmly against her flesh in a heart-even beat. Then she entered the chamber beyond.

∴

There stood a high-backed chair of presence, such as her Mother and Father had used at times of ceremony. In it the Lady who ruled Noth (and perhaps elsewhere also) sat, her long-fingered hands smoothing back and forth across her knees the edge of a cloak which was the black of a stormy night, thick in its folds. Yet there ran across it runes of silver which came and went as do the ripples on a pool into which one casts a pebble or two.

Judging by her size, she was certainly not of Oddling blood. In fact, standing she might have overtopped Kadiya by several hands' height. Her face was neither young nor old, removed from the touch of age, but her eyes showed both weariness and determined will.

"Kadiya!" She inclined her head, but not in any warmth of welcome.

The anger which Kadiya held within her nearly broke its bonds. She wanted to hurl both her ire and her hurt at this untouched stranger, to demand from her own lips why her magic had failed. Could she not have in some way restrained the enemies of Ruwenda? Was this proud Lady of Noth so much less than Orogastus? Her magic certainly had failed when it was needed the most! The girl was able only with effort to forbear voicing those harsh thoughts. Instead she inclined her head, streaked as it was with swamp grease.

"Lady."

She had no chance, she sensed, for either accusation or reproach. There was that here which held her emotionally prisoner, no less than her body would be had chains wrapped about her wrists at the entrance to the tower.

"There comes an end to everything," the colorless voice continued. The near transparent hands had ceased their smoothing of the mantle. "Time is of our making, so it varies. What is the passing of a year to one of the mountains? What is sunrise to sunset for the draffer-fly, which lives for a single of our counted days? To each of us — plant, bird, insect, stone, proud man and woman — time brings an end. Thus, for those of us who still foresee a purpose, there is much to be done in what seems the narrowest of measures."

For the first time her eyes no longer locked with Kadiya's but moved, as if she were looking about her in surprise, finding missing what should be there, or else seeing that which had no place. "I have held wardship here. Yes, here I have guarded that which is of the Light. Once there was a great spread of water, graced by islands, each of which was a

∴

gem of beauty. And there were those who dwelt there. By them"—her hands came together as if to suggest a roof of protection—"I was called upon for a great task, for evil came, and change, and I labored to raise strong wards."

She sighed. "That time of trouble and sorrow passed. Then those you call Oddlings ventured out, and to them, though they were not of my people, I remained Guardian. Time became heavier and heavier, chipped away at what had been. Last of all arrived those of your blood. I searched their minds and hearts and found they were worthy of the Way of the Light and my day was not yet done . . ."

"And then came Voltrik, who is of the pattern of the Skritek!" blazed Kadiya. "Where then was your Guardianship?"

"There rose once more the Dark Powers," the Archimage corrected her. "Against such my kind must always contend. With these invaders was one well learned in the Oldest Lore." She bowed her head a fraction. "This time may be his. Only one defense could I raise when I foresaw the design. You are one of the three, and each of you holds a talent untrained, a gift unrecognized. It will be you who bring down the Dark Powers in the end—if you can pay the price of time."

"And what price is that?" Kadiya's chin was high. She still fought against giving any outward sign that the Archimage might believe her to be overawed.

"That you find your talisman . . . and use it in time."

"Talisman?" Kadiya held out the amulet, though she did not take its chain from about her neck. "But this I have already—and from your own hand, Lady, if the story is true."

"No, that has been but your guide hither. You must use your own strength—and wit—to find the talisman that will give you power. Steel has ever been your choice: that is direct and quick, but many times the most perilous route to success. There are other ways of winning battles."

The Archimage arose from her throne, standing straight and tall. Her movements were not constrained by old age, but rather the determined ones of a person who has a task to do and would get it done. Kadiya found herself lagging a step behind, and lengthened stride so that they came out of the tower of Noth together.

Now the Archimage threw back the folds of her cloak. In the light of day the silver rippled across the folds. She was holding a plant,

∴

though from where she had plucked it Kadiya could not guess. By the flower at its tip it was the fabled Black Trillium. Swiftly the Archimage broke the stem halfway down, three fingers' length above the hair-like filaments of the roots.

"This now will be your guide — and with it you shall seek the Three-Lobed Burning Eye."

She tossed the stem forward toward the water where the punt idled and Jagun lay as if asleep. Kadiya watched it fall straight, break water as might a well-aimed arrow. But what was a Three-Lobed Burning Eye? The Archimage must explain! Kadiya was tired of tracking through the Mires, following a magical gleam to the home of an incompetent enchantress. She needed more information if she were to pursue her quest . . .

Kadiya suddenly stood alone on the pavement. There was no longer anyone beside her and she had a strong feeling that if she were to go storming back into the tower and search it from top to bottom, she would not find its mistress.

Reluctantly and angrily she went to the punt. Jagun had roused and was sitting up, but Kadiya looked to the open water beyond. There she saw, among the murky ripples which the swaying of the craft had aroused, a filament of light. Green it was, but no shade of green that she had ever seen in the swamp: this was clearer, lighter, glistening like a gem, and yet the very forepoint of it was black, to be seen only in the light reflected by its length. When she got into the boat and reached for a pole that rod of green and sable moved. Not with the darting swiftness of something alive, but slowly, so that it would match the speed of their poling.

Kadiya uttered a great sigh. "We have a new guide, Jagun, and a new quest. Let us be on our way."

∴

20

The mountain wind roared down the defile, already carrying a few sharp grains of sleet. The late afternoon sky still had areas of blue, although clouds had been massing all day in the south above the highest pinnacles of the Ohogans—Mount Brom, Mount Gidris, and Mount Rotolo. There would surely be a storm before night, one of the harbingers of the winter monsoons that were due in only two weeks.

Orogastus was unspeakably weary after his eight-day journey from the Ruwenda Citadel. He had left his armed escort in the lowlands of Labornok and now, all alone, he approached his sanctum high on Mount Brom. Huddled deep within his fur cloak, he bespoke his weary mount and the two pack-fronials that trailed behind.

Onward! Ahead is a warm barn, and rich mash to eat, and water to drink. See—I show it to you! . . . Follow the path! Climb strongly! We will catch sight of it once this switchback rounds the outcropping yonder. There! There! Hurry!

The three fronials lifted their heads, and the gilded tips of their antlers gleamed in the dying sunshine. Their nostrils flared, for thanks to the sorcerer's art they already smelled the food that awaited them in the stronghold at the head of the steep trail.

A shining white tower with black crenelations and ornate black tracery about the windowframes was in sight now, tucked against a flank of Mount Brom. The revitalized animals broke into a trot and then into a rolling canter. With their leg tendons clicking and their tails high in anticipation they raced up the last few hundred ells and skidded to a stop, snorting and blowing, at the precipice that was the trail's end. Below yawned a sharp cleft in the mountainside nearly a league in depth and perhaps fifty ells wide, having a thundering glacier-fed torrent in its depths. The sorcerer's stronghold lay on the opposite side of the gulf, and seemed to be completely inaccessible. The sky was now completely overcast and it had become very cold.

Orogastus took a small silver pipe from his belt-wallet and blew a high, thin note that was almost lost in the howling of the wind. At once the dark windows of the tower sprang alight, and light also shone from the opening door of the distant gatehouse. There was a rumbling sound. In the cliff wall directly beneath the gate a square opening appeared, and from it was extruded a narrow bridge with an underside most strangely framed, which thrust out as the rumbling continued and eventually closed the gap between the trail and the tower.

Orogastus dismounted and blindfolded the three fronials. Then he led them on foot across the slender juncture, which had only a low railing and was scarcely a pace in width, while the rising wind tore at his fur mantle and caused the structure beneath his feet to tremble violently. A false step by the man or the animals would have sent them all tumbling to their deaths. But Orogastus exerted his magical powers to steady the bridge, and bespoke the fronials in reassurance. They followed him readily even when the first swirls of snow began to fly, and they all came safely into the gatehouse at last. The sorcerer then barred the door and pressed a device on the wall that caused the magical bridge to vanish back inside the mountain.

Home!

He threw off the heavy furs with a shout of relief. The fronials squealed and ramped a bit, and he laughed as he removed their blinders, unsaddled his mount, and took off the loads from the pack-animals. Then he led the faithful creatures down a corridor lighted by peculiar lamps that shone without flames, into a stable carved from living rock that was nevertheless dry and equipped with all things necessary for the comfort of the fronials. His grumbling as he fed and bedded them was good-humored. Normally such work would be done by his three dedicated acolytes; but they were back in Ruwenda Citadel, tending King Voltrik and awaiting his orders, and so the Master would have to cater both for the beasts and for himself. He knew how to manage the homely duties full well, for the three Voices had been recruited only ten years since. Before that Orogastus had tenanted this elaborate lair, built on his direction by Voltrik's craftsmen, all alone.

Now, as he climbed the winding stone stairway to his apartments in mid-tower, he felt glad that no others were here. The past ten weeks had been the most arduous and stressful of his life — first with the old King's death and Voltrik's accession, then with the preparations for the invasion and the march into Ruwenda. The victory itself had been paradoxically easy; only the freakish wounding of King Voltrik and the escape of the three Princesses had marred the sorcerer's grand scheme.

Well, the Voices had assured him that Voltrik was on the mend at last, and if all went well, the girls' hiding places would shortly be secret no longer. He would take care of *that* business immediately, postponing his own human needs until he had consulted the ice-mirror.

He came into his rooms and left the bundles of supplies near the hearth of the dining-chamber, pausing only long enough to light the pre-laid fire with his magical sparker. Then he hurried into his bedroom to change from his soiled traveling garb into the silver-and-black vestments and headgear that he wore for the most solemn incantations.

He did not want to take the time to bathe, but he sponged off the worst of the grime and begged pardon of the Dark Powers — then chuckled as the thought struck him that They might actually prefer him to commune with them in a grimy state. The fine metallic mesh of the ceremonial robe was shockingly cold upon his bare skin, and he winced while donning it and forgot to say the appropriate prayers. His silver-glacé leather gauntlets and the dramatic star-burst headpiece with its half-mask were warmer, but he eschewed his usual ritual sandals and slipped his feet into fur-lined boots before heading for the tunnel that led deep into the mountain to the Cavern of Black Ice.

His breath was visible in the cold, humid air of the rock tube. He walked briskly along the lamplit shaft, praying that the ice-mirror would grant him his boon promptly, without balking. One never knew with the marvelous devices of the Vanished Ones. Even if the proper rituals were observed and powerful enabling spells chanted, the magic could be capricious. But please — not tonight, when he was so weary and hungry and cold!

He came to the massive door, frost-covered even in the warmest weather, braced himself, and uttered the first incantation. He asked pardon of the Vanished Ones for disturbing their ancient tranquillity,

∴

but admonished them sternly in the name of the Dark Powers to serve him. Then he opened the door.

The Cavern of Black Ice was as always. As he had found it — summoned to it! — when he first arrived in Labornok with then Crown Prince Voltrik. (Only later had Orogastus commanded the stronghold to be built, to shield the Cavern and provide ready access to its wonders.) It was a large vaulted chamber hewn crudely from the quartz-veined granite of Mount Brom, having intrusions of black ice here and there in the walls. The floor was paved with strange black tiles like glossy obsidian, and the same material — itself closely resembling the ice — had been used to construct a myriad of inset niches and tiny rooms, all fitted with doors. In these he had originally found the fantastic devices that had seduced him from the more abstract magic he had learned from Bondanus, while paradoxically guaranteeing his influence over the Kingdom of Labornok. Many of the compartments were equipped with arcane locks that he had been unable to open. Others — including the room of the ice-mirror — had yielded their secrets willingly.

He raised his silver-gloved hands and intoned aloud: "O Dark Powers! Once again I thank you for your great gifts. Let me use them without coming to harm." Then he slid open a narrow obsidian door and entered the mirror-room.

It was only a few paces deep. Most of the inner wall was a lumpy mass of thick hoarfrost, which effectively hid whatever mysterious devices flanked the circular mirror itself. Trembling from cold and apprehension — for he knew that if the mirror refused to respond, his great scheme for world-dominion was very likely undone — he spoke the spell:

"O mighty mirror of ice! Farseeing eye of the Vanished Ones! Awaken and respond to my request!"

He waited.

At first, the grey, glassy surface only reflected his own image: a tall robust man draped in fluid silver and black, crowned with a star-burst diadem and with a silver mask hiding his upper face. Then there was a dim glow within the mirror's heart . . . and a voice. It was faint, raspy like that of a dying man, and its accents were not human.

"Responding. Request, please."

Orogastus stood stark still. In spite of the fact that he was half-freezing, perspiration rolled down his forehead behind the silver mask and into his eyes. This was the most critical moment. If he posed the request incorrectly, the affronted mirror would wink out and remain dormant for at least two days while it "recovered" from the insult. Mentally, he offered a fresh prayer to the Dark Powers. Then he said in a neutral tone: "View three persons. Locate present position of the three persons on map."

The mirror brightened. A maelstrom of silvery-blue shadow materialized in the center of its disk. It said: "Request validated. Names of three persons."

"Princess Anigel of Ruwenda. Princess Kadiya of Ruwenda. Princess Haramis of Ruwenda." As he spoke, he was careful to form a mental picture of each girl.

"Scanning," said the mirror. And Orogastus nearly fainted with relief. It was going to work —

The mirror said: "Subject One: Princess Anigel of Ruwenda. Location: Sa fourteen two, Lo seventy-one ten on Grid Oma." It spoke the usual incomprehensible gibberish; but this was immediately followed by a beautiful map-diagram showing a blinking light on the Mutar River below the Citadel, just a few leagues above Lake Wum.

Orogastus restrained himself heroically. A false word or movement could throw the mirror off irretrievably. The sorcerer concentrated upon memorizing the indicated location. A moment later the map winked out and the mirror showed instead a full-color portrait of the girl, all in motion as though she were alive inside the grey ice. Anigel was seated in the bow of a punt, holding two straps that appeared to be reins. The craft was being towed through water at a high rate of speed. Behind the Princess sat an Oddling woman, who glanced back over her shoulder at a red sunset and then said clearly: "We'd best put in for the night, sweeting. There should be plenty of fish for the rimoriks in the lagoon over there."

And then the picture disappeared.

"Subject Two: Princess Kadiya of Ruwenda," said the mirror softly. "Location Mo twenty-nine four, Vi ninety-five five on Grid Oma." The blinking light placed the fugitive just west of the Skritek-infested jungle known as the Thorny Hell.

Orogastus stifled an exclamation, then looked on in fascination as the mirror showed the second of the triplet girls kneeling on a mud bank in deep twilight, attempting to kindle a campfire of vine-bark, and in the background a single Oddling was taking something from a native boat.

Kadiya said: "I've puffed till I'm blue, Jagun, but I can't get this perverse stuff to light. You'd better try."

The picture disappeared.

"Subject Three: Princess Haramis of Ruwenda. Location: Pa forty-two three, No sixteen eight on Grid Oma." The indicator light on the map blinked in a most extraordinary position—high on the slope of Mount Rotolo, the second-loftiest peak in the Ohogans, near the head-waters of the Vispar River and only a league or two away from the secret settlement of the Vispi Oddlings.

The sorcerer held his breath as the final picture appeared on the mirror. It was very obscure, a purplish dusky scene that he finally recognized as a snow-cave interior overlooking the slope of a twilit glacier. A shadow detached itself from darkness and became the sil-houette of a young woman wrapped in a white cloak, gazing outside.

Haramis said: "Will I live through the night? They are out there, waiting for me—the Eyes in the Whirlwind—and the trillium seeds that led me to this place of icy death are all gone save one. It is the end. I have no more food and the snows are becoming so deep I can no longer proceed. Unless the Vispi themselves take pity on me and come to my rescue, I shall have failed in my quest for the Three-Winged Circle."

The picture vanished.

Then came the inevitable fateful words from the magical device: "Bahkup Power temporarily exhausted. Hiatus for recharge." And the ice-mirror's light and voice died.

"Thanks be to all the Dark Powers—Aysee Lyne, Inturnal Bataree, and Bahkup," Orogastus intoned, making a deep obeisance, "and to the Great System operated thereby, forever and ever, so let it be."

Then he withdrew, walking humbly backward, closed the obsidian door to the mirror-room, and fled to his own apartments.

Much later, after he had eaten and soaked in the tub, Orogastus consulted the ancient *Book of Peninsular Prophecies* while seated in front of the cheerful fire in his study, sipping a mellow brandy. Outside, a snowstorm howled among the tower battlements.

The Three-Winged Circle . . .

Yes, it was mentioned here, together with two other obscure symbols — the Three-Lobed Burning Eye and the Three-Headed Monster. The reference was unclear, but it seemed that the three were destined to come together, and thereby precipitate some climactic event.

"Might it be," the sorcerer mused, "that the other two Princesses also seek their talismans, even as Haramis seeks hers? And having found them and become reunited, might the girls *then* be so potentialized as to overthrow Labornok?"

He stared into the flames for some time before deciding what to do. The need to dispose of Kadiya and Anigel was straightforward enough; but Crown Princess Haramis was quite another matter . . .

He straightened in his chair, closed his eyes, and placed his fingertips on his temples. "My Voices!" he intoned. "Hear me!"

In his mind three shapes took form, blurs of red, blue, and green that assumed the aspect of his three hooded minions. They had no eyes but their expressions were full of eagerness.

"Master! Have you succeeded?"

"Yes. Be alert for the Sending! Here is the present position of Princess Anigel . . . and here is Kadiya."

"We have received your Sending, Almighty Master. And the Princess Haramis?"

"I have found her also. But listen! General Hamil is to set out with at least half of the army in pursuit of Kadiya, who has gone into a very dangerous region. The Red Voice is to meet and accompany Hamil, and consult with me every other day until she is taken."

"I will obey," said the Red Voice.

"The search for Princess Anigel," Orogastus continued, "is to be conducted by Prince Antar and his knightly cohort. The Blue Voice will accompany him."

"The Prince and his party returned to the Citadel from Trevista four days ago," the Blue Voice said. "It should be easy for us to find Anigel if she is as close by as you say."

"Nothing is easy where the Archimage Binah is concerned," Orogastus admonished him sharply. "Keep in mind that the girls are guarded by the last of her magic. And should they be successful in finding certain powerful new talismans called the Three-Lobed Burning Eye and the Three-Headed Monster, their magic will certainly be greatly enhanced. It is imperative that the Princesses be captured and killed, and the talismans be saved for me."

"We understand," said the Voices.

"There are further instructions for the Blue Voice," the sorcerer added, "concerning Prince Antar."

"I believe I already know your mind, Master." Blue uttered a mirthless chuckle. "It would be sad if the Prince were to perish through misadventure after having done his duty."

"There must be no hint of your involvement," Orogastus warned.

The Green Voice then said: "And shall I join the force that will pursue the Princess Haramis, Master?"

"No. You will remain with King Voltrik, taking care that he recovers fully, reassuring him when I transmit to you reports of progress."

"But Haramis —"

"I intend," Orogastus said, "to take care of the Princess Haramis myself."

21

H aramis cast forth the final Black Trillium seed on a
morning that saw the slopes of Mount Rotolo enveloped in pearly mist. When she woke, it had
seemed strangely warmer. The walls of the tiny cave where she had
slept — surprisingly soundly — glistened with melting snow. Her fur-
lined mantle, which she had wrapped around her sleep-sack, had been
completely soaked, making it at least twice as heavy as usual and quite
useless, since she had no way of drying it. Using her small knife, the
Princess had then cut the water-repellent sleep-sack along one side and
across the bottom, fashioning a kind of cape that was stiff but weatherproof. After a breakfast of cold water, she had freed the last seed
and stumbled out of the cave to follow it through ankle-deep wet snow.

It floated languidly, adjusting its flight to her slow steps, drifting not
an arm's length before her. She could see nothing beyond that distance,
so thick was the mist, and she tramped along leaning heavily upon her
iron-shod stick. She realized dimly that she was becoming increasingly
giddy from the thin air, but this did not seem important to her. Everything was far off and hazy. She hardly cared where she placed her feet,
so long as the floating seed stayed within view.

Many times she stumbled and fell, her white wool suit and boots and
mittens becoming more and more sodden. Moisture crept into the exposed plant-down lining of her sack-cape as well, and before long it
was achingly heavy. The next time Haramis fell, she left the thing
behind. The air was now so warm that she did not need it.

The seed. The winged seed. It was all she saw, all her fogged mind could concentrate upon. She went on and on, climbing ever higher. Sometimes the snow was knee-deep and sometimes more shallow; but it was always heavy and wet, clinging to her boots so that her legs seemed made of lead.

It must have been three or four hours before the weather suffered an ominous change. Haramis was too dazed to take note of the fact that the mist had lost its pearly color and turned to an increasingly gloomy grey, nor did she notice as the air grew steadily chillier. Her hands and feet had lost all feeling, but this was as unimportant to her as the dull pain in her empty stomach.

And then it began to snow.

She halted, unable at first to realize what was happening. Seeds? Was the world alive with floating fluffy trillium seeds? And which was her own magical guide? That one — ? No . . .

The mist was thinning as the snow increased and Haramis could see once again the rearing cliffs and crags of the mountain she climbed. The wind rose, blowing snowflakes into her face. She became aware of having lost her stick. The guiding seed? It was gone.

Gone as all the others — but not at day's end, having first led her to a safe shelter, but here, near the crest of a knife-sharp rocky ridge that the wind had blasted clear of snowpack. The last Black Trillium seed, blown away; and so she came to the quest's end . . .

Flying snow stung her face, brought tears to her unfocused eyes and caused her cheeks and nose to tingle, then grow numb. A mortal lethargy crept over her and it seemed that the most desirable thing in the world would be to sleep. Why struggle further? Each breath was a swordcut. Her heart thudded as though it would break her ribs. Her hands and feet were frozen.

I will go to the top of the ridge, she told herself. *Just twenty more steps. And there I will look out on my kingdom for the last time.*

The wind tried to foil her. Like some huge, resentful creature, it howled and pushed and seemed almost a wall forbidding further progress. She crouched, lifted one foot and then the other, thrust her body forward, leaned into the wind with all her fading strength.

Father! Mother! Soon I come to you, having failed. I wanted so much for the dream to be real, for the mad quest to have a magical fulfillment, to believe that the poor old Archimage knew my destiny. But it seems that she did not know, and so there was no magic after all. I suspected as much.

Wind.

Snow.

Cold.

And her body still moving, almost beyond pain now. With her teeth, she pulled off one frozen mitten and let it drop; then thrust the icy bare hand inside her snow-crusted overtunic to touch the trillium amulet one final time, begging for a last modicum of physical strength.

Let me only make it to the top of the ridge. Five more steps, the most arduous, most terrible actions she had ever accomplished . . . *God, help the one who trusted Thee* . . . one more step . . .

Done!

At the ridge-crest was a rocky parapet only lightly covered with snow. As she straightened up, the wind's blast seemed to abate, the blizzard no longer lashing her. Back the way she had come, the air was still roiled with tempestuous grey; but ahead there was blue sky and a dazzling panorama of snow-clad peaks extending far into the west. The steep front of the ridge fell away at her feet into an abyss that seemed to plunge to infinity before its depths were lost in haze.

"Here I am," she whispered, and dizziness overcame her, and she swayed and nearly lost consciousness. But her hand gripping the amulet was no longer without sensation, but felt a growing, painful warmth; and rather than succumb to welcome death, she forced her eyes to open one final time.

On the ridge, not a stone's-throw to her right, a great snowy whirl-wind spun, all sparkling in the sun like diamond-dust.

Haramis dropped to her knees and stared at it, completely helpless. It swayed and swirled and grew into a gigantic fluid white cone that spun on its point. And within the whirlwind there were Eyes.

Eyes green as ice. Scores of them. Looking at her.

"I seek the Three-Winged Circle," she whispered.

We are its guardians, come to meet you.

"I greet you," said Princess Haramis, with dignity. Then she fell forward into a profound and welcome blackness.

There followed a time filled with busy dreaming, during which she suffered great pain and then found a deep and soothing release. The Eyes in the Whirlwind inhabited her dreams, only sometimes they were fearsome and sometimes gentle, belonging to tall and graceful beings

∴

clad in pale-tinted flowing garments and adorned with extraordinary quantities of jewels, who whispered to her and ministered to her and admonished her to do this thing or that, while she obeyed like a tiny child.

She asked them who they were, and they told her that they were the First Folk, who had been keepers of the great Sceptre of Power of the Vanished Ones from time out of mind.

She asked them if this Sceptre was the talisman she sought, and they said: *In a manner yes, and in another manner, no. For in dark ages past the Threefold was sundered and its members scattered so as to prevent it falling into the hands of evil.*

Dreaming still, the Princess asked the Eyes if they were in truth the keepers of the Three-Winged Circle, her own talisman.

Yes, for this portion of the Threefold we kept safe in an ice-cave. The other two parts were sent far away by the White Lady, to be cared for by others until the time when her powers should fade, and the Sceptre would be needed to restore the great balance of the world.

Harmis said: "My sisters seek two other talismans."

And so does the evil one of this age, who even now looks upon you, hoping you will succeed in your quest . . .

It seemed to Haramis that one pair of watching Eyes changed from ice-green into star-white, blazing; and she saw the beautiful face of a man smiling at her, and she asked: "Is this he?"

And they said, *Yes.*

In the dream this man reached out to her, and she returned his smile; and he said: "I am not what they say I am. Be not deceived. These little ones understand only a part of the great whole. Reserve judgment until you can know me truly and make up your own mind."

Haramis woke in a narrow bed with gauzy hangings all about, and she marveled that she was so warm, until she realized that heat emanated from the mattress beneath her.

The hypocaust warms the base of the bed and the floors, said a soft voice. *Through its flues steam comes from the hot springs, and in this manner do we heat our homes.*

The bed-drapes parted, and Haramis saw an aboriginal woman of a race heretofore unknown to her. Her face was narrower than that of the familiar Nyssomu, and her mouth and nose more human. Her huge

∴

eyes — green rather than golden — and the ears that emerged from a wavy mass of platinum hair, marked her as of the Folk. She had hands with three digits also; but the talons were vestigial, and very much resembled fingernails — save for their thickness, and an apparently natural tendency to come to a point.

When she smiled at Haramis, her teeth were not fanglike, but were small and even. The Princess recalled the melodious timbre of the Vispi woman's voice from her dreaming; it was some minutes before she realized that the woman's lips did not move when she spoke.

But of course not, came the cheerful acknowledgment. *You would not understand our language, so we use the speech without words! My name is Magira, and I greet you, Princess Haramis of the Trillium. Now come out of bed and let me help you to dress, for you are quite recovered and our people would meet with you before you continue on your quest.*

"But you can understand me . . ." The Princess still had not fully recovered her wits, and she was not yet certain what was dream and what reality. Magira's talk of "continuing on her quest" was more than a little daunting.

As you speak, so your mind repeats your thoughts, Princess. We Vispi have no trouble understanding you . . . Does this gown meet with your approval? I think you will find it very comfortable, and the black fur edging matches your hair.

"Yes, thank you. The dress is lovely."

Haramis let Magira attire her in a flowing robe of pale blue fabric, like velvet only not so heavy, trimmed with soft black fur. At the neck and sleeve-edges and hem were wide embroidered silver bands all inset with sapphires and moonstones. She put on boots of silvery leather, and a silver belt with a hanging purse all beaded with seed-gems, and let the Vispi woman braid her hair into two thick plaits and tie them with blue ribbon.

Our Vispi blood flows warm and so we require garments much lighter than humankind must wear here. Take this cloak also, and gloves, and I will lead you to the Town Hall of Movis, which is not far from this house.

Obediently, Haramis slipped on the bejeweled gloves while Magira draped a splendid cloak of mingled black and white furs about her shoulders and drew up its hood. The Princess then followed the Vispi woman out of the bedchamber, and down a flight of stone stairs with narrow, glazed windows, and into a vestibule; and thence outdoors.

∴

"So this is Movis!"

Haramis stopped in the portico and gazed about at the city which she had thought only a legend. The air had a golden luminescence and it was obviously near sunset. The Princess had a view of several hundred finely made stone houses, many of impressive size, and a number of other buildings, considerably larger, clustered about a central plaza.

Plumes of vapor rose up on every side — not only from the slate roofs of the dwellings, but also from grates in the cobblestone streets and from boxy small structures standing in every dooryard and forecourt. Little trees and neat gardens surrounded each home, but no people or other living creatures were visible. The scene was oddly lit, shadowless, for no true sunshine reached the valley floor. A layer of bright cloud, like a golden ceiling supported by the hundreds of pillars of white steam, overlay all of the Vale of Movis. The lower slopes were green and terraced; the higher were snow-covered. From a great glacier poured a waterfall like a long white scarf.

The people have prepared a festive evening meal for you, and they are awaiting your arrival, Magira said.

"That sounds lovely," Haramis said, moving quickly to keep up with the long-legged Vispi woman, who now glided swiftly down the twisting streets, her gauzy garments afloat about her like pale banners streaming in a wind. "I seem to be very hungry; perhaps it's the air here."

You slept for five days, Princess.

"Oh!" said Haramis.

During that time our caregivers attended you and healed your frozen flesh, and your other injuries. Doubtless you were aware of their ministrations in your dreams.

"Yes. And I dreamt of another, too."

Magira slowed, turned her emerald gaze upon the Princess, and her thought-tone was uneasy. *We know that the evil one bespoke you. He can scry your presence only through his ice-mirror, and that not constantly, but only at intervals of two days or more, since you are shielded by your amulet from the natural mind-observation of ill-wishers —*

"But he could still bespeak me in dreams?"

Knowing you were here, he could. If you had been awake, you need not have listened, of course.

Haramis forbore to talk of Orogastus further, yielding to a most curious feeling that the sorcerer evoked within her mind. Instead, she said to Magira: "Tell me, are your people self-sufficient in this valley?"

We grow such food crops as can prosper in the low light, and we keep domestic animals as well — togars and nunchiks within the town, and the larger volumnials and a few fronials outside, pasturing them in the dry season, sheltering them in caves during the rains and snows. In the caverns, nutritious luminous lichens and fungi grow, and you would find the nighttime appearance of our livestock droll, for their winter diet makes their teeth and antlers and hooves glow in the dark.

"These are the animals that you obtain in trade?"

Yes, for they breed slowly in the mountains.

Haramis lifted one glove, and the gems sewn upon it gleamed. "You trade jewels and precious metals only?"

Magira laughed. *They are quite enough, Princess, for all races of the Folk crave such ornaments. In earlier years, our trading network spread from the Ohogans to the Tassaleyo Forest, with the retiring little Uisgu ever acting as our middlemen with other races of Folk. Since the advent of Ruwendian humankind, the trade-pattern has altered, with humans now supplying more animals and sweets than the Folk alone ever could. And so the Vispi have prospered.*

"But still you forbid others to enter your land."

Magira gave a delicate shrug. *The hot-spring valleys are few and far between, and the living precariously balanced. We First Folk were made for this climate when it covered most of the world. As it shrank with the passing ages, we diminished in numbers, although we did succeed in retaining our culture. In time, other races of Folk, diverging from us, joined the abominable Foundation Stock in what is now called the Mazy Mire. But the high mountains are ours, and we protect them with fearsome illusions such as the Eyes in the Whirlwind. And since we are People of the Trillium, and obedient to the command of the White Lady, we guard also the Vispir Pass between Ruwenda and Labornok —*

Haramis halted and confronted her companion, speaking reproachfully. "Then where were you when King Voltrik's army invaded us?"

Alas . . . the Lady did not alert us in time to your enemy's approach, and when the Vispi pass-guardians came, their illusions were penetrated by the power of the sorcerer. He bade the Labornoki soldiers ignore the phantasms and strike at the flesh-and-blood persons projecting them. The invaders slew all the Vispi guardians of our villages nearest the pass — some three hundred souls.

"I am sorry," the Princess said sincerely. "I did not know. Very little news of the invasion came to us at the Citadel, for the invaders marched with fatal swiftness, overwhelming our people before they knew what was happening. Even now I know not what befell our people of the Dylex country, or the outlying manors of the south . . ."

They had finally reached a very large building with windows alight in the dusk and the sound of music coming faintly through the walls. When Magira threw open the doors, Princess Haramis was astounded at the great crowd of Folk gathered therein: many hundreds, some seated at round tables, others dancing to a stately tune in a central open space.

At the far end of the Town Hall was a broad dais at which richly attired Vispi sat. Above them on the wall was a banner carrying a great Black Trillium outlined in glittering diamonds. The female citizens of Movis were dressed much as Magira, in pastel flowing gowns and a profusion of jewels. The males mostly wore robes of deepest midnight blue, with undertunics and high boots of white. Their gem-studded belts, collars, and bracelets flashed like rainbow fire in the light of thousands of small cresset-lamps suspended from the high ceiling.

A great clamor went up as Magira escorted her guest to the dignitaries at the dais. Haramis felt her vision dim and her mind reel, and might have staggered had Magira not taken hold of her. The mental and vocal shouting! She had never known anything like this. She felt assailed both inside and outside her body, and even though she knew the aggressors were friendly, she felt overwhelmed.

Stop! Her mind gave an involuntary cry.

Consternation.

Silence, tangibly penitent.

Trembling with relief, she said: "Thank you. I appreciate your welcome, but I fear I have not yet become accustomed to your manner of expressing it."

A male of most venerable appearance, whose eyes were not green but dull white, rose from his place at the head of the table and addressed Haramis. She knew he was blind; she knew also that he saw her.

Dear Princess, forgive us! We would not have affrighted you deliberately. Our joy at your appearance carried us away. I greet you in the name of all Vispi. I am Carimpole, Harkener of Movis. We have long awaited you. It was known to us that the flying seeds would draw you to our town . . . if you were strong enough to follow them. All throughout your journey, from the time you left Noth, we watched you. We saw you suffer hardship and fatigue and discouragement. We saw you come into the snowy high country where all of your great intelligence was useless and only willpower and physical endurance would sustain you.

∴

And then it seemed that you were weakening and would fail, as those who spend much time in thinking often do, scorning the body that seems unable to sustain the burning spirit it houses. We prayed for you in your extremity, as did the White Lady, and from us you drew fresh strength, perhaps, and forced the body to serve the mind, fulfilling your ordeal. You reached our innermost border — at which time we were permitted to take you in.

Haramis heard a great murmuring of minds all about her, touching gently, wishing well. Her voice was barely audible: "You — you were forbidden to help me earlier?"

Yes. For you, the journeying itself was crucial. It was an essential part of your quest.

"And now — have I reached the end of it? You have the Three-Winged Circle and will give it to me?"

On the morrow we will begin to teach you how to command the great birds you humans call lammergeiers. Your talisman lies some leagues from here, in an ice-cave high on Mount Gidris. A lammergeier will take you to the cave. As to your quest's completion, I cannot say. Merely having the Three-Winged Circle in hand is nothing. It must be empowered. We do not know how this is to be accomplished.

"I was told by the Archimage to return to her with the talisman after I have mastered my self. But she also told me that my destiny is linked with that of my two sisters, and that all three of us must succeed, or none will. Am I then to assist Kadiya and Anigel?"

Haramis of the Trillium, we cannot say. I think you will have to decide this for yourself.

"I am the eldest sister, and I have always taken responsibility for the others. There is also a certain prophecy among the swamp Folk that says that a woman of Ruwenda will bring down the throne of Labornok. It seems that this woman must be me, for the Crown of Ruwenda is rightfully mine, and mine is the obligation to liberate our vanquished land."

The great bird will carry you wherever you desire. But we cannot advise you further. Now that you are recovered from your hurts, we can only celebrate your coming and speed your going. But for now, will you sit here at table with us? For five days you have taken nothing but liquids, and we have tried to prepare dishes that will please your human palate.

"I thank you," Haramis said, "and I will gladly join you."

The Harkener clapped his hands. *Then let the festive meats and pastries be brought forth, and honeyed fruit and mulled wine! And let there be more music and more dancing and merriment, for our Princess nears her goal and the world is brought that much closer to regaining its lost balance . . . Praise be to the White Lady, and to the Lords of the Air, and to the Triune over all!*

Cheers filled the Town Hall, and side doors flew open to admit a train of cooks and helpers bearing heavy platters and steaming bowls. The musicians began to play again, while the people all hurried to seats at the other tables.

Princess Haramis pulled off her gloves and unfastened her cape, and sank gratefully into the place indicated by the Harkener Carimpole. Magira sat beside her. Momentarily Haramis felt lightheaded again, and closed her eyes; and it seemed that she could see right through the walls of the hall. The clouds had lowered with oncoming night, and snowflakes were sifting down from them. But these melted when they reached the warm air just above the rooftops, and turned to rain that fell upon the village of the Vispi, softly at first, then with increasing vigor, rapping against the windowpanes as if demanding entrance. Mingled with their pattering was the faint voice of a man calling her name.

Haramis opened her eyes again to the brightness and jollity all around her. She heard nothing but the convivial Vispi and their music — ringing oddly, half in her ears and half in her mind.

Someone handed her a crystal goblet of sparkling wine. She drank deeply of it, and tried to smile.

22

Shut out, the sorcerer was amused rather than angered. "Enjoy yourself then with your Vispi friends, Haramis! But I will call you again and again, and the time will come when you must answer."

Secure in his lair on Mount Brom, with the early snowstorm still raging, Orogastus began to search through his library, seeking further clues to the nature of the three mysterious talismans.

The *Book of Peninsular Prophecies* was his principal source, as always. In one entry it named the talismans and hinted that they would reunite and precipitate some wondrous event. In another prophecy, one he knew of old (and had made certain that King Voltrik knew it also), the Three Petals of the Living Trillium were designated quite baldly as the "extinguishers" of the Labornoki throne; but nothing in the book hinted at a link between the Princesses and the talismans. Setting that ancient volume aside, he undertook a search through his large collection of thaumaturgical and mystical references.

There was nothing to be found in the many books from Labornok, and he had no better luck rooting among the smaller number of volumes from Var and Raktum. The most ancient source of all, the incunabular *Cyclopedia of Dark Powers* he had brought from his own distant homeland of Tuzamen, made tantalizing brief mention of the subject. Under the heading "Threefold Talisman" he found but a single sentence: "A device of great potency, supposed to have been entrusted to the Vispi by the Vanished Ones from time out of mind."

Yes! But what was it intended to *do?*

He continued his search, looking to nonmagical books. And finally, in a slender, lingit-nibbled treatise of aboriginal studies from the island principality of Engi (of all places) he happened upon a reference to "the great Threefold Sceptre of Power which the Vispi race, most ancient of their kind, safeguarded until it should be required in the fullness of time." The reappearance of this cryptic object was ordained by the Vanished Ones, the book averred; exactly what it was intended to accomplish, no human knew, but it would shake the foundations of the world.

"So we have three talismans and three girls seeking them," the sorcerer said to himself, closing the last book and rising from the library table.

Hands clasped behind this back, he moved to the window and stared out at the blizzard. It was not completely unseasonable, the monsoons being due in ten days, and so it could not clearly be attributed to magic — specifically to the mischief-mongering Vispi who were such great friends of the Archimage Binah, and who were, according to tale-tellers, able to exert a certain control over the weather. Nevertheless, this snow-storm underlined the urgency of his researches, the necessity of vanquishing the Princesses before he was trapped up here in the mountains by the great winter tempests.

"Three talismans, formerly together in the form of a Sceptre and entrusted to the Vispi, but evidently now separated and scattered about Ruwenda. And the so-called Three Petals of the Living Trillium, the Princesses, who in bringing the talismans back together may empower some great Three-in-One . . ."

A maddening sense of indecision gnawed at the sorcerer's mind. It was obvious that more than the mere survival of Labornok and its King was at stake here: his own great ambition, forsooth! Would it not be better to permit the Princesses to live until they fulfilled their quests, thus insuring that all three talismans passed into his own hands? Or was his first instinct the correct one — that the girls should be prevented at any cost from succeeding, since they alone could potentiate the magical Three-in-One?

More information! He needed more information before the final decision could be made.

Orogastus whirled about and strode to the fireplace, where the fire painted his white hair with lurid glints. He stiffened, arms thrown wide, closed his eyes momentarily and spoke the spell. When his lids re-opened, blazing stars sprang up behind his pupils and caused the flames to pale.

Then Orogastus bespoke his Green Voice at Ruwenda Citadel, com-manding him to begin a search of the great library there, gleaning whatever knowledge of the talismans, the Living Trillium, or the Three-fold Sceptre of the Vispi might be found. The Voice was to enlist the most intelligent assistants he could find among the Labornoki host.

"But take no Ruwendians into your confidence in this matter," the sorcerer warned, "and swear your fellow-searchers to secrecy by strong oaths, on pain of the royal displeasure."

"I shall obey, Almighty Master."

"Now tell me how fares King Voltrik."

"He continues to mend," said the Green Voice. "The good news that you had reached your tower and scried the three Princesses in your ice-mirror cheered him exceedingly. He congratulates you and ex-presses the royal approbation and his personal good wishes, and looks forward to your continuing zeal in directing the search for the fugitives. King Voltrik commanded that we carry him to the window of his room so that he could give his benison to the two search-parties as they sallied forth, and on that day ate his first full meal."

"Very good, And now report to me concerning the occupation and pacification."

"The Citadel and its environs are very quiet. The noncombatant middleclass Ruwendians and Citadel Knoll freeholders have pledged fealty to Labornok, albeit grudgingly. There is no organized resistance to our rule. Most of the surviving nobles in the southern realm have fled into the swamp, but they pose no serious threat. The unburned Dylex villages are all fully garrisoned now except for the remote en-claves of Prok and Goyk, and the orderly harvest and processing of foodstuffs has resumed. There may be some shortages among the locals during the rainy season, but our army of occupation will be well-fed."

"Satisfactory. And the export trade?"

"The Trevista market has reopened. Trade in medicines, spices, es-sences, and dyes is about one-quarter of the pre-war rate. The Master-Traders expect things to pick up next season. The timber-trade is effectively stalled until the Rains end. Tass Town, where forest products are gathered, was untouched by fighting, and its craftsmen surrendered

∴

bloodlessly, but there have been delays in getting them back to work. Large amounts of lumber and raw logs have piled up at the holding yards at Tass Town and at the northern end of the lake, near the Great Causeway. All that is needed to restore trade is a resumption of caravan movement from Labornok and this will be accomplished during the spring dry season."

Orogastus sighed. "Very good. I am pleased with you, my Voice. You will hear from me again in two days."

"As you will, Almighty Master." The vision of the Green Voice faded.

Orogastus now let his farseeing eye rove briefly westward, where he spied General Hamil's great flotilla of riverboats sweeping upstream toward Trevista. The sorcerer did not exert himself bespeaking the Red Voice. Time enough for that when the force would have traveled as far as the Thorny Hell. By then he would have confirmed Princess Kadiya's travel-route by means of his every-other-day scrutiny of the ice-mirror, and worked out the strategy for taking her.

The Blue Voice had already reported that the first day of searching by Prince Antar's force had failed to find any trace of Princess Anigel. This was no great surprise to Orogastus. His reference books had revealed to him the unusual nature of her transportation — clearly a novelty arranged by the Archimage Binah herself. With the powerful rimoriks hauling her wooden punt, Anigel had undoubtedly put a good distance between herself and the enemy concentration at Citadel Knoll. Now that the two-day interval of rest required by the ice-mirror had passed, it would be possible to scry out her new position, and perhaps deduce where she was heading in search of her talisman.

Enrobing and masking himself, the sorcerer came again to the Cavern of Black Ice and addressed the wonderful device:

"O powerful tool of the Vanished Ones, answer my request!"

The greyness lit slowly — so slowly! — like a candle with the wick cut dangerously short. The voice was a rough whisper.

"Responding . . . request . . . please."

Curse it! The illumination was flickering. Perhaps he should have let it rest longer after that first rather extensive querying. Well, there was no help for it now. He would ask after Anigel, and let the other two Princesses go for the present. They were still inaccessible after all, while there was a good chance that Anigel was within Prince Antar's grasp.

"View one person for as long as the Dark Powers permit," Orogastus intoned. "Locate present position of this person on map."

"Request . . . validated. Name of person." The eery voice strengthened and the maelstrom within the icy mirror assumed an almost normal aspect.

"Princess Anigel of Ruwenda." Orogastus visualized the girl, then held his breath.

"Scanning."

The map image formed. It was not so bright or clear as last time, but it would do. Anigel was on Lake Wum, close to the western Greenmire shore and about halfway down. She had to be heading for Tass Town at the foot of the lake. There was no other place to go. But, what a singular destination!

"Princess Anigel of Ruwenda. Location: Sa fifty-one two, La twenty-two four on Grid Oma."

Then came the picture, its colors dull but clear. The rimorik-drawn punt moved at only moderate speed through the thick Greenmire shrubbery of the western lakeshore, where small arboreal bloodsuckers, slimy flat things the size of coins, bedeviled the Princess and Immu by dropping from the foliage into the boat.

"If you think these suckers are bad," Immu's mirror-image said to the disgusted girl, "just wait until we get into the Tassaleyo Forest!"

"Aha!" Orogastus cried out exultantly. "Now I have you!"

The ice-mirror immediately reproved him: "Bad command. Use debug to review your program. Hiatus for recharge."

And it fell into a sulk and the image died.

But the sorcerer's elation was undaunted. He had the crucial clue that would enable him to plot Anigel's capture, and his voice rang from one end of the frigid cavern to the other as he gave thanks to the Dark Powers.

23

The strange little swimming root led Kadiya and Jagun only a short way back down the River Nothar, and then it turned off to the left to ascend a nameless tributary. They were now heading toward forbidden territory indeed: the treacherous wilderness called the Thorny Hell.

To keep in sight of their frail guide they had to stay in what open water there was. Sometimes that became so shallow that they both waded on foot, dragging the punt with them. Again they needed to cross patches of open water where Jagun fell back on his trailcraft and heaped over the punt a mass of rough-cut reed, so they would appear to be a drift of soggy growth.

Twice that first day Kadiya lay belly flat, peering through the rough thatching of the punt, Jagun stretched with her as they looked upon small groups of Skritek. Kadiya pulled up her wrist to seal her mouth, for her stomach now rebelled. Much had been told of the hideous creatures she spied upon but none of her imaginings were as bad as what she now saw.

The first pack seemed to be hunting afoot, and there were young among them. Here in their own territory they did not always resort to drowning, but walked boldly in search of prey. They had split apart, one section moving ahead to take a stand on one of the rubble mounts while the remainder came toward them, stamping three-toed feet, beating the growth with the butts of crude spears and clubs. Creatures broke from hiding, leapt, or scuttled, or tried to fly, while the Skritek ahead made sure of plentiful captures. Nor did they wait to carry this prey to any camp but ate at once, some of their catch still alive, quarreling over portions. Watching, Kadiya swallowed sickly, sour bile in her mouth. But she made herself look. For she had learned one thing from Jagun: know well the habits of your enemy, his goings and comings, his food, his sleep, all that is his common custom, learn and remember.

While they hid from the fiends of the Mire, their swimming guide appeared — by some instinct, if one might deem it that — to seek safety, lingering near the drooping edge of the thatch which covered them.

The second party of Skritek which they encountered passed later, near sundown. This time there were no croaking cries, no striking at the mass of vegetation. They walked easily, seeming to thread some trail Kadiya could not see from her position. And with these was another! A human being. The girl gasped and Jagun nudged her sharply.

It was certainly a human male walking the trail with Skritek, but he was no prisoner. He was dressed all in red, but with the fabric all muddied from the swamp. His head was covered by a hood which extended down to his mouth in the front, masking half his face. He wore a sword and carried a short spear. He spoke with his monstrous companions in so guttural a series of noises that Kadiya wondered how he could produce them, apparently disputing with one of the Drowners — pointing in one direction while the Skritek wanted to proceed in another. And he won that small clash of wills.

In all history, in the gathered legends, the lore of Nyssomu and Uisgu, polder and Citadel, never had there been any truce between the Skritek and another race. Now Jagun was proven correct: somehow Voltrik or Orogastus had enlisted these ogres into their service. However, their reputation for treachery was well set. It was a brave man who walked with them, even if he served a bloody cause. His confidence hinted that it was certainly more than force of arms or persuasion of words which was his protection.

That must be one of the Voices! Kadiya shivered. Her hand was flat against her breast over the amulet. *Hide us,* she begged it wordlessly. *Protect us!*

As to what — or whom — that party hunted, Kadiya had little doubt. She did not know where Haramis or Anigel had gone, but she was here. This band of Skritek sniffing out trails, companioned by one of Orogastus's servants, were intent upon finding her. That the sorcerer's

∴

acolyte had not been suddenly aware of her was astounding. Certainly Orogastus must have some method of search other than eye or ear. She could hardly believe it when the brutes passed without any alarm being raised. But the Black Trillium's magic was not easily overcome.

Kadiya squirmed a little forward and looked into the water. The root-guide rested there as quietly as if it lay upon a table. She drew forth her amulet. It gleamed with potency and the green light underwater seemed to pulsate in sympathy, quivering into life. Though it had been originally pointed toward that shore along which the trail led, now it shifted course until it was parallel with the opposite bank. Kadiya saw Jagun reach for the sculling oar and felt the skiff answer.

They hugged the shoreline, always alert to any movement, pausing now and then as Jagun used nose and ear to judge what lay about. There was only the usual hum of insects, the peeping of mud-dwellers, the natural sounds of day.

Any confidence which that might have given them was sharply dispelled. They came not only to the end of the wider lane of water but also to a barrier of what appeared to be an islet standing well above the water. Into a grim land the root-guide pointed straight ahead. A few feet above them were tangled the black, rotting skeletons of trees which gave support to a network of what looked like vines. The ground offered bedding to distended ball-shaped growths of reddish blue.

Jagun pointed to the nearest of these. "Those are killers nourished by the foulness of this soil. Avoid them as you would a poisoned knife, King's Daughter."

Here was utter silence, a land which could not or would not support any form of life except evil. Still the root that was their guide did not vary direction. It was straight ahead that they must go.

A putrid odor made Kadiya gag. She did not need Jagun's touch as warning. There was movement among the dead trees, a swishing sound — and a female Skritek came into view.

She did not march with any alert purpose, but rather dragged herself along, leaning on a staff, swaying from side to side. She was not sleek or slim of body. Instead her greenish flesh was bloated, the paunch protruding so that the creature was plainly top-heavy. Once she clutched out at the crooked limb of a dead tree and that crumbled to dust, so she went to her knees. No struggle could bring her upright again and she crawled until she reached a more substantial tree to pull herself up.

Her body twisted. Her open mouth voiced a harsh cry. From beneath the overhang of that huge belly there protruded a white object that wriggled as if it had a life of its own, fell to the ground, and humped away. This was followed by a second, a third, until Kadiya could count ten fat, whitish wormlike spawn, perhaps as big as a human baby's head.

The mother Skritek collapsed against the tree she had embraced and the young, which had been plainly questing for something, turned nearly as one to swarm over her who had given them birth. They were plainly feeding.

Jagun crept up beside the girl. "The newborn spawn are ravenous." His voice was the faintest of whispers. "And that luckless dam had no meat waiting to appease her brood."

Already two or three of the loathsome young had left the carcass of the female Skritek. Two came humping forward. As far as the girl could see they had no sign of real heads, although they carried the front ends of their bodies a little higher. These waved about in the air and then centered on the direction of the punt. They began to crawl toward the water.

Jagun moved quickly. His blowpipe was ready and the first dart thudded deeply into the body of the leading larva. It was followed by a second which as easily picked off its companion. The spawn beat the foreparts of their bodies upon the ground and then were still.

Jagun hitched his hunter's bag toward him and worked out of it a much folded strip of some substance as fine and transparently woven as a festival veil. He split this in two and handed half to Kadiya, gesturing that she was to follow his example in its use, twining the length about the head so it covered eyes, nose, and mouth. He tested the knot the girl had tied to fasten hers before he went ahead.

More of the larval Skritek were turning toward the punt, their fore ends lifted as if following the scent of prey. This time Jagun aimed not at them, but at the reddish-blue bulbous growths springing from the soil around them. The first ball his dart entered exploded as if some force had been imprisoned under its rind. Outward shot a cloud of blue dust, which was joined by another and another cloud until there was a drift of spores across the shore as thick as a fog. Jagun pushed the punt back to mid-water and kept it there until the cloud broke into wisps and settled. Where the Skritek spawn had crawled there were now lumps of slimy jelly slowly sinking into the ground.

Kadiya reached into the water and caught up the stem of the trillium. It tugged, straight-pointing in her hand. Then it slipped from her hold and flew through the air as if she had thrown it. There was no escaping the fact that it now lay on that evilly spotted shore where the Skritek mother's dead body lay, and that it pointed inland. The Princess looked to Jagun. He shrugged.

Then he spoke, his words muffled by the improvised mask he still wore. "There lies the Thorny Hell itself, Farseer. It would seem that we have no choice but to enter in."

That she had no choice was evident. Twist or turn as she might, she could not leave the path the Archimage's magic had designated for her. She crawled stiffly onto the bank. The root of the trillium slid steadily forward, though it made a wide swing about the round poisonous growths.

"What lies ahead?" demanded Kadiya as she shouldered the second hunter's bag.

Jagun shook his head. "Unknown land, King's Daughter. If fortune favors us we may reach the holdings of the Uisgu."

She stepped carefully around one of the yellow balls, taking good care not to look at the tree where lay the Skritek dam's half-picked bones.

"Fortune?" The Princess gave a bitter little laugh. "No one holds the good will of that for long."

They came to a weed-lined channel with green-scummed water. One of the dead trees had fallen to span it and there were prints in the mud showing that it served as a bridge. Kadiya stooped to pick up the trillium-root, fearing that it might glide on into the waterway and be lost. It was stiff and straight in her hand. From its tip sprang an emanation like a thread of black flame; and although there was no breeze, it pointed ahead in the direction they were to go: into a wilderness of towering thorn-ferns twice the height of a man.

They traveled on for hours. Then finally Jagun said: "We will stop here for the night."

The area which the root-guide had brought them to stood somewhat above the level of the rest of the ground. It was bare of the thorn-ferns and there were none of the poisonous balls to be seen. Rough grass with sword-sharp edges surrounded them as they came upon a great irregular mound. Though they had seen very few evidences of ruins since they had left Noth, it was plain that intelligence and not nature had shaped this outcrop. Kadiya clutched a small shrub to help pull herself up and loosed a clod of roots and earth. She looked upon what seemed to be dressed stone. It was not the dark granite which was the common construction material of the ruins she knew, but a mineral much smoother, so slick she wondered that the sod had found root there at all. And it had a peculiar sheen under the setting sun.

"What is this?" She called Jagun's attention to it. It could be that the root-guide had led them to an artifact so huge that she could not begin to guess its meaning or use. As she clawed away more earth to uncover it, it became obvious that the ruin was certainly not made of stone. The surface was sleek under her muddy fingertips.

Jagun looked at her discovery and then hurriedly averted his eyes. "It is of the Vanished Ones." He made a small gesture in the air and stared intently at the trillium-root Kadiya carried. Its black flame, which had indicated their route, still held aslant for a moment; and then it straightened and flared with a green halo.

Suddenly Kadiya felt that the aching burden of doubt which had held her for so long was lightened. She pulled herself up to the top of the mound and found that she was balanced on the rim of what might be a giant bowl. The sides sloped downward abruptly, and apparently frequent slides caused by storms had cleared sod and detritus from stretches of the surface, which as far as she could see was neither pitted nor eroded.

Kadiya was amazed, and suddenly she laughed.

"Hunter, this land holds many surprises. Perhaps fortune smiles after all for I feel—" She flung her arms wide and drew a great breath of air. The Vanished Ones seemed to approve her presence here, even welcome her. She rejoiced in a lighter heart. Here all the darkness and terrors that had oppressed her appeared small and far away. She felt no more of the fatigue of her journey, only a rising excitement and a belief that whatever lay before them would indeed work to her purpose.

∴

24

Prince Antar set out in pursuit of Princess Anigel with an expeditionary force of twenty knights and sixty soldiers, and also the sorcerer's Blue Voice, who would keep the Prince apprised of the girl's position through contacts with his farseeing master. The men of Labornok traveled from the Citadel in three large flatboats equipped with auxiliary punts. The fronial mounts belonging to the knights were left behind by princely order, which occasioned great grumbling by Sir Rinutar and Sir Karon and their cronies, even though they could not say how and where they hoped to ride the great steeds in the trackless Mazy Mire. The flatboats each had three crews of oarsmen to row double-time in sequential shifts, and the big boats fairly flew along the calm waters of the Lower Mutar and Lake Wum.

Following Orogastus's triumphant second scry, the search-party was augmented by the Master-Trader Edzar, who was as experienced in dealing with the timber-purveying Wyvilo aborigines of the Tassaleyo Forest as he was with the Nyssomu of Trevista. Through the intermediary Blue Voice, Edzar had conferred with the sorcerer and devised a plan that he declared to be foolproof.

Now the Labornoki force was fast approaching Tass Town, the only sizable human settlement on the lake. The timber-trading center of Ruwenda was a rather shabby agglomeration of docks, warehouses, and shanties situated on an island, surrounded on all sides by floating booms which formed great pens that enclosed the raw logs. The Master-Trader Edzar explained to the knights that many of these would be

∴

transported to holding yards at the upper end of the lake by forming them into rafts and sailing them north during the rainy season, when the prevailing winds were favorable. The more valuable cut lumber and peeled spars were loaded on flatboats and transshipped at any time of the year to the northern yards, whence they were carted away via the Trade Route during the dry seasons.

Riding on the forward deck of the flagship with the awning shading them from the blazing lake sun, the Prince's men were bored with voyaging and the genial trader's lecture — there being little else to do but drink and watch the scenery — and eager to begin their hunt again.

Their first search for Princess Anigel in the Mazy Mire near Citadel Knoll and the Great Causeway had been a near-fiasco. The men were chevaliers, not sailors, and had no knowledge of how to direct a search on water. The force of twenty auxiliary punts, each bearing a knight-commander, three men-at-arms, and three oarsmen, had milled about the Mire every which way under the orders of their inexperienced captains. There had been squabbles over who should search the near areas and who the far, who the clear channels and who the dense thickets crawling with venomous water-worms, stinging vermin, and voracious milingal-fish.

Several hours were wasted criss-crossing the same easy territory and leaving other places untouched, until the skipper of the flagship had tactfully suggested to Prince Antar that the watermen, rather than the knights, should direct the movements of the boats, with a large reward offered to the crew that should first locate the Princess. An efficient search was then conducted, which unfortunately came to naught. Prince Antar did not seem at all dejected by their lack of success.

Now, as the search party approached the scene of more promising action, Antar became morose and edgy, so that the rough-hewn Sir Rinutar whispered to a few of his intimates that the Prince seemed not to subscribe wholeheartedly to their quest. His remarks were overheard by the bluff and loyal Sir Penapat, who took great exception to them and threatened to break Rinutar's head.

An unseemly fracas was avoided only by the intervention of Antar himself, who restored order with the help of his marshal, Sir Owanon. The Prince then retreated to his solitary position in the bows of the flagship where none dared to disturb him, and remained there until they were about to dock.

∴

At this time, the Prince called upon the Master-Trader Edzar to bring out his maps once again and recapitulate his scheme for the entire knightly party, so that there would be no misunderstandings when they disembarked. Edzar still wore his gold-embroidered green tabard, but he had exchanged his orange robe for a vivid purple one, and his leaf hat for another, even broader of brim, woven intricately of long conifer needles and banded with large cerise flowers.

"As you can see, my Lords," he began, "three large rivers, including the Lower Mutar, feed into Lake Wum. But there is just one outlet, the Great Mutar, which flows into the Tassaleyo Forest and is the only corridor into that howling wilderness. If the mighty Orogastus has interpreted his vision correctly, then Princess Anigel is heading for the forest, and to get there, she must pass *here*."

His finger indicated Lake Wum's southern outflow, which on the map was labeled TASS FALLS.

The lanky, saturnine Blue Voice now insinuated himself forward. He usually kept to the flatboat skipper's cabin, being shy of sunlight as a slug; but their near approach to Tass Town had brought him on deck.

"My worthy Master-Trader, the ice-mirror of my Almighty Master not only sees, but also hears. The farsensing lasts but a minute. Nevertheless, on his second scrying, my Master clearly heard the Princess Anigel's servant remark about their impending journey into the Tassaleyo Forest."

The Prince scowled at the map. "If we miss her at the falls, we'll have to chase her down the Great Mutar. It's less than a fortnight to the rainy season . . . and what in Zoto's Name are we going to use down there for boats?"

Edzar said: "It should be possible for us to lower our own punts via the log-lift. However, the Wyvilo have their own much faster rivercraft moored below the falls. In the normal course of events, humans do not ride in them. Ruwendian humans, that is. But if we find it necessary to pursue the Princess down the Great Mutar we might — er — try to convince the Wyvilo to transport us."

Sir Rinutar gave a wicked chuckle. "Now, how could they possibly refuse to help a fine lot of lads like ourselves?"

He had been sharpening his sword, which he now swept up in a gentle arc, bringing the point to bear on the Master-Trader's bulbous nose. Edzar spluttered and the knights laughed.

∴

The Blue Voice said: "I am empowered to demonstrate certain magic to the forest Oddlings, should they be reluctant to assist us. Between my sort of persuasion and Sir Rinutar's, we should experience no great difficulty securing additional transport, should that contingency arise . . . Of course, if Master Edzar's plan succeeds, we will take Princess Anigel here at the falls."

Sir Owanon, who was Prince Antar's close friend as well as his second-in-command, was a younger man with a humorous, intelligent face. He now lifted an admonitory finger. "Hark! Is that the cascade itself I hear?"

"It is indeed, my Lord," the trader replied. "Tass Falls are quite impassable to rivercraft. They are more than sixty ells high and spew a great volume of water, even in the dry season. Below them, the Great Mutar flows wide and slow to the sea. Wyvilo loggers have no trouble bringing their timber upstream to the falls. It is a droll sight to see the strange inhuman beings perched in a long line atop a floating log of heroic proportions, poling it upstream while singing their barbaric anthems."

"And no doubt planning ingenious ways to slice up the liver of the next unlucky human they meet," drawled Sir Karon. Most of the other knights laughed grimly.

"No, no, my lords," Edzar protested. "For all their horrific appearance, the Wyvilo are — er — relatively civilized. You are thinking of their cousins the Glismak, who live further south. *They* are the ones with cannibalistic tendencies —"

"Stones of Zoto!" somebody exclaimed. "We must fight man-eaters?"

"You can hold our cloaks, Stolafat, if the prospect freezes your guts," jeered Rinutar.

"Enough of this," Prince Antar broke in. "Master Edzar, show us again this so-called foolproof plan of yours." And to his men: "Pay attention and cease this bickering!"

Edzar flourished the map and respread it, beckoning all to come closer. "See here. Tass Town on its island lies near the lake's eastern shore. The eastern channel is completely blocked with log booms. To the west are fewer booms, for there arise the rocks called the Fangs of Munjuno, through which swift currents pour before surging over the rim of the cascade. The western lakeshore at this point is sheer rock and quite impassable, while on the eastern shore is thick jungle, penetrated only by the skid-road that leads from the great log-lift at the precipice edge to the cove opposite Tass Town where the wood is put into the water. This eastern road is the place where we must set up our ambush."

Edzar pointed first to the map, then to the eastern shore, which lay across from their docking place, beyond a great labyrinth of floating timber. The Prince and his men could see numbers of skeletal wagons parked on the skid-road, having wheels taller than a man; but there seemed to be no people or draft-animals moving about over there, and indeed the shore looked deserted.

"The war brought most commerce in Tass Town to a halt," Edzar explained. "The Ruwendian workers who normally staff the lumbermill below the falls, the great lift, and the skid-road have not yet returned to work. Lord Zontil, one of General Hamil's most trusted aides, has been charged with setting up a garrison here. He expects to have the situation well in hand by the end of the Rains. All the logs that you see now in the water will be sent to the northern end of the lake by that time. And by the spring dry season, timber production should be back to normal."

"Cease boring us with your mercantile trivia, trader!" Sir Rinutar slapped the map impatiently. "Do you guarantee that the fugitive wench can get to the Tassaleyo Forest by no other route than this — this skid-road?"

Edzar drew himself up in offended dignity. "I do. There is a vast unscalable escarpment along this border of the Ruwenda tableland. Untold ages ago a narrow footpath was cut by the Oddlings in the cliff east of the falls. The great log-lift and the lumbermill below, that is powered by the falling water, were built by the first humans inhabiting Ruwenda, utilizing foundations that are said to have been left by the Vanished Ones. There is no way from Lake Wum to the Great Mutar River save the lift and the footpath. The Princess must take the skid-road to attain either one."

The three flatboats of the search force were now being tied up at the main Tass Town dock, which also seemed conspicuously devoid of activity. Well-armed soldiers of Labornok stood guard all along the quayside as glum-looking Ruwendians handled the lines and pulled the gangplanks into place. A Labornoki nobleman in elaborate armor, attended by several officers, waited impatiently for the docking maneuvers to be completed so that he could greet the Prince.

But Antar was bent over the map, giving instructions. "This is the way we shall deploy, then. We will divide our force into three companies — Owanon to lead the first, Dodabilik the second, and Rinutar the third — to be stationed at the skid-road landing, midway down the road where the footpath cuts off, and at the top of the log-lift."

"You do not intend to command a company yourself, my Prince?" Sir Rinutar's tone was tainted with the slightest archness.

"No," said Antar coldly. "The Blue Voice and I will coordinate the action from a point of vantage. He is able to farsee for short distances. Penapat will also remain with us, since his foot is not yet healed from the water-worm bite, to handle the signalmen and messengers who will transmit my orders. We must make absolutely certain" — the Prince's gaze met that of the hovering Blue Voice — "that Princess Anigel does not slip through our fingers again."

It was just after noon of their third day on Lake Wum, and the sound of Tass Falls rumbled in the air like faraway thunder, its brink lost in sparkling mist. Anigel and Immu had approached Tass Town's island with great care, and their boat now lay concealed beneath a weeping tree that grew from a cleft in a great precipice along the western shore.

All about their hiding place huge rocks rose from the water. Between them and the island less than two hundred ells away, the five pointed Fangs of Munjuno marked the point of no return above the falls. A small boat could breast the current north of the rocks and safely reach the log booms and the opposite shore; but to pass south of the Fangs meant being trapped in swifter waters and swept over the cataract.

"What we must do," Immu said, laying out a frugal lunch in the green shade, "is wait until nightfall, then cross over above the Fangs. There is a road on the shore over there that runs less than half a league. We follow it to a steep path that leads down to the Ruwendian sawmill at the foot of the falls, and steal another boat there."

"But the rimoriks — !" Anigel cried.

"But but but! We let the good creatures go free, back to their home waters. Did you think you could keep them as pets forever?"

Anigel hung her head. "I did not think at all."

Immu patted her shoulder. "Never mind. The Great Mutar is very shallow, aside from the main channel. We can make a log raft and pole downstream if need be — and at least one of your great fears will be left behind. The troops of Labornok will never think to look for us in the Tassaleyo. With luck, the Wyvilo will respect your trillium amulet just as the Uisgu did, and they will help you on your quest."

Anigel looked up dubiously from munching her dried roots. "Do you really think so? I have heard that they are very hostile to humankind, and fearsome to look upon as well."

"They're not the kind of Folk you would invite to a grand ball at the Citadel," Immu conceded. "Some Nyssomu say that aeons ago members of our race were stolen away by the Skritek and forced to consort with them, and from the mating arose both the Wyvilo and their more primitive neighbors, the Glismak."

"What do they look like?" Anigel asked, licking her fingers.

"I have never seen one, but they are said to combine Skritek features with those of Nyssomu or Uisgu."

"Ugh!" said the Princess.

"Whatever their aspect," Immu continued reprovingly, "the Wyvilo are also subjects of the White Lady who revere the Black Trillium, and so we may hope they will receive us kindly."

"These Glismak — they are unfriendly to humans?"

Immu sighed. "Like the Skritek, those fiends of the Mazy Mire, the Glismak hate all beings save themselves. We must pray that your talisman —"

"Look!" cried Anigel, pointing across the water. "Oh, look! A whole fleet of punts coming out from behind the island — *and the leader bears the banner of Labornok!*"

Immu shaded her eyes and peered into the shimmering glare. The air was windless and it was very hot. "Are you sure?"

"Oh, I am. The miton sharpens all senses." She shrank back, terror blanching her face. "It's a search-party come looking for me, and they are heading for the eastern shore."

"By the Flower!" Immu growled. "They have cut us off. If we had only arrived sooner."

"They must not take me! Is there no other way down?"

Immu screwed her face into a scowl as she thought. "Down down

down. I know only the one way." But then her expression changed, and she seized the girl by the shoulder with one small taloned hand, while the other pointed over the side of the boat. "But *they* might know another."

"The rimoriks?" Anigel whispered.

"Try them," Immu snapped.

The Princess leaned over the gunwale. The traces of the harness that the water-creatures wore had been greatly lengthened for lake travel, and the water here was deep. The rimoriks were out of sight, seeking coolness.

My friends. I have a most important thing to ask you.

First one dark shape appeared, then another. The two sleek green-spotted heads lifted out of the water with hardly a ripple and the animals bared their fangs in a manner that Anigel had once thought ferocious, but now knew to be their fashion of smiling.

Human friend, ask your question.

Do you know where we are now?

Certainly. On the brink of the Great White Falling Water. Do you have any other questions?

Is there a way down? Into the Great Mutar River?

Yes. There is a way from the Wide Flat Water into the Water Flowing to the Sea.

"Immu!" the Princess cried. "They say there is a way!"

"Ask them if they can take us." Immu's voice was strained, harsh.

Can you take us down there in the boat?

If you wish it.

There are evil humans on other boats round about the island over there. Can you take us so that they can't catch us?

Oh, yes. Do you wish to go now? If so, we must first share miton.

"They say yes!" Anigel exclaimed, radiant with joy. "They want to know if we'd like to go now! Oh, it's wonderful. What should I tell them, Immu?"

The Oddling woman's great yellow eyes blinked slowly. Her gaze was fixed on that of the human whom she loved, seeing the once delicate skin now sunburned and insect-bitten, the hair that used to be compared to spun gold now turned to frowsy straw, the blue eyes, once brimming with fear, now eagerly aglitter . . .

"My sweet child, of course you must tell them to take us." Having spoken, Immu calmly set about repacking the food, then tied their two packs by the cords to one of the punt thwarts.

Anigel had taken the miton gourd from her belt-wallet. Sipping first, she then shared the liquid with the rimoriks. "Now we are ready. Take your place, Immu."

The Princess returned to the driver's thwart in the bows of the punt and took up the reins, wrapping the leather straps once about each well-calloused hand to keep a good grip. Her mind called out:

My friends, let's go!

The two powerful beasts submerged, thrust forward with their clawed flippers, and hauled the long slim boat out of its hiding place and into the open lake. Tracing a long curved path, swimming with all their prodigious strength, they turned south — heading straight through the Fangs of Munjuno toward the brink of the huge waterfall.

Leaning on the stone rail, Prince Antar watched his knights and the men-at-arms disembark from the punts and begin to spread out along the skid-road. He and the Blue Voice and the limping Sir Penapat had taken up a position in the loftiest structure of Tass Town, a lighthouse about fifteen ells high on the western side of the small island settlement.

The Prince and the knight stripped to tunic and buskins because of the heat, and surveyed the scene from the outer parapet of the light-house, while the skinny Blue Voice was not only robed but hooded, seated upon a stool next to the great unlit lamp while his farseeing mind's eye followed the deployment of the forces on shore.

"I wouldn't like to live here," Penapat said.

"Why not, Peni?" Antar was idly scanning the roofs below, from which only a few threads of smoke arose. Lord Zontil had told him that most of the population save for the log-raft sailors abandoned Tass Town during the rainy seasons. The war had simply started the exodus sooner.

"Too noisy," the big man stated. "The waterfall. Hurts my teeth."

"Your *teeth* —"

"Can't you feel it? A sound that's so deep it's hardly a noise at all. It comes up through the rock and makes the whole lighthouse shake, and my body too, and hurts my teeth."

Antar began to laugh — and then he suddenly cut short, having caught

∴

a glimpse of something out on the water. "My God!" he breathed. "Peni, will you look out there? Do you see what I see?"

"A little boat," Penapat affirmed. The big man's expression was sweetly quizzical. "It shouldn't be going beyond those rocks. The trader said there's a strong current out there, that'll take you over the falls."

"Blue!" roared the Prince. "Get out here, quickly!"

The Blue Voice rose with evident reluctance, only to be dragged unceremoniously to the lighthouse rail by Antar, who pointed out the vagrant punt.

"That boat! Who's in it?" Antar demanded.

The Blue Voice pursed his lips. "You roused me from my trance, Prince. That's a *most* dangerous thing to do — "

Antar's hand, which was very strong, tightened on the scrawny blue-clad bicep. "The boat, you worram-scat! Quickly!"

The clairvoyant's eye-sockets were abruptly black and empty. His thin lips trembled. "My Lord — I — *I can't tell who rides within.*"

"Anigel!" the Prince cried. "It's the Princess!"

The punt, moving with astonishing speed, was now well beyond the Fangs. There were two small figures in it, one far forward and stiffly upright, the other huddled amidships. A light breeze had sprung up, wafting away the mist that curtained the lip of the cataract. It could now be seen clearly from the lighthouse, a nearly straight line of blue-black, fringed at the fatal edge with white. Beyond it was a void of sky and distant, haze-shrouded trees.

As Antar watched, the racing punt seemed for a moment to be preceded by two dark forms arching through the spume at the brink. Then the slender vessel hovered for an instant, its front half in thin air, its stern still supported by water, before it tilted and slid out of sight.

∴

25

The lammergeier flew tirelessly over the peaks and icefields of the high Ohogans, so high that Haramis found the clear thin air difficult to breathe. She became drowsy not long after the huge bird left Movis, and was content to snuggle down within her thick fur cloak, sheltered deep in the feathered hollow between the lammergeier's wings, and sleep.

She was unaware of their passage over Mount Rotolo and the slow approach to towering Mount Gidris, which was enshrouded in thick clouds. The lammergeier breasted strong winds for hour after hour, but by nightfall it still had not reached its goal.

Haramis woke when it began to descend through thickly falling snow. As the Vispi had taught her, she first brought to mind a clear picture of the creature's striking black-and-white crested visage, with the glittering eyes like polished jet and a great beak edged with sharp teeth. Then her mind spoke its name: *Hiluro!*

I hear, Haramis.

She heard its reply in a place in her mind that Magira had patiently taught her to use. Haramis had found learning the speech without words a strange experience; her first attempts had been complete failures. Then, almost by accident, she had managed to bespeak Magira. After several more semi-accidental successes, she had worked out what she was doing, and after that the process was simple, almost automatic. One simply rendered this part of the mind "open" after first calling out mentally to the desired person. After Haramis had learned to bespeak reliably, Magira introduced her to the lammergeier who would become both mount and companion in the next stage of her quest.

The great bird had glided down and landed on the slate roof at Magira's summoning. Its wingspan was as wide as the house, and its gigantic black-taloned feet could have seized a full-grown man in armor with the ease of a night-caroler snatching a tree-vart. But for all its ferocious demeanour, the colossal flyer had greeted Magira with great-hearted affection.

I tell you now one of the great secrets of the mountain Folk, Magira had said to the Princess, stroking the lowered head of the bird. *You know that we were made for lands all girt about with ice and snow — but so were these great creatures. When the Vanished Ones refashioned the abominable flesh of the Foundation Stock into the First Folk, they engendered at the same time the voor, which you humans call lammergeiers, from a lesser sort of bird. Folk and voor were thus newborn upon the world together, since the Vanished Ones knew we Vispi would need helpers in order to move about over a world locked fast in ice. Our towns are few and widely separated, but with the help of our great friends, we journey over the long distances in safety. As you shall, in fulfilling your quest . . .*

The lammergeier, landing with confidence in spite of the blowing snow, pecked with its great beak at the white frozen cliff-face, whereupon the ice cracked and revealed a dark opening.

"Is this the place where my Three-Winged Circle is hidden?" Haramis asked.

No. This is shelter for the night. We both need food and rest, and you will be safe here while I hunt. I shall return soon. Hiluro lofted back into the sky.

Haramis drew out her Black Trillium amulet from her bodice. It glowed like a lantern, casting light ahead as she stepped over broken bits of ice into the cavern.

It was a huge place, mostly dry, although the wind swept flurries of snow in after her. Several tumbled blocks of dark stone all shot through with thick veins of white quartz mingled with another material reflected back the amulet's warm glow. Haramis realized she was looking at a lode of gold.

The Princess left her pack and wandered for some time by the light of her amulet, finding outcroppings of gold everywhere, and sometimes great nuggets lying on the floor.

But it was far at the back of the cavern that she made her most interesting discovery.

Within a rough alcove, the amulet's golden light had flickered on something very dark and shiny, and when she approached she found a wall of perfectly smooth black ice, in which she saw herself, holding the glowing amulet.

An ice mirror . . .

And was it not some such thing that the sorcerer Orogastus was rumored to use for scrying?

She asked the question of her image within the dark ice, a tall and beautiful young woman whose pale face, framed in black hair, was haloed in the white fur of her mantle's hood. The glowing amulet at her throat had a reflective radiance that drew back her eyes whenever she would look away.

She stared at the amulet's golden glow, and it seemed that her vision swam, and the image of herself became that of another: a man, attired in strange robes and crowned with a headpiece like a great silver star. He smiled at her and held out his hand, offering to show her his secrets, to share his knowledge, his magic . . .

Haramis!

"Orogastus," she whispered, petrified with sudden recognition. He seemed to reach out to her, through the mirror of black ice —

Haramis!

The mental call was inhuman, familiar, urgent.

Hiluro?

Haramis, come back. Now!

She saw her own face again reflected in the sheet of ice. Chilled to the bone, she turned and hurried back to reassure Hiluro, whose calling of her name by the speech without words still resounded in her head, driving away all other thoughts.

26

Jagun made no attempt to start a fire. Instead he stood with his hands hanging by his side. He might have been one who had come to the end of a trail to find nothing but a wall over which there was no climbing. Kadiya watched him uneasily. This was a Jagun she had never seen before.

She was about to ask him what was the matter when he turned quickly and clawed and fought his way up to her, to the top of that bowl-like opening. Slowly he paced around the broad rim, but he did not look down at the path his feet followed; instead his head was up, turning slowly from side to side, his tense body expressing the need to hear, to see, to know. When he completed the circle he came back to her and she asked:

"What is it, Jagun?"

For a moment she thought he would not answer. The he raised his head to face her squarely.

"Farseer, for us all there are hidden things. This is a strange land, as much so to me as to you. But I think we come now to an even stranger one."

"There is something to be feared?" she demanded.

"I do not know." Now he drew his bag to him and rummaged quickly in it, bringing out food—some dry cakes and two small smoked fish so brittle that they broke when touched. Again Kadiya wondered over the lack of fire but some caution kept her from asking. Though night in this water-logged country was apt to be dank she did not feel that chill now. Rather it was as if the bowl still held about them a little of the sun's heat.

The full burden of the day settled upon her. Although thought about the larvae and those poisonous balls they had passed flitted through the sudden descent of fatigue, she could not raise energy to suggest guard duty. The sensation of safety which had closed about her when she had first climbed up here was like a warm robe promising sleep without fear.

Did she sleep or did she wake? She could not have truthfully sworn to either. As the night darkened and drifts of mist floated over their heads from one side of the bowl to the other, she lay quietly.

Their root-guide she had set up by her head, butt in drift of soil, black tip up. There was no flame from that. However, it was not completely dark after all. She was first aware of a shimmer which she could catch only in the corners of her eyes. If she shifted quickly to view it, it disappeared, or seemed to move enough out of sight to remain only a suggestion.

So it went for a time. Then those shimmers rooted themselves. They were at least as tall as Jagun, thin pillars in which swirled faint colors, so pallid that one hue might hardly be distinguished from another.

At first they only stood still, not in any pattern Kadiya could discern; then they wavered and floated free. She could not understand why they moved so, but she was sure they were weaving an intricate pattern whereof she and Jagun were the heart. Yet no fear stirred in her. Finally she did not see the pillars anymore, except as a whirling mist which spun slowly about the opposite slope of the bowl.

The mist glowed, and within it she saw a beautiful city — the same city she had dreamt of before reaching Noth! It seemed also that she had once known that city and found happiness and contentment there, and she wanted nothing more than to go seeking it.

Somewhere there was singing, a music different from any that a Ruwendian bard could draw from a harp, raising in Kadiya a new longing. And then the vision disappeared.

Kadiya sat up, suddenly chilled, her hands going to her amulet. That feeling of being guarded and comforted was gone. Instead she had a sudden vivid mental glimpse of the diseased land through which they had come to this place . . . and then she realized that it was early morning.

∴

There was movement nearby. Jagun stood ready for the trail, beckoning to her, that strange bleak look still on his face. Kadiya arose, took up the root, shouldered her bag, and prepared to set off once again. The two wayfarers looked down and away from the great mound which enclosed the bowl. Swamp mist swirled about, and there seemed to be no sign of a rising sun to burn it away. In Kadiya's hand the trillium-root came to life, slipped easily through her fingers and started to glide downhill on the slope opposite that which they had yesterday climbed.

"We go." Jagun's voice held as little expression as his face and he said nothing of food — rather pointed on toward more of the tall thornferns and the bulbous horrors which had taken root among them. They trudged on, slowing as they wove a zig-zag path to avoid the poisonous balls.

After a time they came to an open space carpeted with a furry yellow scum. There were no trees here, only a series of columnar projections, almost like miniature clay towers, leading out into what looked like a cleared and leveled field stretching ahead of them. But Jagun warned her that it was a quickmire. A single misstep here and one would be swallowed forever.

Jagun delved into his hunter's bag and drew out a packet. Freed of its ties, it proved to be four dish-like ovals. Once released from their fastenings the ovals opened, took on thickness in the humid air, and became boat-shaped leaves curling up about their outer edges. Skimmers, the hunters called them.

Kadiya had used these before, always cautiously, and only when she was with Jagun. Seating herself on a rounded outcrop she made fast the lashings of the skimmers around her ankles. She stamped to test the tightness of the cording before she started carefully after Jagun, making sure she followed his path. The root-guide had already slipped out ahead of him upon that treacherous ground. Under her feet Kadiya was aware of the give in the surface, and their pace was now swift. Always flanking them were the lumpy columns, taller than either she or Jagun.

The mist swirled so thickly now that she caught only a very hazy glimpse of the shore of the Thorny Hell from which they had set out. Sometimes even the stubby pillars were nearly blotted out. As they went on, she became aware that the footing became steadily more

∴

secure. Then suddenly a large veil of mist hovered as if it had been caught on something, and then freed itself, and drifted away.

The last of the pillars was revealed. Only it was not a pillar. Chunks of mud as hard as if baked had scaled away, and what stood there was unmistakenly a figure — though certainly no monstrous one.

It had been made to represent no Oddling. The proportions were as human as her own, although the image was masculine. Save for an elaborate crown-helm and three scarves or belts the statue wore no clothing. The belts were drawn one over each shoulder, crossing on the breast and ending in a wide waist belt latched together. The body itself was of an ivory shade and possessed a sheen as if highly polished. Scarves and belt were covered by small flakes or scales, green, gold, blue, shaded from the palest to the darkest in each hue.

It was what was gripped in the image's outstretched hands which drew and held their eyes.

Kadiya had seen great savagery in the days just past. But the severed head that the figure held was so foreign to the feeling that the rest of the statue aroused that it startled and sickened her. For that was the head of no Skritek nor Oddling. In spite of the fact that it was utterly hairless and the rounded skull bulged overmuch, it might have been the head of a man of her own kind!

She moved a little away, the better to see the face of the statue, expecting somehow to witness there a fierce countenance such as the Labornoki had worn when they dabbled in horrors at the Citadel.

But the face overshadowed by the elaborate helm was calm, full of strength and serenity. The image might have been fashioned as a dire warning, or a monument to some victory; but the longer Kadiya looked at those eyes — which stared to her right, as the head was slightly turned — the more she was sure that what she saw signified some ancient justice, intended to stand as a warning for all time.

The eyes themselves were not blank carving. Instead the hollows were inset with dark stones and in each, even as in the heart of the Black Trillium flower, there was a hint of gold.

"The sindona!" Jagun sprang back a little from the statue. "This is the Forbidden Way!" He wore an expression of awe which held more than a tinge of fear.

Kadiya's eyes did not leave those of the figure. "Who?"

∴

Jagun did not answer her. Instead he stooped and caught up one of the shards of baked mud which had plainly been scraped from the figure.

"This was done not long ago. But — not by the Skritek. They would not lay claw to this! Then who?"

"Please, what does this statue represent?" Kadiya raised her voice.

Jagun blinked. "Sentinels of the Vanished Ones — they who could command the earth and water . . ." His words trailed off as he caught Kadiya's arm.

"Look!"

Resting on a nearby chunk of the hard mud lay the trillium-root. Its small candle was aflame, pointing not in the direction they had been traveling but that in which the figure was looking. Jagun sank the butt of his spear into the yellow muck. It penetrated for about a finger's length and then met resistance, though the surface looked no different from the morass they had transversed so carefully. Kadiya watched as the hunter moved on, tapping the end of the spear before him. The root wavered back and forth as if it wanted to take the path Jagun followed, but would not leave Kadiya behind.

Magic — all magic! Her old impatience flared. But so far the guide had not played them false. Though she inwardly shrank, the Princess strode behind the hunter in this new direction. The skimmer-leaves sank a fraction under her weight but no more, and the root raced ahead as might a hound unleashed.

At length the yellow morass was broken here and there by what might once have been pavement. They came through the last of the thinning mist to a place covered with clean, coarse turf such as grew in the polders to the northeast. There was a straggle of other vegetation and Kadiya gained smarting thorn scratches as she took the trillium-root into her hand.

Her back and legs ached with a steady pain, for she had unconsciously tensed her body through all their journey over the morass. Now she stumbled twice and then went to her knees. Jagun was beside her at once, water-bottle in hand. Kadiya gulped gratefully and then sank down to rest among the tussocks of grass. In less than a minute she was asleep.

Light shining in her eyes awoke her and she stared up at the open sky, bewildered. She had dreamt she was in her own chamber in the ladies' tower of the Citadel. But there was no carven roof above her. She sat up and groaned at the stiffness in her back.

Trees surrounded the turfed area where she lay. Their smooth trunks were greenish bronze and their green-edged, bluish leaves rustled at the tug of a breeze. She was alone, though Jagun's pack lay in sight. A blabat-bird perched on an arched stem of bramble, snatching at a bright red berry. It paid no attention as Kadiya got to her feet and stretched. The trillium-root was planted stem-up near where her head had lain and it was quivering.

"Na . . . na . . . na . . ."

That sound the girl recognized at once. The Nyssomu were never loud or free of speech, but they sometimes voiced a croon of content. Jagun rounded a big bramble bush, carrying in one hand a vine from which hung some oval scarlet fruit, swollen near to the bursting point with ripeness.

Kadiya nearly swallowed the first fruit whole, and had a second ready to eat before she was able to ask a question.

"Where are we?"

Jagun was carefully peeling more of his spoil, a long length of sweet-cane. He shrugged, indicating that he did not know. The girl was so used to crediting him with all Mire knowledge that she could not believe they were lost. He chewed a bit of cane core and then spit out the pith which had been drained of its sugary juice.

"We are beyond all trails I know, Farseer. I know only that there is stone under this." He thumped the turf with the end of the cane. "And that," he nodded to the upstanding root-guide, "has brought us here."

"More ruins."

Laying aside his piece of cane, Jagun carefully used his knife, levering up a patch of sod. Beneath was indeed a dark-stained stone surface. "A roadway. That is what this is." He gestured ahead, where there was an opening in the trees.

"A road made by the sindona?"

Jagun looked away from her. Instead he stared at the hole he had dug as if the uncovering had been a mistake.

He spoke hesitatingly with pauses between his words, as if the information came from him unwillingly. "The Vanished Ones — and with them, their sentinels, the sindona — once ruled the water and the isles. We were of their making, fashioned by their minds and their hands. The Dark Powers arose and there was death in the land. But before the ancient ones left they called us forth and told us that we were free. Only certain oaths they asked of us . . ."

Jagun looked down at the knife in his hands, turning it over and over.

"The sindona remain to watch over what was left by the Vanished Ones. There were certain things — and certain knowledge which they could not take away with them, nor were they able to destroy it. This roadway" — he waved to the rows of clay-covered sentinels — "leads to one such guarded place."

He dropped the sod he had dug up back into its hole. "King's Daughter, your Father had Oathed Companions who served him even unto death. Though we Folk owe allegiance elsewhere, our oaths bind us as fast. But Farseer, I have now broken that vow! Yonder, through those trees, lies the Forbidden Way. Last night I sent forth the Great Call. There was no answer. I could not link with any scout of the Folk. We have come past the barrier set up for my own race. That goes" — he pointed to the root with his knife — "and you must follow. I do not know if I will be able to accompany you. I thought we were going to the Uisgu, but instead we are here. And someone uncovered the Captain of the Sentries — Lamaril, the great one not even the Skritek would dare to front . . . No, I had no answer to my call. But yonder" — again he waved the bared steel, and even under the faint sun it gave off an ominous glint — "there was a fire in the night. Off in those trees, along the Forbidden Way."

Kadiya was startled. "I slept . . ."

For the first time Jagun looked less grim. "Farseer, you slept part of a day, and all the night which followed. This is the second day."

She frowned. "You should have awakened me."

"Not so. What lies before us I do not know, save perhaps it may be greater peril than we have yet faced. Any hunter would choose fronting a Skritek over traveling the Forbidden Way. You need to face the future with all possible strength of mind and body, and so I let you sleep."

∴

"This fire you saw . . ."

Jagun looked grim. "The fires our people use are small. What I saw was great. To feed it must have been a task for many hands."

"Voltrik's men?"

"If so they await where that," he gestured to the root, "would lead us." The two of them walked on in silence, but it was clear that Jagun was becoming more and more agitated.

Kadiya was also unnerved. She was almost ready to snap the little guide in two. Only she could not destroy it. She was ensnared by the Archimage's magic and her quest for the talisman, the mysterious Three-Lobed Burning Eye, and she could not gainsay it.

Suddenly Jagun gave a loud cry and reached for his hunter's bag. From it he snatched a golden armlet inset with red stones. Only twice had Kadiya seen such a thing before: first when he had come to the Citadel to receive formal greeting from her Father; and again at a sing-chant of his people when he had worn a similar thing on his upper arm. He must have obtained the sacred object at the Nyssomu village.

Now he turned it around in his hands, groaning as his fingers caressed its smooth surface. Then he grasped the armlet tightly, the straining muscles of his shoulders betraying the effort he made, his face a mask of dread.

The armlet snapped. Jagun hurled the pieces from him. An eerie warbling sound issued from his lips. That, too, she had heard, always when one of his own clan had died and the raft bearing the body had been poled away to the secret place of interrment.

"Jagun?" she ventured.

His face had stiffened.

Never had she viewed such coldness in his expression.

"Jagun is dead," he told her tonelessly. "This one is no longer named. I am oathbreaker, castoff of Kin, one who cannot Speak and to whom none will Speak again. We go to break the forbidden silence. The Lady of Noth has the right to wring the life from us."

"When we follow her own guide?" Kadiya demanded hotly. Did he hold *her* at fault when it was certainly none of her doing? Against her breast the amulet heated. "I am going on!" she cried. But an instant later she stumbled and caught her balance with an effort. The feeling that flooded through her was so alien that she tried to scream and found she could not make a sound. For that single moment she had a sensation of such overwhelming fear that it shook her whole body.

Fear of what? she demanded of herself. She caught at a nearby bush to steady herself. As ever, fear awoke rage in her.

Dagger out, she turned around. Near her Jagun lay on the turf which covered the ancient roadway. His thin fingers clawed feebly at his chest and he was breathing in short fluttering gasps.

"Jagun!" Kadiya went to her knees beside him. His mouth opened and a trickle of moisture oozed from one corner.

"Back!" His voice was only a thread of sound. He threw out his arms in a frantic gesture and strove to pull himself upright. "Take me . . . back!"

Kadiya sheathed her dagger and took him by the shoulders. Exerting her full strength she pulled him a full fifty ells along the turf, back from that ancient roadway which the root-guide urged her to follow.

The root had halted, but it wavered as if beckoning her on. Her own fear was now gone as if a door had been shut. She caught at her amulet. It was blazing with color and warmth, but not as if it were giving forth a threat. Instead, it seemed to encourage her.

Wind arose, coming at them through the trees. Jagun coughed and levered himself up to a sitting position.

"A barrier — " the hunter wheezed. "I cannot go that Way." His head drooped forward. There was a blankness now on his face. He faced something which was beyond his power to fight and he had no weapon left.

"Farseer — " There was pain in his voice. "It is forbidden — only you can go on alone. But I swear that if there is a way I may come to you, I shall discover it!"

"I — " Now it was *her* lips which had frozen. "Jagun — take care."

His hand went up in a gesture of reassurance and encouragement. Then he turned and crept away, and after a time got to his feet and waved to her. She guessed that he would indeed range wide to discover whether there was a way past that which held them apart.

There was movement in the grass. The root was switching back and forth as if expressing exasperation, beckoning her on to action.

She shouldered Jagun's bag and unwillingly and with a lagging step she followed her root-guide forward into the trees. There was a nauseating whiff of something in the wind which now blew steadily at her, a stench which was neither like that of the Skritek, nor the bog. Twice she looked back hoping to catch sight of Jagun, but he was not to be seen.

However, there was something ahead, a dull gleam at the foot of one of the trees. She stooped to pick up an arrow, well made, with a shaft and feathering the color of dried blood. She had seen such before, yes . . . and during the siege had helped to gather all which had not hit marks or shattered against walls, to replenish the stocks of archers at the Citadel. This arrow was not of the swamp but of the intruders! How had it come here? And why did it lay so balanced — as if, like her root, it was a guide?

She nearly threw it from her and then thought more clearly. It took but a moment to replace it, with the point set in the opposite direction.

How had the Labornoki been able to pass the barrier which had defeated Jagun? Her amulet must have been the key for her — but Hamil's men, what did they carry except the steel they had already so foully bloodied? Was this more of Orogastus's dark magic?

Within a couple of strides she came upon the impression of a boot in a wet patch of earth. And beyond that — Kadiya fought down the rise of bile in her throat as she saw a dead Skritek lying to one side as if the body had been kicked out of the way. The creature bore no wound that she could see, and there was no puddling of blood.

She turned determinedly away and continued on, counting steps under her breath, trying very hard to keep her attention alert to all which lay about her. Then a new noxious odor fouled the air. She looked to the right. An Oddling, its thick body pelt revealing it to be Uisgu, was bound to a tree. This time there was evidence of how death had come and it had not been easy.

Not far beyond the first Uisgu victim, there was further disturbance of the ground, and the smell of fire was strong. Bushes were torn from the ground, and the turf was scuffed up. There she found another tortured Oddling. She could not make herself look closely, until there came a thin cry, and she was forced to go to the Uisgu. A crooked hand strove to rise, an eye looked at her from a broken face.

Once more Kadiya called upon the brace of anger.

"Who did this thing?" She hesitated — how could she ease such terrible hurts? She had nothing . . .

∴

The hand moved. It would seem that the wounded mouth could no longer shape words. The Uisgu made a greater effort: a small gesture toward her knife.

At last she was able to guess the nature of his plea. Kadiya's heart raced. She had always been fascinated by weapons, and had once or twice indulged in swordplay when she could get the Master-at-Arms into a good mood. Jagun had also taught her Oddling knife-tricks — but *this* she was not prepared for.

Once more that faint cry, the small gesture . . .

Kadiya set her mouth firmly and took her dagger hilt in both hands. Something else came to mind, words she had heard Jagun say when he had found a strayed fronial so entrapped in a suck-vise it could not be freed.

"Go safely beyond . . ." She brought down her blade and felt it enter living flesh. Then she swallowed and swallowed again.

Getting to her feet the girl stumbled on, wanting to be away, free. Yet when she glanced down she saw the root-guide still sliding ahead. That she went into danger she could guess, and her preparation for it was as woefully small as had been those of the Citadel garrison when the invaders had stormed in upon them.

She became aware of mist gathering between the trees ahead, edging out now and then into a tongue of fog. The root bore steadily onward. She was startled when the tip of the trillium-root lifted, blazed green, and then spun to the left, now pointing between two of the largest trees she had yet come upon.

There was a thin, high-pitched whistle. Kadiya instinctively leaped to one side as something struck the trunk of the tree just ahead of her. A spiral of thick and oily smoke arose, and she threw herself belly down and thrust her way, in spite of the pain, into the shelter of a great bramble-bush.

Again came the whistling cry, followed by what might have been a muffled answer. Kadiya was caught face down on the ground by Jagun's bag, which had snagged on a bramble. Aroused to a frenzy, she fought to free herself. Smoke blew into her face and she choked and then coughed without relief. But that deep-lunged coughing saved her. The brambles gave away as she struggled and she fell forward into what seemed like a dark hole. Her outflung hand scraped against stone, not bark or branches.

As the hunting cry sounded for the third time behind her, she wormed forward into the dark. In her panic, one part of her thought she might be pushing into a trap, yet she continued to crawl ahead.

Any moment she expected her pursuers to catch up, to seize her by the ankles and pull her out of this hole as a sucbri could be jerked from its shell by a skilled hand. Somehow she managed to keep going until her outreaching hands met only emptiness and she plunged down and down . . .

Water closed about her and with it light. But this was not the turbid murky liquid of the swamp pools. It was crystal clear, except nearest her own body where swirled the muck and soil she had picked up during her crawl. Though Jagun's bag pulled her down she refused to rid herself of it. Rather she kicked and fought her way to the surface. A gleam of green caught her eye. So she had not lost her guide! The root was swimming before her.

There was a wall about this pool, over which she splashed and struggled into the air. She crept on hands and knees over a pavement of metallic blue mosaic. There was no growth of weed, nothing to sully the pool and the limpid water it held. Before her was a flight of stairs, on either side of which stood ranks of statues.

She got to her feet. The utter silence of this new place struck her first. Once she had pulled herself out of the water and her own splashing ceased, the smooth surface of the pool was undisturbed.

Kadiya ventured to look up the flight of stairs. There was not a hint of greenery to be seen — only the rows of statues that Jagun had named sindona. The light which appeared to pour into this place struck an eye-tormenting glitter from the ornamentation on the motionless figures. Not all the sindona who seemed to regard her so calmly were male, yet they were clad alike. And there was about them such a feeling of life that she would not have been surprised had they moved and spoke — perhaps to refuse her entrance, perhaps to bid her welcome.

She looked down at her bruised and scratched body, the tattered Nyssomu garments which had not survived too well her battle with the wilderness. Strangely, she felt renewed, stronger. She wanted to press on to see this place, of which no legend or traveler's tale had ever spoken.

At the top of the stairway Kadiya paused before one of the figures. It was taller than she — perhaps life-size for the race whose hands had modeled it. She looked up into the face beneath the shadow of the helm.

"Who are you?" Her words sounded abrupt, too demanding for this place of silence and beauty. And how could she expect any answer from the silent sentinel?

Of course there could be no answer. Nevertheless she was aware of an odd sound, as if a deadening curtain had been pulled aside. There came a crystal tone as if small bells chimed. Birds twittered, and a breeze wove a breath of scent about her which banished the last of that choking horror which had driven her into cover.

She looked further. Here was another flight of stairs even wider, but without the guardian figures, and it led up and out into such a stretch of parkland that no one born in the swamps encircling Ruwenda might have imagined. It was a place of rich and paradoxical growth. Unfamiliar kinds of ripe fruit hung beside the very blossoms from which they developed. Above was an azure sky. So enchanted did the garden seem, so enwrapt in magic that Kadiya dared not venture into it. On the top step of the second stairway lay the root-guide, the green halo at its point sparkling as if it had been fashioned from an emerald.

Kadiya blinked, and blinked again. She was no longer alone.

The one coming across the garden to meet her was plainly one of the statue people, even though helm and military belts had been exchanged for a gauzy robe.

Woman — truly? Kadiya could not have said. But she knew that here was one to whom even the Archimage would make obeisance. Princess Kadiya sank to her knees.

"Daughter of the Threefold, what have your people done that the great balance of the world no longer holds firm? That death and pain have come into this — the last stronghold?"

Kadiya could not believe that she was actually being accused — it was only that this being wanted the truth. Slowly, Kadiya arose.

"Firstly" — she strove to give her words the same easiness that the other's held — "I am the daughter of King Krain of Ruwenda. Those of Labornok, under Voltrik, using treachery and force of arms, and above all, the talents of an evil sorcerer, have laid waste my country. By the aid of the Nyssomu hunter Jagun I escaped from the Citadel at its fall. Then I went to the Archimage who rules at Noth, and this was given to me." She picked up the root and held it out. "On me she set also a solemn task — that I must search for a certain talisman. It has been foretold that only through a woman of our house may justice be wrought for Ruwenda. The Archimage named me and my sisters Petals of the Living Trillium. There are three of us — although I am not sure now that the others still live. And this small trillium-root has led me here."

"The Archimage of Noth," the robed one said slowly. "It has been long years since she sent one here to the Place of Knowledge. But if she does, we can well believe that there are shadows abroad in the land. By the ancient ways life must here be so —" The stranger held out one hand horizontally and set the other under it vertically. "Dealing with the Dark Powers upsets the balance. Once before this happened, and there was a mighty battle and a rending of the earth. Dry land became water, water became land, and the Conquering Ice formed a shroud over all."

Kadiya asked: "How did those of blood find the road to this place, and pass the barrier which holds back the Nyssomu?"

"King's Daughter, once the smallest opening is made in a wall, it may spread to a tumble of stone. This sorcerer you have spoken of as your enemy reaches high and has learned much. He has given certain protection to his followers which have proven keys for the unlocking of our ancient gates. King's Daughter" — the woman pointed to the root still in Kadiya's hand — "finish out your journey here. If the Archimage of Noth has chosen you, then you will indeed go into battle. Whether you stand alone or not, that will also come from your own actions."

"There is no safety here in the Place of Knowledge?"

"Not from what has come — for have I not been summoned by the threat of the Dark Powers?" Her head went up as if she listened. "So! They do not have quite as much power as they think. The secret way which led you here is closed and they must now cast back and forth blindly with their Skritek. The old protection holds after all."

"What do they seek?"

"That which they deem treasure, King's Daughter. But what the troops of Labornok and the Skritek are greedy for is not what moves their master. He seeks what is forbidden and his followers are greatly wearied. They would return to the Citadel without that which would appease him."

"And what about the talisman that I seek?" Kadiya cried. She

∴

dropped the trillium-root and it did not move; its color had faded. "Where is the Three-Lobed Burning Eye that the Archimage commanded me to find?"

"Look within you, King's Daughter — open wide your heart and mind."

Kadiya stared. "I have no magical talisman! I have no army! I have not even a sword — "

"All these exist, King's Daughter." There was a chill in that answer. "Look within yourself and you shall see!"

And she was gone.

Kadiya sank down onto her knees. Nothing in that wondrous garden charmed her now. She was spent, lost. Only the shriveled-looking root of the Black Trillium was left to her.

Magic! She pounded both fists against the pavement until the pain of her bruised flesh broke through the consuming rage. Look within her, look within her! Within was fury! Leaning forward she snatched up the stem which had mocked her and led her to this useless place and strove to shred it between her fingers. But it resisted.

One of three.

Out of nowhere came the phrase which rang in her head. Kadiya looked up quickly. Had that sentinel-woman returned? No, only the silly garden lay before her and the worthless root-guide.

With all her force the girl threw the root from her. It flew through the air with the precision of one of Jagun's darts, turning but once in flight so that it landed, root end down, upon a patch of open earth in front of her. There it stood upward, quivering a little. Kadiya scrambled up, thinking to finally crush it. But she held back. Before her eyes it was growing thicker, taller, wider. Wondering, Kadiya crouched before it, watching. Two smaller stems sprouted from near the top and straightened into bars. Below them the stem enlarged even more, forming a thick dark cylinder. At the very tip it budded — or so it seemed, for there three spheres grew, closely conjoined.

Kadiya watched, amazed, hardly daring to believe what she now saw. There was movement in each of those spheres, a splitting of their black covering. What was revealed were —

Three eyes.

One was an eye of the Folk, yellow-green. One was gleaming brown — and Kadiya had only to look into a mirror to see its like in

∴

her own head. The third was silvery blue, with its pupil enormously wide, and in the depths a spark of golden fire.

Her amulet burned at her breast.

Before she could put hand to it the trillium amber sprang up as though it were a thing alive, and the golden chain about her neck broke, and the amulet flew toward the Three-Lobed Eye and became fixed at the place of the spheres' juncture.

Even as those three eyes had opened, so they closed again, leaving three featureless black globes behind. The girl took hold of the stem just below their swell and above the outthrust leaves, then with a certainty that this is what must be done, she pulled.

What she drew forth from the earth was not the root end of the broken plant, but a gleaming sword! And one whose hilt fitted so well into her hand that it might have been forged for her alone. Kadiya fingered the three spheres on the pommel.

"The Three-Lobed Burning Eye." She was overcome with delight. But then she noted that the bright weapon was dulled at the edges and lacking a point! "Lords of the Air, what manner of sword is this? How can I use such a thing against my enemies?"

A soft voice, hardly more than a breath in her ear, said: *Learn.*

∴

27

"What are you doing?" Anigel shrieked to the racing rimoriks. "We cannot go this way — we will be killed!"

But the animals made no reply and only swam faster, so that the boat fairly tore through the water and it was all the Princess could do to brace her feet against the bow-wood and hang onto the reins. Her mind refused to accept that these animal friends, these loyal creatures who had brought her so far, were now pulling the punt with her and Immu in it straight toward the brink of Tass Falls.

Anigel saw the drop-off coming closer and closer. She was incapable of uttering a sound now, unable to form one single coherent thought that she might have flung at the minds of the rimoriks to turn them aside from their suicidal folly. Even the trillium amulet was out of reach, since the reins wound around her hands were so taut that she feared her arms might be yanked from their sockets. She thought not at all of Immu, so convinced was she that her own death was approaching.

The sound of the waterfall grew to a roar. Air-borne droplets of water thrown up by the cascade soaked her clothing and her hair. Her eyes were locked on the approaching rim, where the flowing water changed from the near-black of the deep lake into a glorious medley of blue, aquamarine, green — and finally white. As the punt finally neared the brink it slowed abruptly. Anigel unwound the reins from her hands, threw them down, and gripped the gunwales. She gasped as two great dark bodies leapt up, throwing a shower of diamond-bright spray, and then plunged out of sight.

The bow of the punt where she sat thrust out into mid-air. For an instant she was able to look down, beyond the tumult of whiteness that was the face of the cascade, and see a great azure pool with tiny buildings on the lefthand shore. From the pool flowed a wide, many-channeled watercourse that shone like a silver braid in the high sunlight, winding away through the dark green expanse of the Tassaleyo Forest until it was lost in purple haze.

She saw this picture with her keen eyes, and her mind seemed to hear Immu and the two rimoriks say: *Trust!*

And then the punt tipped forward, and there was flying spray all around her and a hundred circular rainbows, and she began to fall through a terrible crashing white world that soon faded into blank nothingness.

In the new dream her Mother, Queen Kalanthe, was walking swiftly along a path in an unfamiliar landscape that Anigel somehow recognized as a dryland forest, wearing her coronation robes and the awesome Crown of State. Anigel was a long distance behind, running to catch up with the Queen, crying out for her Mother to wait — but Kalanthe could not hear. There was nothing else to do but run faster, and Anigel did this with her heart thudding in her breast and her lungs burning and her legs hurting so badly that she would have cried out at each step except for lack of breath. She should have given up, thrown herself to the ground in despair, and let the Queen hurry away; but instead she forced herself to go on.

And then the miracle: the Queen stopped, and turned, and waited smiling while the girl staggered up with the last of her strength and collapsed into her Mother's arms, weeping with happiness.

"Dear little daughter," Kalanthe said. "I was so afraid you wouldn't come either. Your sisters have gone on other roads, you know. But all will be well now, just as soon as we get you ready."

Then, amazingly, the dream-Queen led Anigel to a nearby brook, opened a velvet pouch, and took out soap and a soft cloth and an ivory comb. "We must clean you up," Kalanthe said, "and dress your hair, and find you rich robes to wear so your subjects will recognize you."

The wash-cloth rubbed away at the dirt on Anigel's face. Rubbed

∴

harder and harder until the flesh stung and the Princess cried out —

And woke up.

She was lying on soft ground heavily carpeted with moss, near a riverbank. A tiny creature with striped yellow fur, a pointed face, and big black eyes was licking her cheek with its rough tongue. When she uttered a cry of surprise, the little thing squeaked in alarm and scuttled away into the dense undergrowth. An unfamiliar white bird was singing on the lowest branch of the tree she lay under, its complex song threading like a bright ribbon through the sound of distant thunder. The river a few ells away had numerous small channels flowing and intermingling on either side of a broad, twisting mainstream, and there were mudflats and low-lying islands everywhere.

I'm alive!

The realization came to her slowly, and she moved each arm and leg in turn, and her fingers, and then slowly sat up. Her woven-grass garment was in tatters, as was the worn linen shift beneath. Her feet were still shod in the Discerner's stout leather sandals, but her buskins were mostly torn to shreds. She still had her belt with its wallet attached, and the trillium amulet hung about her neck. Her skin was caked with mud but quite dry, which meant that she must have been lying on the bank for some time. She had no memory of how she had got there.

Walking carefully over decaying driftwood, she went down to the riverside. From the water's edge she had a clear view upstream. Along the entire northern horizon was a high green rampart, rearing up out of the forest and cloven in two by a silvery swatch — the waterfall. It looked like it was at least a league away. The great blue pool at its base was not visible, nor were the buildings she had glimpsed momentarily before plunging over the brink. There was only the broad, shallow river, its flow dissected into scores of braided channels, and the dense forest on either bank, which had vivid blue-green foliage very different in hue and texture from the jungle woodlands of the Mazy Mire. Even the smell was different — sharper, more resinous, with occasional whiffs of unfamiliar flower-fragrance.

"I'm alive," she said, wonderingly. Then she flung out her scratched and mud-smeared bare arms and cried: "Alive!"

In that same instant, guilt smote her. Immu! Where was Immu? And her two loyal rimorik friends? She peered up and down the riverbank, but saw only long-legged vermilion birds with spearlike beaks, dabbling in the shallows. For a moment panic threatened to overwhelm her. She was alive, yes; but all alone in the Tassaleyo Forest with no notion of what to do next.

Should she call out? What if the Labornoki searchers had followed her and were lurking somewhere, listening? There was no place she could go, no path along the bank, only the small clearing with its decaying driftwood, surrounded by dense shrubbery, and further inland the massive trunks of soaring trees.

Were Immu and the animals dead?

A terrible thought struck her. She recalled Immu's strange, almost resigned attitude as she repacked their lunch things back on the lake. Immu had tied the packs to the thwart! She had never done that before. Had she known what awful escape route the rimoriks would take?

"Did she stay with me out of love," Anigel asked herself in a whisper, "hoping that I would survive the plunge, since I had been given rimorik-strength by the miton — but knowing that she would surely die?" She felt her heart contract. Oh, Immu. Dear old friend.

But she mustn't start blubbering uselessly! It was time to get on with it . . . Why not take some of the sacred drink to build up strength, then try again to summon the rimoriks.

She found a moss-covered rock in the shade, opened her wallet, and took out the scarlet gourd with its net covering. Removing the stopper and lifting it to her lips, she closed her eyes and uttered an unspoken prayer. Then her mind called: *Friends!*

There was a sudden splash.

She opened her eyes and saw two sleek heads out in the main river channel a stone's throw away. Rising, she waited for them to haul themselves over the shoals and rivulets, their glossy pelts getting more muddy with each awkward shove of their flippers. Finally the pair of rimoriks reached her and rested in the shallows, regarding her solemnly with huge black eyes.

Human friend, we have searched for your friend of the swamp Folk.

"Immu . . . did you find her?"

No. We went a long way, looking. But the Water That Flows to the Sea is wide and has many backwaters where your friend's body might have been washed.

Anigel's eyes stung and she pressed a knuckle to her lips to stifle a cry. "Her body! . . . You do not think she survived the falls?"

We searched. We did not find her. Now it is time to go on. Your human

enemies are coming down the Great Vine That Takes Trees to the Sky. They
will catch you if we do not take you away.

Anigel understood at once that the Labornoki were descending via
the log-lift into the Great Mutar Valley. For a moment she was tempted
to command the rimoriks to resume their search for Immu; but in her
mind's eye she seemed to see her good old Oddling nurse shaking one
taloned finger and scolding her. Was Immu's sacrifice going to be
wasted? She had not died on a whim, to comfort an ordinary girl. Her
great gesture was intended to show her loving support for a Princess
on a quest, who must not shrink from facing the worst tragedies or
dangers. Immu had gone bravely to her death. It was up to Anigel to
press on, now that she was so close to her talisman.

"Did you find the punt?" she asked the rimoriks.

Your boat is smashed into small pieces. We found your friend's pack, but
not yours. We have taken a boat belonging to the forest Folk. It is hidden over
here.

They waddled and wallowed downstream for a dozen ells before
turning into the deeper water of a narrow creek. There was nothing
for Anigel to do but wade into the river and follow them. The bottom-
mud was as soft and tenacious as glue, and she dared not stop moving
lest she sink down and become trapped. Splashing along frantically,
she caught up with the rimoriks as they nosed a fairly large, oddly
made watercraft out of the creek mouth into waist-deep water.

It was perhaps twice as long as the wooden punt had been, but
narrower in the beam. Its white frame looked like it was made of soft
bone or ivory-wood, lashed together with dried sinews. The hull was
translucent, hard but resilient, almost like dull, flexible glass. Pieces of
this strange material were stitched together in nicely sewn patchwork
and the seams smeared with some shiny, waterproof resin. The craft
rode high in the water and must have been of negligible weight.

Anigel flopped in. Immu's sodden pack lay on the bottom. "There
are no reins, friends. And you seem to have lost your harnesses. How
am I going to drive?"

They grinned at her. *This boat need not be pulled. It floats as easily as*
a dry seedpod. We will swim along on either side, pushing, and you shall tell
us which way to go.

The Princess settled herself and opened her belt-wallet. From it she
took the unwilted leaf of the Black Trillium. For the first time, she

∴

noticed that the upper portions of the golden vein, those representing the part of her journey already completed, were beginning to fade to brown. Below a large tan spot that represented Lake Wum, the golden vein twisted and turned over a distance about as long as Anigel's little finger before entering the very short, sharply bent stem.

"There is some distance to go yet," she told the animals, "but it seems to be entirely on the Great Mutar River. I suppose we must simply travel on as fast as we can, keeping ahead of the enemy soldiers, until I receive some magical sign."

Do you wish us to take you to the forest Folk of the River?

"Why—" Anigel hesitated. "I never thought of that. Perhaps you had better. Those would be the Wyvilo, I suppose. Do they have villages?"

There is one place only where they live. We will take you there.

"Very well," said the Princess.

Growling and woofing with the effort of moving out of their element, the rimoriks nudged and shoved the boat over one mudflat after another, sliding it along through subsidiary streamlets whenever they could, until it finally reached the main channel. There the big creatures rolled about in the dark clean water for a few minutes in evident relief before settling in on either side and beginning the journey down-river. Without any urging from Anigel, they propelled the craft rapidly along.

She guessed that it must be late afternoon. Opening Immu's drenched pack, the girl laid out her nurse's sleep-sack and a few pieces of extra clothing to dry. Fortunately, Anigel was a small person, so she would be able to use the things. There was a soft, wide-brimmed grass hat, a little leather raincloak, and an extra pair of buskins to wear under her sandals. The supply of trail-ration roots was now running very low and Anigel carefully set out the remaining ones to redry in the hot sun. The fruit leather had been eaten up long ago, and they had been living mostly upon wild fruit and nuts, augmented with the shared prey of the rimoriks. She would have to be very careful about sampling unknown plant-food. So many of the most tempting-looking things had been designated deadly poison by Immu. Thanks be to the Lords of the Air and Immu's ironshell fire-making kit (which would be serviceable again once the damp tinder dried out), she would be able to broil her fish instead of eating them raw. The rest of Anigel's treasury consisted of her own small knife and the other items in her wallet: a comb,

∴

a handkerchief that she rinsed out each day, a small cup, and a sliver of soap.

"My riches, my royal robes, and my sumptuous foods," she declared, surveying the poor collection of things laid out on the bottom of the boat. "And two faithful retainers to stand by me. What more could any princess ask?" Sighing, she found a clear space in the bottom of the boat and lay down with the hat shading her face. *My friends, I think I am going to sleep.*

They said: *It is a good thing for you to do.*

Freed from the chore of driving for the first time since they had left Noth, Anigel fell into a dreamless doze, too weary even to mourn Immu. She woke hours later, when the rimoriks beached them on a small, narrow island where the grass grew in soft, clean sand instead of mud. The evening was very warm, but the island was swept by a cool breeze that kept the stinging insects at bay. The bed of the Great Mutar had widened as they traveled downstream and now was almost too wide to see across. The forest on both sides was nearly lost in the deepening haze. From far away came a trumpeting sound, the cry of some large animal. But Anigel was confident that her friends had chosen a safe place for her to spend the night.

One small bruddok shrub grew on their island. She drowsily congratulated the rimoriks for having found it. They bared their fangs briefly and swam away to hunt. The Princess ate a few of the sweet, juicy fruits, made a nest of the sleep-sack beneath the "traveler's friend," and burrowed into it.

Once again, her sleep was without dreams.

Prince Antar's force spent all of the next day searching the great pool at the foot of Tass Falls, but had no luck finding the bodies of Princess Anigel or her companion. The remains of her wooden punt were found washed up near the deserted sawmill, and the consensus among the knights was that no one could have survived the trip over the cascade. Their opinion counted for naught, however. The decision whether to call off the hunt rested with the sorcerer Orogastus. The Blue Voice would confer telepathically with his master on the morrow, when fresh intelligence would have been vouchsafed by the all-seeing ice-mirror.

The search-party made camp at the pool's edge — knights, men-at-arms, and the flatboat crews who had been pressed into service for the

∴

body-search. Sitting around their bonfires that evening (the sinister chorus of nocturnal hoots and roars emanating from the forest behind the mill insured that no one strayed far), the Labornoki commoners were in a mood of suppressed cheerfulness. With the Princess surely dead, they looked forward to returning to the civilized comforts of the Citadel. Most of the knights felt disappointed, cheated of their chance for glory. It seemed unlikely that the force would go any further down the Great Mutar, searching for the mysterious talisman that the sorcerer had set his heart on.

Contrary to expectations, only three Wyvilo boats had been found at the lower landing, and there were no aborigines in evidence to serve as guides. The Master-Trader Edzar feared that the forest Oddlings had retreated to their large village, called Let, when the Labornok invasion brought a halt to the timber trade. There was small hope they would come back up-river before the next dry season.

Prince Antar sequestered himself in his pavilion that night, refusing even the kindly overtures of Sir Owanon and his other loyal friends. His grief at the apparent death of the Princess was an open secret, the simple Sir Penapat having blabbed to all hearers how distraught Antar had been when the punt was swept over the falls.

The following morning, the Blue Voice was alerted mentally by Orogastus and retreated to his own small tent for a long telepathic conference. Antar was left to cool his heels meanwhile, and with Sir Owanon took the opportunity to study more closely the water-powered mill, and the lift mechanism that had transported them all down the escarpment.

"The elevating device is most cunningly made," the Prince remarked, craning his neck for a better look at the woven-steel hoist cables. "All one need do is load a single giant log, or a batch of lumber, onto the platform. The huge counterweight and the system of pulleys insure that the draft animals at the top are able to lift the heaviest load without a great exertion of energy."

"Ingenious, these Ruwendians," Owanon said. "Still, we have similar machines in the shipyards at Derorguila, even if they be not so large."

Antar said in a low voice: "Large though it is, the lift can hardly handle the great flatboats that brought us down the lake, even if we could wrestle the things along the skid-road. We could lower the punts, certainly. But they would be inadequate to transport our entire force and its necessary supplies down the Great Mutar."

Owanon nodded agreement. "Effectively, our expedition is stalled."

"This is what I have instructed the Blue Voice to tell the sorcerer. I have no intention of leading a blind search into the Tassaleyo for this magical talisman he covets so greedily. Yet I would not put it past him to press such an adventure upon us. I will depend upon you and Dodabilik to support me when I decline to take our force any further."

"This goes without saying, my Prince."

Antar's face was grave within the open visor of his blue-enameled helm. "I fear the sorcerer will use this expedition's failure to further diminish me in my Royal Father's eyes. The insidious spellmonger knew full well that I have no stomach for this harrying of helpless women. And there was also my breakdown at the lighthouse yesterday . . ."

Owanon was tactfully silent.

The Prince eyed his friend with an expression that was both sad and self-mocking. "Do all of them know that I had fallen in love with her, Owan?"

"Aye, my Prince. But the better men think none the less of you for it. One cannot help the inclinations of the heart. And you have carried out King Voltrik's commands meticulously. No true-spoken man can say that you shirked your duty."

"Orogastus can," the Prince retorted bitterly. "He has always hated and envied me, convincing the King that I am too immature to grasp great matters of state. This damnable invasion . . . the monstrous cruelty with which we treated the vanquished Ruwendians . . . all the sorcerer's doing! He has turned my father into his creature, playing upon his fears and encouraging his basest instincts."

Again Owanon forbore to speak.

"King Voltrik was not always a cruel man," the Prince said. "When I was a small boy and my dear stepmother Shonda yet lived, he was a noble Crown Prince, a loving husband and father, and a man of sanguine and kindly spirit. It was only after the coming of Orogastus that his soul became envenomed. Father had to wait too long for his throne, and the luckless Shonda was barren, and the sorcerer encouraged and abetted every wicked and extravagant ambition that stole into Father's mind. Even the contriving of Shonda's death."

Owanon said gently, "These sad matters are common knowledge, my Prince. But your father brooks no criticism of Orogastus — and he is King."

"Yes," sighed Antar. "Only sometimes, when I remember the awful scene when he ripped the regal diadem from the brow of the dying King Sporikar, and his terrible glee anticipating the bloodshed that our invasion of Ruwenda would occasion, I fear that the sorcerer has driven him mad. But to suggest this would be high treason, of course."

Owanon's face was somber. "You would not be alone in your belief. There were many in our army who thought the invasion of Ruwenda unwise. But I fear these matters must worsen before they can be bettered." At that moment he spied a man running toward them, and cautioned the Prince to silence.

It was Rinutar rushing up, his armor clanking and his face alight with a malicious grin. "My Prince! Amazing news! The Lord Orogastus has determined that Princess Anigel yet lives. She is on her way down the Great Mutar. You are commanded to follow her, but only with your body of knights and a servant for each. And here is the strangest part! The sorcerer no longer commands that the girl be hindered from her quest and killed. On the contrary — she is to be given free rein! And only after she has secured her magical talisman are we to seize her and put her to death."

Antar stared at the knight thunderstruck. "She lives," he whispered.

"So says the ice-mirror." Rinutar's smirk was insolent. "I had a feeling you'd be pleased . . . at being given another chance at her."

28

The lammergeier said to Haramis, *There is the cave you seek.*

On this morning, the storm having blown away, the fresh-whitened southern face of Mount Gidris was so dazzling bright that Haramis was almost blinded. Even shading her eyes with her gloved hand, she could not see the place Hiluro pointed out. But the great bird spiraled down, down, down, and what had been a featureless glare became a vast bowl just beneath the mountain's summit, from which a colossal glacier flowed.

The river of ice poured over a steep precipice before beginning its gentler descent toward the Ruwendian basin, fracturing into a mass of titanic ice-blocks that were partially buried in new snow. The cracks and chasms of the icefall glowed with a hundred varied shades of blue . . . but in the midst of the tumble shone an unexpected golden gleam.

As the great bird flew closer, Haramis saw that this was an upthrust spire of rock, milky in color but flecked with gold. What had seemed a fragile needle viewed from afar soon became an outcropping some eighty ells high and five ells in width, apparently formed of white quartz with sparkling inclusions of precious metals. The glacier had so abraded it over the ages that it resembled a slender tower making a valiant effort to remain above a chaotic, frozen sea. Halfway up the spire was an opening, with a narrow rock shelf just below it.

I can only hover while you alight, Hiluro told Haramis. *The ledge is too narrow for me.*

The huge black-and-white bird descended. The mouth of the cave was twice the height of the Princess, but seemed smaller because of the dangling icicles that fringed it like diamond fangs. Almost all of the small ledge was slippery ice, in which gold nuggets and chunks of white rock were embedded.

Haramis touched her amulet, offered a wordless prayer, and clasped Hiluro's feathery neck. Her hands just met, and she locked her fingers tightly together. She hung blind, her fur cloak billowing and the toes of her boots pointing down. And she heard not only the shrill piping sound of air rushing through wing-plumage, but also a thunderous growl, and along with it a deep, eerie ensemble of musical notes, as if some giant's fiddle were being bowed.

Her feet touched a firm surface. She relaxed, sank slowly with hands still holding the bird's neck, then let go. Opening her eyes, she saw the huge form shooting skyward while she rested precariously on her knees at the entrance to her goal: a cave of glittering ice with its entrance gold-framed —

Or so it seemed.

Overcome with awe, Haramis looked about her. The rock-spire in the midst of the glacier vibrated like a tuning-fork to the constant scraping flow of the ice, which filled the air with an immense musical sound. How many thousands of years had the ice ground away at this hard, gold-veined quartz mass before diminishing it to its present slenderness? Seen from close by, the rock tower looked incredibly fragile. The cave's mouth, bordered with large amorphous lumps of gold, was partially barred by icicles that were beginning to melt in the brilliant sunlight.

Haramis climbed to her feet, slipped cautiously through the dripping tusks of ice, and came into the interior chamber, whose walls and ceiling were streaked with flows of black ice.

A pale glimmer behind the ice-sheet at the back of the cave attracted her attention. She moved toward it, on realizing that the trillium amulet she wore was warm against her breast, as if it were calling to something. Was the glimmering object the talisman destined for her?

She moved closer to the great dark mass of ice and to whatever it was that glowed beneath it. She still could not see it clearly, but her amulet continued to grow warmer against her skin. Might her talisman itself be trapped in the ice? If so, how could she get it out?

She moved still closer to the mysterious gleam. Her trillium-amber was now so hot that it was burning her breast. She pulled off her gloves, hooked a finger around the amulet's chain, and pulled it from under her tunic. The flower flashed as if it were afire, and the amulet was so hot she could barely touch it. She slid the chain carefully over her head and held it so the amber dangled in front of her face. Instead of hanging at the end of the chain, however, the amulet pulled away from her, drawn to the glow in the wall. The blazing light from the embedded trillium turned an entire section of the wall bright gold. The glare was painful, filling her eyes with a large gold spot encircled by a bright blue corona.

The amulet dragged her several steps closer to the wall. Now it gave off such extreme heat that Haramis turned her head away from it. Out of the corner of her eye, outside of the area where the light blinded her, she could see water flowing in a thin stream down the wall. The amulet was actually melting the ice!

Suddenly there was a flash of silver amid the gold as something melted free and slid to the floor. The amulet's glow faded and it cooled rapidly, falling back against her clothing. Haramis bent quickly to grasp whatever had been freed before it could refreeze into the puddle on the cave floor. Before she could focus her eyes on it she felt its weight in her hand.

She waited patiently for her vision to clear. Her eyes hurt, and she fought the impulse to rub them. But even through the pain, deep within her heart a tremendous sense of *rightness* bloomed. For an instant, she understood the pattern of the world and her place in it. She knew all, had power over all, commanded all. She had become what she always knew she could be . . .

. . . but for a moment only. And then the transcendent feeling was gone.

She stood in the ice-cave, now lit only indirectly by the sunlight outside, and realized that she could see normally again. She held a wand made of silver metal, about half the length of her forearm. At one end was a small ring to accommodate the chain, and at the other, a kind of hoop, much larger, that she could have passed both her closed fists through. At the circlet's top was a projection that she at first took to be a flower made of the same white metal; but when she looked more closely, she saw that what she had mistaken for petals were instead three small wings, upright.

The Three-Winged Circle.

∴

Her talisman. At last.

Then you will know that the final struggle for Ruwenda, and for your own soul, is at hand . . .

The words of the Archimage seemed to echo in the gold-and-crystal cave, and Haramis gave a great start, crying: "Who's there?"

But immediately she knew that she was still alone, and her mind harked back to the feeling of incredible power that had suffused her when the talisman was first freed from its icy imprisonment.

The amulet and talisman both flared to light simultaneously. Reflexively Haramis dropped them both and brought both hands up to shield her eyes. But even through the palms of her hands she could see glowing radiance. She kept her hands in place until the light faded, then slowly lowered them. Her vision was a little blurry, but this time she was not completely blinded. She knelt quickly to look for the amulet and talisman, hoping they hadn't decided to freeze themselves into the floor. *Do they think I'm unworthy of them?* she wondered anxiously.

To her vast relief they lay loose on the surface of the ice. But now they had fused together, with her trillium amulet nestled within the wings of the wand.

It was a source of power. Of magic . . .

Yes — *this* was magic!

"And how will I learn to use this power?" Her gaze was fixed upon the three wings. "The White Lady said that there were two other talismans for my sisters, and if all three of us succeeded in our quest, then the resolution would come. But that doesn't tell me much."

Within the silvery ring beneath the wings, pearlescent vapors seemed to flow. Almost dreamily, Haramis found herself commanding the talisman: "Show me if my sisters have succeeded!"

And she saw Kadiya.

Her sister stood in the midst of a great crowd of Oddlings — Uisgu, judging from their small stature — holding up in one hand a shining thing like a Sword of Mercy, a blade lacking a point, with a pommel resembling three conjoined black fruits. The Folk were cheering her.

"Yes," Haramis murmured, "you were likely to win through. But poor little Anigel . . . Where are you, timid one?"

The Circle was wiped clear of Kadiya's image. In its place, another formed, at first unrecognizable — but then Haramis gasped.

Anigel! Golden hair streaming, face no longer plump-cheeked and sweetly pale but lean, flushed, exultant. Sapphire eyes narrowed and flickering from side to side with a keen alertness Haramis never would have thought possible. Ani, dressed in muddy rags, sitting in an exotic boat that fairly flashed down some wide river, leaving a white wake behind it. Ani, timid little Ani, smiling grimly while some fierce-looking water-creatures pushed the boat along at breakneck speed . . .

"Impossible!" Haramis exclaimed.

And the vision winked out.

Haramis stared at the empty Three-Winged Circle. "Are these true visions? Is the talisman so easy to command?"

A third vision: the Archimage, lying in bed, distinctly weaker than when Haramis had seen her in person, her eyes closed and her skin waxen. Although the creased and sunken lips did not move, Haramis seemed to hear her speak:

All three of you must accomplish your foreordained tasks, mastering your own selves above all, before Ruwenda may cast off the yoke of Labornok and the balance of the world be restored. And if one fails, all fail . . .

"But that doesn't make sense!" Haramis protested. "I am Queen of Ruwenda; the duty is mine. And the prophecy of your own Folk says that *a* woman will bring down King Voltrik — not three of them!"

The dying Archimage opened her fathomless eyes. Still her lips were unmoving.

But I told you also that Voltrik was not your greatest enemy . . . The vision of the Archimage disappeared.

Something flickered in the icy mirror of the wall where the talisman had been. Haramis looked up and saw the smiling face of a white-haired man.

His age was unguessable; the passing of years had left no trace upon his fine features. He wore robes of black and silver, and sat at a table on which several strange devices rested, with a great book and a tablet half-covered with writing. He held a stylus in one strong hand and a half-eaten rosy ladu-fruit in the other. It was this last homely thing — hardly to be expected of a devil in human form — that made Haramis begin to return his smile.

"Princess Haramis." His voice was as clear as though he stood beside her. "Welcome to our company."

"And what company is that?" she retorted, tightening her lips. "That of Labornoki murderers? Unlike you, Orogastus, I am particular about the company I keep!"

The sorcerer laughed and put down pen and fruit. "You have a rare

∴

spirit, Lady. I must admit that King Voltrik and General Hamil and their ilk are not the companions I would have chosen — had it not been that I had no choice."

"No choice?" Haramis asked skeptically.

Orogastus continued with perfect amiability. "The company I welcomed you to was that of magic-wielders. I confess that our number is somewhat reduced in these latter days, consisting of only you, me, and Binah — she whom you call the Archimage. And I fear that soon only you and I will remain."

"Are you planning to kill the White Lady, now that she is too weak to defend herself?" Haramis spoke coldly.

"My dear child — of course not! I am no wanton killer. No, what stalks Binah is old age and death." He looked saddened and pensive. "I fear it comes to all of us in time. Some thirty years ago, there were left in the world only two persons of power: my mentor, Bondanus, and Binah. Bondanus passed his power on to me. Binah, against all logic, would dilute hers by bequeathing it to three of you."

"In order to save Ruwenda!" Haramis cried.

"Ruwenda . . ." The sorcerer shook his head in gentle mockery. "Your talisman has the potential to do so much more than rescue Ruwenda! Binah's vision, like her life, is dimming. She truly does not know what power the Threefold Talisman can command! But you, Haramis, have centuries ahead of you in which to study and use it."

"Centuries?" Haramis blinked. This had never occurred to her. *Does using magic prolong life — and by that much?*

"Centuries," Orogastus repeated firmly. "Always assuming, of course, that you don't accidentally kill yourself with it." He gestured to the talisman she held.

Idiot! Haramis told herself. *You would sit there holding it in plain sight. Apparently he recognizes it. But how? How much does he really know about it? The Archimage seems unable to teach me, and I don't have time to discover its use by trial and error — not if I want to save my kingdom and my sisters.*

"The Three-Winged Circle." Orogastus was smiling. "I am happy that you found it. I have several books that speak of it, and I have always wished to see it."

"You have books about it?" Haramis asked. *I wish he'd go away and leave me to study his library!* "What do they say?"

"Quite a lot. Too much, I fear, for me to explain to you now — you would be an icicle before I had told you a sixth of it." He gestured at her surroundings. "You have been so engrossed in our delightful conversation that you have ignored the passage of time."

Haramis looked quickly around her. He was quite right; the sun was low in the sky, and the cave was getting dark and cold. She looked back at the mirror. Orogastus's clothing appeared lightweight, and there was plenty of light around him.

He beckoned to her. "Come to my home, Haramis, to my mountain tower. Let me teach you to use the talisman. It would be pleasant to have company here. Mount Brom is rather out of the way, and I seldom have visitors."

"You don't want my company," Haramis said, looking him straight in the eyes. "You just want the talisman."

To her surprise, Orogastus actually laughed, and seemed to mean it. "I forget how new this is to you. No one can take your talisman away. It is bonded to you, and for one who would try to take it there is only death. But you know next to nothing about the talisman's use. You scry with it!" He laughed. "The merest Oddling conjurer can do the same with a leaf-full of water . . . No, Haramis, you don't understand. But I will teach you. I have a great library and so many magical devices of the Vanished Ones that they defy numbering. I ask only the joy of sharing my knowledge with you. You are reputed to be quite a scholar — do you not know the joy that comes from the pursuit of knowledge? The exquisite satisfaction when what was unclear suddenly falls into a logical design and you comprehend it?"

"Yes." Haramis found herself nodding in agreement. "I do know what you mean."

"Then come to Mount Brom," Orogastus invited. "With the talisman you can summon your lammergeier to carry you to my tower — and be here in time for supper."

So he doesn't know Hiluro is here, Haramis thought. *At least he is not omniscient.*

Orogastus's face grew grave. "I swear by the powers we share that I will not seek to wrest the talisman from you by force, nor cause any harm to come to your person. May my powers leave me forever if I prove false to this oath." He laid his hand over his heart.

"So be it," Haramis murmured automatically, the formula familiar to her from years of witnessing oaths. The ice-mirror went dark.

∴

Well, now what? she wondered. *Do I go to him, go to the Archimage, stay here, or wander off somewhere and see what I can do on my own?*

Neither of the last two alternatives was in the least appealing. Also, the Archimage had not exactly ordered her to return immediately. "When you achieve your goal of the Three-Winged Circle, return to me," was what Binah had said. Had she meant simply the physical possession of the talisman, or was the ability to use it part of achieving the goal?

Since Binah did not command me to return when she bespoke me just now, perhaps she intends for me to master the talisman's use—and perhaps now is the time I should confront Orogastus . . .

While the sorcerer was undoubtedly dangerous, at least there would be warmth and food at his tower. *The Archimage did tell me that I should learn his weaknesses,* Haramis thought. *Presumably it is part of my destiny—and it will be a nice change to have my destiny taking place in comfortable surroundings! . . . And if I do run into trouble at Mount Brom, I can always ask Hiluro to carry me away.*

She suddenly became aware of an increased vibration of the rock spire and sounds coming from outside the cave. The thundering bass-notes of the grinding glacier blended with the clarion-cries of the lammergeier screeching a warning.

Haramis! Come out! Danger! Great danger!

She threaded the small ring of the talisman onto her neck-chain, tucked the wand into the bodice of her dress, and stepped over to the cave entrance. The icicles had all broken off from the tower's shuddering, and the chamber within the spire abruptly began to pitch and rock like a boat on a choppy river. Haramis lifted her arms. A familiar black-and-white form rocketed down out of the sun and something closed about her body, snatching her off the icy ledge. She saw a brief flash of gold, a clashing collapse of rainbow prisms, and a wheeling sky, violet-blue, behind a great crested head.

Then the lammergeier went into a slow glide, lifted its claw, and carefully held her while she climbed into the soft hollow between its outspread wings. Haramis risked a quick glance at the place where the quartz spire had been. Now only rock slightly less white than ice marred the glacier's surface, and only a few bits of gold glinted in the setting sun.

∴

There passed a night, and Kadiya slept between the sindona at the head of the stairs. She had made free with the bounty of the garden for food, but she had a feeling that to linger there was wrong. The living sentinel had not come again. Kadiya did not expect her as she lay, one hand tightly gripping her amulet. It was not true sleep into which she drifted, awoke, and drifted again.

That the invaders had somehow gained a way into this forbidden land she had already found proof. And there was Jagun — would he fall captive to some scouting party and end as had the poor remnant of a Uisgu who had besought her mercy?

Where should she go now? Retrace her path — face those who had hunted her here and might still wait to pull her down? That was sheer stupidity. Yet she had no guide, and to wander out into that strange garden would do her little good. To her right ran a lofty wall; she would follow it.

Jagun's hunter's bag, which had gotten hard usage, she had emptied and dried last night. She had had to discard some of the small packets in it, for by the time she had fished the bag out of the pool they were thoroughly soaked. She had gathered edible tubers from the garden, woven a lopsided net of grass to carry fruit, and refilled the water bottle. There was nothing more to keep her here, yet Kadiya turned once more to look into the garden. Forbidden it might be, yet there was something here that reached out to her — that had seemed to welcome her even in spite of the chilly demeanor of the sentinel.

Kadiya sighed and shouldered her bag. For her talisman she had devised a temporary sheath and slung it across one shoulder, and its steady weight there continued to reassure her that at least she had fulfilled a part of her quest. One sword — when an army was what she truly needed!

She walked for some ways along the high wall; and then it ended at a mighty gateway, and she saw within a broad stretch of park, and beyond that a gleaming city. Awed, she entered the gate and approached the place. Greenery half-smothered the silent houses, and grass and vines carpeted the streets. Yet beneath that assault of vegetation there was no sign of decay. The walls which showed through the shaggy drapery were not made of stone, she was certain, but rather of that same peculiar substance that had formed the bowl in which she and Jagun had spent the night.

Kadiya suddenly realized she was seeing the city of her dream. More walls rose beyond, enclosing it. She came into a wide avenue and walked on, marveling. The buildings on either side were well proportioned, and about their doorways and windows were indecipherable patterns in high relief. The avenue eventually led her to a gate nearly as tall as a three-story building. It stood ajar, and Kadiya walked out into a far different world where once again the swamp ruled — though the much worn remains of a road led off into it. What time had not touched within the city walls had been conquered here.

Luckily that eroded path had not been totally obliterated. She caught glimpses of the ominous yellow scum on either side of the roadway, but footing upon it appeared substantial enough. She stopped to cut a sturdy branch from a bush and use it to test the ground before she trusted her weight to it.

She had come well out into the Mire when she turned to look back — and then shook her head, unable to believe her eyes. What lay behind her now were broken ruins. Even the wall was tumbledown and over-grown by rampant jungle growth. Illusion!

But *which* was the illusion then — the mysterious garden and the dream city, or this? Had everything that had happened to her been enchantment? Yet, there was the weight of the talisman on her shoulder, and she raised her hand to feel the knobs of the Three-Lobed Burning Eye.

She walked on for what might have been several hours, seeing noth-

∴

ing unusual and hearing only the normal sounds of the swamp. Judging by the light of the sun, which always seemed to be in a haze here, it was midday or a little later. There were thickets of thorn-fern and high brambles ahead.

And then she heard it — the distinctive chirp of a ras beetle, voiced three times in a familiar rhythm. Jagun! It must be!

There was a slight movement in the bushes, and then she saw the face of her dear old friend grinning out at her. A dark spot of bruise puffed around one eye. That he had had no easy time of it was clear, for he wore a mass of pulped leaves tied with reed strings about his upper arm near the shoulder point, and he moved awkwardly.

Nor did he waste any time on greetings:

"They are here — the Skritek and soldiers."

She thought of those pathetic figures she had seen along the other road — and also of the distant bonfire, and the arrow that had marked a route . . . for someone. "I have seen signs that the enemy is near at hand."

Jagun's face was a mask, and his attention was not really on her, but on his own thoughts. "The Feast of the Three Moons nears," he whispered, "and the darkness gathers! But soon there will be fire aplenty, and it will be quenched only by blood . . ."

The Feast of the Three Moons. They had always celebrated it at the Citadel with feasting, and strange old songs had been sung by the bards, and a raft loosed on the river laden down with flowers and lighted by three-pronged candles. It was a time when the threat of ancient evil was driven away by the will of all. And when the three orbs shone high in the sky, close together in mystic conjunction, the people rejoiced beneath their benevolent radiance, and sang. But what did Jagun mean? Might he have foreseen some great battle upcoming at the time of the ancient celebration? A battle in which she might wield her talisman to the liberation of Ruwenda?

Before Kadiya could question him further, Jagun said: "The Skritek — and with them the sorcerer's Voice and a party of human soldiers — have fallen upon a Uisgu village. Fire they used, and magic summoned out of the air. The Folk they still hold captive will soon be meat for the Skritek."

"They seek me!" Kadiya cried. "This is why they harry the poor Uisgu!"

"Your capture would be a great triumph. But more than that draws them." He nodded back toward where the city of the garden lay hidden by illusion. "You have been there. And have you also fulfilled your quest?"

Wordless, Kadiya took the talisman from behind her back and held it up for him to see.

Though she had known Jagun since she had first begun walking, she had never seen such an expression of joy and exaltation upon his face. He half put out his hand as if to touch the weapon, but then held back. The black lobes at the hilt remained closed, dull, but the blade drew what weak sunlight there was to it.

Kadiya held the sword closer to him. Tears were pouring down his cheeks. He fell to his knees before her. "The talisman! Oh, Farseer . . . you have found it!"

"There is a custom of my people," she said slowly, "that a sword with a broken point stands for mercy." She shook her head. "To some I will not offer mercy. But to you —" She hesitated and then the sword gently touched Jagun on the head, and from some place she did not understand there came words of absolution:

"My dear friend, be of good heart. Take back your own name! Wear again the sacred armlet of the Nyssomu. You have broken no oath — you have only followed the course of things as they had to be. Bear no soul-burden from this time."

Then Jagun did what Kadiya had never seen before. When he had first come to the Citadel and spoken to her Father King Krain, he had saluted the monarch with both hands high in the manner she had seen him greet the First of the House in the village where they had stayed. But now his whole body inclined forward until his arms and forehead touched the earth.

"All service to you, Light Bearer, Hope Carrier, Protector and Defender — heart-kin of the Vanished Ones!"

Bemused, she held up the talisman. It was as if a far off echo reverberated his words. Yet something in her shrank, wanted nothing more than to thrust the magical blade back into the ground, to return it to what it had been — the root of the Black Trillium.

"Jagun, I do not know what you mean —"

He climbed to his feet and looked her eye to eye, the sturdy Master of Animals and royal huntsman of old. "Lady of the Eyes, learning shall be yours. And none will be called where they were not meant to serve."

"I do not know how to use this talisman," she protested. Never had she felt so at a loss. Even the rage which had always given her strength before was now missing.

"That knowledge, too, will come. Now you must begin the true work you were destined for."

She took a deep breath, then returned the talisman to its improvised sheath. "Very well. These beleaguered Uisgu," she said now, briskly. "Where are they?"

"Near the Upper Mutar. I heard them send out the Call, but it will be too long before they can be answered by other Folk. The Skritek"— his lips flattened, showing the sharply pointed small fangs so unlike her own teeth—"are not easily kept under control. They must be rewarded by blood . . . and flesh."

Kadiya swallowed. But she asked, resolutely: "Is there some way that we can aid the captive Uisgu?"

"Farseer, I would say such a deed is impossible. But to you the Forbidden Way was opened, and you bear that which is threefold. We shall see."

"Then let us be off," she said.

They no longer followed the road but took to a tortuous path through the broken lands of the Thorny Hell. When evening was near they sought a campsite, since they could not follow the trail through the night on land. But before they could bed down, a familiar and terrifying stench came faintly to them on the breeze. The Skritek were nearby!

Jagun had them both rub down with wads of acrid-smelling leaves that would mask their scent. Then he dropped belly down while the girl followed his example, and the two of them slithered through the underbrush. Moments later they crouched shoulder to shoulder, hidden behind the trunklike stems of the giant ferns, to look out on an open area.

It was a camp of sorts. A handful of men in rusty armor were gathered there, Labornoki soldiers. Between them and where Kadiya and Jagun crouched in hiding spears had been driven into the ground and roped together by twisted vines to form a pen. A pen filled with captives. None were males. About a dozen aboriginal women sat or lay in small groups within the cage. Two had children in their arms. There was about them such an air of misery and fear that Kadiya felt her heart contract. Her hand sought the talisman-sword and she stealthily drew it.

There came a faint wail, and one of the women clapped her hand over the mouth of a child. Four Skritek stood guard at the corners of the pen. One flung up his long-jawed head and bellowed, then took aim with his spear at the Uisgu woman holding the crying child.

Kadiya lowered the sword, although she still kept her left hand on its hilt while her right went to her knife-scabbard. There was a way of throwing her dagger she had learned only last season by watching a performer at a fair, and she had made it her own by much practice. She was sure she could hit the throat of the nearest Skritek guard! Oh, if she had only three or four archers at her back!

But she did not . . . and perforce controlled herself. The other Skritek laughed, and seemed to urge their fellow to fling his spear at the cringing mother and child.

Kadiya took hold of Jagun's arm. Could they not do *something?*

He opened his own left hand for an instant. On his palm rested a green lump which he held with the greatest care. It was an aworik, a strange fungus, hard to find but a good friend to any pursued by one of the large predators of the swamp.

But the enemy moved first. Two human soldiers came out of the thorn-ferns, dragging a Uisgu male between them. The Skritek menacing the mother hesitated, then lowered his spear.

While the attention of the invaders was centered on the new captive, Jagun drew out his blowgun. Rising to one knee, he flung the aworik with all his might, aiming at a place between the human soldiers and the prisoner pen. The brittle fungus shattered as it hit the ground, and from its shell flew a myriad of whirling spore-carriers, each one sharp-edged as a razor for all its buoyancy. Instantly, all of the captive Uisgu dropped to the ground, shielding their great eyes. But the Skritek and the Labornoki were taken by surprise. Those who were not blinded at once fell into a frenzy as the tiny aworik-blades slashed the vulnerable parts of their flesh before finally settling to the ground.

Jagun already had his blowgun ready and Kadiya heard the hiss of the first poisoned dart even if she did not sight its swift passage. One Skritek fell. With her talisman in one hand and her dagger ready in the other, the Princess leaped to her feet. The Skritek nearest her staggered sightless, waving his spear. The girl sent the dagger in the

∴

whirling throw she had practiced so long. It struck the soft throat of the monster and he crashed to the ground, thrashing in his death-throes. More poisoned darts from Jagun's pipe downed the other two Skritek. A bloody-faced soldier came at them with a short-sword, but Kadiya was ready for him, her talisman-sword upraised as if she were a trained Oathed Companion. She swung and felt the jar throughout her body as the talisman crushed the man's voice-box. He fell, strangling in his own blood. She stood stunned for a moment, unable to believe that she had been so able to use the magical sword.

There was a din of screams and cries. Jagun's darts were taking a toll of the remaining Labornoki soldiers. Dying Skritek roared and flailed their great limbs, gouging the earth with their talons. Kadiya raised the sword a second time and brought its dull edge down on the netting of rope which formed the wall of the pen. The vine parted as if melted, not cut.

"Out!" she screamed to the females inside, most of whom were already on their feet. Kadiya pointed with the sword. "Run! Into the thorn-ferns!"

They fled, Kadiya at their heels ready for any attack from other Skritek or soldiers. Jagun followed, having retrieved the Princess's dagger from the flesh of the monster she had slain.

Kadiya and the Uisgu came to a great river, undoubtedly the Upper Mutar, where a raft floated beside a large barge such as traders used. There were four soldiers there, slightly bewildered by the clamor they heard in the distance, and a single Skritek just rising out of the water with his jaws closed upon a writhing fish.

"Jagun!" Kadiya took in their peril in a second. They needed the hunter with his poisoned darts. She was no match for what faced them. But Jagun had lagged behind, making certain they were not followed.

The Labornoki soldiers, swords drawn, were moving to ring her round. Screams of terror came from the female Oddlings as the huge Skritek splashed toward them.

The girl felt a sudden warmth against her hand, so much that she shifted her grip from the hilt of the talisman-sword to the pointless and dulled blade, bringing it up before her. The three eyes on the pommel were open, regarding the nearest of the swordsmen moving in on her.

He gave a hoarse cry and staggered back, dropping his weapon and holding his hands to his own eyes. Kadiya did not know what had happened, she could only guess. She turned the talisman toward another soldier. This one screamed and blundered into his blinded fellow, who immediately whirled and cut at his third comrade, striking a mortal blow. Kadiya turned the sword to the last man. But he had seen what had happened to the others and he ducked, throwing himself forward to tackle her. Then he twisted and screamed. From the back of his neck protruded one of Jagun's poisoned darts. A tremendous splash came from the river as the Skritek was struck by another dart. As Jagun ran up, the two surviving sightless soldiers continued to hack at each other as if they had gone mad. Jagun shouted for them all to climb onto the raft. He sliced its mooring rope with Kadiya's dagger and tossed the blade on board. Two of the Uisgu women had picked up swords, and others readied the raft's poles.

"Quickly!" Jagun shouted. "More Skritek are coming! Cast off!"

Kadiya hastened to help the wounded climb aboard. The poles dug in and the raft responded. One of the women started a droning chant of the riverpeople, and the ones at the poles responded with accelerated swings. Then the powerful current took them.

"Jagun!" the Princess screamed. But he only shook his head, and then turned to confront five howling Skritek that burst out of the ferns. Helpless, the girl watched him lift his blowpipe against the charging monsters . . . and then the raft floated around a bend in the river, and Jagun's brave little figure was lost to sight.

The only weapons they had were the two swords, Kadiya's dagger, and the talisman. The Uisgu females did not even wear much in the way of clothing save their own bedraggled fur. There were eleven of them all told, and the two tiny children. Four of the aborigines wore leaf bandages matted with bloodstains, while many of the others nursed cuts from the aworik spore-cases or bruises dealt by their former captors.

"Lady?"

Kadiya had been mourning Jagun, but now she lifted her head. One of the Uisgu women had seated herself nearby.

"I am Nessak of Dezaras, once First of the House and Speaker of the Law. These" — one outflung arm indicated the others — "are also of the village of Dezaras. Misfortune came upon us as we journeyed. Our men the human soldiers gave to the Skritek and we were made to watch. These invaders seek secrets, Great Lady, which we have no knowledge of. For it is oath-bound upon us that we must not go into the forbidden place of the Vanished Ones — this place which has ever and ever been closed. When we could not speak of what we do not know, the human who led the others, one dressed all in red, ordered that we be held for the coming of more humans who walk with Skritek and seek to raise Dark against Light. This man went away down the river shortly before you came and rescued us . . . Now we are your servants forever, Lady, and we thank you for our deliverance. Will you tell us who you are and whence you come?"

"I am daughter to King Krain who was — and my name is Kadiya. These workers of evil have taken our land. My Father died of their cruelty, as did all those who followed him. My Mother also."

She caught her breath for a moment, looking dull-eyed down at the talisman. If she had only had it when the Labornoki invaded the Citadel! It had in some way defeated those soldiers — what might it have wrought upon King Voltrik himself?

"There was a prophecy," the Princess continued, stroking the closed eyes of the pommel, "that the defeat of these evildoers would come through a woman of my house. My two sisters and I journeyed forth, commanded by the Archimage Binah, she whom you call the White Lady, in search of that which would avenge our kin."

For the first time in what seemed like days, she thought of Anigel and of Haramis. How had they fared? Were both dead, and she the only one left to demand death price for their house?

"Anigel . . . Haramis . . ." She spoke their names aloud as if she called to them.

Under her hand there was movement. She snatched her palm from the pommel of the sword. Two of the eyes were opening! Eyes? No, not this time. Instead she saw two tiny pictures — visions! There was Haramis, in her hand a Black Trillium full opened. And Anigel next, cupping in her palms a similar one. Kadiya had no doubt now that her sisters did live, and that somewhere they awaited her and the hour of their mutual trial. Even as she was assured of that the eyelids closed and she looked once more on the blank spheres of the pommel. Kadiya sighed.

∴

"Lady," the Uisgu woman said gravely, "it is plain that you are the Light Bearer, the Hope Carrier — the Lady of the Eyes who is kin to the Vanished Ones."

Kadiya shook her head vehemently. "No, Speaker of the Law, I claim no kinship with the great ones of old, although this" — she drew her hand down the talisman — "might well have come from out of their far time. I do not know how I can bear light or carry hope. All I am sure of is that I must bring down King Voltrik and his sorcerer Orogastus, even if I must do so alone."

"Lady," Nessak said softly, "you do not stand alone. Those wicked ones who took us broke the great oath and met their punishment. You have been into the Place of Knowledge and passed harmless before the guardian sindona. You have been sent to *us*. You are the Lady of the Eyes — the one long awaited. So shall the Uisgu rise to your aid, though war has ever been forbidden us. Darkness walks the land, the great balance has been destroyed, and from the struggle ensuing no one stands apart! Once we reach Dezaras the Call will go forth and the Folk of the Uisgu race will march beside you."

Kadiya caught her breath. What she had suggested to Jagun, what she had been told could never happen now would come to pass. If the Oddlings arose they would turn the very Mazy Mire into a weapon against the invaders. Her will hardened. This would be full war, and if her talisman's secret could be mastered, the war would be won . . .

Her clenched hands dug nails into her palms. Time — she needed not only time but knowledge. She prayed her new allies might somehow deliver that.

∴

30

The rimoriks swam down the river pushing Anigel in the boat for three more days. Sometimes the main channel twisted near the forested bank, and the Princess gazed with awe at the strange trees. Some were very tall, with branches that looped and curved upward like a dancer's sinuous arms. Some had quaintly corrugated trunks, as if thousands of rings were piled one upon another, and slanted off-center this way and that in a manner that seemed to defy gravity. There were massive, squat trees like gargantuan tubers, broad at the ground and pointed at the top, sprouting a ludicrous crown of tiny branches with leaves that never ceased to tremble. There were groves of splendid gonda-trees, highly valued for construction, larger than any that grew in the Mazy Mire. Their huge columnar trunks were each wider than the great main gate of the Citadel, forming hushed green arcades lit by slanting golden sunbeams. There were flowering trees so packed with vivid scarlet and orange blossoms that they seemed afire. There were hulking, shabby-leafed trees with gnarled limbs and gaping holes in their trunks, which harbored noisy colonies of night-carolers. The variety of trees was so great that Anigel's mind was finally overwhelmed by them, and she was glad when the river's mainstream carried them far away from the banks.

It was obvious that during the Rains the wide, nearly empty bed of the Great Mutar ran brim-full in flood. The further downstream they traveled, the more great stacks of driftwood littered the channel, the dry bleached branches often brightly clothed in skeins of flowering vines. Huge flocks of birds inhabited the bottomland, feeding on the mudflats and in the shallows, and rising into the air squawking and shrieking when the boat sped through their midst. There were occasional animals to be seen—fat gray quadrupeds with gaping mouths that fed on aquatic plants in the sloughs, lithe fish-eating carnivores resembling giant pelriks, that the rimoriks greeted as comrades, and always numbers of the harmless little yellow-striped creatures that had awakened Anigel to the Tassaleyo, that swarmed about the shore vegetation and also lived on the river islands.

But no people.

Anigel questioned her friends about this. They told her that the Wyvilo had, for long years now, lived in only one large village. They sought safety in numbers, rather like certain fish or birds, since they were endlessly preyed upon by their Glismak cousins who lived downstream and in the depths of the inner forest.

Long ago, the rimoriks said, the Wyvilo had had no permanent abode and lived in small family groups. They had rather easily avoided their clumsier Glismak foes by never sleeping twice in the same place. But after the Wyvilo began trading with humankind they accumulated many things and were no longer able to wander. They became more and more rich as their lives were more endangered by the envious Glismak.

But they will not go back to their old ways. Such a pass would be worse to them than death. We cannot understand this.

"But I do," said the Princess to the rimoriks. "Humans have had a similar history. There is that within certain people that drives them always to do better, to learn more, to strive harder, to climb higher. Not all people are this way, but the urge is easily passed from parent to child. It is not a bad thing. It is a great mystery that the motive-power of the world drives living things—especially thinking persons—ever to grow more complex—when one would think they would tire of pressing on and fall back into simplicity, as a fire falls into ashes. The very old among us do grow tired. But there always seem to be new young ones eager to drive further on, to live better and better."

Humans and Folk are then akin.

"I—I suppose we are. But I do not know for certain. The aborigines—the people you call Folk—are said by our wise ones to belong truly to this world. We humans do not."

The rimoriks laughed. *Oh, yes you do.*

∴

Anigel chided them. "I am no scholar, but I have been taught this by the finest teachers. My sister Haramis, who is very clever, assures me that it is true. And it is a belief not only of Ruwendians, but of other human nations as well."

Humans walked this world before the swamp Folk, before the mountain Folk, before the forest Folk. Only the great Drowners walked the world earlier.

Anigel was skeptical. "How do you know? You are only animals!"

But the rimoriks only laughed again, and would not speak of the matter further, and a few moments later Anigel caught her first glimpse of the Wyvilo settlement, and she could not be bothered thinking further about mysteries.

The Wyvilo obviously knew that she was coming.

A fleet of more than thirty of the slender, translucent canoes put out from the shore and came speeding toward her. Each craft carried a couple of dozen aboriginal paddlers, with a coxswain standing proudly in the bow, gesturing to direct his crew.

"I think we had better stop," Anigel told the rimoriks uneasily. "By the Flower, there are a lot of them! Will you — will you poke your heads out of the water and look protective?"

Two splashes responded, and the big animals grinned at her, then turned their eyes to the approaching fleet.

The Wyvilo village was spread out over a large cleared area that the Princess later learned was an island surrounded by artificially deepened channels. The shoreline bristled with small docks, at which were tied many more of the lightweight, gleaming vessels. (The rimoriks had told her that the canoe-making material came from the swim-bladder of a gigantic river fish.) The houses, all on stilts, were beautifully constructed of peeled logs, with shake roofs, shutters, and every kind of balcony and surrounding deck — the latter crowded with spectators. Most of the dwellings were connected by rather rickety-looking aerial walkways.

A portion of the village that lay farthest downstream had evidently been struck by fire recently. Blackened structures were in the process of being torn down and new building frames were rising from the ruins. Strangely enough, the Wyvilo had no trees at all in their village; but there were masses of shrubbery and garden plots down on the ground, and many of the mossy shake roofs had flowers growing on them.

When the leading Wyvilo boat was about ten ells away from Anigel's motionless craft, it hauled up short. The others stopped beside it, forming a solid line of boats jam-packed with gaping Oddlings, who were very different in physical appearance from those that the Princess had seen before.

They were taller than the Nyssomu and Uisgu swamp-dwellers of the north, about the size of strapping adult humans. Their heads were elongated, not rounded, and their noses resembled small snouts. Wyvilo eyes were more familiarly aboriginal, being large and yellow; but they had vertical pupils—such as Anigel knew the Skritek also had. The open mouths of the gawking Wyvilo revealed formidable teeth. Their skin was partially hairy and partially covered with dermal plates that resembled shiny brown scales. The forest Folk wore gorgeously painted loincloths and were hung about with a profusion of necklaces, bracelets, stomachers, anklets, and other jewelry—some of it gold or platinum, inset with glittering gemstones. Strung blue-glass trade beads seemed to be as fashionable as precious metal, and Anigel saw one aborigine sporting the ornate steel cuirass of a Ruwendian knight, and another wearing a polder lady's fringed shawl about his massive shoulders.

She had calmly combed her hair while the fleet approached, and put on Immu's leather cape to cover her shabby attire. Now she stood up carefully in the boat, flanked by the rimoriks, and raised both hands. The cape fell back to reveal the trillium amulet gleaming on her breast.

The mob of floating Wyvilo voiced a low cry. Talons pointed, and those in the sterns of the boats crowded and stretched to get a better look, muttering and exclaiming in their guttural language.

"I come here as a friend," Anigel said. "I seek a magical talisman called the Three-Headed Monster."

All of a sudden the forest Folk fell silent. Again their mouths gaped and their golden eyes bulged.

Anigel waited, then finally said: "Is there one among you who can speak to me?"

One of the most elaborately ornamented of the coxswains made an abrupt gesture. His boat nosed out of the ranks and approached that of the Princess.

"This one speaks," he declaimed in the tongue of the Peninsula. His voice was thick and almost unintelligible, and his brown-furred brow knit in a fierce scowl. He wore a collar of beaten gold set with multicolored gems, a fine Ruwendian hat of creamy brocade with a brooch of brilliants and sweeping red plumes, and a brocade loincloth to match. "This one is Sasstu-Cha, Speaker of Let," he croaked. "Who are you? And why do you seek the favor of the Wyvilo?"

"I am Princess Anigel of Ruwenda. You may know that my country has been seized by human enemies from the north." She lifted the trillium amulet as she continued to speak. "The Guardian of our land, the White Lady, sent me to seek a talisman. It will free my people from the slave-chains of the conquerors. Have you heard of this Three-Headed Monster?"

The Speaker hesitated. "We know of one such. But it is no talisman. It lies down the river one-half day's journey, then several more hours' travel up Kovuko Stream — in Glismak country."

The Princess drew in her breath sharply, which brought a smile to the Wyvilo's face.

"Can you furnish me with a guide who will take me there?" she asked.

"No."

Anigel brandished her amulet. "I demand it of you! By the Flower!" The crowd of Wyvilo uttered a great, sighing cry.

Desperately, she pulled the Black Trillium leaf from the wallet at her waist and flourished it. The Folk cried out even louder, and this time their tone was clearly fearful.

"But I must go there! Help me," Anigel pleaded.

"If you go up the Kovuko, you will surely perish," Sasstu-Cha said. "The trees of that place are as voracious as the Glismak themselves. None of our people dare take you there. Even if it were not a place forbidden by the Sky God, we could not go. Four suns ago the Glismak attacked Let and burned many of our houses. As the dry season ends, they always do, knowing we are richest in booty from our trade with the humans. They will return soon and attack again. All Wyvilo must stay and defend our home. Not even the holy Black Trillium can sway us from this duty."

Anigel drew herself up and took a deep breath. "Very well. Then I and my rimorik friends will go by ourselves. Will you at least give me careful directions, so that I may quickly find this Kovuko Stream?"

"Yes, willingly. And also food, and fresh human clothing, if you wish it."

∴

"That would be most welcome. There is also one other boon I would beg. Following after me are other humans, my enemies. I beg that you do not tell them where I have gone."

"We will not," said Sasstu-Cha. He swept his arm up in a gesture to his paddlers. "Now this one asks you to follow, Princess Anigel of Ruwenda. Accept for tonight the precarious hospitality of Let, then go on your way. And if you find your magical liberating talisman, think not only of your own imperiled home, but give some small thought to ours as well."

31

The Uisgu were highly sensitive to the swamp environment, which made them conscious of the smallest change in the life about them. It was twilight when those at the poles (they had changed many times during their journey downstream) suddenly stopped. Kadiya saw them draw together, speaking, in whispers, their own dialect.

Nessak, who had the trade tongue, came to Kadiya's side.

"Lady, there are more of the enemy before us. The greater part have camped at the river bend. We must somehow find a way around them or be taken again for their evil pleasure."

Kadiya nodded. She would have to depend upon their land and water skills as she had upon Jagun's.

Jagun . . . he remained a painful memory. In spite of all their hopes he had not reappeared along the Mutar, nor had the Uisgu women reported picking up any Call from him. But the Princess continued to flinch away from the thought that he was dead.

"There is a way for us to pass around our foes?" Kadiya asked.

The mists were rising again, drifting to veil first this part and then that of the river and the banks. They had encountered no further sign of ruins since they had escaped.

Nessak slowly shook her head. "Lady, the wicked humans have with them Skritek, but it is also true that they are much wearied and there are more dangers hereabouts. This is hunting territory for the looru. Thus—" she made a small motion with her hand, "after nightfall we must go into hiding from more than men and Drowners."

∴

Looru! Kadiya had heard of those savage night-flyers from early childhood. They were what nurses used to frighten any of their charges who lingered in the open after sundown. But since they had fled into this land Jagun had not mentioned them. She had seen well tanned squares of their leathery wings on sale in Trevista seasons back, but only once and then they had been something of a curiosity. Now she looked up into the steadily darkening sky. Looru were bloodsuckers that could latch onto a man or animal and suck it dry, with talons to claw the life out of any prey close enough to be captured.

"Lady!" One of the Uisgu who had been at the fore of the raft called softly. "Look there!"

The river had made several bends, even split into more than one channel since they had taken flight. Now it appeared to be straightening out again ahead and there was a glow on the left-hand bank, one which certainly was not born from any swamp-growth but from a fire or other fixed light. At the same time they heard the notes of what could only be a battle-trumpet summoning an ingathering, and then the shouts of men and a droning sound.

The Uisgu women sent their craft to the opposite shore with hasty pole work.

"The foemen are attacked!" Nessak's voice rose above her former soft speech. "Maybe the looru, Lady."

"If they are such fools as to light the way for those predators," commented Kadiya, "then certainly they are simple as babes in this place. The Skritek should have given them warning—"

Nessak made a sound which was near bitter laughter. "Lady, these men from afar will not listen to the gabble of the Drowners. They would think a warning from a swamp-dweller need not be taken seriously. There is no good sense among them, only the need for the shedding of blood to satisfy their masters."

"If the looru attack them now," Kadiya said, thinking furiously, "can we not slip by them?"

Nessak considered. "Such might give us a chance, Lady. We can but try it . . ."

They touched the shore on the left bank. Kadiya and several of the others grasped swiftly at reeds there and cut quantities, throwing the bundles back to the rest who were busy working to make the raft appear one of the floating masses of debris which were often to be seen drifting down-river. The only barrier against such a plan was the size of the craft they were trying to disguise. Such floating islets were usually less than a quarter the size of the log platform on which they had taken refuge.

Having made the only preparations they could, two of the polers pressed them back into the current, which was lazier here, so they drifted along at a nerve-torturing slowness. The fire in the enemy camp blazed ever brighter. On the raft the Uisgu lay flat, reeds pulled over them, but watched the other shore with anxious eyes.

It appeared the invaders had learned a little something during their earlier battles with the looru for a number of men waved torches, each torchman being flanked by a fellow with waiting spear or sword. Several of the beasts were down struggling on the ground. A Skritek beat in the head of one and a man who wore a reddening bandage about one leg heaved a light sword as if it were a hunting knife to pin another violently beating wing to the earth.

There was nothing proud and self confident about the bearing of these Labornoki soldiers now. Their armor was rusted, their helmet-plumes draggled, and their clothing filthy. A number wore bandages, while the faces and bare skin of near all of them were puffed and reddened by numerous stings of insects. Under one tree which had a rude shelter braced about its trunk were at least four who lay motionless.

It was very evident that the camp, large as it was — for this was no band of scouts — was completely under concerted attack. Kadiya reached out with her pole and drove its end into the left bank, exerting her strength to urge the craft forward faster. Others of the Uisgu women followed her example. But the raft moved on very slowly.

It would seem that the looru were finding their battle more perilous than they had counted on. The swarm sheered swiftly away when one of their number caught fire from a well aimed torch. The burning thing screeched, and then dropped on its attackers determined upon retaliation. The talons on one wing hooked a man's jaw, scraping off his helm. He gave a last cry of terror as the looru dove headlong to the ground, burying its human prey under its own burning body.

Kadiya felt that they had more than a chance of slipping past undetected now. None of the battlers were close to the river and, even though bonfire and torch illuminated the surface of the dark water, none of the Labornoki or Skritek appeared to look in their direction.

∴

But she knew hope too soon. The raft suddenly shuddered under them and was carried toward the right shore. Kadiya struggled with her pole against what she first thought was some trick of the current. Then, hardly more than an arm's distance away, the camouflage covering the logs heaved. She heard a Uisgu scream as a great scaled arm arose from the water to paw at the stacked reeds.

At the same time her pole was jerked from her hands, and she let go just in time to save herself from being pulled overboard. The raft was now moving steadily toward the scene of the battle.

"Drowners!" Nessak gasped. "Underneath—they are pulling us!"

There was no way to marshal a defense against creatures so used to the water that they could lurk for a long time unseen below its surface. Nor did they dare try to leap overboard and swim for it, since their enemies would only swiftly pull them under.

Kadiya guessed what had happened. Most of the canny swamp devils had taken to the water at the coming of the looru attack, leaving the men to do battle. There must be a goodly number of them now in the river, judging by the speed the raft was now making toward the shore.

The chaos in the camp was lessening. There were more looru down, and now the company of vicious flyers had sheered off before making a fresh attack.

And then, as Kadiya watched, into the full light of the fire there came a figure robed in red, a hood pulled up and over his face. This could only be the Voice of Orogastus, who had sought her so long. In one hand he carried a rod, and this he raised vertically, ramming the lower end into the ground. A soldier ran forward and helped to steady the staff. On the upper end, well above the level of the bonfire, was a circular plate. Now the Voice stepped back, and from his hand there shot a beam of light which struck the plate. There was a small explosion. Orange-yellow flames spurted from the plate's rim, and it began to spin, making an ear-splitting keening sound. The swarm of flyers uttered squawks of fear. In a body, they lofted high into the night sky, and a moment later had disappeared. The whirling firework blazed and shrieked on for a few minutes more, then subsided into a shower of sparks and died.

The man in red strode down toward the shoreline to stand watching the incoming raft. Kadiya heard no call from him but immediately

∴

several men wearing the torn cloaks and tarnished insignia of officers came to join him.

There were orders shouted and troops came running from the recent scene of battle. Kadiya saw a ragged handful of archers with arrows at the ready. But an officer in a full suit of elaborate blood-red armor threw up his arm and they did not fire. None of the Uisgu females had risen out of hiding, but Kadiya had no doubt that those ashore were quite aware of them. Clambering out of the river now and setting the big raft to rocking, the Skritek grinned in triumph, their large eyes returning the red gleam of fire and torch.

The officer, whom Kadiya now recognized to be General Hamil, turned to the Red Voice and spoke. Straightway the acolyte of Orogastus shouted in trade tongue:

"Ashore, swamp scum! Or shall these allies be allowed to take what they wish?" He made a small gesture to the waiting Skritek.

The reeds shifted as the Uisgu women crawled out. But Kadiya did not follow at once. She gripped her talisman. Surely there might be just a chance . . . Skritek seized the Uisgu and hurled them ashore. However, the Voice had no eyes for their capture. He stared at the place where Kadiya still lay hidden, frowning. The talisman seemed to be shielding her in some way.

The Voice said something to General Hamil and the officer turned. One of the Uisgu women who carried a child had stumbled and fallen at his feet when the Skritek had thrown them ashore. Hamil stooped and caught the screaming child by one arm, jerking it out of its mother's loosened grasp, and tossed it to one of the Skritek. The monster roared with delight and caught the prize easily out of the air.

Kadiya burst out of the covering of rushes, talisman in hand. "No!" she screamed.

"Take her!" shouted Hamil.

Before she could move, the talons of a Skritek who had climbed up from the river closed upon her, twisting her arms behind her back painfully, and she was dragged off the raft onto the shore. The talisman had fallen in the mud; but when another Skritek stooped to pick it up he yelped and pulled back, while around the now-glowing pommel there arose curls of smoke.

Thrust before the General and the Voice, Kadiya stood tense with

∴

impotent rage. Hamil's helm was open, and he bore very little resemblance to the splendid man she had seen at the Citadel. His bristly bearded jaws and cheeks were lumped with bites, some of which were badly swollen. One beside his left eye had pulled down the lid so that he could hardly see out of it. But he was smiling and now he laughed.

"Well, Voice," he spoke to his companion. "Now here is something that can make all this damned muck-treading worth it. The Princess Kadiya! We have indeed been favored this night!"

A hand shot out and nails cut cruelly into her cheeks as he cupped her face and held it higher.

"Swamp vart," he said with real pleasure. "Far from your silks and pretties now, aren't you? It did not take long to reduce you to a mud-runner — soft meat like all your kind!" He let go his hold and slapped her face, a blow so sharp and heavy that tears came willy-nilly.

Hamil snorted. "Weep your eyes out, girl. There is no mercy for any of your house." He looked to the Red Voice and added scornfully: "So the women of Krain's blood are to bring great Labornok down?" His heavy hand fell again, this time on her shoulder, and he brought her about to face the minion of Orogastus. "This — this is what your great lord sees as death to us? What a joke!"

The Voice was not looking at Kadiya, rather at the talisman, which lay a short distance away. He stooped to take it and then drew back, scowling.

"What frights you, Voice?" Hamil was jovial. "It is the talisman! The magical gimcrack so coveted by your master. Take it, man. What are you waiting for?"

The Red Voice stiffened. He seemed to grow taller, more massive. From the eyeholes of his mask dazzling white beams shone, so that even General Hamil joined his men as they all exclaimed in fear.

"Hamil!" As if borne on the night wind came a new voice Kadiya had heard before. It was the acolyte speaking, but the tones were those of Orogastus. "You have done well, better than you know. But you must take great care. That lying before you is bonded to your prisoner. Neither you, nor any other who has not the old knowledge, can handle it — only she. My Red Voice, obey me! Make Princess Kadiya carry the talisman back to the Citadel, but be sure she cannot use it."

The Red Voice slumped. His eyes were dark again, and he whispered: "Yes, Master."

∴

Hamil spat, loudly and noisily, the spittle striking the mud just beyond the pommel. "So she and that stick are magically bonded. Well, Voice, how do you solve this problem? It is plainly of your master's kind of warfare."

The sorcerer's acolyte produced a length of cord, not woven from any fiber but oddly mottled in color as if it had been the skin of some small swamp-worm. As Kadiya watched, he fashioned a small noose at one end of it. This he proceeded to roll between thumb and forefinger muttering to himself. Then, with the care of a fisherman about to entice some wary pond dweller, he lowered the loop and, with great patience, worked it over the pommel of the talisman, giving it a stiff jerk when he had it in place. Having made sure that his noose was secure, he lifted the snakeskin and so drew the pointless sword entirely free of the ground. As he stood dangling it before him, Hamil reached forth carelessly to touch it, only to have the Voice pull back.

"Lord General, this be truly bonded. Lay hand fully upon it and it may have you entrapped."

The General snorted.

"You heard the orders of my Master," the Voice went on. "This is a thing of great power he wishes to possess, and since it is bonded to Princess Kadiya, he wishes her also."

Hamil eyed the girl thoughtfully. "But what if she contrives somehow to use the damned thing?"

Through the eyeholes of his mask the Voice was regarding Kadiya intently. "Lord General, we do not know what this girl can do. But my Master has given me a device to subdue her."

At the end of the spotted skin which held it, the sword swayed hypnotically back and forth. The Red Voice reached into his robe with his other hand, brought out a small white object, and touched it to Kadiya's forehead.

Kadiya cried out, and then her voice died away. It was as if the biting cold of ice struck her, freezing her very bone-marrow. The cold spread through her body from head to foot. She tried to move, but her body did not respond.

The Voice nodded. "Just so. For a space, Lord General, she will be harmless—though this will not hold forever. The device works but once, and I have but one of them with me. There is another way that we shall coerce this girl. That which is bonded can be released—by willing. But such breaking of another's resolve will take time. We must see that this talisman goes with her until we are in a position to accept it freely from her."

"Accept freely?" Hamil stared and then laughed, "Oh, that can be arranged, oh, yes, it can!"

There was a volley of orders. Kadiya was trussed like an inert bale of goods, with her talisman lashed to her back. Then poles were run through the ropes, and two soldiers bore her off like the trophy of a hunt.

The Uisgu from the raft had been once more herded together and were bound up, their necks noosed one to the next in a line. However, it would seem that their captors had no intention of going farther that night. Perhaps to leave their fire would appear folly after they had beaten off one looru attack. There were a couple of strong-rooted trees growing among the ferns, and to those the neck ropes of the captives were made fast. Skritek squatted nearby, grunting among themselves, eyeing the prisoners greedily.

Kadiya's thoughts moved sluggishly. She had a queer mental picture of one pushing step by step through a great bank of snow. She considered General Hamil. He was a fit and ready tool for King Voltrik. From him there flowed a sense of evil, not of unearthly darkness such as the Voice and his master projected, but rather a brutality which was worse in a way because it was fully human. Nevertheless, it seemed more likely that she might influence *him* than the sorcerer's puppet . . .

She tried to use anger, as she had so often before, to arouse herself out of the deadly cold. But she was trapped. There was no warmth either from the talisman to which she had been so carefully bound. She closed her eyes and willed herself to think clearly, but her congealed nerves seemed only to urge surrender.

Then she was aware of a rustling beside her, and that for some time she had not heard the grunting of the Skritek. She opened her eyes as breath foul with the fumes of brandy puffed against her cheek. Then there came a clamping down of a hand, harsh and hard, across her lips, and strong fingers tangled in her hair.

"Princess!" It was a tainted whisper. "What of the treasure you have seen in the swamp ruins? Where is that beldame of the ancient legends who plays with magic, who is said to have gathered the most powerful tools of the Vanished Ones? Orogastus thinks to gather all into his own hands. Ah, much I know of that! More than Voltrik, who may be dead by now, along with that stupid boy, his son. But the sorcerer is far away in his tower, and this Voice of his but a weakling and a fool when he is not possessed by his master's spirit. Tell me the secrets you have learned! Buy a clean death, King's Daughter. If you gain one you buy it of me, and me only."

Hamil! This man was playing some game of his own . . .

The hand uncovered her mouth but the fingers remained painfully twisted in her hair. Oddly enough, the brutal General's threats appeared to have broken through some of the icy sorcery which held her impotent. So there was no longer a meeting of common purpose among the enemy. How could she turn this to account? It was so difficult to think clearly.

"Would you rather face the Skritek, then, mud-crawler? Well, we can make a pretty show in the morning for you. One you can watch."

His grip on her loosened and she was abruptly alone. For a big man he could move silently enough, though she had been cast down on the ground not far from his tent. And then she saw another shadow moving, one that did not approach closely. But she heard a sibilant whisper:

"So! Hamil believes that he is a match for the Master! As if there was ever any need for him, or King Voltrik, or Prince Antar, once this land was overrun. What you carry, girl, that is what matters! Orogastus would be willing to let you take your blood payment from the Labornoki King if you would meet him with truth."

The Red Voice crept nearer. Then his hand was on her shoulder, very close to the pommel of the talisman. "See, I will play you fair. I can free you from the spell that freezes you. We can be far from here before that morning Hamil prates about if only you will bond the talisman to me."

Exerting all her strength, she managed to gasp: "I am no fool, faithful servant of a foul master!"

"Foul? Ah, no, Princess. You will find Orogastus a most pleasing friend. Already your dear sister Haramis is his cup-mate and learns from him such wondrous craft as your Archimage never even dreamed might exist. She has a taste and a talent for such things, has the Princess Haramis, and already she sees matters through the Master's eyes. You can join her. My Master will not gainsay you if you bring King Voltrik and Hamil down. They have begun to weary him. You can be a queen, if you wish — a ruler of two lands, and your sister will have a thaumaturgical throne to reach the stars."

There was a poisonous reasoning in what he said. That Orogastus might be tired of his Labornoki allies could be understood. That he believed he could use her, a royal Princess, to rule both Ruwenda and Labornok — yes, that, too, was plausible. Of course, he must be lying about Haramis submitting to Orogastus. Still, she might temporize.

"I . . . I cannot give anything . . . when I am so bound," Kadiya pointed out.

The sound that came from the Voice was nearly a snicker. "Princess, you can command your talisman even if you are bound. Release by word and thought what you carry and I shall speedily release *you*."

Of course she did not believe him. But there was so little time to think and her thoughts still seemed sullenly slow . . . Then she remembered — remembered a blade which had grown from a root. She might carry a magical sword, but it was rooted in something else — and that this follower of Orogastus did not know.

"I grant you . . . permission to draw it." She found words coming to her tongue which had not been in her mind a moment earlier. "Plant the blunt end of the blade in the ground."

She could hear his quickened breathing. That he trusted her was a wonder, but one she had no time to consider now. She felt the talisman slide out from between her shoulders. There was no gleam to it now; it remained quite dull. The Red Voice was on his feet. She saw him put the blade into the soil until it stood upright even as she had asked.

Then — there was a radiance, the blade thinned, became as slender as a stem, but the three lobes remained the same. She heard her own voice in a fierce whisper:

"Be, O living talisman, O rootstock of the Black Trillium, the emblem and strength of our house, as you have always been!"

At her order the spheres opened. The three eyes were alive. They turned on the Voice, who had stiffened. For an instant his own eyes gleamed star-bright as the distant sorcerer sought to invade him. But Orogastus was not quick enough.

One eye of the talisman shot forth white light, and to that was joined a green beam from the Oddling eye, and a shaft of gold from the human.

And the Voice burned.

∴

He writhed as the magical radiance enveloped him. A column of tricolored flame entwined about his body sealing him in. He had not even time to scream. And then the fire was gone as suddenly as it had come and cinders lay heaped on the ground, giving off wisps of smoke.

In the place of the Three-Lobed Burning Eye stood the talisman, lifeless and dull.

32

Never had Prince Antar spent such wretched days and nights as those on the Great Mutar. The unrelenting sun roasted him and his armored companions like holiday togars. They had taken only the seven largest of their wooden punts (deeming those of the Wyvilo too fragile and tippy), and these were cramped and crowded when loaded with the reduced force of forty-three men and the necessary supplies.

In their inexperience the Labornoki almost always chose stopping places on the main banks of the river that were too hot and too muddy, and infested with slimy bloodsuckers, biting gnats, and small yellow-striped vermin that gnawed holes in the supply sacks. The meals prepared by amateur soldier-cooks were usually either burned or raw. Two men already suffered the bloody flux from snacking on poisonous fruit. Bereft of their comfortable pavilions and folding beds, which were too large to fit in the punts, the knights had to sleep on the ground as the common soldiers did, covered only by their capes.

And finally, when the unkempt force reached the attractive Wyvilo settlement of Let, which looked by then as inviting to them as Derorguila Palace, the accursed Oddlings refused them permission to land.

Meeting the Labornoki in midstream, the Wyvilo were totally unimpressed by the Prince's offer to reward them handsomely for their trouble. The Speaker declared that the village had no time for guests. It expected to be besieged by its Glismak foes at any time. The humans must move on. Neither guides nor food supplies were available.

Sir Rinutar took it upon himself to revile the assembled flotilla of forest Folk and their Speaker roundly. He threatened them with the thaumaturgical fury of the mighty Orogastus, this same to be delivered via the Blue Voice if the Wyvilo did not accede at once to Labornok's demands.

Rinutar's friend Sir Karon, not wishing to be bested in defiance of the insolent primitives, surged to his feet in his punt, drew his sword, and challenged Speaker Sasstu-Cha to single combat. At this point, the apparently unarmed aborigines whipped out small catapults and bombarded the seven Labornoki boats with a barrage of smartly flung flintstones.

The Prince and most of the knights in their armor were hardly hurt (although the luckless Sir Penapat narrowly missed having his eye put out); but the twenty-one soldiers, having been pressed into service as reluctant oarsmen and shucking most of their armor because of the heat and constraints of rowing, sustained many a bruise and laceration.

Sir Karon was startled into overbalancing when the assault commenced, and his massive flounderings caused his punt to roll over with a tremendous splash. Still waving his sword, the iron-clad stalwart vanished into the depths of the Great Mutar, never to be seen again, as did his knightly companion in the punt, Sir Bidrik. The Blue Voice, who had also been a passenger in the capsized craft, popped to the surface of the water with remarkable buoyancy for one so skinny, and struck out for the Prince's boat, into which he was dragged by Sir Owanon. The three decanted soldier-oarsmen thrashed about pathetically calling for help, since they could not swim and their boat had drifted off down the river out of reach. Eventually they were hauled safely aboard other punts by their mates.

The Wyvilo had watched this spectacle phlegmatically, slingshots at the ready.

"Go away," Speaker Sasstu-Cha commanded once again. "We will not harm you further if you leave at once."

Prince Antar spoke in a whisper to the dripping Blue Voice: "Can you magick yon Oddlings and force our will upon them?"

"Nay, High Lord." The Voice was calmly wringing his skirts over the side. "The instruments of enchantment I might have used are, like the late Lords Karon and Bidrik, now resting on the floor of the Great Mutar."

"Very well," sighed the Prince. And he called to the oarsmen: "Row on!"

Thus ignominiously did the search-party continue down the river,

∴

until it was nearly dark and the Prince deemed that they had gone a safe distance from Let. Then they put in at an inviting small cove, hard by the main channel and smoothly sanded, and made camp by firelight.

There were seven soldiers so badly battered that they were useless for fighting or arduous rowing. These were excused from further duty. "Tomorrow," Prince Antar told them, "you men, and two others more able-bodied from among the wounded, will take one of the punts and make your way back to Tass Town. Tell the boat skippers and the Master-Trader that they are to await our return upon pain of death — even should we not have returned by the start of the rainy season."

There was much murmuring among the knights and the other men at this, but the Prince paid no attention. He then summoned the Blue Voice. "Call upon your dark master to scry for us Princess Anigel, so that we may know where to betake ourselves on the morrow. Tell Orogastus also to inform my father King Voltrik that I continue to follow his orders faithfully, and those of his Grand Minister of State."

With that, the Prince tramped off down the moonlit shore by himself. The other men went about their business sunk in melancholy, excepting the Blue Voice, who retired to a grove of weeping wydel-trees at the margin of the strand, knelt down, and passed into a trance.

"Almighty Master, hear me!"

"I, Orogastus, hear you, my Voice."

"Alas, my Lord, our expedition has suffered a grave setback at the Wyvilo village of Let. The Oddlings caught us unawares with a shower of missiles, upsetting the boat in which I rode. All of the magical equipment was lost, and the knights Karon and Bidrik sank from the weight of their armor and drowned. Also, seven men-at-arms were so badly banged about that they must retire back to Tass Town in the care of two others less seriously injured, and Sir Penapat has a black eye the size of a ladu-fruit from being smote with a flying rock."

Orogastus digested this news. "The Prince and the other seventeen knights are yet hale?"

"Aye, Great Lord. And twelve soldiers — although most are bruised and full of complaints."

"I have scried the Princess Anigel. She is encamped at the mouth of a small stream down-river from you and intends to go up this waterway tomorrow, traveling on foot when she can no longer use her boat. It will take your party about five hours to reach the stream if both the men and knights row double-time. You will order Prince Antar to depart at dawn and pursue Anigel with all speed — but see that she goes un-scathed until she secures the talisman, which must now be very close by."

"I will transmit your commands to the Prince, Master."

"Tell the Prince also the good news that his Royal Father is very near full recovered. Furthermore, General Hamil has Princess Kadiya in custody and will shortly take charge of her talisman, the Three-Lobed Burning Eye."

"Master . . ." the Voice faltered. "This evening, as we made our landing, I felt a sudden brainstorm. It — it seemed as though my Red Brother, who accompanies General Hamil, had met with misfortune."

"My Blue Voice, you must be brave. Your brother has perished in my service."

"Oh, woe!"

"The Dark Powers will receive his life-energies and glorify them. And you two Voices who remain shall share an even greater earthly reward when my great ambition is fulfilled . . . But recall now the other matter, concerning Prince Antar, that you must yet carry out."

"I wait only for the appropriate moment, Almighty Master. The doughty Sir Rinutar, a man after your own heart, will be taken into our confidence after the deed is done. He will surely lead our party back safely once the talisman is secured."

The sorcerer's mental speech now lost all tinge of sympathy and became charged with a dreadful resolution. "It is of the utmost impor-tance, my Voice, that Anigel's talisman be not lost."

"Great Lord, I understand."

"Kadiya's talisman is all but secured. That of Princess Haramis will soon be mine — perhaps even before this night is over! But these two are fully empowered only by the third, the one you must bring to me."

"On my life," the Blue Voice vowed, "I will place it at your feet. And if all goes well, Prince Antar will not see tomorrow's sun set."

"I am pleased. Farewell, my Blue Voice."

The enchanter's minion made his way back into the camp, where one cook-of-the-evening was preparing a stew of dried meat and veg-etables garnished with fatback, while another attempted to bake loaves in a sooty reflector oven. The smells were not encouraging.

The Blue Voice approached the Prince boldly. Antar's preoccupation vanished and he looked almost eager. "You have news?"

"Aye, High Lord. The fugitive Princess is only about eight hours ahead of us. She nears the goal of her questing, and perhaps tomorrow or the next day will see her taken." The Voice went on to tell of the King's recovery, and how the sorcerer had nearly secured the other two talismans. He did not mention his fellow-acolyte's death. The Prince listened with half an ear, then walked away without another word to share the poor supper with his men.

That night a great thunderstorm struck the Tassaleyo Forest, the first genuine precursor of the rainy season which would officially begin in six days, after the Feast of the Three Moons. The men of Labornok were roused by the thunder, and hastened to turn over their boats and take refuge under them. But once again their lack of wilderness experience betrayed them. The sandy flat that had seemed so pleasant earlier was now inundated as the Great Mutar rose in brief flood. Cursing and groaning, the party had to right the punts and climb into them, then paddle into an adjacent thicket, now also underwater, and tie up there for the rest of the night. They dozed fitfully beneath their streaming capes as the storm raged on, bailing out the punts as rainwater accumulated.

Prince Antar was as soaked and miserable as the lowest soldier. Yet he thought not of his own discomfort, but rather sat sleepless as he worried how Princess Anigel fared throughout that endless, blustery night.

Friend, they called to her. *Friend, awaken. It is first light. You asked us to call you. Awaken!*

Inside the hollow tree, Anigel stretched and yawned. She lay on dry, clean wood-dust, the product of the carpenter-worms that still worked industriously around and above her to reduce the dead forest giant to a mound of humus. Her hair, sleep-sack, and the handsome new clothing that the Wyvilo had given her were powdered with the stuff; but it was a small price to pay for snug shelter during the storm.

She had dreamed again, but the memory faded with the rimoriks' call. She had bade the animals rouse her early, knowing that she must be nearing the object of her quest. Last night, awakened momentarily by the crashing thunder, she had seen her trillium amulet glowing like fire; the small floweret within was very nearly full open.

She ran the comb through her hair to dislodge the worst of the dust and took out the miton gourd from her wallet. The Black Trillium leaf wrapped around it no longer seemed so fresh and green; its upper

∴

portion was withering where the vein had turned brown, and only the base was moist and alive. The golden trace that had guided her from Noth now extended only through the short, bent stem.

We have a fish for you, friend. Come out and see.

Gathering her things, she stopped and squeezed out of the hollow tree. The two rimoriks were there beside the punt, which was drawn up partway on the bank of the stream. A fat winju-fish lay on the moss. Rags of mist stole in and out of the surrounding trees, and the under-growth of great ferns and shrubbery dripped even though the rain had stopped. The sky seemed clear and the white birds were singing their welcome to the dawn. The creek, she noticed, ran much fuller than when they had entered it last night. That was fortuitous: it meant that she would be able to travel farther up-stream in her boat.

"Thank you, my friends," Anigel said, "but I think I will eat only this Wyvilo pastie and some of these berries for breakfast. It would be hard for me to start a fire in this dampness, and I would like to be quickly on my way."

That would be a good thing, said one rimorik.

The second one said: *It is known to us that your enemies are fast ap-proaching on the Water That Flows to the Sea. Our comrades tell us that the humans are very wet and very angry, and more eager than ever to catch you.*

Anigel sighed. "For some strange reason, I find it hard to fret over them now. I am no longer even afraid of the Three-Headed Monster! But I don't think this has anything to do with bravery. I am only sick of this quest and anxious to bring it to an end. When I have the talisman . . . well, perhaps *then* I will worry about how to save myself from the foe and return to my sisters."

The creatures took hold of the punt's stern in their strong jaws and pulled it into the water.

Share miton with us, and we will be on our way.

She performed the ritual, then climbed into the boat. They began to move up the stream that the Wyvilo called the Kovuko, and slowly the sun climbed higher and the dense foliage of the Tassaleyo Forest began to steam. It grew so sultry that Anigel shed most of her clothing, save for the new shift she wore under her hunter's tunic and Immu's broad-brimmed hat.

It had surprised her that the forest Folk's homes were so richly furnished with human luxuries. The modest Nyssomu of Trevista had household goods and garments mostly of their own manufacture; but the places she visited briefly in Let had been crammed with all manner of Ruwendian and Labornoki things — iron kettles and silver spoons, fancy oil-lamps and gilt candelabras, expensive leather furniture, seed-poppers and toasting forks, tapestries and paintings, plush toy animals, rugs, harps and mandolins and bagpipes, satin cushions, porcelain and fancy glassware, playing cards, game boards, and every sort of decorative trinket or knickknack that the Dylex crafters had ever invented. Speaker Sasstu-Cha and his wife had even owned a copper hipbath, of which they were inordinately proud. Anigel had soaked in it and washed with perfumed soap. The fresh clothing she wore came from the Speaker's subadult children, who were faddishly fond of certain kinds of human garb.

Once she became used to their forbidding faces and rather grumpy mannerisms, Anigel quite liked the Wyvilo. They were a forthright people who worked very hard during the dry season and fought never-ending battles with their poorer Glismak cousins during the Rains. The Speaker confided to her sadly that the human traders had placed an embargo upon one kind of goods only: no weaponry was ever traded for Wyvilo forest products.

"Both Ruwendians and Labornoki hold fast to this policy in their own self-interest," Sasstu-Cha had told her. "For if we had modern weapons — swords and lanceheads of steel, and powerful crossbows — we would be able to defeat the Glismak once and for all, and extend our sway down the entire Great Mutar into the land of Var, and sell our timber to the agents of King Fiodelon more easily and profitably."

Anigel had not known what to say. "It does not seem fair to deny your people the means to defend themselves. On the other hand, my little country lays claim to the northern Tassaleyo and depends upon its timber-exports to support its economy. Surely there must be a way to compromise, so that both Wyvilo and Ruwendians can live safely and prosperously."

"If there is, only you Ruwendians can find it."

"But we no longer rule. You know that Labornok has crushed us!"

"Are you so sure? What of this talisman you seek? Is it not to provide your salvation?"

"The Three-Headed Monster?" Anigel gave a sad little laugh. "Do you really think I can tame such a thing and send it against our foe?"

"No," the Speaker had said. "Not if your quest ends with the Three-Headed Monster we know."

∴

He refused flatly to describe this thing further. But before Anigel departed from Let, he told her: "Soon it will be the Feast of the Three Moons. You can see, when they rise in the night sky, that the orbs are drawing closer and closer to each other, in the kind of conjunction that only occurs once in a thousand lifetimes. If it happens that this year the moons conjoin, then a great wonderwork will certainly take place. And it could concern you, O Petal of the Living Trillium . . ."

Anigel's boat moved up Kovuko Stream and the forest on either side changed character, becoming dryer and less choked with undergrowth. Many of the lofty columnar trees grew here; but there were others as well, of a most unusual aspect. They were about three times the height of a human being, herbaceous rather than woody. At their base was an open rosette of thick leaves, some individual trees having leaves colored purplish green, while others had leaves swirled with patterns of variegated green-gold. From the center of the rosette grew a stout fleshy trunk studded with short branches, each one of which had smaller leaves, together with brilliant flowers of luscious pink or magenta, and pendulous clusters of fruit having a most delectable smell. Atop the trunk was another cluster of larger leaves curving upward, forming a kind of chalice. The aspect of the trees was exotic but very appealing. They seemed almost like gigantic goblets with elaborately bejeweled stems.

Charmed, Anigel proposed stopping and gathering some of this strange tree's fruit.

Nay, friend. It would be your last meal.

"Oh! Are the fruits poison?"

They are delicious. But the tree uses them to bait its trap.

With a shiver of fear, Anigel recalled certain words of Speaker Sasstu-Cha: "The trees of that place are as voracious as the Glismak themselves . . ."

"They—they would *eat* me?"

Or us, friend. Or any creature foolish enough to touch the tempting offerings that dangle from their trunks.

They moved on up the stream, which now began to narrow rapidly and become more choked with rocks. There were fewer and fewer of the columnar "normal" trees now, and more of the goblets, together with many other species of sinister appearance. The land on either side of the stream rose, and they entered a wide, humid canyon. Strangely, no birds sang nor did Anigel see any animals. The forest was very quiet except for the tumbling waters of the creek and one far-distant scream that she heard, which then stopped abruptly.

When the sun was nearly overhead, the two rimoriks drew the punt up below a patch of whitewater thick with boulders. For more than an hour now they had pushed the boat slowly from behind, squirming and humping through water that was no longer deep enough to swim in, while the banks grew steeper and the country more rocky. Now the two green-dappled creatures turned their great dark eyes upon the Princess and spoke the mental words she had anticipated with dread:

Friend, we can take you no further.

"Yes, I see. The water above the rapids is much too shallow."

Slowly, she put her hunting garb back on. The friendly Wyvilo youths had given her blue boots, a knee-length tunic of blue leather, and an ornate belt that she had hooked her wallet to. The lace trimming of her new shift showed at the sleeves and hem of the tunic in a way no real hunter would have tolerated, but she did not care; she had so longed to feel something soft and clean next to her skin. Checking her supplies, she decided to leave Immu's raincape behind. Her garb was now weatherproof enough if it should storm again, and she no longer cared whether hands or face got wet.

She strapped on her pack, settled Immu's grass hat, and as an afterthought arranged her small dagger where it could easily be pulled out. Then she said to the rimoriks:

"My dear friends, what will you do now? Your home is so far away that I do not see how you can ever return. And this is my doing. Is it possible for you to make a life for yourselves in this forest?"

There are none of our kind here. Only distant relatives. But this does not matter. We will wait here for you, with the boat, until you have fulfilled your quest. Then we will all return together to our own country.

Tears blurred Anigel's vision. Stumbling a little, she stepped into the creek to kiss the top of each wet, glossy head. Then they all three shared miton.

Again, away in the distance but echoing now against the canyon walls, there sounded an agonized scream. Anigel pretended not to hear it as she resettled her pack. A faint trail beginning above the rapids paralleled the creek on one bank and led up-stream. With a last wave to her friends, she set off alone into the forest.

∴

33

It was the most frightful headache Haramis had ever had in all her life, and she moaned as she sat up in the great bed, and clasped her throbbing skull with both hands. She cursed herself for a fool, trying to remember exactly what had happened on the previous night. But pain and nausea defeated her.

Had he cast a spell upon her, sapping her willpower, deceiving and ensnaring her?

"I walked into his trap like a gauzewing flying into a lingit-web! I was as reckless as Kadiya ever could be, and even sillier than Anigel! Oh, my head hurts."

Blearily, she peered about her prison.

One wall of the chamber was cut stone hung with tapestries, and there were two small glazed windows through which she could see grey daylight and snow thickly falling. New candles in gilt sconces lit the other walls of rich wood wainscoting, hung with paintings of strange landscapes. There was a brisk fire in a fireplace framed in colored tiles and having curiously wrought andirons. But she was surprised to feel warm air also coming from a small grille in the wall next to the bed.

She saw the door. It was of heavy gonda-wood, carved in a pattern of stars, and had iron bands and hinges and a massive lock-plate.

Locked in. Trapped.

How?

The canopied bed with its downy comforter, soft sheets, and brocade hangings . . .

She remembered Orogastus leading her to it when her senses had begun to fail, after they had sat long together by the fire conversing and sipping cup after cup of warm brandy. He had laughed as he closed the door, and the click of the lock had followed, and for some strange reason she had burst into tears. Then dizziness had overwhelmed her as she sat on the bed's edge, and with her last strength she had pulled off her outer garments and retreated into blackness.

Poison. Had he tried to poison her, to steal —

She lifted one shaking hand. But the talisman still hung safe between her breasts, suspended by its golden chain. The wand. The Three-Winged Circle.

"Thank the Lords of the Air —"

There was a knock at the door.

"Go away," she moaned. "Can you not let me perish in peace?"

"Haramis, you are not dying," Orogastus said calmly. "Open the door."

"You have locked me in yourself, villain!"

"Look on the table in front of the fire, Haramis."

Slowly, to prevent her pounding head from breaking into pieces, she rose and slid out from under the covers. There were black fur slippers on the rug beside the bed, and a dressing-gown of heavy quilted black velvet lay neatly folded on a nearby bench. Having managed to put these on, Haramis tottered over to the fire.

A graceful little table and a chair upholstered in red leather stood there. On the table was a basket of bread-rolls and a silver-gilt stand with crystal pots of jam. There was also a tall silver ewer, steaming spicily from its spout. And lying on a folded napkin of fine linen was a big brass key.

"Please let me in," the sorcerer said. "It grieves me that you are suffering. I swear that I mean you no harm."

Was he lying? Did she care? Whatever he did to her, she couldn't feel much worse than she did already.

She picked up the key, staggered to the door, and after some fumbling managed to turn the key in the lock.

He turned the latch-ring and entered, tall and dressed all in white. She felt one strong arm support her and lead her to the chair in front of the fire. She collapsed into it.

"You could have opened the door quite easily yourself," she mumbled, accusing. "Don't deny it! You would not even have had to blast it with your lightnings. What lock could restrain a sorcerer? You or one of your attendant demons must have been in the room already, for the fire is lit and the table laid!"

He was pouring some of the hot liquid into the cup. It was darci tea, and the smell of it raised her spirits the merest bit.

"I have no attendants in this place. And I was not in the room, although I did cause the fire to burn and the food to appear. That was what I would call necessary magic." His deep voice was cheerful. "I admit I could have forced the lock, but that is hardly the way to treat a guest. Now drink your tea and eat your breakfast. I assure you that you will feel better after that. Then, if you feel you can forgive me, come again to my library in the main tower and we will resume our interrupted conversation of last night."

She regarded him with deep uneasiness. "And if I decline to accept your hospitality any longer?"

He bowed his head, concealing his face. "Your lammergeier sleeps on the top of this turret. It would come if you called. In the chamber across the corridor there is a balcony — covered with snow and ice, but with plenty of room for you to mount and fly off to wherever you choose . . . if that is really what you want to do."

He went out the open door and closed it softly behind him.

Haramis got up from the table and went to one of the windows. In spite of the blowing snow, she could see the dark chasm that split the flank of Mount Brom and isolated the tower of Orogastus from the passable region opposite. How had *he* gotten here from the Citadel? Surely he could not fly! And what *had* they talked of last night?

Haramis remembered clearly coming to the tower yesterday evening, and Orogastus standing in the open doorway of the gatehouse, silhouetted against the light, welcoming her as a guest long expected. He had been polite but not presumptuous, seeming no sorcerer at all but only the well-bred lord of a rather unconventional manorhouse.

His hair was the bright white of summer clouds, worn long to frame a countenance mature but unlined. The eyes that had blazed like baleful stars in her dreams and fancies now seemed to be the color of very deep water. He wore a loosely belted tunic, narrow trews, and soft shoes — all spotlessly white. Around his neck was a platinum chain with a large medallion bearing the emblem of a many-rayed star.

He had played the gracious host, showing her through certain parts of the tower such as the solar, the music room (this had surprised her), the great library, and finally his personal study. There, a crackling fire had banished any thought of the snowstorm howling outside. The floor was covered with fur rugs, and a candlelit table was set for two.

Orogastus had cooked her a simple supper with his own hands. And then they had sat together on the rug before the fire, drinking brandy . . .

"What did I tell him?"she asked herself. But she could not remember. She ate one bread-roll, slowly, and finished most of the tea.

A small door she had not noticed earlier led to an adjacent bath-chamber, cleverly fitted and sumptuously designed. Flameless lights within crystal shells flashed on as she stepped into the room. Both walls and floor were tiled in pale green and warm to the touch — heated by a central hypocaust, she supposed. There was a tall gold-framed mirror and a dressing table with golden combs and brushes, a large collection of other exquisitely made toiletries, and little pots of cosmetics, bottles of fragrant essences to perfume the water, and body powder with a down puff. Hot and cold water came of itself from gilt spigots and poured into a greenstone tub almost large enough to swim in. The water shut itself off when the tub was full. There were stacks of soft towels ready. Instead of a garderobe there was a water closet, an exotic luxury she had heard of, but never seen.

Haramis sank happily into the warm water. But even in the water, she kept the talisman secure on its chain around her neck.

She went to Orogastus later, dressed in the riding clothes the Vispi had given her and with her black hair hanging in a single braid down her back. She found him in the library, poring over a great book, making notes on a strange glowing tablet with a stylus. When she approached, he laid a fringed leather bookmark on the page and closed the volume. The tablet he touched with a finger at one corner; it dimmed, and the writing upon it disappeared.

"Do not let me interrupt," she said civilly. "If you wish to read on, it would give me pleasure to examine some of your rare books more closely."

"Your scholarly inclination is famed throughout the peninsula, Lady. It was one reason why my royal master, King Voltrik, proposed marriage to you."

She uttered a small laugh. "One reason, forsooth!" She bent, casually, to examine the tablet. "What is this? I saw you inscribe words upon it, and yet the tablet is now blank."

His expression was neutral. "It is a device of the Vanished Ones, and all such are magic."

"I am not so sure of that," she said slowly. *It doesn't feel magical,* she thought. Orogastus was looking at her suspiciously, so she hastily changed the subject. "You told me you have many of their things."

"Yes."

She picked up the tablet idly. "How does this work?"

"Another time," he said pleasantly, and tried to take it from her. But Haramis kept a firm hold on it, pulling back, and it slipped from his fingers and struck lightly against the talisman hanging at her breast. A spark crackled from the wand to the tablet, and the tablet's glow vanished abruptly.

Haramis hastily set it down. *Oh, no,* she thought uneasily. *I didn't mean to break it, but will he believe that—or care?*

Orogastus seemed to be controlling himself with great difficulty. Haramis edged nervously backward, away from him, and tucked the Three-Winged Circle away into her bodice.

He picked up the tablet and pressed his fingertip to it in several places, but the glow did not return. "It's dead," he said between clenched teeth, lifting his eyes to glare at her.

Haramis, who had been considering an apology for the damage she had inadvertently done, lost her temper at that. Her eyes glittered, and her voice sharpened. "Dead?" she snapped. "That device was never alive! My parents are dead—and at your instigation!"

He was silent.

She whirled away from him and went to the great library window. The mad dancing of the wind-driven snow reflected the turmoil that had suddenly broken out in her mind. Since the fall of the Citadel she had not had much leisure to remember the events of that day, and they were certainly something she had preferred not to think about. But now, suddenly, the memories flooded back: the squire's account of her father's murder, the sight of her mother, bleeding to death . . . Tears streamed down Haramis's cheeks.

"Haramis—"

She cut him off. "What an idiot I have been! You lured me here with your black arts, and because I am young and a fool, you were able to lull my fears and make me forget who you really are. And who *I* am!"

He had come up behind her, and now he laid a hand on her shoulder and turned her about. He spoke softly, almost sadly, and there were tiny silvery reflections from the blizzard deep in his eyes.

"Do you not also remember that I kissed the palm of your hand, and told you how I had loved you ever since the wretched Voltrik showed me your portrait? And do you not remember my telling you how I recognized you as the one destined to share power with me?"

"You are the enemy of the Archimage who has protected our kingdom so long against its enemies. Deny it if you dare! You are the one responsible for destroying the great balance of the world, the one who worships the Dark Powers! You would steal my talisman, and those of my sisters —"

He kissed her.

For a moment she stood rigid in his arms. But his lips were sweet, and warmth from them flowed through her body. She felt dizzy, as if everything were whirling madly about and he was the only solid thing in the room. Her arms encircled him and she clung to him. The talisman against her breast warmed with the surging and unfamiliar energies, passing first from him into her, and then back and forth in mounting intensity until her lips and body seemed they would burst into flame.

In her mind, she heard his voice. *We are both wielders of magic, Haramis — born to command the stars! They have lied to you, who say I am evil. I am not. I seek wisdom, truth, and the power and joy that goes with them. Only listen to me! Let me explain why your poor parents died, why I have suffered King Voltrik to carry out his conquest, why you and your sisters were pursued. Let me show you the true importance of the three talismans and the Threefold Sceptre of Power! And then make up your own mind . . . your mind so akin to my own. I have called out to you over the leagues and drawn you to me. You came freely! You know you did! You know I love you. Now dare to love me in return! Now, Haramis. Now . . .*

Haramis stirred. She lifted her head, and gently disengaged herself from his arms. Her body felt strange, her mind bewildered. "What have you done to me?"

"Haramis, you love me. Your body tells me so even as your heart tries to deny it —"

∴

"No! No . . ."

But she was clinging to him again. "I am cold. So cold."

The flying snow lashed at the window, seeking to penetrate the glass, to reach her, to cover her with its pristine whiteness and quench the last dwindling embers that had awakened and blazed within her. She saw the White Lady, dying in solitary pain. She saw herself reflected in a mirror of black ice.

She saw him.

"Let us go to your study," she whispered at last. "It's much warmer there. I will listen to what you have to say."

But that night, alone in her chamber, she remembered her parents and cried herself to sleep.

nigel walked slowly but steadily, going gradually
uphill alongside the dwindling watercourse. It
struck her after a time that she was moving through
the very kind of strange woodland she had dreamed of after going over
Tass Falls. And—yes!—she had dreamed the same dream again last
night, only forgotten it: the forest where her Mother the Queen, wearing
her Crown of State and all the royal regalia, walked far ahead and she,
Anigel, ran after, trying with all of her strength to catch up.

Today in real life, there was no Queen. Her poor Mother was dead.
And the Crown was with Haramis, heiress to the throne—if she still
lived.

Anigel's heart pounded now with exertion as the trail became steeper.
Thank God the terrible goblet-trees no longer grew so thickly! But a
new kind now became commonplace, having a most horrid appearance,
that she was careful not to touch or even come close to. These trees
were tall and robust, crowned by a heavy head of wiry green foliage.
All up and down their smooth trunks were ovoid openings nearly an
ell in length, like vertical mouths. These were studded with polished
green spikes all around the edges, like teeth, and constantly opened
and closed from side to side as though the tree were breathing. The
movement was accompanied by a soft sound like the murmuring of a
breeze or discordant, chilling music. She knew at once that these trees
were carnivores, even worse than the goblets. Their yawning dark
mouths sought prey: they only opened and closed and sang as she
passed. The trees sensed her. Wanted her.

"Lords of the Air, what awful things!" Anigel took hold of her amulet as fear gripped her once again. And then a new and terrible realization came stealing over her and she began to shudder, unable to take another step forward, and felt the flesh crawl on her bare arms.

Where was the path?

It had disappeared.

Only pristine vegetation lay beneath her feet. How long had she been walking off the trail? She had no idea. She had only thought of following the creek. She stood paralyzed with fright, surrounded by the monstrous trees, not knowing which way to turn.

"White Lady!" she cried impulsively aloud. "Help me!"

The amulet inside her clenched fist had become very warm. When she let it fall free at last, the honey-amber glowed brightly even in the broad daylight. The terrible fanged trees hummed and moaned all around her, nearly drowning out the brawling little brook.

The leaf. Cast the leaf.

"What? What did you say?" She swung about, seeking the one who had spoken. But there was no one. "Lady — is that you?"

The Black Trillium leaf. Cast it from you. Let it lead.

Her hands shook so that she could hardly open the wallet. Clouds had come over the sun, bringing a gloomy dusk to the canyon. She felt as though she were freezing. The leaf —

It crackled as she drew it forth. The entire broad blade was dry now, dun-colored instead of green. Only at the very tip of the stem remained a tiny fleck of gold that glittered even in the deepening shadows.

Cast it forth —

Rising on tiptoe, she threw the leaf into the air. There was no wind, and yet it soared slowly away, leading her up the creekbank. As though she were sleepwalking, she followed. The leaf drifted along faster. She began to run. Uphill. The way ever steeper. The undergrowth thicker, darker. There was only that dancing bit of gold on brown, wafting ahead, drawing her on —

She came into a clearing. It was the canyon's head, all framed in moss-grown rock. The stream had its source in a wispy little trickle of water that fell from a tremendous height, blanketing the clearing in thin mist.

And beside the waterfall grew a tree.

It was the most immense living thing she had ever seen. Beside it, the other forest giants were insignificant. Mere straws. Thirty men could have stood shoulder to shoulder in front of this tree without giving the measure of its trunk. It was of the same species as the thorn-mawed carnivores back along the trail, but its mighty bole had only a single opening in between the buttresses of two roots, and this was of the same size as that of its lesser kin. Princess Anigel stood before it utterly amazed, forgetting her fear. Her gaze lifted and she saw that its height exceeded that of the cliff from which the water fell.

And instead of one leafy head, the tree had three.

She approached it, seeing the fanged mouth constantly open and close, open and close, faster and faster. Its breath was a soft roar of a note so deep that it might have escaped ears less keen than hers. And inside the mouth was not darkness, as in the mouths of the smaller trees, but a rich golden glow that was twin to the color of her own amulet.

The Three-Headed Monster held her talisman.

And its breath came faster and faster because it was afraid.

"Of me," said Princess Anigel. "Afraid of me!"

It was part of the wonder that she knew exactly what to do. At the foot of the little cascade lay piles of dead wood, the remains of trees that had been swept over during the season of flooding. She took up a sound billet, about as long as her arm but thicker, and walked directly to the gaping mouth between the roots.

The glow from the cavity intensified and her amulet blazed. Calmly, she held the small log in both hands, horizontal in front of her. She studied the rhythm of the opening and closing for a moment, then with one quick movement thrust her arms into the thorny jaws.

The mouth began to engulf the wood. And could not. The log was wedged against the cavity walls, propping them open.

The tree roared.

But Anigel knew that it was voicing fear, not fury. She had let go of the wooden billet, and now the tree exerted its great strength to crush the foreign thing. The log buckled and began to splinter, but for a moment more the mouth was propped open —

Quite long enough for Anigel to lean forward over the bristling teeth, snatch the thing that lay within, and leap back out of reach before the log broke with a great crack and the mouth snapped tightly shut and remained so, the edges of the bark pursed into a knot hardly as broad as her two fists.

∴

Anigel held a coronet, a C-shaped open tiara of brilliant silvery metal, having six small cusps and three larger. It was strangely and beautifully wrought with rocaille-work scrolling, shells and flowers, and within each of the three larger points was a stylized grotesque visage. One of the monster-faces had an opening beneath it — and she knew what fit there.

Withdrawing to the streamside, she sat upon a rock, took off her hat, unfastened the chain of her trillium amulet, and slipped the gold-framed bit of amber off. It went perfectly into the hole at the front of the coronet, and when it was in place it could not be removed. The fossil flower within the amulet was now completely open except for a slight curling of the petal edges.

Anigel put the coronet on, and went back to stand before the tree.

It was silent, and its mouth remained tightly closed.

"Now the talisman is mine," Anigel told it. "You guarded the treasure well, but I am the one for whom it was intended. You do not have to be afraid. I will leave you here in peace."

She turned away. Strangely, her eyes had filled with tears. She felt a new heavy weight in the pit of her stomach and a sense that something else — something terrible — impended. She thought: I have my talisman — but it is only one of three. What of my sisters?

Instantly, the tree and the clearing and the waterfall disappeared.

She saw in a flash another place, a scene deep in a swamp overgrown with huge thorn-ferns. Kadiya!

Her sister was crouching, tear-stained and screaming defiance, in the midst of a crowd of armed men, knights of Labornok. She wore no trillium amulet, but she held close against her heart something like a sword, with a pommel that glowed with a throbbing amber light. And in the background stood a tall hideous being with glaring orange eyes and bloodstained teeth.

Before Anigel could draw a breath to cry out at the awful sight the picture was gone. She saw instead a cozy tower room in some keep, with rich hangings and fur rugs upon the floor and a table spilling over with stacks of ancient books. A handsome man with snow-white hair wearing a robe of black and silver sat on cushions before a fire, with a lovely young darkhaired woman beside him.

He kissed the palm of her left hand. In the other she held a wand of bright metal, topped by an open silvery circle, with three folded wings surmounting it. And the woman was Haramis . . .

∴

No! No!

Anigel tore the coronet from her brow and dashed it onto the mossy forest floor.

No — the visions lied. Brave Kadiya in the hands of Labornoki, threatened by Skritek? Wise Haramis consorting with the foul sorcerer Orogastus? Never! Never!

If these two were indeed lost then who was the woman prophesied who would overthrow Labornok and restore Ruwenda? Herself? How ridiculous! What a joke! What a cruel, cruel joke . . .

She flung herself on the ground and sobbed as though her heart would break, cringing away from the discarded coronet as though it were truly as loathsome as its name. So this was her talisman! The end of her long quest, the fulfillment of the White Lady's solemn command! The talisman was a liar — a spinner of nightmares worse than any her own craven self could ever concoct. It was nothing but a Monster.

. . . But in her dream, Queen Kalanthe had said that her sisters had gone on other roads. It was she, Anigel, who was being washed and readied for — what?

Gradually her sobbing eased, her breathing slowed and became more regular, and she fell fast asleep.

She woke suddenly an hour later. Had there been a sound? Perhaps one of those mysterious screams? She was unsure. At any rate, she felt much better. She bathed her face in the streamlet, washed her hands, and ate a bit. Then she picked up the coronet and studied it for a long time. The three grotesque faces on it seemed to be smiling slyly.

It is a sign, she decided, *and a tool. I know one thing it can do; conjure visions. But whether those visions are the embodiment of my own fears or true things I cannot tell. But I am going to find out.*

She put it firmly on her head, and Immu's hat over it, and started back the way she had come.

"My Prince, the punts can go no further."

The sergeant who had been poling the lead-boat up Kovuko Stream called out the unwelcome news, whereupon the straggling string of overloaded craft all gathered together in a rocky pool below a stretch of rough water where the creek ran hardly calf-deep.

Antar, his knights, and the Blue Voice gathered in one group to confer, while the exhausted soldier-boatmen refreshed themselves by sloshing about in the stream, munching some of their meager rations, and lying in the shade of the peculiar goblet-trees. None of the Labornoki knew the true nature of the goblets; but they had learned well the lesson of avoiding unknown fruits, and so left the offerings of the trees unmolested.

"From here we must walk," Antar said. "Since the heat is so oppressive, I suggest that we doff all armor save for our helmets, breastplates, and backpieces — "

"My Prince!" the sergeant shouted from the opposite side of the stream. "I think I have found traces of the fugitive!"

They all went splashing over, and there beneath the great drooping fronds of a patch of fodderfern they found one of the oddly made Wyvilo boats. In its bottom was folded neatly a small leather raincape of Nyssomu design.

"This cape is of the style worn at Trevista," the sergeant said. "I remember well the stamped decoration about the hood. Such were offered for sale in the market of Lusagira Square. It may belong to the Princess."

The Blue Voice pushed forward through the crowd of knights. "Give it to me. I will subject it to a test."

With the garment held tightly in his bony hands, he threw back his shaven head and closed his eyes. "Dark Powers, hear me! Reveal to thy suppliant who has worn this cape." He lifted the thing to his nostrils and breathed of it, and then intoned in a very different voice: "It has been worn by Immu, servant to the royal family of Ruwenda, and Anigel, Princess of Ruwenda."

"Zoto's Tripes!" cried the delighted Sir Rinutar. "A true sign of the wench at last! I had begun to think we pursued a phantom."

The Blue Voice opened his eyes, restored his hood, and tossed the cape back into the translucent canoe. "The Princess had it close to her not more than two hours ago. We must be nearly upon her. It behooves us to move on and waste no more time."

"Very well," said the Prince. "Sergeant, assemble your men. And you, my companions, prepare to — "

A scream came from the grove of goblet-trees across the creek. With an oath, the Prince whirled about. He saw a single soldier come running down to the shore, yelling and cursing. The sergeant hurried to see what had befallen, followed by the noble party.

"It ate poor old Gomi!" the wild-eyed fellow declared. "Swallowed him slick as fogberry jam!"

Everyone began to shout at once, but the sergeant called for two of his soldiers to take up their weapons, and said to the Prince, "Let me go and investigate."

He returned in a few moments stone-faced and reported: "It was one of the strange cup-shaped trees, my Prince. The man-at-arms Gomladik ventured to relieve himself against its trunk, and according to the witness four slender arms like great worms issued from the tree's open crown, laid hold of him, and hoisted him aloft."

The Prince and the knights now accompanied the sergeant deeper into the grove, where the goblet-trees stood innocuous as a display in a bizarre jeweler's shop. But one tree was guarded by two soldiers, and its upper leaves had now closed in upon themselves, giving the appearance of a large ball. From the interstices of this oozed red blood and bodily fluids, which flowed down the trunk and puddled within the other leaves splayed on the ground.

They all regarded the sight with horror and revulsion; but before another word could be said more shouting broke out among the men left at the creekside.

"To arms! To arms! Hostile natives approach!"

The devoured Gomladik was forgotten. Antar, Sir Owanon, and the sergeant led the race back to the water, shouting orders. In moments, soldiers were manhandling the wooden punts out of the stream as fast as they could and piling them up to form an improvised barricade. Knights clapped on their helms and drew their swords while the soldiers armored themselves as best they could and readied their crossbows. Sacks of supplies, discarded clothing, and odd bits of equipment littered the bank and even drifted slowly downstream.

And it was at once very quiet.

"Blue Voice," whispered the Prince from behind his overturned boat. "Have you farseen the foe?"

"A moment . . . a moment." The sorcerer's minion lay near the barricade's end, squashed between Sir Rinutar and a soldier, in an attitude uncongenial to trancing. He pulled himself together, his eye sockets seemed to empty, and he froze. "Yes, I see them! Across the stream, lurking among the killer-trees. There are twenty . . . forty . . . Dark Powers forfend, so many I can scarcely count! And they be not Wyvilo, my Prince. These natives are larger and altogether more terrible in aspect — beyond doubt, the cannibal Glismak!"

"Enough," Antar said. And to the others: "My men, have courage. They are Oddling savages, for all their fearsome look, and inferior to us. We can yet win the day."

"Look," Owanon said quietly. "The first of them."

Six beings stole through the ferny undergrowth and stood poised on the opposite bank not ten ells distant. They were less humanoid than the Wyvilo and taller than men, and carried long spears pointed with flint. They wore no clothing, but a few had jeweled ornaments and all wore belts, from which stone maces and other implements of war hung. Their heads were muzzled and their teeth, especially the two protruding tusks in front, very large and sharp. Deepset eyes of a burning red were armored about the orbits with shining skin plates; these plates also covered their heads and extended down their shoulders, backs, and upper arms, and were a natural part of their bodies. The three-digit hands and feet had both webs and formidable claws. Only a few scattered plates guarded their bellies, and these and most of the limbs and face were clothed in thick rusty-red fur. Scanty fur also grew around the margins of the plates, which were, in each individual, of a slightly different color and patterning. In truth, the Glismak had a savage beauty about them — as well as an air of supreme confidence.

One of the six stepped forward and began a croaking harangue, waving his spear. When he finished, he tossed the weapon with all his strength and the stone blade sank deeply into the tough wood of the Prince's dugout. The other five Glismak cocked their arms.

"Crossbowmen," Antar said, "missiles away."

A hail of iron quarrels shot across the stream. Five of the Glismak fell, screaming hideously. The sixth uttered a trumpeting howl, which was answered by hundreds more, and came bounding over the water. His fellows poured from the goblet-forest behind, whooping and screeching, flinging their spears and brandishing their other weapons.

Within seconds the small force of Labornoki was engulfed by the horde. The crossbows became useless at close hand and soldiers fought with short-swords or daggers, while the knights laid about with their great two-handed swords, hacking and hewing until the sheer press of Glismak bodies toppled them.

∴

The sergeant managed to gut two of the monsters before a third came up behind him with open jaws and delivered a fatal bite to his neck. The few soldiers who were not overwhelmed in the first minutes ran for their lives, only to be chased down by the long-legged brutes, who clawed their flesh from their bones. The fallen were immediately rent limb from limb and in the midst of battle a diabolical feast began. Eerie Glismak howls drowned out the dying cries of the soldiers.

By then Prince Antar and all of his knights were downed. But strangely enough the fiends did not mangle them nor strip off their armor, but rather took away their swords and trussed them hand and foot with rawhide cords, and picking them up like dolls tossed them clanking and cursing into a great bloodstained pile.

Several score of the victorious Glismak now began to dance and chant about the heap of helpless humans, who subsided into hopelessness and began to say their final prayers. Others of the maneaters set about to gather dry driftwood from along the creek, which they made into a great stack, together with the Labornoki punts, and prepared to set it alight. It was evident that the next course of the Glismak feast was to be cooked.

"God have mercy upon us all," moaned Prince Antar, who lay at the top of the tangled mass of prisoners, "and may he damn the sorcerer Orogastus, who sent us to this ignoble death, to the deepest of the ten pits of hell."

The chanting and the howling of the Glismak abruptly broke off.

The dancing stopped. Those of the mob who were still finishing off tidbits of raw flesh desisted from their gruesome feeding and stood astonished. Every savage without exception now was motionless, open-mouthed, staring at something that seemed to be approaching from upstream. Antar wriggled his fettered body about and finally gained a position in which he could see for himself who was coming.

A woman.

She stood on the small creekside path, a dozen ells from the pile of knights and within arm's reach of the nearest Glismak. She wore a hunting outfit of sky-blue leather and had a pack on her back, and in one hand carried a broad-brimmed grass hat and in the other a sapling cut for a walking-stick. Her hair was golden and fell below her shoulders in shimmering waves. Resting upon her head was a strangely wrought coronet of shining white metal, with trillium amber inset at the front.

∴

Her face was a mask of horror and outrage and tears were trickling down her cheeks.

Prince Antar's heart turned over in his breast. He knew that face, and it was the most beautiful he had ever seen and the only one he had ever loved. It was Princess Anigel herself come by mischance into the scene of slaughter, and surely the fiends would fall upon her next —

But they did not. They shrank back as she walked into their blood-stained midst, and some uttered low grunts and even whimpers. She looked upon the human bones and torn remnants of clothing and the heap of bound armored knights who now lay frozen in their contemplation of her audacity and peril.

"What have you *done?*" she demanded of the Glismak. Tears still shone on her face, but her voice was steady.

There were scattered growls, and an uneasy hissing.

One individual came forth from among those who had danced. He was taller than the rest, and his belt had golden studs, and a gold sheath enclosed his flint dagger. The scales of his body were richly adorned with painted designs of green and yellow and scarlet.

The Glismak chieftain pointed at Anigel's coronet with one bloody claw and roared a challenging phrase in his own language.

"I have a right to wear it," the Princess said unflinchingly. She dropped the hat and wiped the tears from her eyes with the back of one hand. "And I say you have done a wicked thing. These men were my enemies, not yours. They did you no harm and yet you massacred them and ate their flesh like beasts! But you are not beasts, you are persons meant to serve the Triune God and one another, and what you did was evil."

The Glismak chieftain uttered a terrible sound that could only be laughter. And then he lifted clawed hands, opened his mouth so that his knife-like teeth shone in the gloomy late afternoon light, and advanced upon the helpless girl.

Anigel pointed her walking-stick at him and said calmly, "Lords of the Air, defend me."

From out of the overcast and louring sky came a blue bolt of lightning. It blinded the captive knights and its thunder pained their ears so greatly that they nearly lost consciousness. When they regained their wits they saw the Princess standing wide-eyed, and the Glismak chieftain blasted to a smoking cinder.

∴

The entire horde of cannibal Oddlings fell on their faces from fear and awe.

"Go away!" Anigel said in a high, clear voice. "Go away, and don't come back."

A fierce head or two lifted from the ground. The Glismak hesitated — and then they were up and running, the entire mob of them, howling at the top of their lungs, and a few still growling defiance. They crossed the stream and raced into the forest, and were lost from sight, and the Princess looked down upon the fuming carcass at her feet with both astonishment and fear.

Now Antar cried out: "Princess Anigel! We here yet live. Will you set us free?"

She snapped out of her reverie and came running, and with her small dagger cut the rawhide thongs. The knights sorted themselves out, and the unhurt among them helped the wounded unstrap their armor and go down to the water. Prince Antar, when he had done what he could, went to Anigel and lowered himself to his knees before her.

"Princess, I have no sword to surrender to you. So I, Antar, Crown Prince of Labornok, surrender my body and soul. I cannot be your enemy. You are noble and good and those who commanded me to pursue you and put you to death are evil. If you would blast me to death as you did yon brutish wretch, then that is only the punishment I deserve. But if you will spare me I will serve you faithfully as your slave, for the rest of my days."

"And I," said Sir Owanon, coming forward and also kneeling.

"And I," groaned Sir Penapat, who was having his wounds washed.

This knight and that echoed these two, and the ones who were able-bodied came to kneel, until only Sir Rinutar and two of his henchmen, Onbogar and Turat, stood back.

Suddenly the mass of ferns that had concealed Anigel's boat parted, and there sitting concealed in the craft was none other than the Blue Voice, who climbed out, waded the stream, and approached the Princess with an ingratiating smile.

"Great and powerful Lady," quoth he, making a profound bow, "I am slave to another Master who has bound me until eternity. But I vow to you on his honor to serve and follow you as well as I may, and I place my poor powers at your command if you will condescend to accept me."

∴

As the Blue Voice spoke he turned to Rinutar and their eyes met for an instant. "And perhaps these three brave knights, who shrink from rescinding their oaths of fealty to Labornok, will join me as I pledge a truce to you. We are humans together, beleaguered in a strange land, and we should not be at odds while so terrible an enemy threatens all of us."

"Aye," Rinutar growled. "I will pledge a truce, as will my men."

Anigel gazed upon the Blue Voice for a moment unspeaking, and also studied the three. Then she said: "Very well. Rise, Prince — and also you men who now deem me your Lady. In a few hours it will be nightfall. We have nothing more to fear from the Glismak, but nevertheless we cannot camp in this place of disaster. I will confer with the Prince and decide what we are to do. Meanwhile, you must gather up what weapons and supplies you can, and remove your punts from the bonfire stack. But do not tear the woodpile apart. Rather place on it the sad remains of your comrades, and before we quit this spot we will fire it to their honor."

Murmurs of approval met her words. She beckoned for Prince Antar to follow her as she walked a ways down the bank of the stream, and when they were beyond earshot of the others said:

"The tall man in blue is not to be trusted."

"I know. He is a Voice of the abominable sorcerer, Orogastus. We shall have to keep close eye on him as we make our way back . . . You do intend to return to Ruwenda, do you not, my Lady?"

"In time," said she. Her blue eyes were solemn and the pupils wide in the shadow. "But first I have another duty. The Glismak horde will surely go now to the Wyvilo settlement of Let and attack it. They were on their way when they encountered you. We must hurry there as fast as possible to warn the forest Folk, and do what we can to help them."

"Aye!" said the Prince in admiration. "We knights shall guard you with our blades while you call down thunderbolts to slay the devilish Glismak!"

Anigel drew back from him with a gasp of horror. "No!"

"But how then shall we save the Wyvilo, Lady? We are sixteen men — twenty if you count the three unpledged and the sorcerer's lackey — and some of us are wounded. The Glismak must number in the hundreds. Do you suppose we can counter such a vast army of savages without your magical assistance?"

∴

"I did not know the talisman would kill," she whispered. And there was terror in her eyes. "I did not know . . ."

Antar took her hand. The tears were starting again. He lifted her calloused, scratched fingers to his lips. "Don't worry. Perhaps you can try the powers of the thing as we travel, and find gentler means of defense."

She drew away impatiently, again thinking only of the task ahead. "We shall rest tonight, then press on tomorrow even until night, so that we reach Let ahead of the Glismak."

"Travel at night?" Antar was nonplussed. "Lady, we amateur boatmen cannot possibly navigate the Great Mutar by the light of the Triple Moons — and it may well storm again."

A tiny smile curved Anigel's lips. "We shall have the services of excellent guides."

She went down to the streambank, still smiling, and called: *Friends!*

35

Hamil came striding up to Kadiya, two of his troopers flanking them with torches. His hand again gripped her hair, and pulled her to her knees.

He was laughing and she heard other voices join him. "Now you are showing the proper spirit, Krain's daughter: humbly — on your knees. What game has been played here?"

His eyes darted about — to the straight-standing sword and then to that odious blackened pile. One charred, skeletal hand seemed to point to the object of power its owner had coveted.

There was a long moment of silence and then Hamil laughed again, but less assuredly. Several score armed men now had gathered, but all carefully avoided the thing lying on the ground.

"So, it looks as if the Voice told the truth and yet did not believe it himself! Was that the way of it, slut?" The General shook Kadiya back and forth by that tormenting hold on her hair. "He strove to take the talisman and it was bonded to you, and thus it slew him."

He loosened his hold on her and ran a finger back and forth along his lower lip. Kadiya had heard enough of the General to know that he, brute as he had proved himself to be, was also wily and keener-witted than he looked.

Some of the men fell away from the edge of the circle about them, giving way to another officer, a huge man. His ragged cloak had once been as ornate as Hamil's but he went without a helmet and there was a dirty bandage about his head, a bristle of grey stubble on cheeks and chin.

.:

"What now, my General?" There was a sharpness in his voice which argued that they might be fellows in a fight but no shield brothers.

Hamil had no chance to answer before a voice from somewhere among the ranks cried:

"Lash the witch to the sword, and into the bog with her!"

There was an answering hum of assent to that. Then another trooper gave different advice:

"Turn the Skritek on her!"

To that there was even firmer agreement. The gathering of men had moved farther away from Kadiya, the edges of the crowd melting into the dark where the torch and firelight did not easily reach. It would seem that the import of that blasted body was making itself stronger and more widely felt.

Hamil swept the assemblage with a glare which apparently his men knew only too well, for the murmur ceased as if a door had been suddenly slammed shut. Then he turned to the big officer.

"What now, Osorkon? Why, we obey orders. Always we obey orders! We came to find this." Again his grip on Kadiya's hair caught her tight enough to make her sway back and forth. "Well, we have found it. We have something else, too —" He pointed to the talisman. "If King Voltrik rewards well those who bring one of these royal wenches to him, what kind of gift will he bestow upon those who produce a treasure our Grand Minister of State mightily wishes to own?"

"A *treasure*," Osorkon accented the word strongly, "which has already disposed of one who knows far more than any of us about its dangers."

"Yes." Hamil's tongue tip ran across his fleshy lips. He dragged Kadiya up from her knees so he had not so far to look down to meet her eyes squarely. "I think you will be more truthful with us now. There are ways we know well how to handle those who are all courage and zeal, so that in the end they are only too glad to do our will even if that means slaying one very near to their heart." He snapped his fingers and again the crowd of men opened as one of the Skritek slouched forward in answer.

"Pellan!" Hamil made an order of that name. From the back rows of the troops tottered a skeletal figure. Kadiya, who had seen the merchant-guide in the days of his well-fed and honored life among his fellows, could not recognize him at first. It was a human wreck who fell to his knees rather than make formal obeisance, and looked up to the General with a face like one belonging to the dead.

Hamil leaned forward to gaze intently at the talisman. Now he nodded as if he had been answered with just what he wanted to hear. "It is still there . . ." In spite of the transformation the sword had undergone, the snakeskin twist the Voice had produced for its handling was still safely looped about it.

"Pellan, tell this stupid brute to take that sword up, and put it back on the girl's back, using only the cord."

The man gulped as if he found it difficult to speak. Then he voiced a stream of gutturals. The Skritek looked at him, at the sword, then at Hamil. Fanged jaws opened and the creature made an answer in his own grumbling speech.

Pellan's face was white beneath the grime of swamp travel. Kadiya saw that his hands were shaking, and that he put them hastily together in a tight grip.

"Well?" demanded Hamil, after a long moment of silence.

"Lord General — he will not touch that." The guide nodded toward the sword. "He says it is of the Vanished Ones and holds their force."

"So?" Hamil's expression did not change. He caught the loop of snakeskin, jerking the blade free from the ground. Then he wheeled slowly, as if to make very sure that all men gathered there were perfectly aware of what he was doing.

"The Vanished Ones," he commented. "We have heard a great deal about these Vanished Ones since we started plowing through this bog. See you, all of you! Need one wearing the emblem of great Labornok be fearful of legends?"

Osorkon coughed. "And what of him?" He pointed to the charred remains. "It would seem that some legends hold legitimate warnings."

Hamil did not even blink, but Kadiya was very sure at that moment that the General held no liking for his immediate subordinate. Through witnessing the slow indrawing of the soldiers, she was also aware that their General's gesture had banished some of their fear-inspired awe.

"That one," Hamil nodded to the cinders, "was one who played with such magical toys. Perhaps those of his master are safe enough, but this thing here is of a different source. A man who handles certain weapons without hurt grows careless. I think this Voice took too much on himself."

∴

The General was back at Kadiya's side now. His heavy paw on her shoulder spun her around so that she might have fallen again. But she was able to keep her feet as she felt the sword slipped slowly back among the ropes that bound her.

Hamil had already turned away. He beckoned to a trooper who stood immediately by the nearest torchman. Leveling his hand, he pointed to the Skritek who had refused his order.

"That one we do not need," he commented.

The Skritek roared and crouched. An axe with a wicked double head appeared in one scaled fist. The creature's defiant cry was answered by several others of his kind.

The soldier Hamil had summoned took a leap forward, his sword up and ready. It appeared that this was not the first time the Labornoki had faced one of their unpleasant allies in combat.

As the axe left the claws of the Skritek, it moved with such force and speed that it was but a blur in the uncertain light. But the soldier had already launched himself forward, not to meet the weapon but in a fighting stance. At the same time his sword flashed, and there was a spurt of dark blood. The Skritek threw up his head with an ear-splitting bellow, his left leg half hewn from his body. The forearms with their sharp talons out. One paw, perhaps more by luck than intention, caught in the mail on the soldier's shoulder and dragged him down. It did not need his shout of pain and terror to bring his comrades' steel out, nor were the other Skritek long in joining the fight.

Labornoki soldiers and Skritek fought and died as the battle whirled around the bonfire. One of the torchmen drove off a monster within claw's range of Hamil himself by thrusting the fiery end of the torch he held into the creature's half-open jaws. The melee was fierce while it lasted, but that was not long, for the mob of Skritek faded away into the swamp night, leaving three of their own number dead, two still living. Four soldiers lay unmoving, and a number of others nursed bloody gashes and the like.

Osorkon had reached out at the beginning of the embroilment, caught Kadiya, and dragged her back toward Hamil's tent, which half collapsed as a guy rope gave way. He himself made no attempt to join in the fight but stood watching. When it was over he studied Hamil with a brooding look. However, he waited to speak until the General, wiping blood from his sword with a handful of leaves, came close enough so that perhaps only Kadiya was also able to hear.

"Our allies must truly have second thoughts on the matter of service," Osorkon observed dryly. "You had that two-tongued pack-vart"—he nodded at Pellan, who had crouched into a ball as close to whatever shelter the tent might offer—"play guide to the last point on the river he knew three or four days back. Since then, we have been guided by the monsters." Now he nodded toward the general area where the Uisgu women lay roped closely together. "All around us the swamp boils, nor have we had any word from our advance scouting party for two days. I say, let us turn back now that we have achieved our goal and you have the girl and that which she carries."

Hamil scowled. "There may be more treasure to be found."

"And what if the Oddlings rise? We have taken Uisgu prisoners and our handling of them has been enough to turn all of their blood against us. And now we have antagonized the Skritek. If we must depend for guides on those who have good reason to hate us, we are fools."

"Oddlings—slimy devils! Have any showed themselves willing to take up arms? No! They are puny cowards, spiritless as barnyard togars. The Uisgu rise—? Impossible! They can't and won't fight. Is that not so, worm?" Hamil prodded Pellan with his boot toe. "Did you not tell us from the beginning that these swamp-sulkers are cravens?"

Pellan raised his head, and also his skinny arm as if trying to ward off a blow. "It was always true before, Lord General. The Skritek they will fight, but only if the fiends of the Mazy Mire attack them. Between themselves there is no quarreling, nor have they ever raised weapon against any of us humans who entered the swamp. I have heard that an ancient oath was laid upon them forbidding warfare, and they are pledged to it."

Hamil snorted. "This girl has managed to find her way about the Thorny Hell, and the Uisgu have helped her or she would not have been able to reach this point. With her and those"—he gestured to the other prisoners—"with us, the Uisgu will not impede us."

The next morning they broke camp and marched upriver, following a faint trail. General Hamil did not speak again to Kadiya, although he kept her close by as he listened to reports brought in by flankers and

∴

scouts. Thus she first learned in truth that the Labornoki force did not travel alone. Something — or someone — skulked along with them, although the men were never able to get a good look at it. Were they being followed by swamp-dwellers who had at last arisen to avenge the murder of their people? Dared she hope for so much?

Kadiya roused from her state of frozen lethargy to hear a badly bitten and mud-stained soldier say:

"Gam's. I'd swear by Zoto's Shield to that! Just his head agrinnin' from a pole planted by a fern patch. No sign of them monsters either. Just some blurry little footprints showin' in the mud — an' this."

He held out what Kadiya recognized as a dart — longer than any she had seen the Nyssomu use. Still, the shaft was painted with two tiny bands, one blue and the other yellow, and those she *had* seen before. Jagun! Or at least his hunt sign.

"Gam," Hamil repeated. His mud-caked fingernails grated across the stubble of beard on his jaw. "I saw him take on the Westlinger pirates — two of them with one blow. Well, I am sure he did not die cheaply. Was he done in by the Skritek?"

"That dart is not Skritek." Osorkon had taken the thing from the scout. "They don't do work as fine as this."

"What has our lady Princess here to say?" Hamil inquired of Kadiya. Her bearers had rested her bound body on the trail. "Do you have some other friend waiting to take a hand in our affairs?" He poised his hand to slap her.

She could answer him with part truth. "I . . . have not seen the like . . . of that before."

Osorkon did not give the General any time to force another answer out of her.

"She may serve as bait, if they do have other weapons to use. Don't waste time mauling her here. Let us get on to some solid land if a fight threatens. We can't put up any show of force floundering around in this demon-cursed mud."

Suddenly, a resounding roar came from ahead. Hamil's sword was in his hand instantly and the soldiers behind bunched about their commander.

"Skritek!" the scout yelled. "And from the sound of 'em, they've got some poor devil on the run!"

"Move along!" Hamil ordered. "Close up! There's higher ground ahead and we need firm footing."

∴

Once more the cry of the Skritek sounded. Kadiya's ears buzzed and she was near unconscious from the jouncing as her bearers ran along. Her arms had lost all feeling from the bindings. Even if she were free and had talisman in hand, she was not sure she would be able to use it. However, behind the pain, the helplessness — and yes, the fear, she still held grimly to the old core of anger. There must be some way she could strike back! If only the magic paralysis would wear off . . .

They raced ahead, depending on flankers for warning. The land now became dry and fairly open except for some low-growing vegetation, but at the same time it had the dire look of that stretch of country Kadiya had crossed with Jagun earlier. Here and there grew networks of fat greyish ground-vines, with leaves which looked hardly more than shriveled buds and which were surrounded by clouds of insects. Crushed underfoot, the vines gave off a putrid smell.

And then they came upon a building.

It was not of stone — but rather of that same sleek material which had formed the bowl-like camping place she had shared with Jagun and the place where she had acquired her talisman. One wall was pierced by a doorway, and recessed on either side was a tall statue in the form of those same sentries which guarded the Forbidden Way. Each sindona held a sword. Kadiya blinked smarting eyes. The swords — they were pointless like the one she now bore on her back. The weapons were outstretched and crossed to forbid entrance.

Hamil halted to eye what lay before them. There was an eager note in his voice. "By Zoto — the very thing I hoped to find! A stronghold of the Vanished Ones, and probably full of treasure! Captain Loskar, you go and give a tickle to those." He nodded to the statues. "The rest of you men get ready with your arrows!"

It proved the measure of Hamil's power over his troops, in spite of all the recent disasters, that he was promptly obeyed. A young officer raised his own sword so that it touched that point where the pointless blades of the sentinels crossed. The metal rebounded with a harsh clang. Loskar's weapon flew out of his hand and he gave an agonized howl and caught at his sword arm, falling to his knees.

"Arrows — inside!" Hamil snapped.

The whistling of the Labornoki war-bolts, meant to afright as well as kill, was loud. Into the opening behind the two sentinels they sped. It was dark in there, with no hint of what lay beyond. Neither was there any answer to the attack Hamil had ordered. He called to the men who carried Kadiya: "Wunit! Vor! Push her beneath the statues' swords!"

The soldiers slung her, carrying poles and all, through the doorway. When the sentinels remained motionless, Wunit and a dozen men ducked down and followed after.

"It's safe, my General!" Wunit called. "We need torches!"

Brands were quickly kindled and passed through. The interior of the building was featureless except for a single inner door at the end of a narrow hallway. Above it was carved a great trillium.

"Wait — I'm coming myself," Hamil said. Grabbing a torch, he stooped and entered.

Immediately, all the torches of the Labornoki went out. There were masculine screams, sounds of floundering bodies, and then utter silence.

Kadiya lay face down, unable to help herself. No daylight penetrated this place. The dark of the open outer door might have been a curtain, although she had felt none such as she fell through. She drew a gasping breath. Oddly enough that paralysis which had gripped her so strongly now seemed to be receding. She thrashed about like a landed fish, trying to rise. The blackness around her was thick and complete, but she was aware of a lessening of that fear which had walked with her since she had been taken captive.

The girl wriggled violently. Suddenly her arms were free at her sides, and the talisman lay loose under her body. She tore the remaining rope from her legs. The surface under her felt clear of any dust or drift from the outer world. Instead it was slippery and now slanted downward at an ever-increasing angle. She began to slide, as she used her numbed arms to lever herself upright. Faster and faster she fell, and then she crashed, still holding the talisman, into an unseen barrier, only to continue her slide in a new direction and crash again. Half-conscious, she clung to the magical sword . . . until she struck one last barrier, flew through the air, and landed senseless on a level surface.

The toe of a boot caught her in the side and woke her.

Kadiya blinked and blinked again. Darkness no longer locked her in. She was in a large room, lit dimly by no discernible source of illumination.

"She's a tough one, General."

Three men stood in a close triangle about her. One was Hamil, the other two Wunit and Vor. The other troops stood sullenly behind them. Kadiya saw that the Labornoki were bruised and trying not to show fear.

She lifted her head. Though her arms were strong again, her hand was not quite able to reach the hilt of the talisman which lay partly beneath her.

"Do you think she knows the way out of here, sir?" Vor asked.

"That may well be," Hamil replied. At any rate we can use her to test for more damned man-traps as we look the place over. Get her moving."

No one touched her. She took hold of the talisman and climbed slowly to her feet, her head aching from the battering it had received. Dully, she wondered why they had not tried to take the sword from her, and then she remembered that they had good reason to fear touching that eerie weapon.

The grey light shone upon a kind of indoor courtyard. Before them was a fountain flowing with water. On the other side of the fountain was a staircase leading up. She walked over to it, but darkness hung above and Kadiya could not see where the stairs led.

On each step was a footprint glowing red.

Hamil showed no hesitation. "Onward!" he commanded. He set foot squarely on the first print, then began to tremble violently like one afflicted with marshfever. White-faced, he staggered back, drew his sword, and brandished it at Kadiya.

"Magic!" he croaked. "Let *her* lead the way." He pulled Kadiya before him so it was her foot that touched the print on the next stair.

By the trillium, she was going to scream! There shot through her a sensation like a blast of flame. Then the talisman she held echoed the feeling of burning heat, but she could not throw it from her. She heard an astounded cry from Hamil. She had reached the fifth step, beyond his reach, and the glowing footprint awaiting her there abruptly vanished. What she placed foot upon was a circle of silver centered by a Black Trillium. Hamil did not expect the sudden move that followed. She was free, completely recovered from her injuries and the enchantment, and each step before her was marked with the same enheartening symbol. As her foot fell quickly upon each in turn new strength built within her.

Anger boiled up. Let her but turn and she could kill them all! No, that was the response of a fool. Armed men watched her, some armed with bows and arrows. She had only this talisman of which she was still unsure.

A moment later she had reached a long room at the head of the stairs. Each wall here was crossed and recrossed by a netting of red light. The chamber was centered by a single block of the strange pale building material, and there only did another color show. For, rising as if from a bed of well tended earth, stood a carven image of a tall plant made of silvery metal. A trillium plant. The stalk ended in a single large tightly closed bud.

Hamil had followed warily, his men behind him. Now he stamped forward to look up at the plant, one hand on sword hilt. He might be in the heart of enemy territory with his army whittled away, yet there was nothing in his stance to suggest that he did not fully believe in himself and his own power. He glared at Kadiya, who stood facing him resolutely with the talisman gripped in one hand. "We will go no farther," she said calmly.

The General glanced back over his shoulder. He did not speak, but Wunit and Vor moved in quickly on either side of him, swords drawn.

"I have heard," Hamil's voice was low and charged with hatred, "that blood is power. This is certainly a place of power." He gave an order: "Drive her over to that altar!"

They harried her with their blades, forcing her back against the stone from which the Flower sprang.

"I," Hamil's voice rang loud now, "am a man of blood. I have learned to pay with blood for what I want. When you die, Princess, you will no longer be bonded to that magical talisman. Orogastus no longer has power here. I do! And I intend to hew off that hand of yours that holds the talisman, and when your life's blood is drained, take it for my own."

His sword swung up. Over her loomed the giant Flower. To Kadiya's sight it seemed to quiver and burst into bloom. Was it a flower or something else — such as the sentinel? She could not be sure, for around it a dazzling green glow radiated.

The truncated sword length of her talisman blazed a vivid green also, sharing the potency of the Flower.

From the pulsing of the light about her she was sure some change had come in on the altar. For Wunit and Vor and the soldiers fled back down the stairs, their faces fear-stricken and ghastly.

∴

Hamil was dusky with rage. He charged at her. By no knowledge she had ever possessed before, her talisman answered, blocking the General's own blade. It seemed to her that time moved oddly — first as fast as a whirlwind, and then as if leaden weights hobbled both of them. Each time he thrust, she parried. He was thrice her bulk, but he could not beat her down, nor thrust past the invincible guard of her talisman.

He howled, throwing back his head and giving voice like an animal. Then, to her complete astonishment, he turned to run heavily down the stairs.

Kadiya steadied herself at the altar. Above her, a huge Black Trillium bloomed on a silver stalk. She dared now to look up. She raised the talisman and the three eyes on the pommel opened, facing three greater ones at the center of the altar flower.

Now it was as if a window in the strange room had been flung open to the full day's sun. The eyes blazed. They seemed to reach deep into her soul.

She herself was no longer of any importance. There was no more Kadiya of Ruwenda . . . only the Lady of the Eyes.

And then all the glory vanished. What had been a pillar of light on the altar flared and was gone. There was no Black Trillium. The room was empty except for her, and her now-dulled talisman.

Kadiya turned to walk to the stairway. The wall colors were fading, all was a dusty grey. She went down the steps and found an open door, and heard the shouts of men and of others, and the ringing of weaponry outside. As one totally renewed in spirit and body she leapt forward into what was a full battle.

Labornoki were falling with poisoned darts stuck into any exposed part of their bodies. Now from the brush erupted hundreds of Uisgu, nimbly dodging arrows with curious half-hopping, half-dancing steps. There were Skritek, too, laying about at the Oddlings. Hamil, his tattered cloak of office shorn from his shoulders, was engaged with three diminutive Uisgu, wielding spears. The General aimed a sweeping sword-cut to cut down Oddlings, but Kadiya sprang forward, barely clearing another body, to face him.

Always afterward she would swear that some spirit had possessed her. She nearly dropped the talisman, but with both hands she grasped the dull, truncated blade and swung the hilt up just as Hamil was about to strike her down.

∴

"To what you have made yourself," she found breath to shout, "return, man of blood!"

Hamil twisted. He dropped his sword to raise both hands to his throat. His eyes were aflame, flame lapped from between his lips, ran down his body. From him came such a cry of torment as made Kadiya shudder. The Three-Lobed Burning Eye looked upon him with all its power, and he fell heavily to the ground. Like the Voice before him, what remained of Hamil was only ashes.

From the talisman pommel there now licked another great tongue of flame, which split into streams and menaced the Skritek. They broke away to follow the fleeing Labornoki soldiers. The flame vanished.

"Lady of the Eyes . . ."

Kadiya looked toward the mass of jubilant Oddling warriors. "Jagun!" That name seemed to come from some other far off memory, part of another time. "You're safe!"

But another voice also spoke now, one that silenced even the moans of the wounded.

"Daughter!"

Kadiya turned back to the sindona at the door. Above their noble heads was a circling of silver, and within it a familiar face, smiling.

"White Lady! Have — have I done what I should?"

"Not yet."

Kadiya drew a breath which was close to a sob. "What, then? Must I carry this" — she held out the talisman — "to the finish?"

"That is so," the calm voice replied.

"I am what I have been fashioned for . . ." In part that was a plea.

"That, too, is so."

She still had so much to learn!

"What lies ahead?"

There came no answer. The vision faded, and Kadiya stood with tears running down her scratched and wounded face. She had been allowed a glimpse of something beyond her understanding, that she must even now hunger for; but now all she could do was carry on. She turned then to face the battlefield. The Uisgu stood there with Jagun smiling among them. They raised their small hands in salute. They had forsaken the old ways; they had gathered clan and tribe to a single purpose. It must be her will and cause to unite them.

∴

36

After he had been introduced to the rimoriks and acquainted with their abilities, Prince Antar decided that the party would travel fastest by taking only two wooden punts, Anigel's translucent Wyvilo canoe, and a minimum of supplies. Before anyone was allowed to sleep, a new set of harnesses and traces for the rimoriks was braided from cut-up leather military cloaks, and holes were bored in the vessels to link them together. After only five hours' sleep the party was off.

Since the rimoriks knew exactly where they were going, there was no need for reins. They pulled the three boats hitched in line while still in the narrow stream, and reached the Great Mutar in only three hours. Once in the big river, the animals were able to pull more strongly abreast while the knights also rowed. Princess Anigel's lightweight canoe trailed the wooden punts in which the men hauled away; and with her rode Prince Antar, the badly wounded Sir Penapat, and the Blue Voice, who had proved to be a hopelessly inefficient paddler — perhaps bungling his strokes on purpose. Having the sorcerer's acolyte in their boat at least gave Anigel and Antar the opportunity to keep an eye on him. He behaved in an exemplary fashion, sponging Sir Penapat's feverish brow in the boat's stern while the Prince and Princess conversed in low tones for hour after hour in the bows.

The rimoriks hauled the humans along so swiftly that they found themselves approaching the village of Let just as night fell on that same day, only barely ahead of a second great rainstorm.

But not ahead of the Glismak.

"Lords of the Air — no!" cried Anigel, as she caught sight of towering clouds of smoke rising against a somber sunset. The boats were still moving along at such a rate that she dared not stand.

"Use your farsight to scan the scene, Voice!" the Prince commanded. "Tell us what has happened."

Anigel had gone very pale and when she spoke it was nearly in a whisper. "Wait — let *me* try."

The Blue Voice gawked at her in astonishment as she closed her eyes and sat still as a stone. But her lovely face acquired nothing of the repellent empty-eyed look that accompanied the trance of Orogastus's symbionts. After a few minutes, she said:

"The Glismak attacked the village from the landward side about an hour ago. I cannot tell if it is the same horde that fell upon your men. There seem to be at least three times as many Oddlings as we saw up the Kovuko . . . They have set many buildings on fire . . . I see Speaker Sasstu-Cha and I will try to bespeak him . . ."

The Prince and the Blue Voice waited. Sir Penapat said eagerly: "If it is to be a battle, you may count on me to do my part! Even one-eyed, one-legged, and one-armed I can outfight any of the rest of the lads! You know me, my Prince."

"Indeed I do, Peni." His countenance was sorrowful. "But I fear there is little any of us will be able to do if the savages have already overrun Let."

Princess Anigel's eyes opened. "The Speaker thanks us for our kindly intentions," she said dully, "but the fighting is now hand-to-hand, and nearly a third of the homes are on fire. He is about to capitulate, as is their usual custom when overwhelmed, and pay a large indemnity of goods to the invaders, who will then withdraw for some weeks."

"But, Princess," the Blue Voice protested with a fine air of reproach. "You have it in your power to save them. If only you would."

"Silence, you misbegotten rascal!" hissed the Prince. "How dare you address the Lady in that presumptuous way?"

Anigel stared at the Blue Voice, eyes wide, and her lip caught between her small white teeth, regarding him as though he were a venomous swamp-worm that had just slithered into the boat. But an instant later she said:

"He is right. I could save the poor Wyvilo, if I but had the courage to call down killing force through my talisman. If I could conjure up

∴

cold-bloodedly the same hate and revulsion and desire for obliteration that I inadvertently focused upon the Glismak leader at the scene of the massacre."

"Then do it," the Blue Voice urged, "and save your friends!"

"I — I dare not." She began to weep.

The Blue Voice shrugged and smiled. "They are only Oddlings."

"They are rational creatures who do not know any better!" she cried. "The Glismak are like wicked children and must be punished and taught to do better — but how can the dead learn lessons?"

"While you cavil and shed foolish tears, your friends die."

"I can't help it!"

"Oh, but you can."

She screamed at the top of her lungs: "I can't! I don't know how and my heart is sore pained, and I'm so horribly afraid and I just can't —"

She bit off her words as though she had spoken the most appalling blasphemy, and looked so frightened and despairing that Antar was near to smiting the wheedling Blue Voice with his large fist. But before the Prince could act her face changed yet again, like a flipped page in a picture book, and she calmed and said:

"Prince Antar, if I go, will you go with me?"

"To Let? *Now?*" But seeing that she was deadly serious he drew himself together and said: "Sweet Lady, I will accompany you to the trapdoors of hell if you but ask it."

Anigel nodded. In a strange, soft voice she said: "My friends, stop."

The train of three boats slowed, came to a halt, and began to wallow in the choppy water, for there was a gale of wind following them and the sky behind was piled with black and purple thunderheads. They could hear faint rumblings now. Half a league ahead and on their right Let sent up a forest of sooty columns that spread out when they reached a certain height to form a black roof above the village.

"Sir Owanon!" Anigel called out to the Prince's marshal, who rode in the leading punt. "Cut the traces connecting your boat to the ri-moriks!"

As he hastened to obey, she herself severed the line joining her boat to the punt ahead. *My friends, swim back to my boat so that I may re-hitch you.*

We are coming.

Prince Antar and the others still had not grasped what she was about to do, but as she continued to give commands her intent became clear. "You men! Paddle back to us and take Sir Penapat and the Blue Voice aboard. You in the stern of Sir Owanon's boat — cut yourself free of the second punt. Bring me both connecting lines."

They leapt to follow her orders, while she herself took the severed traces from the mouths of her rimoriks, and with her small knife poked holes in the tough upper hull on either side of the canoe's stem, passed the leathers through, and tied a large knot in them. The other two lines she fastened to each animal, improvising reins.

The rimoriks said: *Share miton, and we are ready.*

From her belt-wallet she took the scarlet gourd, and swallowed deeply. The animals licked her fingers as the Prince looked on in amazement.

Sir Penapat had been transferred to the other boat, but the Blue Voice still remained firmly ensconced in his place in the stern of Anigel's Wyvilo canoe. Now he fended off the two wooden punts with the knights in them, so that the three craft drifted quickly apart in the wind.

"I will remain with you also, Princess!" the Voice shouted. "I can be of help!"

Prince Antar cried, "Get out of the boat, you ill-omened knave!" He turned about and began to lurch sternward toward the acolyte, moving so violently that the lightweight craft rocked nearly to the gunwales.

But it was already too late. Princess Anigel signaled the rimoriks and they surged forward. "You men make for the opposite shore!" she called to Sir Owanon. "You must not be on the river when the storm strikes. If we do not come tomorrow, then save yourselves as you can. Farewell!"

The pale canoe rocketed forward with Anigel driving, and soon the two punts were lost to sight.

Antar had been thrown into the bottom of the boat by their abrupt start. For a while he simply clung to a thwart, fearful that they would flip over at any moment, and he in his armor would sink like a stone. But they only zipped and splashed through the chop like a low-launched arrow, traveling faster than he would have thought possible.

The Blue Voice was with them to stay, crouched in as small an area as possible, with his hood pulled down over his face. Antar could hardly cast him overboard. Muttering to himself, the Prince settled down somewhat more comfortably, but he was in a black mood. The Princess paid no attention whatsoever to either man.

Now it came to pass that Prince Antar became chagrined at the way that the lovely Anigel had ordered him and everyone else about — not that he faltered for an instant in his devotion to the Princess; he was as determined as ever to die for her sake. But she who had seemed so pathetic in the Citadel dungeon, so beautiful and doomed going over the cataract, so like a goddess as she smote the Glismak, so young and vulnerable as she battled her inner devils a few minutes earlier, was now the very image of an avenging warrior-queen as she urged the rimoriks onward. And something deep within Antar looked askance at this change and even feared it.

Her eyes were tightly shut, and the Prince doubted not that she studied visions of the carnage going on in Let, and bespoke the Wyvilo that she was speeding to help them.

And yet how lovely she was! How graceful, even in her mannish garb, with her hair flying and the magical coronet firm set on her brow. She stood against the darkening sky, where the fires burning in the village now painted the cloud-bellies with flickering crimson, and Prince Antar's blood quickened within him and he desired nothing more than to die for love of her.

What was to become of Princess Anigel — and of him? He had rebelled against his father, denounced Labornok, and cast his lot with his beloved, who was vowed to liberate her country. But was such a thing possible, even with the aid of the magical talisman? Orogastus could command the lightning, too, and the Blue Voice had assured the Prince that the sorcerer now had in his possession the talisman of one royal sister, and would soon have the other as well.

Anigel would want to return to the Citadel. But surely such a course would be futile. Over half of the Labornoki invasion force of ten thousand men was still encamped there, and the rest of the army, which had accompanied General Hamil on his pursuit of Princess Kadiya, would soon be returning from the swamp. What chance had Anigel, even with her new powers, against the full might of Labornok and the Dark Powers of Orogastus?

King Voltrik was now recovered, and more determined than ever that the three Princesses should die. No doubt he would count the

∴

defection of the son he despised as a small thing. Certainly the damned wizard would be delighted! Orogastus might even prevail upon the deranged monarch to take him as his heir. Perhaps that had been the villain's scheme all along!

With farseeing Orogastus in power and Labornok setting out to conquer the rest of the Peninsula, would he and Anigel be safe anywhere? Or would they two and the handful of faithful companions be forced to flee to some far-distant land where —

A movement.

Antar snapped out of his brown study and turned about, only to see that the Blue Voice had left his place and was creeping forward toward him.

"What do you want?" the Prince demanded truculently. The gale tore his words from his lips.

"Only to speak for a moment, my Prince. I have just now conferred telepathically with my Almighty Master, and he has asked me to pass on to you a message of the greatest urgency."

"I care naught for your foul conjurer's latest falsehoods. Get you back where you were . . . Get back, I say!"

But the Blue Voice came on steadily, his skeletal face split with a smile of such blatant insincerity that the Prince was first infuriated and then alarmed. But before he could react and draw his sword, the minion was upon him, springing like a lothok upon its prey in careless disregard for the Prince's suit of azure armor.

In one hand he bore a long, slender poniard, and he thrust it upward at the gorget of sliding plates that guarded Antar's neck. The sharp steel slid within, and had the Prince not swayed to one side he would have had his throat cut. But as it happened the misericord sliced only into the skin at the side of the neck before the Prince's metal gauntlet grasped the attacker's hand, and the blade was withdrawn. The two men began to thrash wildly in the bottom of the boat.

Princess Anigel pulled up the rimoriks at once. She watched Antar and the Blue Voice struggling, and she clung to the gunwales of the rolling and pitching craft unable to move for fear of causing them to founder. Nor could she call lightning down upon the Voice without sinking them all. She was at a loss and could only invoke the White Lady. But no help seemed forthcoming.

The Blue Voice was incredibly strong, partaking in some way of his demonic master's Dark Powers. He had contrived to get on top of the now supine armored man, one knee on either side of Antar's body, and clutched his long dagger in both bony hands, bringing the point closer and closer to the Prince's face in its open helmet. Antar gripped the wrists of the enchanter's acolyte, but even his great strength was not sufficient to halt the poniard's steady descent toward his eyes.

Anigel tore the coronet from her head and screamed: "Don't! Oh, don't kill him! I will give you the talisman!"

The Blue Voice lifted his shaven head. A long scratch extended from one ear to the middle of his brow and bloodflow made of his gaunt face a gory mask. His burning eyes met those of the Princess and he spoke through gritted teeth, the dagger not a finger's breadth above Antar's right eye.

"Put the coronet upon my head!" The Voice was that of the sorcerer Orogastus.

"No!" screamed Prince Antar. "He will then kill us both!"

But Anigel was leaning forward, the coronet in her hands, and the boat wallowed from side to side, and the first squall of pebble-hard raindrops pelted the three of them and momentarily flattened the surging waters.

And on either side of the boat rose the two rimoriks.

Their sleek bodies came up almost slowly, and their great jaws were wide open, so huge they could encompass a man's head. Their long barbed tongues uncoiled like whips. With the delicacy that they had exhibited taking miton from the soft fingers of the Princess, these tongues now curled about the lower arms of the Blue Voice.

The man shrieked. He was held fast. Anigel fell back, still holding the coronet. Antar released his grip upon the Voice's wrists at the same time that the animals began to swim toward the stern, their great bodies still half out of the water.

The sorcerer's acolyte, still screeching his lungs out, was dragged over the Prince, then hoist further into the air to clear the length of the boat. He disappeared into the black water off the stern with a great splash, and the rimoriks sounded after him. The rain held temporarily in abeyance.

Moments later the two great grinning heads popped up at the bow, near to Princess Anigel. A small shred of blue cloth hung from one animal's tooth.

∴

Oh, friends! . . .

Take up the reins. A great storm is nearly upon us. It will sink your boat if we do not take you quickly to land.

"Are you hurt?" the Princess asked Antar in great anxiety. "I see blood upon your breastplate."

"It is only a scratch. Once again you have saved my life, dearest Lady, and —"

"To Let, then!" Anigel cried, shaking the reins. And they were off in a cloud of spume, with the discomfited Prince again hanging on for his very life.

37

When the Blue Voice perished, Orogastus uttered a mighty groan, and came out of his trance bathed in sweat, and sank back into the great chair in his study from which he had surveyed the tactic's failure.

"It is my fault! Mine only the blame! And now there are two talismans out of my reach."

And if his researches were correct about the Feast of the Three Moons, then only three days and four nights remained in which he might salvage his great scheme . . .

Because he had been bespoken by his Blue Voice, Orogastus was able to watch with his mind's eye the struggle between the Voice and Prince Antar. The boat appeared to be driven by a person invisible, however, since the Princess was still shielded from the sorcerer's preternatural Sight by the amulet now inset within her talisman coronet.

The Blue Voice had wanted to postpone his attack upon the Prince until they reached dry land; but it had seemed to the sorcerer that a better chance of success obtained if Antar were menaced out in the stormy water, with no friendly Wyvilo or loyal knights about to give warning or come to the Prince's assistance. Orogastus did not tell his assistant that if the worst happened and the canoe was upset in the river, Antar would have perished together with the Blue Voice, being heavily weighted by his armor — while the rimoriks would surely have rescued Anigel and her talisman.

But now Orogastus's agent was dead and Prince Antar still lived, besotted with the Princess and quite capable of drawing uncertain numbers of Labornoki to his new cause. Alive, he remained a stumbling block of no mean proportion to the sorcerer's own ambitions.

Thinking furiously, Orogastus rose from his chair and prowled about his study. The snow had stopped and the damned Triple Moons turned the fastness of Mount Brom into a scene of breathtaking silvery beauty.

Princess Haramis had retired. Their conversation this day had been most satisfactory. She now seemed to accept his version of the Labornoki invasion, which thrust responsibility for the atrocities upon King Voltrik and General Hamil, with himself as only a reluctant confederate. Almost everything he had managed to explain away or justify. Fortunately, Haramis had not thought to scry Princess Kadiya during that sister's confrontation with the late General Hamil. Orogastus judged that any scrying of either sister that Haramis might now attempt would be unlikely to harm his cause.

Because whether she admitted it or not, Princess Haramis was in love with him.

This emotion the sorcerer was most disinclined to scrutinize. Of course it was impossible that he himself would fall in love with her! . . . And yet some snickering small demon deep within his soul warned him to be on guard. He had not lied to Haramis when he told her he had been celibate. He would have to take great care. His mind was invulnerable to her, but his body certainly was not; when they two had set each other afire, the brief joy had exceeded anything he had ever known before.

And it had frightened him to the core of his being.

Sexual love was traditionally forbidden to the wielders of magic — and for good reason. It distracted one from great goals, blinded objectivity, sapped the will, and drained away energies that must be hoarded and concentrated if one would become truly powerful . . .

But he needed her! And not only for the talisman she owned. She was the magical partner he had searched for through long years, infinitely superior to the toadying Voices. She held the key to the Sceptre of Power that even the Vanished Ones had feared.

And so he would use Haramis, share with her, even take pleasure in her. But he must ever be on guard not to love her.

Tomorrow he would dazzle the Princess with more ancient devices, then wring her compassion by telling her more of his life-story. If she still did not succumb, as was possible in such a strong-minded young woman, then would come the delicate loosening of the snare — so that it could be tightened again once and for all, at the crowning moment . . .

Orogastus left off his pacing and his face relaxed into a smile. He returned again to his chair and, sitting, passed into a star-eyed trance and bespoke his single remaining acolyte at Ruwenda Citadel.

"My Green Voice!"

"I hear, Almighty Master."

"Have you found aught new among the books in the Citadel library?"

"A number of references that may be of import, Master. An ancient history of Ruwenda speaks of a belief among the early human settlers that they lived in the 'Age of the Trillium.' And this first age's ending and the beginning of the new would be signaled by a notable disaster, and events would culminate on a Feast of the Three Moons when the Sky Trillium would manifest itself . . . One presumes some kind of unusual astronomical event is being described."

"No doubt. That is most interesting, and confirms one of my own theories. Go on."

"In a book purporting to describe the magical practices of the Uisgu was given a rough translation of a certain chant. I will quote it:

One, two, three: three in one.
One the Crown of the Misbegotten, wisdom-gift, thought-magnifier.
Two the Sword of the Eyes, dealing justice and mercy.
Three the Wand of the Wings, key and unifier.
Three, two, one: one in three.
Come, Trillium. Come, Almighty.

Apparently, the Uisgu sing the chant at their own Triple Moon Festival each year without knowing its exact significance."

"I can guess its significance," Orogastus said tersely. "Again, you have found material that helps to confirm my own researches. Well done! And is there more?"

"Master, one last finding. Of — of inauspicious portent."

"Say on."

"It concerns the so-called Threefold Sceptre of Power, which we have agreed is the combination of the talismans. In a mouldering chest we chanced some days ago to find a scroll that was near illegible. Only today was the vellum carefully steamed open. I realized at once that

∴

the document was written in Tuzameni, the language of your own land."

"That is most unusual. Hardly any Folk of the Peninsula even know of my country's existence. Go on."

"Most of the scroll is indecipherable. But a portion mentioning a so-called 'Great Sceptre' can be read. It says: 'The Great Sceptre that was broken and hidden by the Ones Gone Away will reappear and shake the roots of the world, making the old new and causing a great star to fall.' "

"I see." Orogastus did not speak for some moments. Then he said, almost lightly, "There are millions of stars in the sky, my Voice."

"Yes, Almighty Master."

"How has King Voltrik reacted to news of Prince Antar's perfidy?"

"He fell into a rage when he heard that his son had pledged his sword and heart to Princess Anigel. But in spite of your wishes, he would not agree to disown the Prince immediately. Antar is popular among the common soldiers because of his good nature and physical prowess, and he has numerous noble adherents among the relatives of his late mother. His Majesty wants to postpone the disinheritance and deposition of the Prince until the return to the Citadel of General Hamil's force, which will increase the number of men loyal to the throne."

"Our King is acting wisely in so doing." And Orogastus added to himself, *More wise than I, and I am spared making another great blunder! Dark Powers, what has gotten into me, that I should miscalculate so grossly?*

But the Powers declined to enlighten him; and he said to the Voice: "I fear you will now have to give the King more bad news. Hamil is dead. His army is mostly intact, however, and now under the command of Lord Osorkon. You need give Voltrik no details — say that the situation is as yet unclear — but the mission of capturing Princess Kadiya and her talisman has unfortunately failed, even as that mounted against Princess Anigel."

"Master — !"

"And both my Red Voice and my Blue Voice are dead."

"May one ask how my brethren and the Lord General perished?"

"You may tell King Voltrik that both the Red Voice and General Hamil died during a bungled attempt at forcing Kadiya to surrender her talisman. The device was magically bonded to her, and it slew the pair when they tried to take hold of it. You must tell the King that

Princess Kadiya escaped, but say that she fled into the deep swamp and will be no longer a threat to Labornok."

"And shall I also tell His Majesty the fate of the Blue Voice?"

"Say nothing. For your own information, the Blue Voice attempted to overcome Prince Antar while the two were on a boat. The Voice failed and was drowned."

"Alas! Blue was the bravest of us, and Red the shrewdest manipulator —"

"But you are the most intelligent, my Green Voice, and to you remains the most ticklish of tasks: keeping King Voltrik from doing anything irremediably foolish until I can return to the Citadel. Lord Osorkon is leading his force back at double-time. With the river flowing faster from storms already taking place in the mountains, his boats should arrive within three days. You may tell the King that."

"The monsoon winds have already brought the first rains to the Citadel region as well, Master. Soon the land-trails and waterways through this wretched kingdom will be nigh impassable. Because of a certain restlessness among Ruwendians in the outlying regions, King Voltrik has decided that his entire force will remain here during the rainy season. He and his staff have already worked out plans to quarter half of the army in various Ruwendian manors and villages, and the other half on Citadel Knoll."

"That is wise." *And another contingency I should have foreseen myself, and advised the King on!* "I wish you to continue, my Voice, to deplore Prince Antar's treachery to the King at every opportunity. Urge His Majesty to disown the Prince as soon as the loyal officers arrive. I need not stress the point that if anything should happen to Voltrik, my own plans would be in the deepest jeopardy."

"I appreciate that, Master. I will do my best to counsel the King. But he grows increasingly uneasy with the approach of the Three Moons Feast. Certain Ruwendian servants in the Citadel have slyly made known to His Majesty the dire prophecies concerning this event. He would like to return to Labornok —"

"He must not leave the Citadel! He would be caught on the Trade Route by the Rains!"

"Master, I have told him this. But even so, he thinks this Citadel is a place of ill-omen, being so ancient and so pervaded with Ruwendian magic —"

"Nonsense! Reassure him. He knows that my own Dark Powers, those that brought him victory, are superior! And I will be with him myself before the Triple Moons conjoin."

"Master! But how? It is an eight-day journey from your tower to the Citadel even during fair weather."

"Never mind how I shall do it. Only expect me before this Moon Feast, and tell King Voltrik that I am coming, and that all will yet be well."

"Almighty Master, I will reassure him, and make light of the doleful happenings, and he will greet you and be eager to follow your counsel."

"Excellent. Farewell, my Green Voice."

"Master, farewell."

When the vision of his acolyte faded, the sorcerer sat with his head in his hands for some time. Then he came to himself, a grim expression hardening his features.

"Everything *will* be well. First I shall consult the ice-mirror to descry Princess Kadiya, and then I shall make sure of Haramis."

On the next evening, upon returning to her chamber after having supped with Orogastus, Haramis found a gift awaiting her — a large flat package wrapped in black cloth and tied with a silver cord, together with a note from him:

My Dearest One:

Tomorrow I would show you my most precious possession, the ice-mirror with which I can scrutinize the farthest reaches of the world. I have showed it to no other human being. In order not to offend the Dark Powers who cause the mirror to operate, I ask you to accompany me attired in the vestments within this package, which I myself have made especially for you, daring to hope that you have come to share my own delight in these occult mysteries, as well as some small regard for the one who would lay them at your feet, in company with his own heart.

If I presume, dearest Princess, and you would rather leave here early on the morrow, then forgive the boldness of this note and excuse the foolish one who has been alone so long, waiting for you, never knowing love until now.

I am ever thine, with the most profound respect,

OROGASTUS

∴

Haramis was uneasy at the letter's overly intimate tone. *Does he think that I am bewitched by him, ready to hand him my heart on a platter? Am I a peasant girl, to become the slave of the first man who touches me? Or does he think me dazzled by all the ancient devices he has collected?*

Haramis considered the things he had so far shown her.

Who knows what those machines might be capable of? They did not look at all like toys to me . . . and that one he particularly fancied, with the look of a crossbow-stock about it, had a distinctly sinister aura.

On the other hand, perhaps he is not quite the villain I believed him to be. Poor man — what a horrible childhood.

Of course his support of King Voltrik's invasion is inexcusable. But I suppose he could not have directly opposed the monarch's madness without being driven away from Labornok. And he knew that his destiny lay not in his own distant homeland but here, in these very mountains, where the Cavern of Black Ice called out to him and surrendered to him its treasures.

Had I been in his position, she wondered, *what would I have done? Would I have been able to comport myself more cleverly and ethically? Would I have declined to become the Court Sorcerer of a corrupt ruler, if it meant ignoring the summons of my greater destiny?*

She opened the package and began to examine the vestments that were alleged to make one acceptable to the Dark Powers. Once she had seen them, she could not resist putting them on, just to see how she would look.

There was an underrobe of some fur-lined black material, and matching boots. Over this went a robe of silvery mesh with panels of a gleaming black, very cold to the touch. There was also a black cloak, lined in silver, with an ornate clasp and the star motif on the back. Finally she took up a most awesome headpiece that she hesitated long minutes before donning. This was a silver mask that fitted closely to the front of her head and beneath her chin, leaving the lower face uncovered. Around its perimeter, beginning just above her shoulders, were sharp-pointed rays, very tall at the crown, that haloed her head with a great shining star, leaving her long black hair falling free behind. The mask was not metal, but some softer material resembling silvered leather. There were also matching gloves with long cuffs.

Fully dressed at last in these garments, Haramis felt an urgent desire to tear the things off, flee from the room, and cry out for her lammergeier to carry her away. Her talisman, which hung at her breast as always, had become cold as ice and the amber without luster.

∴

What am I doing? she asked herself. *This garb feels strange. The devices he has shown me thus far are not magic — I am sure of that — but there is something about this clothing . . . Do the Dark Powers he speaks of truly exist? He obviously believes in them, and, whatever they may be, something gives him abilities beyond those of ordinary men. He might very well be able to rule the world, in time, as is his ambition.*

Is this why I am so strangely attracted to him? He does possess power, whatever its source, but what kind of power? Is it anything I can learn and use?

A spasm of dread shot through her. She lifted the Three-Winged Circle, fixed her eyes on the area within the Circle, and said: "White Lady! Answer me!"

For a long time, nothing happened. Then she thought to take off the silvery gauntlets, whereupon the wand warmed in her bare hands and the trillium amber pulsed with a dim glow when she called. Slowly the pearly mist gathered within the Circle, and in it the ravaged face of the Archimage appeared, resting upon a pillow. She looked up, obviously in pain. Her eyes, dark slits with tears slowly trickling from them, regarded Haramis clad in the garments Orogastus had given her.

"So soon?" The voice was faint as a zephyr rippling a field of flowers. "Has he won you over so easily? . . . But no. I misjudge you, dear child. I see that you have not chosen his way as yet."

"Of course I haven't!" Haramis's anxiety over the White Lady's appearance faded into irritation. The old woman's tone had been that of an adult chiding a misbehaving child. Haramis had not called the Archimage because of guilt. She had done nothing wrong, nor was she ashamed!

"I came here because I was invited," the Princess said, with cool courtesy, "and because I wondered whether anyone at all knew the truth about Orogastus. I came to see for myself what he was — and to search out his weaknesses, as you yourself bade me!"

"It is true that such knowledge may prove useful," the Archimage said gently, "but is it wise to remain under his roof?"

"I am in no danger here," Haramis broke in heedlessly. "My lammergeier is free to carry me off at any time. Orogastus cannot steal my talisman. He treats me with courtesy —"

"More than courtesy."

Haramis flushed behind the silvery mask. "Yes," she admitted.

"I can see that you are intrigued, Haramis, fascinated both by the man and by his power. And you think you know a great secret about the devices of the Vanished Ones that Orogastus does not suspect — a secret that will make him vulnerable."

"Yes," Haramis said. "That is, after all, why I came here, to search for knowledge. There is a great deal to be learned here. And the more I learn, the more questions arise about Ruwenda and its magic. But I am learning, and all will come right. I am certain of it."

"Yes, all will come right . . . But you must come to me soon and hear *my* vision. It differs greatly from that of Orogastus, and to some people it would seem less glorious. But you must make up your own mind. Between my path and that of Orogastus and his ilk, there is a great gulf. You should know both ways before making your choice."

"Yes," Haramis agreed. "I shall come to you soon."

"Do not wait too long."

The aged face faded. The Circle was empty.

Haramis let the talisman fall on its chain. Then she went to the tall mirror in the bathchamber, and looked upon the unfamiliar figure reflected there. Black and silver. The eyes unreadable, the figure tall and imposing. And, yes, frightening.

She turned away from the mirror and began to take off the dark vestments. But she knew she would put them on again tomorrow, and go with him to the Cavern of Black Ice.

∴

38

aving been warned through the speech without words of the boat's imminent arrival, Speaker Sasstu-Cha and a delegation of village elders met Princess Anigel and Prince Antar at the riverside landing, not too far distant from the scene of fighting. The Wyvilo led the two humans into the shelter of a nearby storehouse, since the rain was now coming down in torrents.

"It will put out the housefires," the Speaker of Let remarked, "but the Glismak warriors will not be deterred. We have already received a deputation of them demanding the ransom. And we agreed to pay. This one fears, Princess Anigel, that you have come too late."

She did not speak, only sat down wearily on a bale of goods, still wearing Immu's hat and her raincape which she had assumed when they landed. Since she was apparently irresolute, the Prince stepped forward.

"You may remember me. I am Antar, Crown Prince of Labornok, whom you harried from your town a few days ago. I am now the servant of this great Lady, who twice saved my life, and so are those of my men who yet live. We have come here at great risk to our lives in order to help you. Before you surrender to your foes, you might let us explain what manner of assistance we are prepared to offer."

"Say on," said Sasstu-Cha, in his deep, inhuman voice. "But you should know that the invading Glismak number over a thousand, and some one-third of our fighters have been captured, and some have already been eaten, and we can fight no more this night."

"That should not be necessary," said the Prince. He took Anigel by the hand and gently bade her rise. Then he untied the raincape and removed it, and took off her hat.

At the sight of the talisman the Wyvilo were all dumfounded, and one grizzled elder burst into oily tears.

"The Three-Headed Monster!" he exclaimed, also speaking the human language. "Praise be to the Flower, she has taken it from the tree!"

"And through it," the Prince added, "slain the leader of a mighty Glismak horde and routed its warriors, through calling down lightning from the sky."

Sasstu-Cha asked Anigel: "Is this true?"

"It is," said she. A new light had come into her eyes and new strength into her tired body. The trillium amber glowed in the white metal of the coronet and the open black flower within was plain to see.

"You will blast the flesh-eating fiends to charcoal?" asked the tear-stained oldster eagerly.

"Take me to the Glismak," Anigel said, "and you shall see what I will do."

At another quay on the far side of the village, where a narrow channel separated Let from the mainland, an enormous fleet of crudely made Glismak canoes had assembled to accept the booty. By the time Anigel arrived, mountains of food sacks and heaps of other riches had been gathered together by the defeated villagers, and were being inspected by the Glismak chief, Hak-Sa-Omu, and his underlings.

A hundred or so of the Glismak host were gathered on the pier, heavily armed and smirking with bloodstained fangs, oblivious to the pouring rain. A few of the victors prowled the still-smoking alleys in the vicinity, seeking the scorched bodies that they claimed as the rightful spoils of war. Others manned the canoes, while the vast majority of the Glismak army had regrouped on the mainland, awaiting the dividing of the loot.

Speaker Sasstu-Cha addressed the Glismak chief in the aboriginal dialect. There was a brief spell of wrangling, and then Anigel was led forward. She removed her hat. The amber in her coronet lit up the rain-lashed dockside like a signal beacon, and at the sight of the talisman all of the Glismak voiced a deafening howl of defiance.

∴

"Be silent!" Anigel commanded. And the fierce Folk subsided.

Then she began to address them in her own language, but Antar doubted not that her words were intelligible to all of those assembled. She said:

"You know who I am. Your brethren of the Kovuko Valley have bespoken you over the leagues, telling what I have done. The talisman is mine, and since you are all People of the Flower you know that I must be one of the Three Petals of the Living Trillium. I am indeed. And I intend to bring peace to all this land."

Her words were drowned by a great chorus of roars and hisses, but she lifted her arm and a mighty bolt of lightning slashed across the sky above, and the simultaneous blast of thunder stunned all the Glismak to silence.

"You Glismak are poor. Your Wyvilo cousins are rich. You rob and kill them because you have done so from time immemorial, and you also eat their flesh because this is the custom handed down from your cruel ancestors. But I tell you that you will do so no longer! A new day has come. The old ways are ended and will not come again . . ."

Watching and listening to her, Antar felt a sudden thrill of terror. Before his very eyes, the slender, lovely young girl was changing. She grew taller moment by moment. Her garments melted away and she was clothed in a robe of bright lightnings, red and blue and dazzling white. Her stature exceeded the height of the nearby warehouses; she towered into the stormy sky, arms stretched wide, her hair on fire, the amber at her brow as incandescent as a small sun, her voice like the sounding of a thousand trumpets.

"I will have peace between the Glismak and Wyvilo! Peace between your race and humankind! Good things will be shared. The children of the Glismak will not make a profession of war as their fathers did, but will learn to work. No person will kill another under pain of my wrath, nor will you eat one another's flesh!"

As the apparition had grown, the Glismak cried out more and more, and now they were affrighted to the pits of their savage souls. Those in the boats covered their eyes and cowered, and those on the dock and on the opposite shore fell on their faces, groveling. Only the chief, Hak-Sa-Omu, still stood upright, his glaring eyes starting out of their sockets and his great jaws agape.

"The goods on this dock will not be taken!" Anigel declared. "The

Glismak will withdraw empty-handed and remain in their home places until the dry season, pondering my words. If any Glismak force dares to emerge and make war, we will pour our wrath upon it" — three great thunderclaps hammered the air in quick succession — "and the disobedient warriors will not live to see the good things that will be given to those Glismak who obey my commands!"

The towering giantess now had three heads. And each one was crowned with the trillium.

"We speak now to Hak-Sa-Omu, chief of the Glismak! Do you hear, wretched one?"

The leader uttered a small whimpering phrase. Prince Antar could see that he was shaking from his plated head to his taloned feet.

"Will you take your people away and do as I have commanded?"

The feeble reply could only have been affirmative.

"Will you wait in peace for me to come again?"

Again affirmative.

"Then go!"

There was a final detonation that blinded and deafened all the spectators, and then the apparition was gone and so was Anigel.

Hak-Sa-Omu uttered a quick word, and he and every one of his Folk remaining in Let went scrambling pell-mell into the canoes, which set out with frantic haste for the shore. The Glismak then abandoned their boats and scurried away into the night.

Out from behind a stack of fine furniture came small Princess Anigel, dressed again in her hunting garb and with her wet blonde hair straggling down her cheeks. She smiled up at the Wyvilo elders and the Prince, who hailed her.

"Powerful Lady," the Speaker exclaimed, bowing profoundly, "you have indeed saved us as you said you would! Forgive this lowly one for doubting you."

"You did it!" Antar cried. "And without killing a one of them!"

"I was stupid not to have thought of the way sooner," she said calmly. "The Glismak are like children. You do not argue and attempt to use sweet reason with children, especially when they are in a willful and murderous mood. Unfortunately, all you can really do under such circumstances is frighten them into behaving. Then later, they can be reasoned with and educated."

"It is so." Sasstu-Cha nodded his head. "Any parent knows it."

∴

"I could not have killed them," Anigel admitted in a much lower voice, so that only Antar and the Speaker could hear. "But it was not necessary. It seems that all kinds of thoughts can be made manifest through the talisman. And so as the Glismak fled, I told them that they would be my people and I would love them."

"So will we also be yours," said the Speaker. "And this one declares to you, conquering Princess, that we are now your debtors, and our honor demands that we repay you for the unprecedented thing you have accomplished here tonight."

All of the other Wyvilo standing about joined their voices to that of the Speaker, for even the ones who did not know the language of the Princess somehow understood what had been said.

Anigel lowered her eyes for a moment. The rain still fell, but not hard, and to the southwest the sky showed stars. There would still be a few clear days before the Feast of the Three Moons.

"Dear friends," the Princess said. "Your Glismak foes were grown-up children. But I now must face enemies who are fully mature — not only in the ways of war but also in the spinning of evil enchantments. They would not flinch before my silly horror-show, nor be moved by my profession of love. I was sent on my quest by the White Lady, whom we all revere. Long ago, at the time of my birth and that of my two sisters, she said that we three Petals of the Living Trillium faced a terrible destiny. But she also said that all would be well. Throughout most of my quest I could not believe that this last was possible. But now I am willing to trust."

She took one of Antar's hands and drew him close to her.

"Here is Labornok's next rightful King. He is a good man. In Ruwenda Citadel is his wicked father, Voltrik. I shall set out for the Citadel at dawn tomorrow, and there I will cast King Voltrik down from the Ruwendian throne he seized. Sasstu-Cha, if you and your people would truly repay me, then accompany and defend me as I regain my kingdom."

"We have some five hundred surviving warriors, Princess, and they will go where you bid them. Our war chief, Lummomu Ko, was slightly wounded and rests in hospital. But he will be eager to pledge himself to you tomorrow. Anything that you desire of us, you may have."

Anigel said: "Prince Antar will be in command of those who follow me. I thank you and your people with all my heart for rallying to my cause. But I must warn you that my enemies are powerful—"

"So is the talisman you wear," said Sasstu-Cha.

The Princess sighed. She took the coronet off her head, opened the front of her tunic, and slid the little tiara inside. "For the rest of this night, I will let it rest. And so must I, for I am weary beyond telling."

"You and your Prince must accept my hospitality," the Speaker said at once. And the other Wyvilo elders smiled and bowed, and with many a gesture and word urged Anigel and Antar to come along. So they went off down the street of blackened, steaming ruins into the untouched part of the village, and after a while the clouds passed on and the Three Moons shone down and were reflected on the quiet river.

As she undressed and lay down to sleep in the room of the Speaker's oldest child, who had given up her bed joyfully to the savior of Let, Anigel could not escape the feeling that someone was watching her. Arising, she looked out the windows, into the closet, and even under the bed, but no one was there.

And then she saw the talisman's light throbbing beneath the clothes she had piled on top of it.

Reluctantly, she took the coronet up. She did not want to put it on. Had she not done enough for one day? What if another dreadful vision should come to her, spoiling the sleep she needed so desperately?

Put it on.

"Oh—oh, *lothok-ðung!*" the Princess cried petulantly. Sitting on the edge of the beautiful Ruwendian-style bed, she placed the coronet lightly on her hair.

"Kadi!" she cried. And she nearly fainted with happiness, for there in the vision was her sister, her eyes dancing and a great smile upon her dirty face. She sat by a campfire with large numbers of grinning Uisgu gathered round, and in her lap was a glowing thing like a blunt sword with a pommel of three dark balls conjoined, and at their center was the shining amber of a trillium amulet.

"Well, it's about time you responded to me!" Kadiya said with some irritation. "You've been so involved with yourself that you paid no attention whatever to my bespeaking. And I never thought to hear such words from your mouth, either."

∴

"Kadi, Kadi!" Anigel was laughing and weeping at the same time. "You are alive and safe!"

Her sister flourished the glowing thing. "Thanks to the Three-Lobed Burning Eye, my talisman."

"I saw you —" Anigel hesitated. "My own talisman vouchsafed me a vision showing you the captive of General Hamil."

Kadiya's face became sober. "They took me, a band of scouts of Hamil's force, not long after I secured my talisman. I had yet little idea of what this" — she held up the sword — "was capable of doing. The Red Voice of Orogastus learned first, to his death. After that no one dared try to take it away, but Hamil hoped to force me to give it up. There were Uisgu women under his power he could use to coerce me."

"Oh, Kadi — how monstrous!"

Kadiya was frowning now. "There is nothing merciful about the war we fight now, Sister mine. Have you not yet learned that for yourself? There is power in this." She glanced at the pointless sword she held. "But power is a burden — one must use it sparingly, Anigel, and only with a clean mind. Even anger can serve, but it must be controlled: that is a part of wisdom which I have gained."

"Then your talisman," Anigel whispered, "changed you, as mine changed me from a whimpering craven . . ."

"My talisman gave me power which I must learn to temper with justice. Hamil, and those of the Skritek who stood to be his monstrous weapons — they were judged and shall not walk these ways again. For even a sword of mercy such as I now bear can deal death."

"I — I also used my talisman to kill," said Anigel haltingly. "But only once, and then by accident. I could not possibly do it again."

"I could," Princess Kadiya said very quietly, "if it again became necessary. And it may. There is still a remnant of Hamil's force heading back toward the Citadel. But meanwhile, the Uisgu and the Nyssomu gather. There is a small army which grows hourly. To me they have turned for leadership. May the talisman grant that I serve them as well as they would serve us."

"Would they help us to regain our kingdom?"

"They say that they will. The Uisgu seem so timid and frail when you meet them at the Trevista Fair — but they are really brave little things, and stronger than they appear. They can travel very speedily in boats pulled by a kind of giant pelrik —"

Anigel laughed. "I know. I have become a blood-sister to such creatures myself and driven their boats."

Kadiya smiled. "So I saw. And tomorrow you will set out with your own army toward the Citadel. And your princely sweetheart is your new general!"

Anigel flushed, and said crossly: "He is not my sweetheart! But he is a noble and loyal man, and he has declared himself my slave forever."

To this Kadiya said nothing, but only smiled.

Anigel now had thought of a more important matter. "Kadi, besides my sight of you captured, I had another awful vision. My talisman showed me Haramis with Orogastus, and she seemed to be bewitched by him!"

Kadiya became deadly serious. "There is more than enchantment at work between those two . . . Ani, I envisioned Haramis myself, and I greatly fear that our sister has fallen in love with the foul sorcerer. Or perhaps fallen in love with the power he has offered to share with her."

"It's not possible!"

"Yes, it is," Kadiya stated, her face grim. "I bespoke the White Lady through my talisman tonight. The Archimage is very close to death and wishes Haramis to attend her, but Haramis is determined to remain with the enchanter. I tried to bespeak Hara, but she did not answer me. You might try to reach her, but do not be surprised if she will not talk to you, either. Persons who are deeply in love have room in their minds only for one person."

"This is dreadful. The poor White Lady! And our sister. If she has been seduced by Orogastus, then her talisman may be under his control! What can we do?"

"Nothing at all. The Archimage has accomplished the task she set for herself. We three have our talismans. Still, we are free spirits, you and I and Haramis, and must make our own choices."

In a voice trembling with foreboding, Anigel said: "You — you know that all three talismans must come together if they are to work their great magic properly. And there is a potential in them for evil as well as good."

∴

"Yes. So I learned from one I met on my quest — a servant of the Vanished Ones, I believe."

"Vanished Ones? But how —"

"It is a long story that will have to wait. Rest now, my brave little Sister, and so will I. We will meet soon at the Citadel."

After the vision of Kadiya faded, Anigel tried to bespeak Haramis. She saw a vision of her sister asleep; but as Kadiya had predicted, Haramis did not hear the mental call, being totally rapt in a dream of Orogastus.

Anigel removed her coronet. Its light had dimmed. "I shall never be able to sleep," she said to herself. But then she thought to touch the silvery tiara and ask it to grant her rest, and a moment later fell softly into slumber.

In the morning, she and Antar and a great fleet of Wyvilo warriors went to fetch the group of knights encamped across the river. Then they sped up the Great Mutar to Tass Falls, where they discovered that the rest of the Labornoki force had abandoned their camp, ignoring the Prince's earlier order.

A third great storm was threatening as Anigel and Antar and their people paused at the foot of the cascade and discussed what they would do. The Princess used her talisman to summon a vision of Tass Town, and the place was nearly deserted. All of the Labornoki flatboats of the Prince's search-party, as well as those of the garrison, had departed for the Citadel in anticipation of the approaching monsoon. There would be no foemen waiting at the top of the waterfall; but there would be no large watercraft capable of transporting Anigel's Wyvilo army to the Citadel up there, either.

"We will ascend on the log-lift," Prince Antar said. "It will easily carry the Wyvilo canoes if we make many trips. At the top, we will have to wait until the big tempest subsides and then paddle up Lake Wum to the mouth of the Lower Mutar —"

"No, Prince." The Wyvilo war-chief named Lummomu-Ko stepped forward. "There is a much better way to travel up the lake. And we will not have to await the end of the storm." He told Antar what was in his mind.

Even though he was a man of stout heart, the Prince blanched.

"Such a thing is possible?" Princess Anigel asked, overawed.

∴

"Even humans have done it," Lummomu-Ko said loftily. "There is a certain peril, of course. But if we win through we could be at Ruwenda Citadel in only a few hours."

"Then we will do it," the Princess decided.

The first raindrops began to patter down on the little army. The Wyvilo took no notice. They were equally at ease in sun or shower.

The Princess called out to the knights: "My human friends, pack up your armor for now, since you will not need it for some time, and then we will be on our way. We will go to the vicinity of the Citadel and secrete ourselves in the Mire nearby. From there we will summon all the fugitive nobility and common people of Ruwenda who fled into the swamp to join us in retaking our country. My sister Princess Kadiya is likewise speeding to the Citadel together with a large army of Uisgu fighters. If God wills, we will be ready to engage the foe on the Feast of Three Moons."

Anigel put on Immu's broad-brimmed hat to keep the mounting rain out of her eyes, and then was the first to mount the log-lift.

Later on that same day, a pathetic, starving creature paddled into stormbound Let on a rickety reed raft and then fell into a swoon. The people of the village recognized her as being of the Folk, and hence Kin, and agreed that she must be given aid. When she came to her senses the following day and asked after Princess Anigel, the Wyvilo were astonished.

"The great Lady is rushing on her way to her own Citadel," said the forest Folk, "with her magical talisman on her brow and an army of our people at her command. Our warriors have bespoken to us that they ride up the lake on the wings of the tempest, borne on large log rafts with sails widespread to run with the wind . . . But why might a wretch such as you ask after her?"

"Wretch wretch wretch!" shouted Immu. "Because she needs me, that's why!"

And she made such an outcry and commotion that they agreed at last to let her take a canoe when the storm abated, with three strong Wyvilo youths to paddle. And thus Immu went off in pursuit of her Princess.

∴

Orogastus and Haramis went together to the Cavern of Black Ice. She was eager to learn whether his vaunted ice-mirror was truly magical, or only another ancient device, as she suspected.

Outside the frost-covered door, as he was about to deliver his incantation to the Dark Powers, he chanced to look down upon her, and saw her bright blue eyes shining wide in the silver-masked face, her lips softly parted in a smile of anticipation.

Orogastus thought that she had never seemed so beautiful or exciting as she did now, star-crowned and dressed in the same silver and black that symbolized his own commitment to the Dark Powers. He could not help himself, but took her face in his gloved hands and kissed her mouth.

In time their lips reluctantly parted. The sorcerer sighed. "I hope that the Powers will not be angry. But the sight of you, so lovely and mysterious and so close to me . . . Oh, Haramis, stay with me!" he pleaded, his arms tightening about her. "I know that the White Lady has called you. But she would take you from me, tell you the same old half-truths and untruths, try to bend your will to hers —"

"Except for her help, I would not have been born," Haramis reminded him. "I must hear her dying words. She gave me my Black Trillium, sent me on my quest. I am sure that she guided and guarded me when I would have perished in the high mountains. I cannot ignore her plea. If you have spoken the truth, you have nothing to fear from my going."

.·.

"She keeps the Crown of Ruwenda from you!"

"No. She keeps it *for* me. And with or without it, I *am* Queen of Ruwenda — no matter whose soldiers occupy the Citadel!" She looked challengingly straight into his eyes.

Orogastus sighed. "Why do we tarry out here in the chill? The ice-mirror awaits."

He began his solemn invocation of the Dark Powers, beseeching deities that Haramis strongly suspected to be nonexistent to look kindly upon each of them. Poor deluded man! But she did not smile. Let them seem magical to him, while she continued to weigh his sincerity. She was becoming increasingly convinced that many of the extraordinary powers wielded by Orogastus had nothing whatsoever to do with magic. But even so, he did use these powers. *Can they be countered by my magic?* she wondered, remembering his "magic" tablet. *Quite possibly they can, but I had best not experiment on his precious ice-mirror — he would surely kill me at once if I damaged that. No, I shall watch, and learn.*

Haramis did not have to feign awe when he led her into the chamber of the great ice-mirror and summoned its resident demon. Orogastus had proposed that they use the mirror to scry her two sisters, and she had agreed at once, feeling guilty at having neglected to look for them herself, through her talisman. But having done it that first day and seen them safe, she had forgotten Anigel and Kadiya in her own preoccupations, which seemed so much more momentous . . .

Now, having been cautioned to keep silence, she waited as Orogastus intoned his request and the mirror (which she could see clearly was some sort of machine, and not even in the best working order) responded with gibberish and produced first a map and then an amazing fully colored image of Kadiya, followed by a similar manifestation featuring Anigel. Both sisters were voyaging on the water, in heavy rain, and neither spoke, although the mirror gave forth the natural sounds that accompanied each vision.

Kadiya traveled with a veritable army of Uisgu Oddlings and rode in a native vessel cleverly fashioned of reeds. The map-plot of the mirror showed that this Uisgu flotilla was in the Upper Mutar just above Trevista. The great river flowed turbulently and was laden with uprooted trees and other flood debris; but neither this nor the steady downpour seemed to inconvenience Kadiya or her small companions. Some of the Uisgu wore armor of golden scales, as did the Princess, and all of the Oddlings carried primitive weapons. But Kadiya had not even her little dagger anymore, but bore only her talisman, that strange thing like a pointless Sword of Mercy.

The vision of Anigel was more alarming. The mirror showed a massive raft built from great logs lashed together with stout ropes. It was equipped with a stubby mast and a broad square sail, which caught the wind-blast and sent the big craft charging and crashing through mountainous waves. There was a tiny cabin, little more than an open box, in which Anigel crouched quite calmly, drenched to the skin, her talisman coronet clamped on her head. Crude railings were fixed around the perimeter of the raft, and many knotted ropes fastened to these and to the mast gave hand-holds to the numerous passengers. Some of them were prone and bedraggled humans, while others were Oddlings of a peculiar and formidable appearance, tall in stature, who actually seemed to be enjoying their wild ride.

Haramis was careful to say nothing until the mirror went dead, although her mind teemed with questions. It was clear from the maps that both of her sisters were en route to the Citadel, and both had found and were using their talismans. Had the White Lady given them special instructions, or were they acting on their own? Could they possibly be intending to attack King Voltrik's heavily armed troops with their mobs of aborigines? Did their talismans make them think such a lunatic course of action might *succeed?*

It almost seemed that Orogastus could read her mind. "Your sisters," he said, after the ice-mirror had winked out, "have both used their talismans to kill."

Dumb with shock, Haramis could only stare at him. He led her from the mirror-chamber through the cavern and out into the tunnel that led back to his tower.

"Kadiya and Anigel mistakenly think that they will be able to liberate Ruwenda using the talismans as magical weapons — with help from their Oddling friends and from Prince Antar, who has denounced his father and pledged himself to the cause of Princess Anigel. She saved his life back in the Tassaleyo Forest, and he is now hopelessly smitten with her. Of course, neither of your sisters has the faintest chance of success against Voltrik. They do not yet fully understand the workings of their talismans nor their limitations. They undoubtedly think they have only to wave their talismans at the Citadel, and all their enemies will fall down dead . . . But this will not occur. Voltrik is protected by my own strong magic, under the command of my Green Voice."

"Oh, the silly fools!" groaned Haramis. "I cannot believe that the Archimage has ordered them to attack the Citadel. They are doing this on their own!"

"The talismans that Kadiya and Anigel hold were not intended to be used alone. My researches have made this very clear. The Vanished Ones used the three devices as one, in a great Sceptre of Power, to establish some mysterious great balance of the world. It is your duty, Haramis, to bring together once again the Three in One. Wielding it, you alone can rule over a world reborn into peace and prosperity."

"I? Rule the world?" She laughed. Her mind had frozen at his words, rejecting them even as he spoke. She asked herself what might be the great scheme that the White Lady had held back and was now prepared to reveal. *I shall go to the Archimage as soon as I can,* she decided.

As they hurried along, she glanced sidelong at Orogastus through the eyeholes of the silver mask, and saw that his mouth was tight-lipped. He had not spoken frivolously. He believed what he had told her, and she had best take it seriously. She would have to go to the Archimage at once and demand an explanation of this Sceptre of Power. But what of her sisters? If he did not know already, Voltrik would soon learn from the sorcerer of their advance upon the Citadel. He would send his army — and doubtless the Green Voice also — to meet them.

"Orogastus," she asked, "could you keep Voltrik from sending troops after my poor sisters? Let *me* convince the two of them to turn away!"

"If they withdraw at once into the depths of the swamp, they will be in no immediate danger. Voltrik's soldiers would be hard-pressed to fight an offensive war or even mount an effective pursuit during the rainy season. But do you think your sisters will listen to you?"

"They always did before. But now, having their talismans . . ." Haramis's voice trailed away into silent anxiety.

"I can order my Green Voice not to smite your sisters with my lightnings, or other occult weaponry. But there is no way that I can stop King Voltrik from dealing with them or their Oddling rabble as he chooses. Their talismans will not protect them. If I were there at the Citadel, I might prevail upon Voltrik. From here, working only through my Voice, I cannot."

∴

They came to the tunnel's end and entered the tower, where welcome heat enveloped them. Haramis stopped inside the small foyer and took Orogastus by the hands.

"There is yet time. For both of us, and for my sisters. I do not know what plans you now have. I do not *want* to know, until I have finally made up my mind about us. But — if I fly at once to the Archimage and then decide, will you meet me at the Citadel to receive my answer? And while you are waiting for me, will you prevent Voltrik from sending his army out against Anigel and Kadiya? I can make them turn back! I know I can! But I must first learn the intentions of the Arch-image —"

"Let *me* guide you! I already have a plan —"

"No!" She took off the star-mask, and stood there pale and trembling, and she was unbending this time as he embraced her and kissed the top of her head.

"My dearest one, you will do as you must do," he told her. "But there *is* one serious flaw in your strategy. I have no way to go quickly to the Citadel. Unlike you, I cannot command the lammergeiers."

"I will ask Hiluro to summon one of his fellows to carry you there."

His hands tightened about her. "You would do this? Trust me so far?"

The face she lifted to him was wet with tears. "You are a man who has long guarded his secret heart. Perhaps you have built such strong ramparts about it that you are no longer sure what lies within . . . I think that you are not certain which way to take. Like me, you will have to make a choice."

"Yes," he admitted. His arms fell away, and he did not meet her eyes.

"The lammergeier will come for you," she said. "We will meet at the Citadel, just before the Feast of the Three Moons. Expect me."

And then she was gone, leaving him standing alone, and her silver star-mask lay on the floor looking up at him with empty eyes.

40

hen the wild voyage of the log rafts up Lake Wum ended late on the same day that it had begun, the Wyvilo steered the fleet of ungainly craft into the Greenmire forest islands of the Lower Mutar delta, still under cover of the storm.

There the Nyssomu met them with a hundred punts, and greeted Princess Anigel with much deference. The little swamp Folk ferried her and the knights and the Wyvilo warriors via secret backwaters to a large hummock unknown to humans. This place, which would become the staging area for Anigel's army, was located a few leagues away from a manor on the River Skrokar that had belonged to the late Lord Manoparo of the Oathed Companions. The castle of the manor had been seized and occupied by Labornoki troops; but the outbuildings and dower house still sheltered Manoparo's large family and most of his servants and domestic retainers.

The mistress of the manor, Lady Ellinis, had been advised by the local Nyssomu of Anigel's coming. The Lady was brought out to the isolated hummock long after nightfall, and she greeted the Princess with tears and guarded enthusiasm.

Lady Ellinis was a grey-haired dame whose fine face was now deeply lined with bereavement. In addition to her husband, two of her sons had also perished in the futile defense of the Citadel. She sat with Anigel inside a shelter that the Wyvilo had set up in a dripping grove of gondas, and the two of them discussed the Princess's plan for besieging the Citadel together with her sister Kadiya and the latter's force of Uisgu.

"That you would dare such a thing so soon after the conquest amazes me," Ellinis said. "And perhaps it is true that Voltrik's forces are not yet completely entrenched, and his army is divided, and they are on unfamiliar ground with the rainy season upon them. But still—! You two girls are so young! Utterly inexperienced in warfare! And even if our scattered nobles and freeholders rally to you as you hope, your army is yet composed mostly of Oddlings. My darling Princess Anigel, I wish nothing more in the world than your success. But the Labornoki are hardened fighting men, and the odds are greatly against you."

Anigel only touched her coronet, where the trillium amber glowed. "I know not why I am convinced that victory will be ours, but I am. Perhaps this talisman is the thing that gives me the confidence to attempt such an audacious endeavor. All I can tell you, dear Ellinis, is that I felt impelled to come here now, with the Three Moons converging, and engage the Labornoki who hold the Citadel. My sister Kadiya is of like mind."

Lady Ellinis drew her heavy cloak more closely about her. A small brazier burned in the shelter and on it Anigel was brewing darci tea against the penetrating dampness. Ellinis said: "I was astounded when a Nyssomu came secretly to me and informed me that you were sailing up Lake Wum. Of course, the Oddlings can bespeak each other without words, and I suppose they will have passed the news all over the Mazy Mire by now . . ."

"To all the Folk—yes," Anigel agreed solemnly. "My Wyvilo allies have never, up until now, had much dealings with their Nyssomu or Uisgu cousins. But the conquest of our country by Labornok was a disaster not only to Ruwendian humans, but also to the aborigines who dwell among us. And so the Wyvilo have put aside their ancient customs, and even the peaceable Nyssomu are willing to join us and do what they can."

Outside, where the rain had stopped and night-mists now hung thick, the Wyvilo were busily constructing more brush-and-bamboo shelters for themselves and for others who were expected to arrive at the hum mock later. Like all Folk, they could see readily in the dark and went about their work as efficiently as though it were broad daylight.

Catching sight of a tall Wyvilo axeman, Lady Ellinis shivered. "I

∴

have never seen Tassaleyo Forest Oddlings before, and I confess that
their mien is rather frightening. They are not as dreadful-looking as
the Skritek, of course, and they seem fairly civilized. Nevertheless, I
wonder that you are able to put such trust in them."

Anigel smiled. "Their faces are terrifying, but at heart they are noble
and revere the Black Trillium just as their smaller kin do. Thanks to
the Wyvilo, we were able to send word via the Nyssomu to the scattered
bands of free Ruwendians, who are hastening here from all directions
to join my army."

"My own people and my three surviving sons are yours to command,"
Ellinis said, "and you are welcome to what stores of food we were able
to hide from the enemy. But there are at least five hundred Oddlings
here already, and you say that you expect three or four times that
number of humans and Nyssomu to gather here within the next two
days. I fear that we will not have victuals enough to feed such a throng
for more than a few days."

"We will not be here for very long. If we are not victorious during
the Feast of the Three Moons, we will have to withdraw," Anigel
confessed. "But we *will* win out. I know it!"

The Princess was on her feet, stern-faced and still dressed in the
blue hunting kit that the Wyvilo had given her. Lady Ellinis marveled
at how greatly the girl had changed from the giggling little person she
had seen at a royal ball scarcely five weeks earlier, before the invasion.
That Anigel had been a shy ornamental with hardly a thought in her
pretty head that did not involve court gossip or the latest fashions. This
new young woman was frightening in her dedication, and Ellinis hardly
knew what to make of her. But the Princess poured tea for her guest
without a trace of her old flightiness, as gracious and confident as though
the sooty crock were a silver pot, and the damp and drafty shelter the
Queen's solar in the Citadel. Gradually Ellinis lost her misgivings and
began to think that the impossible venture might not be utterly hopeless
after all.

"This Prince Antar." The older woman lowered her voice to a whisper. "It was clear to me when you introduced us that the young man
is deeply in love with you. Nevertheless, I feel it is my duty to caution
you about placing too much reliance upon him."

Anigel nodded and sat down again, her face without expression. "He
has pledged fealty to me, and so have most of his men. But there are

three of his knights who withheld their troth, and these the others watch closely and exclude from our councils of war."

"But Antar and his knights are Labornoki, after all!"

"Dear Ellinis, I am no longer as simple and gullible as I once was, and it is true that Prince Antar must still prove his loyalty to me. You say he loves me and this may also be true. But I have only a fond respect for him, and even that is yet wary."

"Good!" said Ellinis sturdily.

"But I must trust Antar in some matters, since I know nothing of fighting. If we are to succeed, we will do so under his generalship. I know not what lies deep in his heart, but I am convinced that he is a good man, and one who deplores the cruelty of his father, King Voltrik. He has told me that there are many others among his people who feel as he does, and it may be that we will, through him, divide our foe's loyalty."

"I shall pray that you are right."

They spoke for a while longer, and then it was time for Ellinis to go. The Lady kissed Anigel, which the Princess quite expected; but Anigel was quite taken aback when Ellinis also bowed deeply to her before going away with her servant and her Nyssomu guide.

To Antar, who had come in when Ellinis was taking her leave, the Princess remarked: "She never showed me such deference before. In fact, being a woman of serious bent, she rarely paid much attention to me at all!"

"The more fool she," said the Prince, smiling. "But I have come to tell you that our camp is growing apace, and there is now adequate shelter should the rain commence again." His face sobered. "The Wyvilo war-chief Lummomu-Ko feels that the Nyssomu, even though willing, will make poor warriors. They are so small, and the only weapon most of them can use with facility is the blowgun. In a frontal assault, they would be useless. We can only utilize them in skirmishes and irregular actions."

"Then plan to do so," Anigel said serenely. "Do you have any estimates on the number of humans who might follow us?"

"With luck, seven or eight hundred free Ruwendians might be able to join us here or reach the river below the Citadel by the Feast of the Three Moons. These will be mostly knights and soldiers who escaped into the Mire when the Citadel fell, together with some lords

∴

and men-at-arms from outlying manors south of here who never engaged us — I mean, never engaged your enemies — during the late invasion."

"Very good. Now if only the Count of Goyk and the other free lords of the far Dylex can arrive in time — " She broke off, suddenly turning away, her face darkened with chagrin.

Antar, who had never heard of the Count of Goyk and knew nothing of that worthy's place in Anigel's plan, at that moment realized that she still feared to confide in him completely. He dropped slowly to his knees.

"My Lady, if you command me, I shall say nothing of this Count to my loyal companions. I beseech you to have faith in us — but if you cannot, perhaps it would be best if you placed me and my knights under arrest. Then you would be freed of any anxieties our presence might engender."

"I do trust *you*," Anigel said unhappily, "and most of your knights as well. It is Sir Rinutar and his cronies Turat and Onbogar whom I feel might betray us. I know they have pledged a truce, but I fear it was a grave mistake to bring them here to this secret camp. We should have left them on the lakeshore, as Lummomu-Ko advised."

The Prince bowed his head. "Perhaps. But marooned in the midst of the storm, in a swamp full of unknown perils . . . they would surely have perished before finding their way to a Labornoki garrison. As you yourself agreed."

"I would not have them die! But neither can I let them betray us to King Voltrik."

Kneeling yet, he took hold of her hand. It was icy cold. "Be of good cheer. The three would be lost in minutes if they attempted to leave this hummock and range out into the Mire, and there is no one here who would aid them to escape. My fifteen true companions and I will see to them. Have no fear."

She sighed and turned her eyes back to him. "I suppose you are right. I am taut-drawn as a bowstring, anxious about what will befall us in the next three days. The Count of Goyk that I inadvertently spoke of — he holds the most distant fiefdom of Ruwenda, far to the northeast of the Dylex, in the foothills of the Ohogans. Neither he nor the Count of Prok nor the other lords of the eastern manors were ever subdued by you Labornoki."

"I know. It was to be our first priority after the Winter Rains. To pacify that country and also the south."

"When the Wyvilo agreed to help me, I asked them if they would use their speech without words to discover what humans were unconquered. Through the Nyssomu I then made contact with those who fled the Citadel, and also certain nobles of the garrisoned manors, such as Lady Ellinis, and a few free manors of the south. This you already know. But my Wyvilo friends also bespoke the Vispi, the aborigines of the high mountains. And the Vispi told us of the counties of Goyk and Prok being yet free."

He nodded. "I see. And then of course the mountain Oddlings called upon those lords to come to your aid."

"The Count of Goyk is a hardheaded man, and he is also my Great-uncle Palundo. At first he would not believe what inhuman Folk told him—that my sister Kadiya and I were ready to attack the Citadel. But I myself bespoke the Vispi, imparting to them certain homely secrets that only members of the royal family know, and at last Uncle Palundo was convinced. When we and the Wyvilo quit the village of Let, two thousand armed knights and men from both Goyk and Prok set off from their remote enclaves in fast riverboats. They had a long way to come—but the waterways are already in flood and yesterday they safely skirted the castle of Bonor, about sixty leagues west of here. If all goes well, they will arrive in time to help us."

Antar's eyes were shining. "Better and better! Oh, my Lady, I cannot tell you how you have lifted my heart! No longer does our position seem so forlorn. We are still outnumbered, but at least we will have greater numbers of experienced human fighters on our side!" And he kissed her hand in a transport of joy.

Anigel stiffened. Then, seeing his dismay, she smiled upon him.

"Is my touch then so repulsive?" he asked sadly.

"No. By no means. I was only—surprised. There are so many things on my mind, you see."

She looked so small and bemused, this young woman crowned with magic, perched uncomfortably on a mossy rock with her face lit only by the brazier, that his heart was ignited from pity and love and he rose to his feet and turned away so that she should not see the tears that had sprung to his eyes.

∴

"Yes, my Lady. You have much to think on. Too much for a person of such tender years and great sensitivity —"

"I'll manage," Anigel said, rather briskly.

He turned back to her. "Now I have offended you. I apologize most humbly."

"And I accept." For an instant, their eyes met. Then she looked away and seemed abstracted again, and the rapport that had seemed to spring momentarily to life died aborning.

Had he really seen it? Or was it only wishful thinking? He would have cried out to her that very minute, professing his adoration — but she had her eyes blindly fixed on one wall of the tent and seemed lost in a dream, one finger lifted to her silvery coronet.

"I bid you goodnight, then," he said.

But Anigel did not reply. She was listening to a vision of her sister Kadiya that had just sprung into her mind.

"Haramis said *what?*"

"Ani, she told me to turn back. Ordered me! As though I were still a naughty child refusing to come in from playing in the stables!"

"Did she give a reason?"

"She is afraid that Voltrik knows we are on our way, and that he will send troops out to engage us. But that's ridiculous! The Nyssomu would know at once if any large body of Labornoki left the Citadel. They would give warning, and we could easily hide away in the sloughs and backwaters of the Mire where no flatlander would have a hope of catching us. Of course I told her that. But she got all in a swivet, and started swearing upon her amulet and talisman that I was floating to my doom and sure to ruin some great scheme. When I asked if the scheme was hers or one of Orogastus, she became all huffy."

"Can she have fallen under his dark spell, Kadi?"

"Who can say . . . Has she bespoken you with the same line of tosh?"

"Nay. But I have been so busy and distracted this day that I scarce had time to draw a quiet breath."

"If she does try to bespeak you — don't answer!"

"Kadi!"

"I mean what I say. And tell Hara nothing more of our plans. She has gone to the Archimage at last, supposedly to hear the White Lady's

version of our destiny and the purpose of our talismans. Perhaps our
love-sick sister will recover her wits in Noth. But I shall not count on
it. Bespeak her not again. She must know nothing of our plans until
we all three meet in person and have this out."

"Well . . . I suppose that is the sensible thing."

"She also told me that the sorcerer will arrive at the Citadel tomorrow."

"What — ? But he was there with Hara, in the mountains!"

"She is lending him one of her magic birds as a steed. When I
remonstrated with her — actually, I called her a besotted muck-for-
brains — she insisted she was acting in our best interests."

"Now we shall have his enchantment to contend against, as well as
the armed might of Labornok! Oh, Kadi . . ."

"Now, don't lose heart. Hara seems to believe that Orogastus has
very little real magic at all. According to her, his thaumaturgy may be
based upon nothing more nor less than some fabulous machinery of
the Vanished Ones! The bolts of lightning, the gouts of flame and hail
of steel pellets that destroyed the hill-forts, the ear-bursting horror that
afflicted the Dylex townships, even the panic that seized the war-
fronials of our knights — all some sort of mechanical trickery and not
real magic at all! . . . If Hara is telling true."

"Kadi, I just don't understand this. There *must* be magic! Our Black
Trilliums . . . our talismans . . . the Archimage herself! Magic pervades
the entire world!"

"Never mind, Ani. The only important thing to remember is that our
sister must not be allowed to stop us. So give no heed to her lunatic
admonitions. I am still well ahead of Osorkon and his army, I have
more than three thousand Uisgu following me, and I have worked out
a plan for penetrating the Citadel and avoiding a pitched battle outside
on the Knoll, where we would surely be cut down by Voltrik's cavalry."

"Oh! Tell me!"

"And have you blab it to that witling Antar? Nay! You'll learn of it
when our armies meet on the Eve of Three Moons."

"You misjudge me, and also Antar —"

"I hope so. And I hope I misjudge our sister as well! Meanwhile,
take great care and meet me in this place that I show you . . . When
we confer, we will arrange for King Voltrik and Orogastus to join us
at a very special celebration of the Moon Feast!"

41

Day was dawning rapidly when Hiluro began his descent toward Noth. Haramis had cried herself to sleep, then dreamed a conversation with a scandalized Kadiya, expressing disapproval of her dealings with Orogastus. No doubt Kadiya would have tried to stab him and been struck down with lightning for her pains—how dare she call Haramis's conduct reckless! Now Haramis felt horribly bleary-eyed as the growing light woke her. She was stiff in every muscle, but her position on the bird's back did not encourage much movement, so she looked forward to landing.

As the bird circled over the small stone tower where the Archimage lived, Haramis looked down in bewilderment. The last time she had seen the place it had been covered in greenery and surrounded by a lawn dotted with wildflowers. Now only a few skeletal branches clung to the tower, and what remained of the lawn was brown and scattered with spiky weeds. The moat was low, and the little water that remained in it was covered with a foul-smelling scum.

"What has happened here?" Haramis asked aloud. Hiluro twitched, and for a moment she thought he was about to answer her, but he remained silent.

Could King Voltrik's soldiers have come this far? she wondered. *No, there would be a different kind of destruction if they had. They would have burned and torn down, but this looks as though everything simply died. But there is no natural reason for everything to dry up like this, not at this time of year!*

She thought of the great number of gardeners formerly employed at the Citadel. Perhaps with the Archimage dying, her few servants — and Haramis had heard her mention only one, her steward — hadn't had time to take care of the plants. *But even so, it shouldn't look like this!*

The lammergeier landed at the end of the drawbridge, and Haramis climbed off his back, her mind busy speculating on what she might find within. Was the Archimage already dead? *She was still strong enough to speak to me last night,* Haramis thought.

A feeling of urgency possessed her, and she hurried across the drawbridge, along a mosaic floor almost covered with dead moss, past the now dry fountain, and across the garden, now barren ground with dead flowers strewn about, their roots still clinging to the earth which no longer nourished them. When she came to the black wooden door which led to the Archimage's chamber she was not surprised to find it standing ajar.

The room was stifling hot, and an Oddling — a Nyssomu she had never seen before — crouched by the fire adding more peat. He looked up as her shadow, cast by the sun rising behind her, fell across him. "Lady Haramis," he said. "Welcome to Noth — she said you would be here in time." He nodded toward the bed.

"Greetings . . . You must be Damatole," Haramis said. The Archimage had mentioned his name only once during their last meeting, but Haramis had been taught all her life to remember the name, face, and salient characteristics of everyone she met or heard of. Her parents had considered it an important part of royal training.

"Yes, my lady." The little steward bowed to her. "It is my honor to serve the Lady Binah — and you. She sleeps now, but she should wake soon. Would you care for some tea?"

"Yes," Haramis said gratefully, "I would indeed. Thank you, Damatole." The Oddling hurried from the room, and Haramis picked up one of the padded stools and quietly moved it to the side of the Archimage's bed. Sitting on it, she studied the sleeping woman.

Binah looked even less well than she had in the scrying bowl, her flesh parched and sinking down about the bones of her face. She woke just as Damatole came in with the tea. "Haramis," she said slowly. "You came."

"Of course I came," Haramis said. "You called me. Besides, I need more information on how to use the talismans. Unfortunately, finding my Three-Winged Circle did not automatically teach me how to use it.

Orogastus's library had some information on them — including a book that said the three of them should be joined together to form a sceptre —"

"Not yet," the Archimage interrupted her. "You are not yet ready to control that power. That requires more wisdom than you have — much more."

"Where am I supposed to learn this great wisdom?" Haramis snapped impatiently. "Grubbing around in the swamp while Voltrik's army plunders my kingdom? Or am I to find it in my sisters — who use their talismans to kill?"

The Archimage looked sorrowful. "They do not yet possess wisdom either," she sighed, her voice trailing off into silence. It was several moments before she spoke again, and her question was unwelcome. "Why did you stay so long with Orogastus?"

Haramis frowned, trying to find the right words to explain. "I was trying to learn what he was like — you yourself bid me find out his weaknesses. It's odd; he seems to think that the devices of the Vanished Ones are magical — he actually said as much! He was very upset when I broke one of them — he said it was dead. But machines aren't alive, are they?"

"No," the Lady replied. "And do you think his devices are magical?"

"No," Haramis said. "I cannot explain it precisely, but they don't *feel* magical. But, magic or machine, they give him power, and that power, whatever it is, can be used to do great harm. And while that power exists, I want to know how it works!"

"So you went to Orogastus to learn the use of power? Was that wise?"

"What is wise?" Haramis retorted bitterly. "You lie here in bed while my home is invaded and my parents horribly murdered and hundreds of Vispi are slaughtered because you summoned them too late against a foe they could not withstand. Is that wisdom? If so, what good is it?"

"I know that you are confused and in pain, Haramis," the Lady said gently, "but you must learn to look beyond the moment and see the larger pattern."

"That," Haramis retorted, "is *exactly* what Orogastus said. As if my parents were nothing, and their deaths didn't matter . . ." She found herself crying again, hurt and angry and bereft. *And now you'll die, too,* she thought despairingly, *and I'll be alone with my kingdom occupied by enemy soldiers, my sisters who knows where, and King Voltrik trying to kill me and them. And I don't know what to do and nobody else seems to know either!*

"I have watched over Ruwenda for a long time," Binah said softly, "far longer than you realize. I have loved the land and its Folk and I have guarded them and helped them to grow as they should. It is a great work, and there is much joy in it. But now my time is ending, and yours is beginning." She turned her head to meet Haramis's eyes. "You said that Orogastus invited you to come to him. Tell me, Haramis, why did he invite you, and not your sisters?"

Haramis gazed back at her, startled. "I don't know — I never thought to ask that."

"And now that you know the question, what is the answer?"

Haramis frowned, trying to remember exactly how Orogastus had worded his invitation, as well as what he had asked of her while she was with him. "I think he's lonely," she said slowly. "He spoke of my reputation for learning and of his desire to share his knowledge with me . . . I think he's looking for someone else like him, someone else who can use magic and think the way he does, someone who can understand what he talks about."

"And are you like him?" the Archimage asked quietly.

"In some ways I am," Haramis admitted. "I don't want to blast anyone with lightning, or invade someone else's land, or kill people — but I can understand the desire to search for knowledge, to try to make sense of the world . . ."

". . . to see the pattern of life around you?"

"Yes," Haramis said, "exactly."

"And when you have this knowledge, what do you do with it?"

"What do you mean?" Haramis asked.

"Would you use knowledge to hurt and destroy, to manipulate and bend others to your will?"

"Of course not!" Haramis replied indignantly. "That's wrong. People are supposed to be free to make their own choices, not used as puppets for the amusement of those stronger or more intelligent than they are. But why should I have to *do* anything with knowledge? Why can't I simply study and learn and rejoice in the knowledge and vision I achieve? Why should I have to use it?"

"Because you are what you are, and it shows. I can see it, Orogastus can see it, and any other with a knowledge of magic can see it." The Archimage's voice grew intense. "Haramis, you understand words. Most people never realize that words are important, that they matter, that to say a thing is to give it at least a shadow of existence — and to name it truly is to give it life. You hear, you listen, and you remember, and that is a rare gift. Without it, you would never understand magic, most of it would literally be inconceivable to you. Kadiya possesses great ardor and determination, and Anigel has compassion and a loving heart, but these gifts, while they are great in their own right, are not what is required for the full use of magic. Your passion is knowledge, Haramis, and that, combined with the royal blood of Ruwenda, will make you a magician. If you try not to use your abilities, you — and they — will be used by people like Orogastus."

"Is that why I feel like a pawn in some game you and Orogastus are playing?" Haramis demanded.

The Archimage's eyes burned in her face, as if all the life in the old woman were contained in them. "You feel like a pawn because you have been one, Haramis. But you are reaching the last square, where you can choose what to become."

"A queen, of course," Haramis said in surprise. "Wasn't that choice made for me long ago?"

"No," the Archimage said softly, almost in a whisper, "that choice is not made until *you* choose it. The important thing is for the world to be brought back into balance, which can only be done if you and your sisters can find your own balance. The Crown may not be your destiny."

"What do you mean?" Haramis asked in horror. "Will we lose the kingdom to Voltrik? Will I be killed? Or has something happened to the Crown? I left it with you for safekeeping — did I do wrong in that?"

"By no means." The Archimage's voice was feeble, but still audible. "The Crown is here, and safe." She turned her head toward the fire. "Damatole."

Haramis would not have thought the Oddling could hear that whisper, but he hurried to Binah's side. "The time has come," the old woman whispered. He nodded, crossed to one of the cupboards on the far wall, took out a white bundle, and brought it to the Archimage. She slowly reached out a hand, grasped a fold of the cloth, and extended it to

Haramis. As the bundle started to slide off the bed Haramis grasped at it. It fell open across her arms, and she saw in surprise that it was the Archimage's cloak.

"Put it on, Haramis," Binah commanded in a whisper. "It is yours now."

"Do you mean *I* am to be Archimage?" Haramis asked in surprise. *I don't want this task,* she thought in dismay. *It's difficult enough to be Queen — and at least I was trained for that! But to be the new Archimage — she can't ask* that *of me!*

"You have the ability," Binah whispered, "but it must be your choice. I give you my blessing and my love, and one final warning. Remember that the line between self confidence and over-confidence is narrow and easily crossed. Guard yourself always. Choose wisely." Then her breath rattled in her throat and she lay still.

Haramis stared at her body in shock. *This can't be happening,* she thought. *I'm dreaming. I'm in my bed in Orogastus's tower and I'm having a nightmare, I've been reading too many books of magic, I —*

Haramis became aware that Damatole was speaking to her. "White Lady?"

She turned slowly to look at him. "What is it, Damatole?"

"What are your commands, Lady?"

Commands? He thinks I'm the new Archimage. Why, oh why, did I ever get out of bed this morning — yesterday morning — whenever it was? She should tell him something; after all, he was only trying to do *his* job. Unfortunately, nothing came to mind.

"Let me get you some water to wash with and bring breakfast," he suggested. "You must be hungry."

Hungry. Yes, now that he mentioned it, she was hungry.

"Thank you, Damatole," Haramis said blankly, "that would be very nice."

Damatole served her a simple meal, then led her away to a small chamber where there was a cot. She lay down and slept, and when she woke it was afternoon, and there was a meal set on a small table next to the cot. Haramis ate every bite, and then went in search of Damatole.

She found him in the Archimage's chamber, but she was surprised to see that the bed was empty. "Have you buried her body already, Damatole?" she asked. "I would have helped —"

"There is no body," he replied. "Do you not remember? . . . No, I see you do not. The flesh that once enclosed Binah's spirit has gone to dust, as will this place, once you leave it."

Haramis looked more closely at the bed. Yes, there was dust on the pillow where Binah's head had been. "Where is the Crown of Ruwenda?"

Damatole opened the cupboard in the far wall and took out a bundle, wrapped in white fabric, which he handed to Haramis. When she unwrapped it, she saw with relief that the Crown was whole and undamaged. *Would it turn to dust if it stayed here when I left?* she wondered.

"I shall get you a bag to carry it in," Damatole offered, hurrying out of the room without waiting for her response.

Haramis tried to think of what she should do next, but when Damatole returned with a leather sack, she had not yet decided. Since he obviously expected her to leave, however, she summoned the lammergeier. Then it occurred to her that she was not the only one with no home. "Damatole, do you have a place to go?"

He nodded. "My kin will fetch me away. It is arranged. There is only one last thing." He picked up the Archimage's cloak, which was still lying on the stool where Haramis had left it, and put it into the bag with the Crown.

"Why have you given me this?" she asked as they left the building together, fearing she already knew the answer.

"Because it is yours, White Lady," he replied. "And now I bid you farewell."

A rising wind blew her hair back from her face. She looked up at the thickening clouds and wondered if it would rain tomorrow, on the Eve of the Three Moons.

Hiluro dropped out of the clouds and landed beside her. *Where would you go, White Lady?*

"Do not call me that," Haramis said in a low voice. "Not yet." She mounted the lammergeier, holding tightly to the bag with the Crown and cloak, and Hiluro rose into the threatening sky.

King Voltrik and the Green Voice waited on the parapet of the Citadel's High Tower, and the dark clouds seemed to billow only a few ells above their heads, hiding the flag of Labornok on its staff. Below, the extensive fortress and its outbuildings and courtyards were peculiarly silent, even though it was mid-afternoon and a time when the surviving Ruwendian servitors and freemen were usually hard at work. But on this day only the steady clang of a blacksmith's hammer broke the stillness, tolling like some discordant bell of evil omen. King Voltrik shuddered.

"Is it the wretched feast upcoming tomorrow," he asked the Green Voice, "that has caused the conquered ones to shirk their duties? Full half of the usual Citadel staff claimed today to be stricken with ague and could not leave their beds — and those who are at work skulk about listlessly and seem barely able to carry on."

"Something is in the air," the Voice admitted. "Certainly there is bound to be another great storm soon."

"That's not what I meant," Voltrik snarled. "Something nasty is brewing, and I think you know what it is, and you are afraid to tell me!"

The Green Voice lowered his hooded head in submission. "My Almighty Master will soon arrive, Great King, and he will put your mind at rest and answer all questions."

The King uttered a guffaw of humorless laughter and abruptly turned away from the acolyte, to gaze out upon the expanse of land that lay to the north. The peculiar light made the lush green of the jungle seem especially intense, and the mire-smells were also much stronger than usual.

"If my mind is to be eased," Voltrik growled, "then why has the sorcerer commanded you to have all but a handful of our troops fall back to the Citadel and alert themselves for battle?"

"A mere precaution —"

"Liar! Both of you! Conniving traitors!" The monarch swung around and took the Green Voice by his shoulder. Even one-handed, he was able to shake Orogastus's assistant until his teeth rattled. "They're coming for me — the three Princess-Witches! That's it, isn't it? I could have been safely away from here, back in Derorguila, but you and Orogastus assured me that all would be well — that the witches were captured and their talismans taken. But you lied! And now they're coming for me, just as the prophecy said!"

"Nay, Great King —"

"I'm trapped here!" Voltrik howled. "Zoto have mercy on me! The army hates my guts because they're going to have to stay in this hellhole through the Rains, and the knights are bored out of their minds from inaction and drunk or wenching most of the time, and there is no one left to serve me but cravens and fools and traitorous tricksters plotting to take my kingdom once the Ruwendian demon-trulls have finished me off!"

The Green Voice dropped to his knees and clasped his hands in supplication. "Not so, not so! My Master will explain all when he arrives."

"*If* he does!" Voltrik bellowed. He drew his short-sword and used the flat of it to mash the Voice's nose painfully against his face. "And if he does not, then your shaven, flap-eared head will take leave of its body, and I will hie me out of this sump of iniquity at dawn tomorrow! Better to risk the perils of the Rains than loiter here like a stupid nunchik in a slaughter-pen."

A great blow of the King's foot sent the kneeling minion sprawling to the pavement.

And there sounded a cry like a brazen trumpet.

Startled, Voltrik flung his gaze in all directions but the correct one, so that he leapt with surprise when a gigantic black-and-white bird burst forth from the clouds, uttered another call, and glided to a landing on the parapet.

∴

From between its still-extended wings, Orogastus looked down at the thunderstruck King and bowed his head slightly.

"Greetings to you, my Liege," he said calmly. "I am here as I promised, and prepared to deliver your enemies to you, as I promised also."

"Zoto's Teeth! It's one of those things that serve the Archimage! And now it serves *you* — ?"

Orogastus slid from the lammergeier's back. He thanked it briefly, to which it merely rolled its eyes and then ascended into the dark clouds with a single flap of its wings.

"The Archimage," said the sorcerer with unconcealed satisfaction, "is dead. And her successor is none other than the Princess Haramis, who once spurned your proposed betrothal, and who is now under my power — although she still does not realize it."

"By the Ten Hells!" Voltrik sheathed his sword, grimacing with relief. "And the other two royal sluts?"

Orogastus walked to the tower's northernmost parapet and sat on the stone coping with his head lowered and his face concealed by the hood of his black cloak. Swiftly, using the speech without words, he gave orders to his acolyte. The Green Voice scrambled to his feet and disappeared down the trapdoor ladder.

Then the sorcerer drew back his hood and smiled upon Voltrik with all of the old charm and compelling self-possession that had bewitched a brash prince some eighteen years earlier.

"The other Princesses are indeed coming," Orogastus said. "Kadiya leads an undisciplined rabble of swamp-dwarves armed with blowguns and stone spears. Anigel's terrible host consists of a few hundred ugly-faced forest Oddlings, some faint-hearted Nyssomu, a troop of grubby Ruwendian partisans . . . and your son, the traitor, with his cadre of gnat-bitten turncoats."

"But the Princesses have their talismans!"

Orogastus nodded. "But they do not know how to use them properly. They no doubt think that all they need to do is to command our destruction. But I vow to you on my immortal soul that this is not the manner in which the magical instruments function. They are subtle weapons, and the Princesses are immature girls, with more spirit than brains, who do not understand such things."

Voltrik sat beside the sorcerer, a scowl denting his brow, and chewed on his mustaches. He gestured out at the Mire. "We can't go out there after them. Not with the Rains starting. We'd never hunt them down in the swamp, not even with the help of those abominable Drowners."

"No," Orogastus admitted. "And for that very reason they have been encouraged to come here to the Citadel, where our superior forces and my powerful enchantments will make an end of them once and for all!"

Voltrik brightened. "You will blast them with your lightning? Devastate them with the sorcery you used in the conquest?"

"I will lay the heads of Princess Kadiya and Princess Anigel at your feet. Haramis, who is my creature, will serve you body and soul."

Voltrik giggled nervously. "I wouldn't mind that . . . if you can magick her into submission, that is. I always fancied tall wenches, and I'll have to breed more sons somehow . . ."

"There *will* be a battle, Sire." Orogastus spoke almost with indifference. "It will take place within two days, undoubtedly at the Feast of the Three Moons."

Voltrik was on his feet again, eyes agleam and voice overloud. "Good! Damn it all, that's what we need to get our blood moving again! Sitting here for a month, half the time sick unto death, has turned my heart as stagnant as this accursed swamp! Do you have the strategy for the fight worked out?"

"Most assuredly, my Liege." Orogastus now arose also. "And this time, there is no doubt whatsoever that we will win. My great powers are honed, and I am eager to defend you. The army here in the Citadel is ready, and Lord Osorkon will soon arrive with an additional five thousand men . . . And lest you fret about the alleged power of the Princesses and their talismans, there is also *this*."

From beneath his cloak the sorcerer took a bag, and out from this retrieved a wooden box carved with skulls and other symbols of death. He opened the box to reveal a dull green sphere about the size of a small ladu-fruit, set within a nest of padded black velvet.

"This is a weapon more deadly than all my others put together. It was the second parting-gift to me of my late Master Bondanus —"

"He who gave you the Golden Pastilles?"

"Yes. They were a gift of life — but this brings only death of the most excruciating kind. It is only to be used as a last resort, for its bane will afflict everyone, friend or foe, who stands at ground level within a radius of a thousand ells. If its use should be required — if there is no other way in which to kill the Princesses — then I myself shall wield it."

King Voltrik had paled, and could not take his eyes from the thing. "What is it called, and how does it work?"

"It is known as the Doomful Effluvium, and it is a weapon older than the Vanished Ones, used against them by the ancestors of my Master, in their great struggle for the domination of the world. The sphere is of glass. Dashing it to the stones releases deadly vapors that bring death if a single breath of it be taken. I am prepared to use it to assure our victory — even though it will kill many of our own men as well as our enemies. You need not fear it yourself, Sire, as long as you remain on the upper levels of the keep. Its heavy vapors cannot rise far above a man's height."

Orogastus closed the box and put it away. "Undoubtedly, it will not be needed. I show it to you only to prove that there is no way that these Princesses can win out. We are invincible."

The eyes that the sorcerer now turned upon the grey-faced monarch seemed to become as brilliant as stars, and his soft voice compelled trust and drove away all fear. "You do believe me, do you not, my King?"

"Yes," Voltrik replied in a tremulous whisper. "Yes."

Knowing that her forces would now have to travel from their secret camp on the River Skrokar to Kadiya's hideout some fifteen leagues away in the trackless Mire just north of the Citadel, Princess Anigel had beseeched her talisman to conceal them from the enemy's magical sight. And lo! The day-mist had thickened to an opaque miasma that blinded the humans but bothered the Oddlings not at all.

The Princess deemed this the answer to her prayer, and her force set out. The fleet of Nyssomu punts carried the entire host safely past Castle Manoparo, to the confluence of the Skrokar and the Mutar. Thence they proceeded up the great river itself, staying in the backwaters along the northern shore until they had turned off to the right into a clogged and twisting little channel. This led Anigel to her sister's staging area, where they arrived at nightfall.

The place was another large hummock, but lit only by ghostly lanterns carrying tiny green-glowing swamp-worms. A Uisgu chieftain with

∴

great circles of red paint about his eyes and a full suit of golden fish-scale mail met Anigel's boat at the hummock shore, saying he would conduct her, Prince Antar, and the other Labornoki knights to the place where Kadiya waited.

In the wan lantern light they disembarked, and followed a path to a simple leather tent where Kadiya and her Uisgu battle-leaders were poring over a drawing of the Citadel keep spread out upon a crude table.

There were females there, for leadership was equal. But no long skirts loaded with fine embroidery were to be seen. One and all they wore woven grass breeches, and tunics overlaid with shells and tough scales, from shoulder to thigh, not unlike chain mail. They wore helms also, some fashioned of metal found in the ruins. Kadiya's hair was braided and coiled under hers. Save for her height, she might have been one of the general company.

When the golden-haired Anigel caught sight of her older sister, she forgot everything else, and burst into tears of gladness, rushing toward the other with open arms.

But Kadiya returned the embrace only hesitantly, and her dark eyes never left the face of Antar, who had remained at the entrance to the shelter, together with his men. The Prince looked from Anigel to her sister and there was the beginning of a frown on his face.

"What is wrong?" Anigel exclaimed in dismay; "We — we are together once more, alive!"

"Yes, I live," Kadiya returned stolidly. "But who are these who come with you, Sister? What pact have you made with them? Trust cannot be rooted in the spilling of kin-blood." She stared pointedly at the Prince. "Have you forgotten so easily whose steel slashed our world apart?"

Anigel gave a cry as desolate as if Kadiya had drawn a weapon against her. "Antar is not to be feared or mistrusted, I will pledge my life on it! My very talisman!" And she lifted from her head the silvery coronet, whose trillium amber had begun to pulsate brilliantly as she approached her sister, and held it out.

"Your Highness." The Prince looked to Kadiya straightly. "What must we swear by that will make you accept the truth?"

Slowly, Kadiya drew from its sheath her own talisman. She reversed it and held it pommel up, so that it faced both Anigel and Antar. The

∴

three eyes opened, and the watching men muttered in consternation.

"Sister, turn about," Kadiya commanded, "and let both our talismans pass judgment."

With a stricken countenance, Anigel did as she was bid.

"O Lords of the Air, great servants of God," Kadiya intoned, "reveal to us which of these knights will grant us loving service, and which would do us harm, and do unto the latter as they would do to us."

There was a soundless blast of blue-white light. Prince Antar and his fifteen loyal companions tottered in their armor, their mouths wide in shock; but on the wet earth lay two other knights, unmoving.

After the space of a few heartbeats, Sir Owanon bent over them. Shaking his head, he said: "Onbogar and Turat. Both stone dead."

Anigel cried out for horror. But Prince Antar asked the others: "And where is Rinutar?"

He was not among them; nor had anyone seen him since leaving the boat in which they had approached Kadiya's camp. Antar would have sent his men searching, but Princess Anigel bade them stay.

"I will find him," she said quietly. And she put her talisman back upon her head, and her eyes seemed to look through all the others, in the direction of the Citadel. "He is mid-river. In a stolen punt."

"Smite him!" cried bluff Sir Penapat. "He will raise the alarm!"

"There is no need for that," said a new voice.

This time it was Kadiya and Anigel who stood stock-still and gaping; for Princess Haramis had pushed her way through the crowd of armored men to confront her sisters. She wore the white cloak of the Archimage, and carried the Crown of State, unwrapped, in one arm.

"Haramis!" her sisters exclaimed in unison.

"Kadiya! Anigel!" Haramis embraced her sisters, then said: "Yes, it is I. You may as well let Rinutar go. King Voltrik and Orogastus already know that you are here, and that you intend to attack before moonrise tomorrow, when the feast begins."

All of them, Uisgu and Labornoki, Kadiya and Anigel, even sturdy little Jagun, began to speak at once.

Haramis lifted her talisman. The trillium amber set within the wand throbbed with golden light, as did the amber of the other talismans. Silence fell.

Haramis said: "Sisters, I know what numbers of followers you have brought to this encampment." She tried not to let her incredulity show in her voice; they deserved her courtesy. "I have seen many more boats full of Uisgu approaching this place, as well as a large fleet of heavily armed Ruwendians coming in from the free northeast. But if you attack the Citadel, all of these loyal friends will die, for this venture is fore-doomed."

"Who told you so?" Kadiya demanded hotly. "Your dearly beloved sorcerer?"

Haramis flushed. She hardly deserved that; though perhaps Kadiya could not be blamed for thinking so. She looked Kadiya straight in the eye. "Whatever you may think has happened between Orogastus and me, it is not I who have brought the enemy to our councils." She looked squarely at Anigel, standing close to Prince Antar. Anigel flushed, but said nothing. "As for doom — I am not blind, I can see it for myself. Your aborigines are only lightly armed. Count Palundo's force probably cannot get here in time — but even if it does, it will be countered by the five thousand men that Osorkon is bringing down the river. The other half of Voltrik's army is already on alert, ready to repel any assault you might mount. The great gates of the Citadel have been repaired —"

"Perhaps," said Kadiya with a grin, "we have the wherewithal to open them. And to defeat your conjurer as well!"

"You are gambling many lives on that assumption," Haramis pointed out. "Perhaps you do not know that you can no longer count upon the assistance of the Archimage."

"Why not?" Kadiya demanded. "She has always assisted us before. Are you trying to tell us that she would aid Orogastus in this battle?"

"No," Haramis said wearily. "I am trying to tell you that the Archimage is dead."

It was Anigel who cried out in dismay. Kadiya said angrily: "How do you know?"

"I know because I was there," Haramis said, and then her grief threatened to overcome her again. As yet she had shed no tears for the Archimage; but she did not dare to give way just now. She forced her voice to remain steady.

"I tell you, Orogastus is waiting for you with all the arcane weaponry at his command, and he has called for the local Greenmire Skritek to walk. They are converging upon Citadel Knoll, and will harry and devour any of your people they can catch! Do you really believe you can face all that — and Orogastus's weapons?"

There was a moment of silence, which seemed very long to Haramis. "You will all be massacred," she added quietly. "Withdraw, I beg of you. They can't follow you into the swamps at this time of year."

"No!" Kadiya smashed her fist onto the table. "Orogastus has bewitched you! That is plain to see, for all that you have usurped the cloak of the Archimage."

"Do you really think I wanted to take her place?" Haramis demanded. All of her fatigue, all of her grief for the Archimage threatened to overpower her again.

"Yes, I do," Kadiya declared hotly. "You have always been greedy for power, Haramis. You cannot bear to think that either Ani or I might have a plan that is better than yours."

The unfairness of this struck Haramis like a blow. She felt as if she would collapse under it. Kadiya surveyed her angrily, but Anigel saw the grief in her face.

"I think you are being unfair, Kadi," she said. "Let us at least hear Haramis's plan."

Kadiya glared at both of them. She said: "What of the Crown, Haramis? Will you and Orogastus share the thrones of Ruwenda and Labornok, after Voltrik is disposed of in this great plan of yours?"

"Of course not! Kadiya, you simply don't understand." Haramis was almost despairing. How could she make her sisters see?

It was little Jagun who said unexpectedly: "Let the talismans prove her true or false, as they did Prince Antar and his men."

Haramis drew herself to her full height. "As you wish. But if your talismans are anything like my own, Sisters, you had best be very careful how you frame your test. For I have no doubt that my talisman, like yours, is capable of killing."

"So be it," said Kadiya, as Anigel looked from one sister to the other in open distress. Their thoughts were easily read even by the Labornoki knights and the Uisgu.

"Dearest Haramis," Anigel said forlornly, "we want very much to trust you, but we have *seen* you consorting with Orogastus." Anigel had tears in her eyes, but her voice was steady. "We have no other course but to ask if you will give us leave to test you."

Haramis regarded her sister with a bemused expression. All of the others in the tent held their breath, and in the stillness could be heard the first patter of raindrops from the new storm, and a quiet murmur of many voices outside. Another band of recruits had arrived.

She said quietly: "I did not ask to test you, though you brought your Prince here." Anigel flushed as Haramis went on. "Let it be as you will." She took her own talisman and held it before her face. "Test me, then."

At that point, all of Antar's knights and the Uisgu left the tent in precipitate haste. Only the Prince and Jagun remained, and the small Nyssomu huntsman sketched the sign of the Black Trillium before each sister. Haramis handed Jagun the Crown; he took it reverently and knelt in a corner with his head bowed.

Kadiya and Anigel still stood side by side, talismans raised. But this time it was the youngest Princess who spoke.

"Dear Lords of the Air, have pity on us three. But also show clearly to us any danger we might pose to the great balance of the world."

The three talismans glowed a deep crimson, filling the tent with brilliant light. The three Princesses were like statues, with eyes wide and lips slightly parted.

Then coronet and wand and pointless sword took on a spectral aspect; they flew from their owners to a point midway above them . . . and there the talismans merged. The shaft of the wand slipped into the three-lobed pommel, and the coronet, with its monstrous visages below the cusps, engirded the Circle and closed; whereupon the three conjoined wings with their amber center were suddenly suspended within concentric rings. A mysterious voice spoke.

In this Sceptre of Power is the potential for permanent balance, as well as for the ruin of this world. Consider most judiciously before commanding the Sceptre, and remember that those who made it were in the end afraid to use it . . .

The blood-red light faded. Each Princess again held her own talisman.

After many silent minutes, Prince Antar spoke. "Did the talismans answer?"

∴

Haramis stared, unbelieving, but it was Anigel who demanded, in the voice of one waking from a dream: "Did you not see and hear?"

"Nothing, gracious Lady, save your own invocation."

The three sisters exchanged glances. Without thinking, all three came together in a triple embrace.

"So it seems I am exonerated," Haramis whispered. "Or am I?"

"Of course you are," Kadiya said sharply, "but we will attack the Citadel nonetheless."

Haramis frowned. "Are you both resolved on this?"

"Yes," said Anigel. "If you will not join us, Sister, then at least do not hinder us, nor give aid to our enemies."

"I will not," Haramis said. "But I must leave you. I must go to Citadel Knoll, and there . . . I do not know what I will do. But I know I must go there."

Little Jagun had come from his place in the corner, still holding the Crown of State. "If you wish, Princess Haramis, I will take you in a punt."

"I thank you," Haramis said. "But before I leave," she said to her sisters, "let me tell you something I learned during my time with Orogastus. Much of his so-called 'magic' comes from devices of the Vanished Ones, and it is possible that your talismans may be used to break these devices. When my talisman touched one, the device ceased to function. This may work with your talismans as well." She hugged her sisters. "Kadiya, Anigel, be careful — and may the Lords of the Air protect you!"

She took the Crown from Jagun. And then white-cloaked Haramis was gone with the Nyssomu huntsman, and only Antar was left with the other two Princesses. A grumble of thunder sounded and the rainfall quickened.

Kadiya frowned at the tall young man in the blue armor. "You really saw nothing? No red light, no merging of the talismans? You heard no uncanny voice?"

"Truly not, my Princess," Antar said.

"The vision was for us, Kadi," Anigel said. "And especially, I think, for poor Haramis."

"Poor?" Kadiya scoffed. "Why, here we stand, outcasts ready to go to war — while she, with Crown and cloak, chooses to watch on the sidelines!"

∴

"If we are able to win out without the Sceptre, then she will indeed be the luckiest. But if we need it . . ."

Kadiya threw back her shoulders, and grasped the pommel of her talisman firmly. "It will not come to that."

And then, speaking briskly, she invited Prince Antar to call in again the loyal knights and the leaders of the Folk, so that she might explain the plan of invasion to all of them.

43

That night Haramis slept safe and dry beneath a tree on the shore of the Knoll, in a small park beside the Citadel Landing. She told her talisman to conceal her from sight, and a mist effectively hid her from the few guards on duty at the docks.

In the morning the storm had passed, but the fog lay heavier, enclosing her within a soft grey room where the only sounds were the occasional chirps and squeaks of birds and insects, and the slow dripping from the margin of the tree canopy. The dock guards, she discovered, had retreated to the Citadel. The road from the Landing led directly to the main gate of the fortress less than a league away, and she knew that one part of her sister's foolhardy plan involved an attack along this most obvious route.

She sat quietly in meditation, and prayed for guidance. It was difficult; other thoughts kept intruding, worry for her sisters, grief for the loss of her parents and the White Lady, anger at Kadiya's accusation that she had usurped the Archimage's robe — *as if I even wanted it! But who else is there? Does Kadiya think* she *could be Archimage?*

As if the thought had summoned her, Haramis saw the slender image of Binah appear before her, robed in her shining white cloak with the hood hiding her face. But the hands that rose slowly to push back the hood were young and unlined, and Haramis felt a sudden pang of dread. What would the face be? Would it be Kadiya's — or some horrible demon?

It was neither; the face was Binah's, but it was transformed: radiant and no longer old. It was as if all that was mortal in her had departed and what remained was her spirit in pure form.

Lady. Haramis bowed her head.

A hand seemed to caress her hair and a clear musical voice which was still somehow Binah's said, *What is it, my daughter?*

My sisters, Haramis replied miserably. *They think I'm in love with Oro-gastus — bewitched by him, in fact — and Kadiya actually accused me of usurping your cloak!*

But you know that is not true, the gentle voice said. *In time they will learn it also.*

Kadiya said I was power-hungry.

And she thinks that is why you wear the cloak. It was not a question. *I gave it to you, Haramis, but I cannot force you to wear it. It is a burden, and other people, even those who love you, will never understand why you do this work. It must be done for itself, not because someone else wants you to do it, or will praise you for doing it.*

The work is well worth doing, Binah continued. *It is always there, waiting for the one called to do it. Someone must care for Ruwenda, must make certain that it grows as it should — or at least that it survives until someone stronger can pick up the burden. There is great joy in the labor: to see the beauty of the pattern and to know that your efforts help to maintain it, to hear the voice of the land and its Folk, to feel the cycle of the seasons and the greater cycle of the ages . . .*

Binah's voice fell silent, but in that silence Haramis seemed to hear and feel Ruwenda in a way she never had before. It seemed as if the land had a pulse, a heartbeat, and Haramis felt her own heart matching the rhythm she heard. It seemed to her that there was a song in that pulse, a song she could almost hear and understand — if she could only reach out and truly listen . . .

She sat entranced for a long time, only dimly aware of Binah's departure.

Then a metal tray appeared before her, and invisible hands lowered it into her lap. On it were four hearts, apparently human, and a pitcher of sea water. *Wash these,* a voice commanded. In Haramis's dreamlike state, this seemed a reasonable request. She picked up the first heart. It fit comfortably into her hand and pulsed gently with life and warmth. She poured the salty water over and through it, and the invisible hand took it from her as she finished. She repeated the procedure with the second and third hearts, which seemed identical to the first. But when she picked up the fourth heart it felt different, odd. Something on the bottom of it pricked her palm, and she turned it over. To her bewilderment, she saw that it was a device of some sort, not a human heart at all, but merely a semblance of one. She reached for the water, but the unseen hand blocked hers. *No,* the voice said sadly, *that one cannot be washed. He has given up his humanity.* The mechanical heart was removed from her hand.

I don't understand, Haramis thought.

You must be able to endure truth, the voice said.

Haramis didn't understand that either.

Then for a time, she let her mind rest in a dreamless sleep.

When she woke, it was near dusk. Using the Three-Winged Circle, she watched the preparations going on within the Citadel, the warriors taking up positions to defend the fortress from assault, and the comings and goings of the knights and officers as they reported to the King. She saw Orogastus and the Green Voice readying the martial devices of the Vanished Ones: two machines that summoned lightning; one that would screech with so overwhelming a sound that those whose ears were unprotected would fall deafened and bleeding; two that sprayed a hail of deadly pellets; one that flung great gouts of flame; and another that shot poisoned needles. But as Haramis watched, it seemed that a small voice whispered to her that these engines of death were more suited to offense than defense, and might actually work to the disadvantage of those who tried to use them inside the fortress . . .

She wondered what Kadiya and Anigel planned to do. The freshly repaired Citadel outworks and curtainwalls could not be scaled; they were steep and overlooked by embrasures through which crossbowmen or the wielders of the sorcerer's weapons might shoot. While her sisters' talismans might shield their followers from the sorcerer's preternatural Sight, Haramis was certain that invaders would be quite visible to the normal eyes of the Labornoki defenders. The new gates were too massive for any ram to burst. Did her sisters think to use the talismans to break in? Pressing her wand to her heart, Haramis asked, *Is this possible?* And an answer formed in her mind.

No.

Her heart sank. *I will give them what help I can, but I will not interfere,* she told herself. *Nor will I offer unwanted advice. They are following their destinies — and I have chosen mine.*

A great feeling of tranquillity spread over her. Sitting here beneath the tree in the evening mist, she had a feeling again of being rooted in the very center of the world, of knowing her place in the greater pattern.

I have become what I always knew I could be.

But will its price be the death of my sisters?

She held the Circle upright, and asked to see them. And when the vision came she watched for hours, marveling.

Most of their army, under the command of the human Ruwendians and Antar's loyal knights, took up a position in the swamp just across the river from her own position at Citadel Landing, which was a league downhill from the fortress itself. Since this put them almost directly opposite her, she listened carefully and looked across the river to see if they were perceptible to normal human senses. Satisfied that they were not, she returned her gaze to the Circle.

Apart from the main body of attackers, a few hundred Uisgu and Wyvilo fighters, led by Kadiya and Anigel and Prince Antar, had rowed up the Mutar until they reached that place where the ancient water-intake tunnel had its opening. Secured from enemy Sight by the talismans, this group had disappeared into the cistern conduit.

"By the Flower!" Haramis whispered in admiration. "If Kadiya and Anigel can open the Citadel gates to their army, then perhaps they *do* have a chance to win!"

Later, when the Triple Moons were rising, invisible in the fog, and the feast had its official commencement, Haramis made her own small ceremony and ate from the bag of provisions Jagun had left with her. Then Haramis asked her talisman where reinforcements of the Labornoki army might be. The Circle showed her a fleet of over a hundred flatboats hurtling down the river with all the speed the oarsmen could muster. Even if her sisters managed to penetrate the fortress and throw open the gates, they would be overwhelmed once this second group of heavily armed Labornoki warriors arrived.

As the picture in the Circle faded, she wiped unshed tears from her eyes. So be it. Her sisters' fate would be as it would be, and she must get on with her own business.

∴

She summoned a vision of Orogastus. "I have made my choice," she told him.

The sorcerer regarded her without expression. "Will you do me the honor of telling me this decision of yours face to face? I regret I cannot come to you; the lammergeier you commanded to carry me here performed its service and then disappeared."

"Very well," she said. "I shall come, to the High Tower of the keep."

"May I meet you in the solar there an hour from now, at midnight?" Orogastus requested. "You know, of course, that none of us here can possibly harm you now that your talisman is empowered."

"I know," Haramis said simply. "I shall come."

"Farewell," Orogastus said, and his handsome face softened in a smile. "Fare thee very well, Haramis, my beloved." His image faded from the Circle.

Haramis began to gather up her things by the dim golden light of the trillium-amber inset in her talisman. The mist began to lift, and a breath of chill wind rustled the long leaves of the wydel-trees in the park. Among the reeds and shore-brush, not far away, some creature was splashing and scrabbling in the dark. Haramis thought nothing of this, and was ready to call her lammergeier, when the bushes parted and two gleaming golden eyes looked out at her.

"Princess," a voice hissed.

"By the Flower — *Immu!*"

Haramis dropped the bag in which she had packed the Crown and cloak, and ran to embrace the old Nyssomu nurse.

"Immu, what are you doing here?"

The little being scowled and showed her diminutive fangs. "Doing doing doing! It is a story too overlong to tell now. My brains are all in a frazzle because I have been hastening to rejoin my darling Princess Anigel, and since noontide today my Sight has refused to show her to me!"

Haramis nodded. "It is magic engendered by her talisman, hiding her from the Sight of her enemies — and friends as well, it seems."

"I came to the Knoll, and spied you sitting here in the park. I could hardly believe my eyes! Do you know where my Princess is? She *needs* me!"

"Yes, I know where she is. But I doubt that she requires your good offices, Immu, for she and Kadiya are at this moment leading an army into the Citadel to challenge King Voltrik."

"Lords of the Air!" Immu wailed, and her eyes popped audibly. "On such a venture, she will need me more than ever! Tell me how I may reach her side!"

Haramis hesitated. "Do you have a boat?"

"Yes, a small punt with oars."

Haramis picked up her things. "I will have to show you."

They embarked, and Immu rowed along quietly in the dark backwaters of the Mutar, following Haramis's guidance. After half an hour, they came to a narrow mudflat with much of its vegetation submerged by the rising flood. Inland of this was the Knoll slope with a high bank cut in it, and the level ground at the base of the bank was thickly overgrown with thorn-ferns.

The mud was roiled and pockmarked with a great welter of footprints.

"Here?" Immu was incredulous. "They've landed *here?* But it is nearly two leagues to the Citadel from this spot, all uphill and on open ground. And I see no traces of them —"

"Immu, they have gone in through the old cistern conduit. My sisters were confident that they could shield their force from Orogastus's Sight at least until they gained the lower levels of the keep itself. From there they will attempt to open the Main Gate and the Victualer's Gate."

Immu was girding up her skirts grimly. "How have they ascended the cistern shaft?"

"A rope with a grapple-iron was shot up. After one Uisgu climbed it, he hauled many rope ladders into place for the others. The ladders are still there."

"Scry them for me! Tell me if Princess Anigel is yet safe!"

"No. I will only pray that the Lords of the Air will fight at their sides."

"Very well, then," the little old nurse exclaimed. "You just pray away. But I'm off!" And she leaped from the boat, splashed across the trampled mud, and was soon lost to sight among the tall ferns.

Haramis sighed, and moved forward to take the oars. There were Labornoki scouting patrols ranging here and there about the Knoll, and sooner or later they would discover this place of entry and give the alarm. *I could bring down the riverbank,* she thought, *burying the entrance to the tunnel.*

She lifted the talisman. The three folded wings assumed an open position within the Circle, and the trillium amber shone at the center where they joined. "Let the earth liquefy and the mud flow to cover this place from hostile eyes."

There was a low rumble. The high bank seemed to ripple in the mist, then slid to cover the tunnel entrance. Where the steep bank and the fern thicket had been there was now nothing but a long glistening muddy chute studded with small boulders.

The boat rocked gently on the river. Tendrils of vapor stole about the surface of the water like ghostly snakes. Far away, she heard the drumming of fronial-hooves. The Labornoki cavalry was patrolling the road to Ruwenda Market. A silver trumpet called faintly; another, closer by, gave brief response.

In Haramis's mind, a voice seemed to say, *The power is within you. And that is the great peril of it.*

She rowed away in the sluggish backwaters until she was a good distance from the mudslide, and then put in again to shore. Tying the bag with its valuables to her belt, she called:

Hiluro!

The gigantic bird did not appear at once, but Haramis was not perturbed. She sat down on a rock and gazed at the distant Citadel, which had finally emerged from the slowly dissolving fog. Bonfires must have been burning within the inner wards and courtyards, for the great keep and its adjacent wings were brightly illuminated. From the flagstaff on the High Tower flew the huge Labornoki banner, blood-red with three crossed golden swords. This was now also lit by fires burning at its base. It was almost as if Voltrik were saying: *Here I am! Take back your castle if you dare!*

"Let my sisters win!" Haramis pleaded, gripping her talisman. "Please let them win."

Haramis. She heard the familiar voice of her lammergeier. *I have seen a dire thing.*

Hiluro landed as gently as a dark cloud, and she ran to him. "What is it?"

Climb upon my back and I will show you.

She did, and the creature soared upward, then flew away along the margin of the Knoll, to where the thick Greenmire met the Mutar River

∴

beyond Ruwenda Market. This region was a lonely one, devoid of houses, for much of the Knoll in the vicinity was bare rock with only meager vegetation.

The sky was clearing rapidly now, and the ground-fog almost entirely blown away. The Triple Moons were still thinly veiled, but enough light now reached the ground that Haramis could see below myriad dark shadows emerging from the Mire in several streams, then converging into a single mass as they moved in the direction of the Citadel nearly three leagues away.

"But, what can they be? Surely the second force of the Labornoki army cannot have arrived yet —"

They are Skritek, summoned by the sorcerer, the lammergeier said.

"Oh, Triune God! Of course!"

Hiluro descended, gliding just out of reach only a few ells above the ground, and Haramis saw the fiends of the Mazy Mire, hissing and snapping impotently as the great bird passed overhead.

I cannot let them devour my sisters' comrades, Haramis thought in dismay. *What should I do?*

A voice in her head said quietly, *You are Lady of all Folk.*

But what does that mean?

The Skritek are Folk.

She understood then, and she knew what she must do. She said: "Hiluro, land in front of them."

The bird banked steeply and flew back. He set Haramis on a mossy rock half a hundred ells in advance of the marching monsters and took up a position behind her, great wings outstretched. She put on the Archimage's cloak and waited. The night-keen eyes of the Skritek spotted her quickly, and they came dashing toward her howling and hissing, moving at such a pace that she was certain she would be trampled.

Instead they halted, and fell silent, a scant stone's throw away. She lifted her talisman and bespoke them.

Who leads?

Nine or ten of the shambling, scaled brutes ventured forward. Their jaws dripped stinking saliva and they clenched and unclenched their talons, and she perceived that their slow brains were all in a state of turmoil.

She said, *Do you know who I am?*

You were dead! He said it. We knew it!

I am always alive, here in my country. All Folk are my children, all obey me. But you have not obeyed. You followed the sorcerer and went to war, which is forbidden.

You did not speak to us! You lost your power! He proved that when he called us and you did not forbid our going!

I speak now. Do you hear?

We do, White Lady.

And every one of the great assemblage of Skritek fell upon the ground before her, penitently.

Haramis said to the monsters, *It was permitted for you to help the human invaders before. But now, it is no longer permitted. Do you understand?*

Yes, White Lady. The response included many a bespoken groan of disgruntlement, but it was nonetheless sincere.

Before you return to the Mire, you will perform a task for me.

We are yours to command, White Lady.

She explained carefully what they were to do, making certain that they understood that there was to be no wanton cruelty. Although this was a keen disappointment to the fiends, they were somewhat cheered at the prospect of even a little amusement, and agreed to do exactly as she had requested.

Hearing this, she gave them her blessing, mounted Hiluro, and flew away to meet Orogastus at the Citadel.

44

King Voltrik was not a complete fool, and fairly early on had recognized the breach in his defenses posed by the old cistern tunnel. But the Labornoki engineers were afraid to meddle with it or with the well itself, because they were somehow connected to the main waterworks of the Citadel. So Voltrik could not close the opening. But for nearly two weeks the King had posted sentries about the mouth of the ancient cistern, and set a relay of men all the way down the long series of stairways leading to it, so that word might be passed upward instantly if any Ruwendian invader attempted to gain entry by the subterranean route.

But the well-chamber was noisome and gloomy, infested not only with the disgusting slime-dawdlers but also with those winged animals of the night whose hooting, warbling cries were so persistent as to drive men half-crazy. And as the days passed with no human intruders detected (but plenty of ghostly ones seeming to lurk in the malodorous dark among the decrepit pumping machinery), the squads of Labornoki soldiers assigned to guard the cistern withdrew instead to the ancient dungeon one level above.

There they used their torches to burn off the worst of the creeping things and incinerate the mouldering skeletons; and with the ready connivance of their watch-sergeants brought down stools, and made a table of the old torture-bed, and enlivened their dreary vigils by playing cards and quaffing contraband beer.

As fate would have it, at the moment when the grapple-iron of the first invading Uisgu clanked and dug in its hooks at the cistern's lip, a certain Labornoki warrior named Krugdal was detected cheating in the game, and his indignant comrades took hold of him to give him a drubbing. The soldiers' row covered the small noises made by the fixing of the Uisgu rope-ladders. By the time the luckless Krugdal was deemed sufficiently punished, nearly forty Oddlings under the command of Prince Antar had swarmed into the cistern chamber and up the narrow stairs.

The Prince himself, attired in his full knightly panoply, entered the dungeon and began to berate the astounded card-players for neglecting their duties. The men were dumbstruck at seeing the King's son appear as if from nowhere, and knowing nothing of his supposed treason stood docile as he tongue-lashed them. When the fierce Wyvilo and Uisgu warriors poured into the room the soldiers were too stupefied to resist or even cry out, and so they were easily bound and gagged and thrown into the old dungeon cells.

Now the two Princesses and the battle-leaders of the Uisgu and Wyvilo companies had a quick council-of-war.

It would take time for the three hundred or so invaders to mount the narrow stairways and reach the ground level of the keep, where they might fight their way to the gates. From the captured sergeant it was learned that the relay of Labornoki strung out along the steps had a changing of the guard less than an hour hence.

"We must mount the stairs before this time," Princess Kadiya asserted. "We shall have to subdue the relay of foemen one at a time, using the utmost care so that they do not raise the alarm. One shout, and we are undone."

A Uisgu battle-chieftain named Prebb said: "I will take two of mine. We will go soft as mire-mist and use blowguns to down the foe."

"But if you are seen by even one of them —" Prince Antar was dubious. "You know that the magic of the Princesses has shielded us from the wizard's farseeing eye. But mortal men may readily see us."

Anigel said: "*I* will take the darts and subdue each guard. My talisman will surely render me invisible, as it did before when I was in mortal danger, so no foeman will have a chance to cry a warning."

Antar was aghast, and tried to forbid her, as did all the other leaders. But she was as determined to go as she was positive of her ability to perform the perilous task. Kadiya, clad from head to toe in golden scale-mail whose luster was barely dimmed by the mud splashed upon it, stepped forward and took her younger sister by the hands.

"You are right, Ani. The mission is one you are best suited for, and no one shall deny you that which your courage demands. Fair fortune to you, Sister mine, and may no evil touch you."

Prebb took a bandolier full of the small darts and draped it over Anigel's shoulders. "You stick dart and leave it in place, man die," he said. "You stick dart and take it out, man sleep for long time but live. But beware! Do not stick yourself."

"I understand," Anigel said, her face calm beneath the gleaming coronet.

"As you dispatch each sentry," Kadiya said, "bespeak me. We will follow after in a body, keeping far enough below you that no noise betrays our movements."

"My Princess!" cried Antar, stricken. "I beseech you —"

"No." She went to him and kissed him lightly on the lips, a caress so fleeting that it was barely a touch at all. But it caused the Prince's heart to blaze like a fanned ember, and paralyzed his body so that it was a long moment before he could voice his elation.

But by then Anigel was gone, and the Oddling warriors were grinning at the Prince, and Kadiya suggested rather tartly that they had better see how things fared down in the cistern chamber.

Anigel's only prayer and command was a whispered: "Lords of the Air, defend me." And then she began the long climb.

She came upon the first guard on a landing a hundred steps above, a lantern at his feet and his arbalest in his hands. He was a tall and well-built young fellow, clad like most of the Labornoki men-at-arms in a steel-mesh hauberk and a pot-helmet, and armed with a short-sword and mace as well as a pouch full of quarrels for his bow. He was whistling softly to pass the time and making bets with himself which of two lingits creeping up the damp wall would reach the ceiling first.

Anigel came soundlessly up to him and lifted a poisoned dart with trembling fingers. Where should she strike? He wore a heavy shirt of quilted leather beneath his mail, and his neck was shielded by hinged plates dangling from his helmet.

∴

She told herself: *He will fall, and if he fall upon me or upon the dart, then I may not be able to remove it and he will die! Oh, I could not bear it if he should die, for he looks a brave and comely youth and is surely some mother's son . . .*

And your mortal foe, a vexed little voice seemed to whisper within her. *Who would rape and slay you without thinking twice, could he catch sight of you. For even though he is not evil himself, he will follow without question the orders he has been given by evil men. And those who choose the warrior role must be prepared to endure the warrior's fate.*

Anigel felt herself cringe, and realized for the first time that she also had chosen the warrior's way, no matter how she had tried to convince herself that she would deal with the enemy without bloodshed.

If I had to kill him in cold blood — could I?

She took a deep breath and thrust the dart into the back of the man's hand. Pulling it out instantly, she dropped it and shrank away from him. He uttered a querulous murmur, as of surprise, and his eyes rolled into his skull and his knees folded slowly. The crossbow fell and clattered a ways down the slimy steps, and his helm clanked as he fell prone on the stones.

But he breathed. Anigel made certain of that before bespeaking Kadiya. Then she hurried upward to the next sentry, her heart pounding and her body infused with a vigor that almost shamed her. Her fatigue and fear fell away like a discarded garment. The eerie passage through the muddy conduit and the vertiginous climb up the swaying rope-ladder were forgotten. She was back inside the Citadel, her home, and at war with its despoilers . . .

All in all, she downed eighteen of them. And then at last she reached the brewery door, and listened at it for a time (not thinking to view beyond it by means of her Sight), and hearing nothing she slipped through —

And came face to face with the Green Voice.

Naturally, he did not see her. But he did see the door open, and he felt the ill-smelling exhalation from the lower cellars. He uttered a colorful curse, and then chuckled and said:

"Yes, come ahead, you bog-skipping scum, and get what is coming to you! Perhaps we cannot descry you, but thanks to my Almighty Master we can *hear* you coming very well — and once your vanguard reaches the top of the stairs, you will meet the welcome your rashness deserves!"

The Green Voice had his hood off, and covering his ears were two objects like small caps with tiny things studding them, and a band running from one cap to the other across the top of his skull.

But Anigel paid no attention to this magical device. What seized her attention was a machine that two sturdy Labornoki soldiers were man-handling into position. It was a heavy grey box with rounded corners and complex ornamentation on the top and back; and from the front protruded a long, slender cylinder of glass with many metal rings and rods strapped about it, and at its tip a peculiar thing made of gold. A thick cord of some shiny black material led from this box to another much larger one, which sat on a wheelbarrow behind a large stack of full grain sacks six or seven ells away.

"Be careful, fool!" said the Voice to one of the soldiers, who had staggered under the weight of the thing and nearly caused it to fall. "This and one other are the only lightning generators left working, and if you damage it, my Almighty Master will flay the skin from your worthless body and deep-fry you in seething oil!"

Anigel choked back a horrified gasp. The lightning of Orogastus came from machines? And now the Green Voice was preparing to aim this one down the staircase where Kadiya and their army were climbing up —

And Prince Antar.

Moving fedok-swift, Anigel pricked each soldier in turn. As they fell, bearing the weapon gently to the stones, and the used darts clinked down beside them, the Green Voice took alarm. Familiar with magic, he must have sensed that someone invisible was there. He hoisted up his robe and ran as fast as his legs could carry him toward the large box on the barrow.

Anigel raced after him and flung herself upon his back. As he strug-gled to manipulate some protuberance on the large box, the Princess clutched a fresh dart and plunged it with all her strength into the back of his neck.

He collapsed atop the magical contrivance, inert as one of the grain sacks in the improvised barricade. The strange headpiece fell from his shaven head. Slowly, Anigel pulled away from him. She could not take her eyes from the dart, and at first her hand reached out toward it, only to fall back. She seemed to hear words spoken long, long ago — or was it only four weeks since? — when she and Kadiya and Immu and Jagun looked out over a throne room splashed with blood, and she had demanded in her innocence an explanation of evil:

Gentle folk may not safely respond to them gently, because evildoers do not know what love is, mistaking it for weakness. For this reason you, who are a gentle and loving Princess, must find a sterner way of dealing with such ones . . .

"And you are Orogastus's Voice," she whispered. And stood over him sadly until Kadiya and the others came crowding into the brewery, by which time the Green Voice was dead.

Then Anigel bade the Wyvilo leader Lummomu-Ko take his massive axe and hack the lightning-machine into pieces. When this was done, the little army made its way up to the ground level of the Citadel, and the real battle began.

In times of peace the giant flatboats serving the traders were manned by crews of free Ruwendian oarsmen who prided themselves on their strength and skill, and earned high wages for speeding their awkward craft up and down the rivers. But with the conquest, most experienced rivermen eloped into the Mazy Mire; and the Labornoki, faced with the imminent loss of crucial transport, speedily enslaved those who remained and pressed into service other inexperienced Ruwendians to fill the empty benches. They were chained to their oars, fed poorly, and whipped if they seemed to shirk. But even at the best of times, the slave-crews were far inferior to those of free men, as both General Hamil and Lord Osorkon had discovered on their ill-fated expedition up the Mutar.

Now, when Osorkon desired to return to the Citadel quickly (knowing from conversations with the late Red Voice that some serious mischief was scheduled for the Feast of the Three Moons), the great fleet of boats seemed to move along barely faster than the current. Scandalous numbers of oarsmen had died under the lash since they had left the big encampment just below the Thorny Hell, and the rest were so mortally exhausted that no amount of flogging would speed their stroke.

Osorkon called for the flagship's skipper to join him in the bows and demanded some remedy; but Pellan only said, cringing: "My General, the rowers are done in and collapsing, and nothing can make us go any faster — unless you wish to follow my earlier suggestion and replace the slaves with soldiers."

"Damn your soul, Pellan, we will lose even more time if we stop and unchain the oarsmen so that my men can take their places! And even then, they will make a botch of it. They know nothing of rowing."

"What can I say?" The scrawny riverman did not look up. "The flood gives us a fair pace. There is naught we can do but ride it."

Osorkon ground his teeth but kept silent. He was a less impetuous man than the late Hamil, whose command he had assumed, and he knew that Pellan told the truth. The flotilla would reach the Citadel eventually even if all the oars were stilled. He cast an eye heavenward, toward the bright fuzzy smear that indicated the position of the cloud-veiled Three Moons. It was near to midnight, and the feast had begun at sundown. Who knew what dark magic the Witch-Princess Kadiya and her Uisgu mob might be getting up to?

Turning his back on the riverman, the officer strode up to the forward rail and stood there with his hands clasped behind his back. He was cloaked and warmly dressed against the chill and damp, but had not donned his armor. "What is yon ruddy glow in the sky, Riverman? Can it be that we are approaching the Knoll at long last?"

"Yes, my General. The docks of Ruwenda Market are a league away. But you ordered us to proceed to the Citadel Landing itself, and that is a full three leagues farther by water —"

"Yes, yes, I know. How long before we arrive?"

"Less than an hour." Pellan had taken up a brass spyglass and now peered through it at the black river ahead. "Strange, the surface is greatly roiled up there. One would think the giant milingal-fish were spawning, but it is the wrong time of year."

Osorkon was immediately alert. "Is it enemy watercraft?"

"Nay, nothing of the sort. There is enough skylight for me to be sure of that . . . And now the same ferment is afflicting the waters abeam — *Holy Flower! Get back!*"

A series of tremendous splashes, mingled with hair-raising roars, split the night's calmness. Osorkon saw rising up above the boat's gunwale a huge head with shining orange eyes and a grinning mouth that seemed half an ell wide, studded with teeth like white knives. A stomach-churning stench smote him like a physical blow.

"Skritek!" Pellan shrieked at the top of his lungs. But it was the last word he ever uttered. The monster climbed nimbly over the low rail, took the riverman in his talons, and snapped off his head with a single bite of his jaws.

Osorkon was beside himself with fear and rage, seeing what his putative ally had just done. What was worse, all up and down the length of the big flotilla throngs of the fiends were boarding boats, and the screams of terrified troops now mingled with inhuman roars and whoops.

"Stop!" Osorkon cried. "Hold off, you misbegotten cornholers! We are Labornoki! Your allies! Your friends!"

The Skritek who had decapitated Pellan seemed momentarily flummoxed, as though he had just recalled something important that had slipped his mind. He howled out a phrase in his own language, to which his compatriots responded with disappointed groans and hoots. Then he dropped Pellan's gore-spouting body, seized Lord Osorkon with particular care, and flung him over the side.

The officer surfaced soon enough, coughing and gagging, only to be nearly brained by an oar trailing limply in the water. He took hold of it and clung for dear life, and watched dumfounded as the monsters tossed each and every Labornoki into the muddy, swift-flowing water. The chained Ruwendian oarsmen they let be. A few other Skritek ventured to nibble on their victims, but these were hissed and roared at by their fellows until they desisted.

When all of the five thousand troops were flung overboard, a very tall Skritek wearing a collar and belt studded with gold and gemstones ripped down the banner of Labornok from its staff at the bow of the flagship and befouled it. All of the other monsters howled with laughter, then jumped merrily into the river and swam away toward the Greenmire shore.

When they were far distant, Osorkon called out: "Ho! Do any knights or soldiers of great Labornok yet live?"

A few score voices responded — some fearful, others obscene.

"Climb back into the boats, my lads!" Osorkon cried. But as he spoke the Ruwendian rowers began to shout among themselves, finally realizing what had happened. The great sweeps dug into the water with alacrity and the boats began to draw away from the floating Labornoki.

Cursing and choking, Osorkon clung like a water-vart to his oar, weighting it down, and after a moment it dangled limp again from the rowlock. Eventually, he was able to make his way to the vessel's side and climb back aboard, together with a dozen or so others. Arming themselves, they regained control. Three other boats of the one hundred and twenty that had left the Trevista garrison were retaken, while the others vanished into the night. These four craft, carrying such warriors as could be rescued, pulled into the main wharf of Ruwenda Market, where they were greeted by the Labornoki dockmaster and the captain of the guard.

"Fronials!" Lord Osorkon raged. "Fronials to carry us to the Citadel, or you are dead men!"

Mounts were speedily procured, and Osorkon led his force off at a headlong gallop along the Market Road toward the Citadel. Of his original five thousand men, seventy-two remained.

45

Hiluro flew to the Citadel's High Tower and alighted there. Dismounting and embracing the great head of the bird, Haramis said: "I do not know if we will meet again, but take my blessing with you as you fly away. You have been a true and loving friend."

The bird inclined its beak almost to the stones. *I am ever at your service, White Lady.* Then he soared off into the sky, where ragged clouds now raced and a high overcast once again veiled the Triple Moons.

Haramis lifted the trapdoor, noting that it had been repaired since her departure, and descended the ladder. There were only a few guards on the tower levels where the treasures were kept, but they seemed not to notice as she went past. More soldiers patrolled the corridor leading to the mid-levels of the central keep, and she also came upon a group of five Labornoki knights, staring moodily out a window that overlooked the river; but none of these men seemed to see her.

It is as though I were a ghost, haunting my former home, she thought to herself. *Has Orogastus commanded them all to ignore me, or does my talisman shield me from sight?*

Am I to be only a spectator in this conflict, standing aloof as the White Lady always seemed to do? What is my part in the fulfillment of the prophecy?

Finally, she reached the solar. The room had been prepared for her. A fire burned, and the sconces had candles lit, and there was a flagon of wine and crystal goblets on a small table next to the open balcony windows.

She went to look outside, and her heart sank at the scene that met her eyes. Ranged about the great forecourt of the inner ward were thousands of warriors — men-at-arms waiting in orderly ranks, knights prowling among them inspecting weaponry or simply standing around the great bonfires that had been lighted. Near the Main Gatehouse, stout barricades had been erected; and perched upon the central one was a strange machine tended by black-coated minions who served the sorcerer. On massive high platforms, flanking the entrance to the keep itself, were four other machines and their operators. Along the battlements of the inner and outer wards and the barbican were lines of crossbowmen, and catapult crews were ready with missiles and engines at the bastions. The Citadel Gate that opened to the road outside was now completely blocked by a great pile of rubble that clogged its Gatehouse to the rafters.

"Hopeless," Haramis whispered. "Hopeless." And she turned away, just as Orogastus entered the room

He was clad in his silver-and-black vestments and a starry silver headpiece; but this mask was different from that which he had worn to worship the Dark Powers, for it enclosed his entire head and hid his face completely. Even the eyeholes were glazed over with black glass, and his aspect was so menacing that she gasped aloud.

The two of them stood unmoving, regarding one another. From some deep and distant part of the keep, a small sound arose that Haramis could not identify.

Orogastus unfastened his headpiece and took it off, setting it and his silver gauntlets on one of the benches next to the fire.

"You have made your choice," he said slowly, "and you have not chosen me."

"No."

"I chose my path long ago," he said. "And I cannot now turn away."

"I know."

From a pocket in his robe he took a small wooden box incised with grim carvings, which he opened, revealing a green ball. Haramis stared at this, uncomprehending. She was dimly aware that the noises that had begun shortly before were now increasing in volume. They were the shouts and tumult of fighting going on somewhere in the lower levels of the Citadel.

"This is called the Doomful Effluvium." Orogastus put the thing away, his expression now unsmiling and implacable. "If I fling it down from on high every soul within the inner and outer wards, and even beyond, will die in unspeakable torment. Call upon Kadiya and Anigel to surrender their lives and their talismans to you. *To us!*"

He seized her and kissed her with a strength that neared ferocity. Then he snatched up his gauntlets and star-mask and went out, slamming the door.

"No," Haramis whispered. "No!" She wasted no more time, but took out her talisman to view Kadiya and Anigel and their invading force. The Circle did not this time grow pearly; instead it glowed and seemed to expand and engulf her within it—

—and she seemed to hover high above the kitchen of the keep, where a mob of tall and hideous Wyvilo, urged on by Prince Antar, pressed into a faltering force of Labornoki warriors and knights. Hewing about with long-hafted axes and inflicting a fearful carnage, the forest Folk demoralized their opponents as well as destroyed them. And as the foemen fell or retreated and the Wyvilo cleared the way, tiny scale-armored Uisgu with crimson-ringed eyes aglow poured forth from the inner corridors like a tide of molten gold, screeching and flinging spears as soon as they had room enough to maneuver.

The invaders passed quickly from the demolished kitchens into the bakery and the scullery, and from there began to swarm into the open area of the inner ward, where the main body of defenders awaited them, yelling and brandishing their weapons.

At first, Haramis could not find her sisters. But finally she saw Kadiya, a gold-mailed figure slightly taller than the Uisgu, urging the small warriors on and holding her talisman on high. And then she made out Anigel, clad in blue leather, who seemed to shimmer in the uncertain light, and who stayed close to the azure-armored Prince Antar. Whenever an enemy came at Antar from behind, Anigel pounced upon the man and attacked him with some small weapon, whereupon the luckless Labornoki would drop instantly in his tracks.

Why, Anigel is invisible! Haramis realized. *That is why she can attack those brutes with impunity. Kadiya must also be screened by her talisman. And they actually seem to be winning!*

It was true. But once the invaders emerged from the kitchen chambers into the open ward, the advantage quickly swung the other way. The small force of the fighting Princesses was outnumbered by more than fifteen to one, and the sorcerer's lackeys were at that moment wrestling with their infernal devices, swinging them about so that they could bear upon the area in front of the scullery door.

Haramis snapped out of her trance and ran to the balcony, where she could look below and see the conflict with her own eyes. She bespoke her sisters urgently through her talisman:

Kadiya! The lightning-machine is on the barricade nearest the Main Gatehouse! Break it! Or better yet, use it to blast through the gates, through the mound of rubble that the Labornoki have used to block the outer entrance to the Citadel!

Kadiya made no reply; but Haramis saw a single gold-clad figure come dashing out from among the mob of Uisgu, and go snaking through the yelling mass of knights with the bonfires gleaming on her fish-scale armor.

Anigel! Near the keep's main door are wooden platforms —

But before she could finish, the sorcerer's lackeys began to use their deadly weapons. Golden-white balls of fire flew from two of the machines into the throng of invaders, and where they struck, they clung to skin or armor and inflicted horrible burns. From two other devices, which made a fearful racket, poured a hail of metal pellets trailing red sparks. These penetrated flesh and bone as easily as skewers pierce mushrooms, and those struck by the terrible things fell mortally wounded, if they were not killed on the spot.

I see the weapons, Haramis! I am on my way!

Anigel! Haramis bit her lip nervously. *Be careful! Even though they cannot see you —*

But at that moment Haramis staggered and was half blinded as the lightning-flinger let loose a tremendous bolt. The thundering blast caused even the keep to tremble, and the wine decanter and crystal goblets on the table behind her fell to the floor and smashed.

When her vision cleared, she lifted her talisman for a view through the darkness and the cloud of smoke and dust. She was amazed to see that almost the entire great Gatehouse had been blasted to bits. What was more, the path of destruction had continued in a straight line, demolishing the gate of the outer ward and that of the barbican. The mound of rubble at the main entrance of the Citadel was larger than ever . . . but the massive piers that had supported the gates and a four-ell section of the wall on either side were crumbling to fragments as she watched.

∴

And Kadiya —

"God have mercy!" Haramis cried.

Atop the barricade, the lightning device was a blackened and twisted ruin. Near to it were three smoldering corpses that had once been the sorcerer's henchmen, and a single small figure clad all in gold, lying unmoving among them, a pointless sword still gripped in one hand. *Kadiya must have destroyed the device with her talisman*, Haramis thought, *but I did not realize she could be hurt doing it! I must warn Anigel* . . .

The fool! The speech without words ringing in her mind, Haramis realized, could only be coming from Orogastus. *She has used the entire capacity of the device in a single stroke! The defenses are down and the enemy is on its way across the river!*

Haramis saw him below her. He stood on a small parapet just above the keep's entrance, the silver starburst of his headpiece flashing as the smoke cleared and the dozens of small fires set by the thunderbolt brightened in the rising wind. His voice, magnified by some magic, called out like a trumpet to the stunned Labornoki warriors, who had no notion of what was happening.

"Stand fast! Men of Labornok, stand fast!"

From behind the sorcerer now stepped King Voltrik, in his gorgeous golden armor with its awesome fanged helm, his long-sword held high. At the sight of him, the troops below uttered a great cheer, and the fighting between them and the invading Wyvilo and Uisgu, which had broken off abruptly when the great explosion occurred, now began again.

But suddenly Prince Antar called out, loudly enough to raise echoes in the ward.

"Men of Labornok, do not listen to that demon! I am Antar, your Prince! And I say that Orogastus has bewitched my father and turned him into a brainless puppet!"

A growl arose from a thousand throats.

"Be silent, traitor!" roared Orogastus.

But other voices were shouting: "He's right! The Prince is right! Look how the King just stands there!" And one cried. "Why isn't the King out here, leading us himself?" And another: "Stand forth, Voltrik! Speak to us!" There were more and more shouts, until Orogastus lifted both his hands, and his eyes flared like twin stars.

Silence fell.

King Voltrik knew he would have to speak. But what could he say? His courage was a thing in rags, his great ambitions fled like silly dreams. Reality was the Ruwendian army breaking into the Citadel in spite of all the magic Orogastus pitted against it. Reality was the voices of his own men wavering in their loyalty. Reality was his despised son Antar defying him openly. Reality, above all, was the failure of Orogastus to destroy the three Princess-Witches, one of whom was fated to destroy him . . .

"Soldiers of Labornok, fight on! Fight, I say!" But the King's voice was more a croak than a clarion command. "It is my wretched son who is bewitched. Strike down the turncoat!"

This utterance of his, far from encouraging the knights and men, caused them to clamor louder than before. And Prince Antar yelled: "To me, sons of Labornok! Down with the sorcerer! To me, I say!"

The fighting began again in earnest then; and in spite of Orogastus's booming admonitions, numbers of the Labornoki tore off their scarlet surcoats and rallied to the side of the Prince and his decimated force.

In the confusion, hardly anyone — and certainly not the furious Orogastus — noticed that those black-clad men who operated the terrible flame-machines and the pellet-spewing machines had slumped down senseless atop their tall platforms. Only Haramis, open-mouthed at her little sister's temerity, saw Anigel fling the last dart and begin to wrestle the heavy machines to the edge of the near platform and topple them to the flagstones five ells below, where they smashed into pieces.

When Orogastus realized what was happening, he roared for soldiers to climb the second platform quickly, and defend the abandoned machines there with their lives. But the men now saw that the sorcerer's henchmen up above had been felled by some magic, and the selfsame magic was obviously still at work, for invisible beings were throwing things down upon them. So no one would move, and Anigel continued from the first platform to the second and finished destroying the weapons that the sorcerer had usurped from the Vanished Ones.

Well done! Haramis congratulated her sister. *But now we must help Kadiya.*

Anigel was jubilant. *Was it not marvelous, the way she flung the thunderbolt? My talisman shows me a vision of our army coming ashore at Citadel Landing even now — and they will have easy entry through the broken wall!*

Anigel, Kadi has been hurt. Go to her. I am on my way down to help.

∴

Haramis caught up the Crown of Ruwenda and the cloak of the Archimage, and hurried down to aid her sisters.

"There! There, my Liege — can you not see her?"

Orogastus pointed through the lurid murk to the barricade before the ruined Gatehouse. King Voltrik strained his eyes, and finally said: "Yes. Wearing some kind of golden armor, is she?"

"Exactly! And knocked senseless by the demolition of my lightning-machine, so that she cannot command the talisman. Princess Kadiya is no longer invisible and no longer protected! She is in your power! All you need do is hasten there and put an end to her before she recovers — or is rescued by her people."

"I?" The King faltered. "Go down there?"

"Are you afraid of an unconscious girl?" The sorcerer's voice became silken, persuasive. "There are no foemen anywhere near her, my King, only your own troops, who would be afraid to touch her. But you can make an end of her! Your greatest enemy! Kadiya is the martial Princess, the woman of the prophecy. She slew General Hamil and routed half our army, and instigated this battle. But she has not won! We still have nearly five thousand seasoned troops to counter the approaching rabble, and their female general lies there awaiting your sword!"

"That's true." Voltrik drew himself up. "Much good her magic will do her now!"

"Go, my Liege. Kill her, then order your men to advance upon the Citadel barbican. Cut down the invaders as they attempt to scramble over the ruins."

"The witch shall die!" Voltrik bellowed. "And as I hold up her severed head, you shall announce my deed with your voice of thunder!"

Orogastus stepped to the parapet edge and cried out: "Men of Labornok! Your King comes now to lead you to victory! To the barbican with you! Prepare for the final encounter with the foe!"

There were scattered cheers.

"You know, we really do seem to have gained the upper hand down there." The King grinned at the sorcerer. "Most of those scoundrels who came up through the dungeons seem to have fallen."

"Your traitorous son Antar is gathering partisans while you stand here, my King. Go down! Kill Kadiya first, then rally the men."

"To victory!" Voltrik roared. He snapped shut the fanged visor of his terrible golden helm.

"Go," said Orogastus wearily. "Go."

When the monarch finally tramped off down the stairway, the sorcerer gave a great sigh. Removing one gauntlet, he reached into an inner pocket of his robe and touched the wooden box containing the deadly globe, at the same time forming an unspoken prayer to the Dark Powers.

Would Voltrik be able to kill Kadiya? Or would her talisman deal with the King as it had with Hamil and the Red Voice? The chance was worth taking. If Voltrik managed to succeed, then it might not be necessary after all to wipe the slate clean . . .

Orogastus stood and surveyed the advancing enemy force — which had just been augmented by the heavily armed Ruwendian brigades of Count Palundo. And then he searched the darkness of the Citadel's inner ward, seeking whatever clues there might be to the whereabouts of the other two Princesses.

He saw neither Anigel nor Haramis, but only a little old Oddling woman, picking her way through the tumult and the butchery as if searching for someone.

∴

46

Immu stumbled through the battle scene, coughing from the smoke, tripping over the dead bodies of friends and foes, dodging around the melees and hand-to-hand combat that made of the inner ward a hell of blood and iron.

"Anigel!" she called. "Princess, where are you?"

But when she questioned wounded Wyvilo or Uisgu about her royal mistress, none of those who had strength to reply knew, for they did not know that Princess Anigel fought among them invisible.

Immu saw King Voltrik emerge from the keep and call to himself a body of knights, after which he headed almost straight toward her.

The fighting seemed suddenly to fall into a lull. Following the orders of Orogastus and their commanders, most of the Labornoki were now streaming toward the ruined barbican and the Citadel Gate, regrouping to repel the advance of the main invading force now rushing up from the river.

But the King, it seemed, had another objective in mind.

"The witch!" Voltrik was shouting. "With me, men! I must kill the witch!"

He had beside him Lord Osorkon, who had arrived just in time for the battle, and Sir Rinutar, who had come to the Citadel the night before with news of the invaders, and two other knights named Lotharon and Simbalik.

The King and these four pushed through the moving crowd of defenders, thrust up their visors to see better in the smoky chaos, and began to clamber awkwardly up the barricade to where Princess Kadiya still lay senseless.

Immu saw her, too. And with all the agility her old bones could muster, she climbed painfully up the opposite end of the smoking structure and ran panting along its top toward the place where the golden-armored form lay.

Invisible hands were easing off the scale-mail hood from Kadiya's head. And Immu clearly heard a tremulous voice call out: "Kadi! Please wake up, Kadi!"

The Nyssomu woman cried out: "Anigel! Are you there, my darling?"

The golden-haired Princess appeared abruptly as she removed her coronet. "Immu! Come quickly! Kadi breathes, but I fear she is wounded."

"Two of them!" came a harsh shout. "Great Zoto, both witches are here!"

King Voltrik and his four knights gained the barricade crest at that instant. Knocking Immu flat, the monarch seized Princess Anigel by the hair, dragging her from her sister's side, and raised his sword to her throat. Her coronet talisman spun from her hand, landing on the charred planks with a dull chiming sound. Immediately the glow of its trillium amber winked out.

Simbalik and Lotharon hauled Kadiya upright. The swordlike object fell from her flaccid fingers, and its amber also went dull. But her eyes opened slowly, and met those of her sister.

"Men of Labornok!" King Voltrik shouted, in a transport of exaltation. "Behold! Two of the witches who threatened the throne of our great country are in my hands!"

A great roar arose from the throng of soldiers, and from the parapet above the keep entrance Orogastus's voice boomed. "Hail, Voltrik! Hail, all-conquering King! Show us the reward of those who would oppose your rule!"

During this commotion, Immu had been creeping toward Anigel's fallen coronet. Now she pounced on it like a lothok and tossed it into Anigel's waiting hand a scant moment before anyone saw her. Two men seized the old nurse and prepared to fling her headlong from the high barricade.

Anigel, still with Voltrik's sword at her throat, cried out loudly: "Harm her, and you are dead men."

The trillium amber in the coronet blazed like a pitch-brand, and the men holding Immu froze. King Voltrik said frantically: "The other magic talisman! That Dark Sword there! Seize it!"

∴

"Wait!" Osorkon shrieked, for he recognized the object and the danger in it.

But Rinutar had already loosed his hold on Immu and bent to pick up Kadiya's talisman. As he did so, Kadiya's hand stretched out and touched the hilt an instant before the knight did. The Three-Lobed Burning Eye opened wide and its beams shone full on Rinutar's face.

His armor turned incandescent. He had not time to cry out or even straighten before the flesh burnt from his skull, which glowed bright as steel in a forge. As Voltrik and his men cried out in fear and horror, the burning knight lurched and rolled to the lip of the barricade, and fell to the ward pavement like a human meteor.

Now there was pandemonium among those watching. But Voltrik, to do him credit, had not moved his sword a finger's breadth from Anigel's throat, even though cold sweat stung his eyes, and his heart thudded fit to burst.

Anigel turned her head to look up at him. "Release us. You are defeated. Surrender and throw yourself upon our mercy."

Voltrik howled with hysterical laughter. "Nay, Witch! First your sister shall die, and then you!"

"My King!" Lord Osorkon pointed down, his face distorted with terror. "The Dark Sword — *it moves!*"

Gaping, Voltrik and his companions watched the Three-Lobed Burning Eye rise slowly from Kadiya's hand, hovering at waist level. Princess Anigel seemed unperturbed by the sight. She opened her own hand, and the coronet floated away to meet the pointless end of the other talisman.

"NO!"

The thundering cry of despair came from Orogastus, on the parapet above. But it was too late.

Princess Haramis became visible, standing between her two pinioned sisters. The Crown of Ruwenda on her head sparkled in the firelight and the cloak of the Archimage billowed about her. Taking her own talisman, she slipped the wand into a channel in the sword-blade, so that the Three-Winged Circle formed a meridian and equator with the Three-Headed Monster. Within this space the wings opened; and a great Black Trillium in amber was at the center.

Orogastus lifted high something that gleamed green. Then he flung it with all his strength toward the courtyard stones.

∴

Haramis pointed the Sceptre of Power — and the flying globe of the Doomful Effluvium flared and vanished in a puff of white smoke.

Now she turned to the two knights holding Kadiya. The girl's dark eyes were alert and her muscles tensed for a struggle.

"Release her!" Haramis commanded. But the men hesitated.

"Let her go, fools!" Osorkon cried.

"No!" King Voltrik screamed. "I forbid it!"

Seeing the two knights stiffen and stand firm, Haramis moved deliberately, but with reluctance, pointing first at Lotharon, then at Simbalik, with the Sceptre.

This time the armor did not flame. But within each visor blue-white radiances bloomed for a split second; and when it flared out, each helm was empty, as was the rest of the armor. Two suits of steel clattered in pieces to the planks.

King Voltrik gave a throat-searing shriek and dropped both Anigel and his sword. He fell to his knees. "Mercy! Lady, have mercy!"

Haramis pointed the Sceptre at him calmly. "Receive as much mercy as you have ever given, and let the prophecy be fulfilled."

Glazen-eyed, the kneeling King removed his monstrous helmet. He bowed his head low. As the throng watched in hushed awe, Voltrik's own sword rose up, and its point thrust deeply into the base of his skull. He fell, with the weapon pinning him to the wood beneath.

All over the embattled Citadel, a sound arose like a low murmur of storm-tossed trees. On the barricade, Lord Osorkon laid his sword at Haramis's feet and knelt with bared head. Then there was a clattering and clanking as, all over the great ward, the knights and soldiers of Labornok threw down their weapons and stood numb, waiting to see what would happen next.

Haramis faced Orogastus across the wide courtyard. He had removed his star-mask, and his white hair streamed in the rising wind. The smoke and dust were carried off, and those fires that still burned blazed brighter for the air fanning them. Over all, the sky was cleared of cloud, and the Triple Moons stood in close conjunction midway between the zenith and the western horizon, seeming to touch and form a single Orb with three lobes.

Haramis lifted the Sceptre and pointed it at Orogastus.

"Now let our lives and our service be judged," she said. "Have we fulfilled what was required of us? Have we done right? Have we acted to restore the balance? Judge us, and judge him, also."

∴

Orogastus gripped the parapet's edge in both hands, and his teeth were set as his eyes again shone star-like with the terrible brilliance of magic. The spectators uttered cries of fear.

Prince Antar, appearing as if from nowhere, took Princess Anigel in his arms. Little Immu stood beside Kadiya, the pair of them steadfast.

"Haramis!" Orogastus shouted, his voice still amplified by whatever device he was using. "I can destroy you yet! I can summon the Dark Powers and move the very earth!"

Haramis closed her eyes, holding tight to the Sceptre; but in her mind she still could see his face. *This isn't working,* she realized. *The Sceptre must need all three of us.* "Kadiya, Anigel," she said urgently, "help me! Take hold of the Sceptre and concentrate!" She felt her sisters close in at her sides and their hands joined hers on the Sceptre.

The power in it flared suddenly to full life. It bound them all together: Haramis, Kadiya, and Anigel at one end, and Orogastus at the other. It glowed with a brightness that blinded physical eyes, even through closed eyelids; but somehow, Haramis realized, she could still see. Kadiya and Anigel were at her sides, so close they seemed part of her, and Orogastus confronted them along the length of the Sceptre. And in the bright power that held them, all illusion was burned away, and they saw themselves and each other as they truly were.

It was terrifying. Haramis found herself aware of all the times she had hurt people, even inadvertently, the times she had looked down on her sisters as lesser creatures, especially in contrast to the beauty and strength she saw in them now. She could feel the same emotions in both of them: regret for all their past failures and mistakes, and awe at what they saw in each other. But around and through the thoughts and memories flowed the sisters' love for one another. Haramis understood now, and she knew that her sisters did too; in a certain manner the three of them made one whole entity, their strengths and weaknesses complementing and canceling out each other's. In spite of their individual differences — or perhaps because of them — they were one, and they were Ruwenda.

This must be what Binah meant by balance.

Orogastus was perceptible to Haramis as well, but the feeling was totally different. The closeness she had felt to him when he had held her in his arms was completely gone; what she sensed now was his isolation — total and terrifying. He had no connection with Ruwenda or any other land, or with any of the Folk, and — in spite of what had passed between them — he had no connection with Haramis.

He seemed to be locked inside himself, experiencing horrors that the Princesses could only dimly sense. Haramis hurt for him, even now, and she could feel Anigel's ready compassion extending in his direction as well; but Orogastus was aware of nothing outside himself. And his self seemed to be unendurable.

Haramis pointed the Sceptre at Orogastus. "Judge us," she whispered. "Judge him."

Again the Sceptre flared.

All of them were momentarily blinded, and so many persons screamed from the shock that it was many long minutes before they realized that the sorcerer was gone.

All that remained of him was a great black splash like soot against the keep wall where he had stood, and on it, high above the parapet, the white silhouette of a tall man's body.

That year, for the first time, the Feast of the Three Moons was celebrated three days late, postponed so that the injured could be cared for and the dead receive their rites of honor. But on the third evening following that of the great battle, when the Triple Moons in their full conjunction rose above the Mazy Mire, all of the Folk camped round about the Knoll, and all of the Ruwendian and Labornoki humans as well, came together once again in the great inner ward of the ancient Citadel.

The Uisgu marched in first, led by Princess Kadiya, carrying three-branched torches and singing their ancient festival song; then followed the gentle Nyssomu, headed by Jagun and Immu; and the surviving Wyvilo, marching behind Lummomu-Ko. Then came the Labornoki, with their new King, Antar, walking unarmored and carrying only flowers in their hands; and last of all the army of free Ruwendians, led by Count Palundo, who had with him as many knights and nobles as could be summoned by Folk passing the news through the Mire by means of the speech without words.

Haramis, crowned and cloaked and bearing the great Sceptre, welcomed them. Antar came forward and knelt at her feet, to offer his nation's formal surrender.

But Haramis said: "Rise up, King Antar, for I cannot accept your

∴

capitulation." She took from her head the great Crown of State and held it high. "I who was heiress to the throne of Ruwenda now renounce this Crown. I call upon Princess Kadiya, my next younger sister, to accept it — for I have been called to a different role, that of Archimage."

Kadiya stood at the head of the great throng of aborigines, the trillium emblem glowing on the breast of her golden mail, and her auburn hair falling free over her shoulders. She said:

"I also renounce the Crown, for my destiny is not to be a ruler of humans, but a leader and friend to the Folk, who have besought me to serve them. I call upon Princess Anigel, my younger sister, to accept the Crown she has so richly merited."

Anigel closed her eyes briefly, seeing again that strange dream vision of herself running through a forest in pursuit of her Mother. And having this time caught up to Queen Kalanthe, she no longer felt apprehension as her Mother washed and dressed and prepared her. That which awaited had been truly hers from the beginning.

She also knew that, of the three, she was the best suited to wear the Crown. She opened her eyes, walked to Haramis, and knelt with her head held high. When the great Crown with its emeralds and rubies and huge drop of trillium amber rested on her head, she rose, turned slowly about, and sketched the three-lobed sign in the air above those watching.

Antar was still standing by, and now knelt to her. "Will you accept my surrender, Great Queen?"

"But it is mine already," she said, smiling, "together, I hope, with your heart. And since I am a Queen who cannot rule without a King, I propose that we rule our kingdoms jointly as husband and wife, in perpetual peace." She took his hands and made him rise and stand beside her.

"People of Ruwenda," said she, "I give you your King."

And he said: "People of Labornok, I give you your Queen!"

A great tumult of cheering and weeping broke out then, and the Folk sang their hymn again, and great quantities of food and drink were brought out; and the real celebration began.

Standing close together, the sisters embraced. Then Haramis took the Sceptre of Power and solemnly separated it. The pointless sword, its Eyes now closed in sleep, she gave to Kadiya, who slipped it into the scabbard she wore and tied it in place with a lanyard. The silvery coronet with the three grotesque visages Anigel mounted inside the

Crown of Ruwenda, which she then resettled upon her golden hair. The wand, with its wings folded and the trillium amber glowing only dimly, Haramis replaced on the chain around her neck.

"We were One," Haramis said, "and now we are again Three. Please God that the world has been rebalanced, and the Sceptre of Power will never be needed again."

"By the Flower!" Kadiya growled. "I should hope not! Peace is what we all need. Just think of how much we three all still have to learn! Ani, the tedious statecraft, Hara the magic, and I intend to go back to a certain Place of Learning and put some very important questions to a being who resides there. There are knotty problems to be solved concerning the future relations between Folk and humankind, and I suspect it will take some time to sort out the answers!"

Anigel asked Haramis: "Will you call your lammergeier after the feast, Sister, and fly away to live in Noth as the old White Lady did?"

Haramis looked away, and for a moment her gaze passed over the parapet above the entrance to the keep. "No. That place fell to dust when Binah died. I shall go to another place — one that I know of, high in the mountains."

Antar came up to the three then, smiling apologetically as he told Anigel that their joint assemblage of subjects demanded that the monarchs lead them in festive dance.

"The terrible duties of sovereignty!" Kadiya laughed. "Go along, Queen Anigel. The Archimage and I will continue our weighty discussions over food and drink, and when Your Majesties have danced holes in your shoes, you can rejoin us."

Hand in hand, Anigel and Antar went away; and the music began.

Hurrying across the twilit Knoll meadow toward the Citadel, the old musician Uzun heard the sounds of celebration and quickened his pace. He could hardly believe his ears. Surely those were the songs of Triple Moons! But had not the festival taken place three days ago, while he and the others on his boat were stalled on the riverside repairing the broken hull? He had missed the great battle; missed the victory; missed seeing his dear Princess Haramis destroy the villain Orogastus — missed *everything*.

Or had he? Oh, if only he weren't so incompetent at the speech without words!

Those were certainly the festival hymns, and the sounds of merriment

∴

floating on the night breeze almost drowned out the calling of the swamp creatures. What a miracle! He would be in time after all —

Something on the moonlit ground caught his eye.

He stopped, and bent down for a better look. The soil was very damp yet from the early Rains, and all kinds of fresh growth seemed to have sprung up, virtually overnight. But this was something different. Something he could scarcely believe was real. Something magical . . .

Myriad small plants were growing in this place that had once fostered only grass and sedge. Plants with small black tripartite flowers.

Uzun the musician picked one of the Black Trilliums, and held it up to the moonlight. Yes! There was no doubt about it. The place was crowded with them. They were everywhere.

Laughing giddily, he gathered as many of the flowers as he could carry, and raced off to tell the good news to the people at the Citadel. Thousands more of the trilliums remained, spreading their petals beneath the light of the Triple Moons.